Only Him

only one series

USA TODAY BESTSELLING AUTHOR
KENNEDY FOX

Copyright © 2022 Kennedy Fox
www.kennedyfoxbooks.com

Only Him
Only One series, #1

Cover designer: Designs by Dana
Cover photographer: Regina Wamba
Copy editor: Editing 4 Indies

All rights reserved. No parts of the book may be used or reproduced in any matter without written permission from the author, except for inclusion of brief quotations in a review. This book is a work of fiction. Names, characters, establishments, organizations, and incidents are either products of the author's imagination or are used fictitiously to give a sense of authenticity. Any resemblance to actual persons, living or dead, events, or locales is entirely coincidental.

only one series

SUGGESTED READING ORDER

ONLY HIM
a best friend's brother, second chance,
small town romance

ONLY US
a single mom, friends to lovers,
small town romance

ONLY MINE
a brother's best friend, roommates to lovers,
small town romance

PROLOGUE
TYLER

As soon as I get out of my rental car, the Alabama heat smacks me in the face. Though I'm used to it and have been in worse conditions, it's still a shock after driving in the air-conditioning for hours.

I haven't been home to Lawton Ridge in four years, and now that I have my discharge papers from the Army, I'll stay here until I decide my next move. I'm hoping I figure it out within the next few months because this small town doesn't have much for me here. Most people I went to high school with work for their family's business, left for college and never returned, or got married and settled down. Truthfully, none of those options had any appeal, especially with an addict for a mother and a father who abandoned my little sister and me. Everleigh is four years younger, and she was the only reason I hesitated to enlist. I was worried as hell to be away, and leaving for boot camp was harder than I ever imagined it would be.

I've looked after her, making sure she was at school on time, ate three meals a day, and did her homework. My grandparents reassured me they'd take good care of Everleigh. They kept their word, and tonight, she's graduating from high school. I'm so damn proud of her for getting good grades and *mostly* staying out of trouble. She's loudmouthed and tells it like it is, but I love her to death.

I wasn't sure I'd make it on time with my flight delays, but I did.

I rush through the crowd until I see my grandparents who saved me a seat. Mimi cries the second her eyes meet mine, and Pops pulls me into a tight hug. Over the years, we've spoken on the phone and FaceTimed a few times, but it's not the same as actually seeing them in person. It's a quick reunion because moments later, the commencement ceremony begins.

After an hour of speeches and a slideshow of the students' baby photos, my sister finally walks across the stage. She looks around, and I know she's wondering if I'm here.

As soon as the administrator announces her name, I stand and cup my mouth with both hands. "Go, Everleigh! Woo!" I clap my hands above my head and cheer as loud as I can.

Her eyes widen, and she smiles before glaring at me for making an obnoxious scene. I laugh and continue applauding as she grabs her diploma and shakes hands with her principal.

"She's gonna kill you for that," Mimi whispers, chuckling.

Moments later, I recognize another name as it's announced: Gemma Reid.

Even though she's sent me photos over the past four years, they did nothing to capture her true beauty. She's stunning, absolutely gorgeous with dark brown hair and flawless skin. I'd be lying if I said I didn't think about her daily. We were just acquaintances when I left after I graduated, but for the past four years, we've written to each other, and it's turned into...*more*.

The first letter she sent was so random that I almost tossed it without realizing it was from her. At the time, she was only fourteen, and it was harmless. She asked how I liked traveling around the world, if I missed being home, and hoped I stayed safe. I replied and gave her as many details as I was allowed. Soon, I found myself looking forward to hearing from her.

Her last letter, though—that one nearly stopped my heart.

Not that I hadn't expected some of it, considering how she's hinted at her feelings before, but Gemma was always the quiet one out of my sister's friends. After a while, she shared personal things, and it helped us grow closer. I spilled more to her than anyone else, and for whatever reason, I felt like I could trust her more with each secret I revealed.

. . .

Dear Tyler,

I hope this letter gets to you before you leave. I know if I don't say this now, I might chicken out when I finally see you.

The way I feel for you has grown over the past four years. It's not just a stupid crush I had in middle school. It's much more than that. A month ago, I told you I wanted you to be my first, and I still mean it, but I have to ask one thing.

If you don't feel the same way, if I've fabricated this whole thing between us, please tell me to my face. If you see me as just your sister's best friend, don't lead me on. I've shared more with you than I probably should've, but it's because I know you'd never judge me. You've always given me great advice when I had problems, and with you, I have a safe space to vent. It's something I'll always cherish, even if it can't be more than a friendship. To be honest, I'm going to miss writing to you. I've looked forward to hearing from you each week, but seeing you in person is all I can think about right now. I'm anxious and excited, but my nerves are getting the best of me. I'm second-guessing everything, and I'm worried you'll break my heart.

So please don't. If you tell me my feelings are one-sided, I'll understand. But if they're not, show me.
Love, Gemma

I hate that I didn't reply before I left, but I know she wouldn't have gotten it in time due to where I was stationed. I'm glad to be able to tell her how I feel in person instead. I want to ease her nerves as much as I can. Thinking about Gemma got me through the long ass days and nights. I've felt guilty because of her age and because she's Everleigh's best friend, but I didn't plan this. These feelings developed over time and grew stronger over the past year. Knowing she feels the same makes me want to make her mine, and now I can't stand the idea of not being with her.

Gemma glides across the stage and smiles wide as her dad stands and claps. Her brother, Noah, is next to him cheering loudly. He's a year older than her, and I didn't know him well in high school, but Gemma's told me so much it feels like I do. He's in love with her other best friend, Katie Walker, but never told her. According to Gemma, by the time she talked Noah into confessing his feelings, their cousin Gabe had moved to town and asked Katie out first. That was two years ago, and they're still together. I've learned more about the people from Lawton Ridge while being away than I did living there for eighteen years. Though I didn't mind hearing the gossip from Gemma because it meant the letters continued to come.

As Gemma walks off stage, she finds me. There's no doubt she heard and saw me earlier, and the smile that spreads across her lips confirms she most definitely did.

I smirk, then shoot her a wink, and she licks her lips, then walks back to her seat.

After the ceremony is over, Everleigh rushes toward me and leaps into my arms. "You made it!" she cries.

I tighten my grip and smile. "With minutes to spare even."

She pulls back and looks me over from head to toe. "No broken bones or bruises?"

"A few bruises from training." I shrug. "Nothing major."

"Thank God."

Though I was honored to serve my country, I want to experience life in other ways too.

Mimi and Pops give Everleigh hugs, then we discuss dinner plans. Of course, Mimi already prepped a home-cooked meal.

"After we eat, I wanna take Tyler to a party," Everleigh tells them, threading her fingers through her beachy waves once she takes off her cap. Though she's tall like me, we look completely different. I have dark eyes and hair while Everleigh's a brunette and blue eyes.

I'm half-listening as I scan the area for Gemma. She's probably with her family, but I'm dying to see her.

"A party?" I furrow my brows and shove my hands into my pockets. "I'm twenty-two. I'm too old for high school parties."

Everleigh scoffs, then swats my chest. "Nonsense. We're technically *not* in high school anymore, so there."

I snort. "Oh, I'm sorry. I forgot that you're a full-ass adult now."

"Language, Tyler," Mimi scolds.

I apologize, and Everleigh laughs.

"Trust me, you want to go. Gemma will be there." She snickers and waggles her brows. Lord knows what Gemma's told her or what she knows about our…*friendship*.

"Gemma Reid? Are y'all dating?" Mimi asks.

"Yes," Everleigh says at the same time I say, "No."

Pops chuckles. "Let's feed you crazy kids so you can go celebrate."

Everleigh rides with me and talks my ear off about some guy she's kinda seeing. After five minutes, I already want to punch his face in or turn the radio up so I don't have to hear about it anymore.

Once we arrive at our grandparents' house, Mimi serves chicken fried steak with white gravy, cornbread, and mashed potatoes as we sit around the table. She even made a pecan pie, and it was still warm when she sliced it. It was a good old-fashioned Southern meal—something I haven't eaten in years—and just what I needed to feel at home. I'll be staying here in my old bedroom, but everyone's aware it's only temporary. Before I got here, I told them I wouldn't be settling in town, and they spent the better half of dinner trying to talk me into staying.

"I'm gonna get ready for the party, then we'll go, okay?" Everleigh says as she skips toward the staircase.

"You only want me to go so I can drive you there and back."

"Well, duh!" She laughs as she goes up to her room.

Over an hour later, she finally comes down all dressed up. Her long hair is in curls, and her skirt is too damn short.

"That's what you're wearing?" I raise my brows, waiting for Mimi or Pops to say something. She moved out of our mother's house the year I left and visits sparingly. I don't blame Everleigh for not wanting to live with her, considering I have no intention of seeing my mom at all. While I was gone, my mother never wrote, called, or reached out to me in any way. She couldn't care less that I'm home, and I don't care to waste my time. She's been toxic my whole life, and it's obvious that won't change.

"You look adorable, Everleigh!" Mimi praises, and I stand in shock.

Everleigh sticks her tongue out at me, then gets her purse.

Inhaling sharply, I grab my keys and walk toward the door. "Alright, let's go then."

The party is being held in her friends' backyards, and I bet it takes all of thirty seconds before one of the neighbors calls the cops. When I was in high school, we always brought booze we stole from our parents and snuck it into our red Solo cups with cola. I wouldn't be surprised if they're doing the same thing.

"Gemma, Katie, Gabe, and Noah are there already," Everleigh says as we turn onto Main Street, then she looks over at me. "You'll be okay if I wander off, or do you need supervision?"

"You mean, do I need to supervise *you*?"

"Puh-leese. I've been supervising myself just fine while you were gone." She flips her hair.

I lift a brow. "Really?"

"I'm not pregnant, addicted to drugs or alcohol, and I graduated with good grades. You should be praising me."

"I'm proud of you for not becoming a statistic." When she furrows her brows, I add, "You didn't become an addict like Mom."

The mood changes, and she frowns, then lowers her eyes. "I invited her to come tonight. No surprise she didn't show up."

Leaning over, I squeeze her shoulder. "It's her loss, Everleigh. You know that."

She nods, then flashes a small smile. "You coming is the best gift I could've ever gotten anyway."

Once we arrive and I find a place to park, we walk toward the crowd of people. Everleigh's greeted by a bunch of her classmates, and she shrieks when she sees her group of friends. There's a huge table set up with snacks and desserts, and of course, several people have red cups.

The moment I see Gemma, I swallow down the lump in my throat and follow my sister toward them. She's wearing a skirt that's so tight it's like a second skin on her petite frame. I was right, the pictures she sent didn't do her justice. She's grown into a beautiful woman.

"Guys, you remember my brother. He's finally home!" Everleigh proudly pulls me closer.

"Hey, man. Lookin' good." Noah gives me a fist bump.

"Thanks."

Gabe gives me a head nod before he whispers in Katie's ear, and the two of them take off. Noah watches them with jealousy but tries to play it off like it's nothing, then brings his attention back to us.

"Noah, can you show me where the drinks are?" Everleigh loops her arm through his. As they walk away, she looks over her shoulder and smirks, leaving Gemma and me alone.

"Congrats," I tell her as she stands in silence. "Bet you're glad to be done with school."

"Thanks." She smiles. "I am."

Awkwardness lingers and the last place I want to be right now is at a party where everyone can see us. "Any chance you wanna get the hell outta here?"

Her face lights up, and she smiles. "Definitely yes."

"Just gonna let my sister know, and then we can head out," I explain, grabbing my phone from my pocket.

I quickly shoot Everleigh a text and ask her if she can hitch a ride with someone so Gemma and I can talk. She immediately sends a response of random emojis—an eggplant, cherry, and smiley face with its tongue sticking out. I'd scold her if I wasn't in a hurry to leave.

She follows me, and when the house is out of sight, I grab her hand and loop her fingers through mine. When we get to the car, I pull her in front of me and grip her waist. We're inches apart as she leans against the door.

"I got your last letter," I tell her as we lock eyes.

"You did? I wasn't sure if it'd make it on time." She grasps my biceps, and I can hear the anxiousness in her voice.

"I did, and I wanted to respond in person…"

"Okay."

"Actually, I wanted to show you."

Her breath hitches.

"However, I get the impression that you're a bit nervous, so maybe we should talk and—"

"Or you could kiss me so I can stop wondering if you're going to."

She sucks in her lower lip, then bites down before releasing it. For a split second, I hesitate, making sure it's what she truly wants. There's no doubt about it as I dip down and gently brush my mouth against hers.

"I've thought about kissing you for way too fucking long," I whisper.

"Probably not as long as I have…an *inappropriately* long time."

The corner of my lips turns up slightly, knowing she wants this as badly as I do. I cup her face, tilt her chin up, and this time, I claim her mouth. We take our time as our tongues slide against each other. Gemma moans, and the desire to have more of her overwhelms me. Lowering one hand down her body, I cup her ass and squeeze, pressing her into my erection.

As we continue, our kiss grows hotter, and my dick gets harder. Gemma arches her back and rocks her hips against me, which drives me even more crazy.

"You need to stop that. People can see us out here."

"Then take me somewhere so they can't."

Fuck yes. I open the car door for her, then jog around to the other side.

"Alright, tell me where you wanna go." I crank the engine.

"I've been fixing up my mom's old cottage. We can hang out there."

It takes us less than ten minutes to get to her house. As soon as we're out of the car, she grabs my hand, and we quietly sneak to the backyard. The quaint cottage needs a lot of work, but it's cute. There's a bed and a small studio area where she explains her mother used to paint. I know her mom passed years ago because she talked about missing her a few times in her letters.

"Now that school's done, I can actually spend more time remodeling. It needs a new paint job and a good cleaning. Then I can decorate it and make it cozy."

"It's nice, actually. You're close to your dad's house but far enough away to have some privacy." I walk around, looking at everything.

"I plan to keep her art hung, at least my favorite ones."

"You never got into painting?" I ask, closing the gap between us.

"I tried. I think I liked it as a child, but then I think I associated it with pain because I was sad she wasn't here."

"That's understandable."

"Yeah, but I don't want to talk about that right now. I'd much rather you kiss me again instead." She grins, grabbing my shirt and yanking me toward her.

I smirk and lower my eyes to meet hers. "I think I can accommodate that."

Our mouths fuse again in a white-hot kiss. The way she makes me feel burns through my entire body. I crave her, and I need to feel more of her. The way our relationship grew over the years led us to a deep connection. The emotional drives the physical, and being with her like this feels even more intense than I could've anticipated.

Peppering kisses down her jawline, I attach my lips to her neck. She shivers against me as I flatten my tongue against her soft, smooth skin and lick up to her ear.

"Fuck, Gemma. You've consumed me for so long that I can hardly control myself around you."

"I don't want you to...I'm yours. Take all of me."

Gripping the bottom of her ass, I lift her as her legs wrap around me. I walk us toward the bed, then lay her down on the mattress and crawl over her body. Our mouths collide as I slide a hand up her stomach, then palm one of her perky breasts.

"That feels so good," she murmurs.

"Better than the tool bag who thought he was fingering you?" I smirk against her lips, and she bursts out laughing.

"Oh my God, how do you remember that? I told you about Benny like two years ago."

"I kept thinking about how fucking hilarious it was, and how much I wanted to be the one who touched you there."

"Trust me, I want that too."

"Should I show you how it's really supposed to feel?" I lie next to her on my side and slip my fingers inside her skirt.

"Yes," she whimpers. "Show me."

I slide under her panties and immediately feel her wetness. Every inch of her begs for my touch. The pad of my finger glides up and down her slit before rubbing circles against her clit.

"Oh my God. That feels way too good." She closes her eyes and hums. "Please, don't stop."

"It might hurt when I push my finger inside you, Gemma," I warn.

"I've fingered myself before," she tells me.

I chuckle at her honesty. "I'll still be gentle."

"I trust you, Tyler." She wraps her hand around my neck, pulling me down until our mouths touch. "I know you'd never hurt me."

The confident way she says those words has my heart bursting. That's the last thing I want to do to her, *ever*. Gemma Reid is everything I've ever wanted but don't deserve.

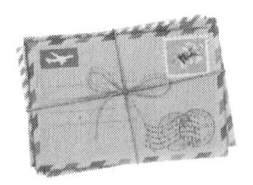

She gave me all of herself that night. I told her we could wait and didn't have to rush, but she was firm with her decision. I was her first, and she was the first woman I ever loved.

But three months later, after spending the entire summer together, I broke both of our hearts when I left with no plans to return to Lawton Ridge. I asked her to come with me—together we could travel and be spontaneous—but she didn't want to leave her dad and the only home she's ever known.

As much as it hurt, she couldn't leave, and I couldn't stay.

Gemma will always be the *one* I let go, the woman I walked away from—my biggest regret.

CHAPTER ONE

TYLER

TWELVE YEARS LATER

THE AIR FEELS different for the first time since I've entered this hellhole. I inhale a deep breath and smile when I see my best friend's truck in the parking lot. After spending five years in prison, it's the best fucking sight ever. Walking out with only the clothes on my back and a new sense of freedom, I head toward them.

Maddie hops out with her seven-month pregnant belly, and I chuckle when I hear Liam calling after her.

"Tyler!" she shouts, waddling as fast as she can to me.

As she approaches, I smile and open my arms, and she cries the moment we embrace. My emotions start to bubble over too, but I hold them back, knowing she's on hormone overload.

"Oh my God, I can't believe you're out!" She pushes back slightly, eyeing me up and down.

Liam joins and pulls me in for a side hug. "Dude. You look buff as fuck."

I chuckle. "Gotta make sure I'm prepared for the real world now, ya know?"

Smiling down at Maddie, I look at her bump. "You look huge."

She playfully pushes at my chest, laughing. "Shut up. I know. And I still have two more months."

I cringe. "Yikes. Good thing I'm only staying for a few weeks."

Maddie's smile drops. "What? That's it? Why?"

I knew she wouldn't be happy about that.

Liam grabs Maddie's hand as we walk to the truck. He helps her into the back seat, and I take the passenger seat.

"You know I didn't even want to go to Sacramento." We all buckle up, and I glance back at their firstborn sleeping soundly in his car seat next to Maddie. "I found a job back home. I need a fresh start. There's nothing here for me," I tell her, not wanting to upset her further, but Maddie has always been vocal for as long as I've known her. I don't actually have the job set in stone yet, but if Maddie knows that, she'll be even more relentless about me staying.

"Ugh. Me! And Liam and baby Tyler."

"And you all have your own lives to live. You won't mind me invading your space for a little bit, but after a while, you'll want your privacy again, so it's best if I try to go back into civilian life the best I can."

Liam starts the truck and drives us out of the parking lot. "Babe, he's made his decision," he tells Maddie.

I glance back at her and see her shoulders slump. "Fine, but I'm using these next three weeks to change your mind."

"You will after you realize my cooking game is weak." I'm rusty from being locked up.

My grandmother taught me during my teenage years since my mother barely got her high, drunken ass out of bed on most days. Mimi and I spent countless nights and weekends bonding in the kitchen.

"I'm happy you'll have time to spend with baby Tyler at least," Maddie says, glancing at him with pride.

"Me too, Mads. I'm ready to get back to normal." *Whatever the fuck normal is.*

I teared up with happiness when they visited me in prison and introduced me to him. After I saved Maddie from the O'Learys and got Liam out of his arranged marriage with the mob princess, they honored me by naming their first son after me. Even though helping them is what put me behind bars, I'll never regret what I did to protect them.

Baby Tyler's almost two now. I wish I could watch him grow up and be in his life every day, but I have to get away. After what happened in Sacramento and Vegas, the last place I want to be is somewhere she can easily find me. Victoria O'Leary ruined my life and stole time that I'll never get back.

Even considering the outcome, I wouldn't change anything I did. Liam's been like a brother to me for years, and I value the friendship Maddie and I formed through it all. They're my family and always will be.

After Victoria kidnapped Maddie and threatened Liam, I lied to get on Victoria's payroll, and she stupidly hired me to be one of her bodyguards. When she sent me to Montana for a "classified job," I had no idea it was to oversee Maddie. After setting a plan into place, I knocked out Eric—the other bodyguard—and escaped with Maddie. Victoria had a rich-bitch hissy fit and planted illegal guns and pounds of drugs in my truck. When I was driving to California to visit Liam and Maddie, one of her shady police officers pulled me over. He knew exactly what he'd find too and stated he smelled pot inside the truck, which gave him probable cause to search.

Fucking bastard.

Though all the O'Learys are fucking ruthless, Victoria takes the cake. In the few months I worked for their family, I saw and heard the craziest shit. Still, it didn't prepare me when I witnessed Victoria murder her brother, JJ, the night Liam was knifed by Victoria's boyfriend, Mickey.

It was the biggest fucking scandal I've ever witnessed. One I hadn't seen coming.

Weeks after that, life had gone back to normal, or so I thought. Liam recovered from getting stabbed, and I moved back to Vegas. A few weeks later, that bitch pulled the rug from underneath me.

Every day was basically the same. I tried to keep my mind busy by working out, but the anger ate me alive. I lifted weights and ran until I couldn't feel my limbs. The only thing that brought a smidge of happiness was when Liam and Maddie came every month. Though I wish they could've visited more often, the drive was six hours round trip, so I understood.

Everleigh flew from Alabama a few times, but I knew she couldn't afford it, so I asked her to stop. She opened a boutique a few years ago and put her life savings into it. The last thing I wanted was for her to spend money on visiting me for a half an hour when she could invest more into her business. Instead, I called her and our grandparents a couple times a week to catch up. I miss her like crazy, and though I'm nervous as hell to go back to Lawton Ridge, I'm excited to see and hug my little sister again.

"So, what kind of job did you get?" Maddie asks as we merge onto the highway.

"Mechanic at a garage," I explain, hopeful I'll actually get hired. "Working on cars, doing oil changes, greasy shit."

"Do you still remember how to do that stuff?" she asks. At one point, I worked on her car and even taught her a few things. Maddie doesn't enjoy getting her hands dirty, but I made her anyway. Thinking back to it has me cracking up.

"Yeah, I know enough. I even read articles and books while I was locked up."

"You did?"

"I had to keep my mind sharp." I smirk. "I read other stuff too. We had access to a small library."

"I feel bad. I should've brought you some of my romance novels."

Liam snorts from the driver's side. "Yeah, sure. If you want him to get his ass kicked."

Maddie leans forward and smacks my arm. "Nah. Look how big his muscles are. They'd be stupid to mess with Tyler."

Grinning, I pat her hand. "Thanks, Mads. I appreciate the ego boost."

"You're very welcome. Now, on to more important subjects. Are you going to see *Gemma* while you're there?"

She emphasizes her name like it's a dirty word, but for me, it ignites a fire in my body. Gemma—the woman who's haunted my dreams for twelve years—the woman I left, who's engaged to another man.

I shrug, though I know damn well I'll see her nearly every day. It'll be my own personal hell, but one I deserve after the way things ended. Her father owns the garage I'll be interviewing for, and although my gut reaction was to say no when Everleigh brought up the idea, I also knew my criminal record would make getting hired at most places nearly impossible. Especially in my small hometown where rumors fly like planes at an international airport.

My sister wanted me to come home just as much as I wanted to start over and was nice enough to talk to Jerry about giving me a job. She thinks I'll get it, and I hope she's right, but if not, I'll be looking until I find something. Working at the garage would help get me back on my feet.

"Maddie..." Liam warns. "Quit pushing him. He hasn't even been out for an hour yet."

She frowns. "Fine, but I will get the juicy details out of you eventually. I'll text and call you every day if I have to."

I chuckle. "I don't doubt that."

"Don't worry, man." Liam turns to me. "As soon as she pops that baby out, she'll forget all about your love life."

"Ha! Love life? There won't be one for a long ass time, *trust me*. You'll be having your next baby before I have a relationship."

"Don't put that idea in his head!" Maddie scolds as Liam laughs. "He'll keep me knocked up!"

"What's the problem with that? You're adorable." I look over my shoulder and smirk.

"I was *adorable* four months ago. Now, I'm just a beached whale."

Maddie talks my ear off for the next three hours, and soon, Liam's pulling into the driveway. They bought a new house, but the picture I saw of it didn't give it justice because it's big and beautiful.

"Home sweet home!" Maddie says, wrapping her arms around me from the back seat. "I'm glad you're here."

I squeeze her and smile. "I am too. Thanks for having me."

"If it were up to me, you'd move in permanently, so don't thank me just yet. I plan to talk you into staying."

Liam opens the door and helps her down. "Babe, you can't harass him the whole time."

"I'm not."

Liam gives me an apologetic look, but I don't mind. Listening to Maddie's antics brings me back to being roommates and hanging out every day. That was before shit got complicated with the O'Learys.

Baby Tyler wakes up when Liam grabs him out of the car seat, and he nuzzles his face into Liam's neck. I take the diaper bag from him, then shut the door.

"Gonna give me the grand tour?" I tease as we make our way to the front.

"Absolutely!" Maddie answers. "I have your room all set and ready. Can't wait to show you."

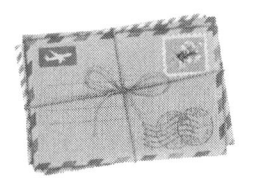

A couple of days after my arrival, we had a cookout and my other friends—Mason, Sophie, Hunter, Lennon, and all their kids—came over. It was the reunion I'd been anxious about for months. Though they all visited me from time to time, it wasn't as frequent as Maddie and Liam, so it was good to see them.

We drank beer, talked about sports, and I played with the little ones. For the first time in years, I felt normal. Though at moments, I'd look around waiting for the guard to tell me time was up, then push me back in my cell.

I hadn't realized the PTSD would kick in so quickly or that I'd actually have it. There's no "therapy session" that walks us through going back to real life. Basically, I'm just winging it. It was often lonely. The only person I had actual conversations with was my cellmate, Archer. We met three years ago, and before him, I didn't talk much to anyone. He has a few years left, and I told him to get in touch with me as soon as he's released. I even left him my new address in case he wanted to reach out.

Tomorrow, I'll fly to Alabama, and Everleigh will pick me up from the airport. I don't have much packed, maybe a suitcase full. Liam was able to grab some things from my old apartment in Vegas, mostly clothes and some personal items. My sister's letting me stay in her spare room, which is great for me, but I already feel like a burden. Though she's told me several times I'm not, it's hard not to feel like a failure at life right now.

"The baby has been kicking all day." Maddie waddles into my room and plops down on the bed. "He's protesting you leaving."

"Is that so?" I ask with amusement, popping a brow.

She crosses her arms over her chest and frowns. "Yes. He wants to meet you as soon as he's here."

"You can FaceTime me on my new phone," I remind her. "After the birth, though, please. Not during."

Liam chuckles as he walks in holding baby Tyler, glancing at Maddie, then me. "Trust me, I wouldn't do that to you."

"It won't be the same." Maddie pouts. "But either way, you better answer when we call. No matter what."

"I will, promise."

She closes her eyes, and tears stream down her cheeks. It guts me to see her upset. I love Maddie and appreciate everything they've done for me, but I can't stay. No matter how much she wants me to, I just can't.

"Mads, don't cry." I lean over and wipe her cheek. "I'll visit. We'll text and talk on the phone. You'll send me photos of your babies. I'll FaceTime you and show you around my hometown."

She sniffs and nods. "You better!"

"I will."

Maddie cracks a smile, and I wrap my arms around her, giving her a hug without adding too much pressure.

"How about I cook one more dinner for old times' sake?" I grin.

"Not that spicy shit, though." She points a finger at me, and I laugh. When I was her bodyguard in Montana and before she knew I was Liam's friend, I made her one of my grandma's Southern pasta dishes. Before I could warn her to stir in the seasonings, she took a large bite, and her tongue went numb.

"Whatever you want. Lady's choice," I offer, standing.

She follows my lead, and we walk toward the kitchen. "Mac 'n cheese mixed with carrots and cut-up Vienna sausages."

I turn and narrow my eyes at her, then glance at Liam.

He shakes his head. "Don't ask. She's had the weirdest pregnancy cravings these past few months."

"It's not *that* weird!" she argues.

"I don't know, Mads. That sounds like prison food." I chuckle, grabbing a pan from the cabinet. "In fact, I'm pretty sure I've eaten it but made with generic shit and old powdered cheese."

"Oh, we're going fancy tonight. Kraft shells all the way and extra cheese on top." Maddie grabs two boxes from the pantry, then shakes them in the air like maracas.

Soon, dinner is ready, and the three of us are laughing as we serve ourselves, then sit at the table.

"This is so good." Maddie moans around a mouthful. "Right, baby?"

We all look at baby Tyler who's half-feeding himself and half-tossing the noodles on the floor.

"He looks just like Liam when he stuffs his face full of food," I say.

"Yeah, and he looks just like his uncle Tyler when he's having a hissy fit," Liam throws back.

"Oh man, low blow." I cackle. "I can't wait until he's older, so I can teach him how to box. He'll be kicking your ass before he's ten."

I miss training in the ring and teaching people how to fight. It was my favorite profession before prison and something I hope to get back into once I'm settled. Even though Lawton Ridge is a small town, and there aren't many gym choices, there's one I can join if it's not too expensive. For the past three weeks, I've been running outside, but I miss lifting and hitting a punching bag.

"I don't think so…" Maddie intervenes. "He loves to dance just like his mama."

"We are not putting my *son* in dancing classes."

"Yes, we are."

"He's going to play football like his daddy."

"Daddy and Mommy also did yoga, so he could do both," Maddie adds with a grin, and Liam groans with an eye roll. Even I know it's no use arguing with her.

We spend the rest of the evening talking shit and playing with baby Tyler. It's surreal to say good night to them one last time, knowing I'll be gone tomorrow. I'm so proud of my two best friends and how much they've accomplished. They fought for each other for a long ass time and endured much drama and many hardships, but it led them to where they are now. They have the picture-perfect family, and no two people are more deserving. I'm truly happy for them.

I hope someday good karma comes around and rewards me with the same.

The next morning, Maddie's in tears again as I hug her goodbye. I kiss baby Tyler, hug Liam, then grab my two suitcases.

"Text me when you land," Maddie calls out.

"I will." I flash her a wink. "Good luck, you two."

"Same to you, man," Liam says.

"I wanna hear all about Gemma. Don't forget!" Maddie shouts as I walk through the sliding doors at the airport. I shake my head at her persistence. This isn't the first time she's asked about her, probably more like the hundredth. It's my fault for mentioning Gemma years ago and then bringing it up a few times in the letters I wrote Maddie. But it hurt too much to talk about her, so I stopped. I didn't want to open that wound again. What happened between Gemma and me was years ago, and I need to let it go.

That was before I decided to return to Alabama. Before I realized I'd be working for her dad.

Before I found out she was engaged to a rich prick.

Before I realized my feelings for her never went away.

But it doesn't matter now.

Too much time has passed and she's in love with another man. I kept her away this long, so it shouldn't be that hard again.

CHAPTER TWO

GEMMA

My alarm blares at six thirty in the morning like it does every weekday for work. I love being the office manager at my dad's garage, but he's an early bird. Me, not so much. However, I've had to become one over the years.

While the coffee maker finishes dripping, I make some avocado toast. Once my breakfast is ready, I sit at the small breakfast bar with a mug full and eat.

> **Robert: Morning, darling. Hope you slept well. Care to come over tonight so I can kiss my beautiful future wife?**

I smile at his message.

> **Gemma: I did, thank you. How about you? I can stop by later.**

> **Robert: I would've slept better with you next to me.**

My stomach drops. It's not the first time he's hinted at me moving in before we get married. Robert and I met a couple of years ago and have been engaged for eighteen months. Though he proposed early into our relationship, we didn't rush to set a date. I've needed time to figure out wedding details, and after finding a venue, we set an official date for March. Though it's seven months away, it still feels too soon.

Gemma: I can sleep over this weekend.

I stay with him most weekends, but he's ready for me to move in permanently.

Setting my phone down, I look over my planner and check my agenda for the day. I have to place a few orders, clean, and file receipts from last week. The garage is typically quiet, but when customers drop off or pick up vehicles, it gets busy. I make many phone calls, return dozens of emails, and search online for parts when my dad needs something specific that I can't find locally.

My dad and I have worked as a team since I was twenty-one, though I worked in the summers during high school and college. I got my associates degree in business management and then started working full-time.

Once I've finished eating and downed my coffee, I take a shower. The birds sing loudly outside, and I smile as I look around my cottage in the backyard of my childhood home. My two best friends, Katie and Everleigh, like to tease me about how it looks like something out of a Disney cartoon. It's quaint and cozy, and all it's missing is a fairy-tale story based around it.

As I wash my body and hair, I think about how I need to start packing soon, and the thought of moving out makes me sick to my stomach. For the past twelve years, I've made this place my own while leaving little parts of it that honor my mother. It gave me all the privacy I needed after I turned eighteen, and my dad was glad I was still close if I needed anything.

Before my mom passed, the Snow White cottage was her painting sanctuary. I don't remember a lot about her, and most of my memories come from pictures and watching old family video tapes. She died in a car accident when I was eight, and there's been a gaping hole in my heart ever since. My father raised me and did his best to make sure I didn't feel neglected by not having two parents. He always did a great job putting me first, but it never fully replaced not having my mom around. During those formative years of boys and going through puberty, I craved a woman's perspective.

Jerry Reid is a great man, but he knows jack shit about cramps and what type of pads I needed or what meds to take. Though he tried his best. Asking him to take me to a gynecologist for birth control to help regulate my periods was another defining moment of my teenage years I don't care to think about.

I have many happy memories here with friends and my dad helping me plant in the garden. I've taken care of it for years, and now, the thought of leaving scares me.

I know it makes sense to move in with Robert, but I want to spend the time I have left enjoying this place before the wedding is here. It's the only time I feel her presence and super close to my mother.

Katie, Everleigh, and I have spent countless nights on my couch drinking wine and watching *The Bachelor*. It became a weekly girls' night tradition. When I'm married, I don't know how often we'll get together. I don't even want to think about it.

My mother's paintings are hung on the walls. I love waking up to them and running my fingers across the frames. Though Robert has encouraged me to pack a few to hang in his house, it doesn't feel right to move them. This cottage is where her creativity blossomed. She'd set up her easel, then open the patio doors that face the little garden in the backyard. She'd paint the sycamore and red oak trees, squirrels, and blue jays at the feeders.

After she died, my father maintained the garden and even added a few birdhouses. While I didn't get her creative gene and can't paint to save my life, I understand why she loved this space so much. The view is awe-inspiring and feels like a little slice of heaven. Perhaps it's why I haven't been able to make the commitment to leave.

Once I've finished getting ready, I grab my things, then lock up. The garage isn't that far, and even though we could carpool, my dad always starts working before I arrive so he doesn't get behind. Lately, he's been doing everything on his own, and it's no secret he needs help in the shop. We open at eight, and I make it with ten minutes to spare.

"Good morning, Daddy." I open the door that separates the waiting area and the shop. I don't see him, but his truck is parked in the back, so I know he's here somewhere.

"Mornin', sweetie."

I finally see his legs sticking out from under a car. "What time did you get here?"

"Seven. Hey, can you call Mrs. Betsy Anne and let her know she can pick up her Oldsmobile at noon?"

"Can do. Anything else you need right away?"

"Maybe some coffee for your old man?"

I grin and shake my head. "Of course. Let me brew some, and I'll bring you a cup."

"That's why you're my favorite daughter." He rolls out from underneath and smirks.

"Nice try. I'm your *only* daughter."

I start the coffee maker and straighten up the cups and napkins on the table for the customers. Main Street Bakery, a few blocks down, delivers fresh pastries every morning at eight and will be here any minute.

As soon as I unlock the front door and flip the sign, the phone goes off. Minutes later, Mrs. Wright comes in with a dozen donuts and chats for a moment about the weather before leaving. I deliver my father a cup of steaming hot coffee and a chocolate eclair before going back to the front desk.

My day is nonstop, and if I'm not on the phone, I'm at the computer or going over invoices with customers. I'm able to take a thirty-minute break for lunch, and that's when I walk to the cafe on the corner and check my phone.

Katie: Tyler's back in town. Have you seen him yet?

I inhale a sharp breath at seeing *his* name on the screen. Everleigh told me he planned to return, and while it's been on my mind, it didn't really hit me until now. However, my anxiety spikes at the thought of running into him and how awkward things will be between us.

Gemma: No. You?

Katie: Nope.

The last time I saw Tyler Blackwood was twelve years ago. I was crushed when he left town after we spent three months together. It was the most amazing summer of my life, and then he broke my heart. I was in love with him, had given him my virginity, and was ready to spend the rest of my life with him.

But I wasn't enough to make him stay.

I knew he was only staying temporarily and had planned to move, but I had hoped he would stay for me. The day he left was the last time I heard from him.

Brokenhearted doesn't even brush the surface of how I felt for months after. Katie and Everleigh picked me up off the floor and forced me to move on. Being his sister, Everleigh was just as sad to see him go. The letters he sent me while he was in the Army were all I had left of him.

When he kissed me for the first time, I swear my heart stopped. As corny as it sounds, I'd fallen in love with him long before that kiss. After years of getting to know him, spilling my deepest and darkest secrets, and complaining about boys and school, he went from being a brotherly figure to someone I connected with on a level I never knew existed.

We hadn't seen each other in years or even talked on the phone, but those letters changed me.

I still have them stuffed in a shoebox in the back of my closet. Though I should just throw them away because I'm engaged, but I can't. Those letters are a part of my past, and at times, when I'm down and get drunk on wine, I pull them out and re-read my favorites.

It's self-sabotage, but I've only done it a few times. When I'm feeling uncertain about my future or want to reminisce about the past, I'll dig them out. The tears usually come so fast I can't even read the words on the paper.

My moments of weakness would happen when Tyler was on my mind and heart. I really believed he'd never return. The night I learned he'd been sentenced to five years in prison, I knew the prospect of seeing him again was slim to none. I'd always held a sliver of hope, but by then, I realized I needed to move on, so I did. I honestly figured after serving his time, he'd go back to Vegas and continue living his life in Nevada. But Everleigh mentioned a month ago he was moving home, and my stupid girl brain got anxious all over again about seeing him. I felt like a teenager again.

Katie: Think it'll be weird when you do?

Gemma: Probably a little, but hopefully I won't run into him that much anyway.

Katie: Well, if he's going to live at Everleigh's for a while, you might. Plus, he'll be around town. It's not like we live in NYC.

Gemma: It'll be fine. It's been years, and I'm engaged now. No reason it has to be awkward.

My words are more for me than her, but they're true. They both remember how stupid in love with him I was and how broken I was after he left.

Walking inside the café, I smile at Angela who's behind the counter. Since I'm a regular, she asks me if I want my usual, and I give her a nod. A few minutes later, she hands me my vanilla chai latte and cinnamon loaf.

"See you tomorrow." I wave as I head toward the door. Angela smiles and tells me goodbye.

A gentleman opens it before I can, and my heart stops. At first glance, I thought it could've been Tyler, but it wasn't. He keeps it open for me, and I thank him as I exit.

Great. Now every time I see a tall, good-looking man, I'm going to think it's him.

I'm fucking *doomed*.

Dear Gemma,

I hate that I can hear you crying in my head even though I'm thousands of miles away. A boy should never make you cry, and one who does isn't worth your time. Derrick is an idiot for breaking up with you. You know that, right? He's not worthy of you.

And before you think it… No, I'm not just saying that. I really mean it.

Derrick's lucky I'm far away right now and can't kick his needle-dick ass to the next county.

But for real, I'm sorry you got your heart broken. I know it can be hard, especially the first time, and you're probably thinking there's something wrong with you or that you aren't good enough, but it's not true. I might not have relationship experience, but I practically raised Everleigh until the day I left for boot camp and know how you teen girls think.

The pain will eventually go away, and soon, you'll wonder what you ever saw in him. Time heals all wounds, Gemma. Don't give this boy your tears. He doesn't deserve them.

I've re-read that letter so much after he left that even after all this time, I still have it memorized.

There's so much irony in the words he wrote to cheer me up. The lie that time would heal all wounds when I spent years shedding so many tears for him.

Tyler and I weren't "friends" growing up. His and Everleigh's childhood was a fucked-up, sad situation. Given what they went through, they avoided being like their drunk mother and deadbeat dad at all costs. Well, except Tyler getting mixed up in some shit with some terrible people. I really don't know the whole story, but from what Everleigh said, he was framed and then sent to prison because of it.

After he enlisted, Everleigh moved in with her grandparents, but Katie and I continued to have sleepovers with the three of us, and we all grew even closer. Since talking about Tyler upset her, she found ways to deal with missing him by writing to him. That gave me the idea to do the same. I figured he could use the company and distraction from whatever he was going through, but I honestly never expected him to write back. Receiving his letters was the highlight of my teenage life. We wrote to each other several times a month for four years, and every letter was like having a piece of him no one else had.

The worst part was that I waited for him after he left me. I waited *years*.

I went on several first dates, but nothing ever came of them because my heart was still hung up on him. I was naïve to think he would come back for me. It wasn't until two years ago when I met Robert that I actually felt like I could give myself to another man.

Robert's a wealthy businessman who owns his own development and realtor company. He's fifteen years older with life experience. He wants children and is eager for us to start our lives together. The man isn't afraid to show me how he feels and has never played games like most guys my age do. Robert has always been open and straightforward about his feelings for me. When he compliments me, I know without a doubt he means it.

After six months of dating, he proposed, and it felt like the pieces of my heart had finally glued back together. I wanted to be happy. I *deserved* it, and Robert wanted to give me the world.

I accepted, and soon, I'll be Mrs. Robert Hawkley. I honestly can't wait to see him later.

The following day starts out the same. After visiting Robert last night, I came home and passed out.

Mrs. Wright arrives with the morning pastries and just as she's walking out, I hear her thank the man who's holding the door open. I look up and see *him*.

No. It can't be.

Blinking, I shake my head to clear my vision. He walks toward me with an intense expression on his face, and I know I'm not seeing things. It's *really* him.

My mouth falls open, and I forget how to breathe. I stay standing as I wait for an alien invasion to come and abduct me. I want nothing more than to be taken out of this uncomfortable situation.

"Hi, Gemma." His deep voice sends electricity down my body. It's even manlier than I remember.

"Tyler. Hi." I clear my throat after the shaky words give away my nervousness. "What are you doing here? I mean, not in Lawton Ridge, since I knew you were coming home."

My gaze lowers down his body, and I take him in. Time has been good to him. *Really good.* My eyes stop on his mouth as he licks his lower lip before plucking it with his teeth.

"I'm here to speak to your dad. Is he around?" He shoves his hands into the front pockets of his jeans.

Swallowing hard, I furrow my brows. While his brown eyes are still kind, something brews behind them like a distant storm at sea. The boy I remember is now a man, and he's rigid like a sharp piece of glass. "My dad? Why?"

Fidgeting with my fingers, I tilt my head as I study him. I shouldn't, but I can't help it. He's really here. When our eyes meet again, there's a sliver of the old him there, but it's gone in a flash when he straightens his stance, and replies, "Because he's going to be my new boss."

CHAPTER THREE

TYLER

BY HER REACTION, it's obvious Gemma had no idea her dad and I had an arrangement. I thought Everleigh would've at least told her, but instead, Gemma's completely blindsided by my arrival.

When I look into her eyes, they still sparkle as bright as they used to. Guilt floods in, but I push it away. I know she's engaged, but it doesn't stop the unfiltered thoughts that flood my mind as I study her. Flashes of our past come in waves. The last time I saw Gemma Reid, her hair was longer, darker, and she rarely wore makeup. Now, her hair is cut and curled to her shoulders, her lips are ruby red, and she barely looks over twenty-five. She's aged well—not that thirty is old—but compared to how she looked at eighteen, she's a grown woman.

"He didn't tell you?" I ask when she doesn't speak.

"Uh, no. He did not, but it's no big deal." She waves a hand in the air with a light chuckle. "Probably slipped his mind. He's constantly on the go these days. Always worrying about his customers."

Her rambling has me holding back a smile. Gemma was a shy teenager. Even when I spent that summer with her, she was on the quiet side. Now, she seems more confident than before.

"Well, sorry. I won't take too much of his time."

"No worries. Just let me grab him." She walks to the door, and I shamelessly check out her ass. It's strange to see her in a tight pencil skirt and blouse. She loved wearing sundresses and running barefoot when we were together. Now she's all business and looks more tempting than ever.

"Tyler!" Jerry booms the minute he walks into the lobby. He reaches for my hand and shakes it.

"Mr. Reid. Good to see you, sir."

"You too, son." He pats me on the back. "Come into my office so we can chat."

Jerry looks over at Gemma. "Did you offer Tyler a drink?" He glances at me. "Coffee? Water? Coke?"

Before Gemma can respond, I hold up a hand. "No, I'm fine, but thank you."

Gemma flashes me a smile, but it doesn't reach her eyes, and by how she fidgets, I know she's uncomfortable as hell. I almost feel bad, considering our history, but I need this job and a fresh start. I'll stay out of her way if that's what she wants. However, if we're working together every day, it won't be easy.

Jerry brings me into the office and shuts the door. "Sit, sit…"

"I really appreciate you giving me this opportunity, Mr. Reid. My past isn't the best, but I'm a hard worker." I could elaborate on the bullshit that got me locked up, but he doesn't seem like the type of guy who cares to hear the whole story.

"Please, call me Jerry. Mr. Reid makes me sound old."

Leaning back in the chair, I chuckle and nod. "Will do."

"I have no doubt you'd be a good fit, Tyler. I've heard some of the stories and whether they're true isn't for me to judge. I just need you to show up on time and not be distracted by your phone all day."

"That I can definitely do." I sit up straight. "I'm very disciplined."

"I know you spent four years in the military, and that's no easy task. So, I'll tell ya what, we'll do a trial run. If you start slacking off or get into trouble, you're fired. If you come to work with a good attitude and get shit done, you can stay. Fair?"

"Absolutely. I won't let you down, Jerry."

"You can start Monday. Gemma will give you a tour, and then I'll put you to work. That okay?"

"Fine with me." That gives me five days to get what I need and settle in.

He stands, and we shake hands again. "Thank you again. I can let myself out," I say so I can have a minute with Gemma before leaving.

"Alright, see you next week."

We say goodbye, and I make my way to the lobby. The door slams behind me, and Gemma jumps.

"Jesus!" She drops her cell on the desk and holds a hand to her chest.

"Sorry. Didn't realize it would be so loud." I tap my knuckles on the counter and lean over, glancing at her phone screen. "Who're you texting?"

She quickly flips it over. "None of your business."

Chuckling, I shrug. "Hope it's not that Derrick guy you were obsessed with or I'll really have to kick his ass into the next county."

Her eyes widen, and for a long beat, I don't think she's going to speak, but then she clears her throat and the corner of her lips tilts up. "That was my sophomore year. How do you even remember his name?"

I've never forgotten what she said in the letters she sent me, even years later. It's something I thought a lot about when I was behind bars. When Liam offered to pack my apartment, I made sure he grabbed them so I didn't lose them.

"Because I remember that little prick made you cry."

"Well, I'm a big girl now. And he's married to Maggie. She owns the salon."

"Wait." I hold my hands above my head to imitate big hair. "The girl who looked like she used a can of hairspray every day?"

Gemma laughs, then nods. "Yep."

"Wow. Guess I have some catching up to do."

"A lot has changed." Her gaze locks on mine, and neither of us blinks. The intensity is thick between us. "I'm engaged," she blurts out, then immediately blushes. "I mean, so you don't have to go laying anyone out."

I narrow my eyes at her, wondering if she's always this socially awkward or if it's just with me. "I heard."

"Right. Of course, you did. I'm sure Everleigh told you."

"She did. Congrats." I shove my hands into my pockets.

"Thank you. We finally set a date, so I'm in major planning mode now."

"That's great. I'm really happy for you, Gemma. You deserve the wedding of your dreams."

She stares at me as if there's something on the tip of her tongue. "I waited."

"What?"

Gemma inhales a sharp breath and looks away before locking her green eyes back on mine. "After you left, I waited. *Years*, actually."

I wasn't expecting her to say that. My throat goes dry, unsure how I should respond, and all I can muster is an apology. "I'm sorry. I didn't know."

"Well, how would you? I never heard from you again."

Fuck.

The hurt in her tone is undeniable, and this is the last place I expected us to have this conversation.

"Gemma…" I step closer.

"No." She shakes her head. "I shouldn't have said anything. It doesn't matter. I'm over it."

The bitterness of her tone has me halting. She never got closure. Neither did I, but honestly, it was my own stupid fault.

"We—"

The phone rings and interrupts us before I can tell her that we should talk in private, but she holds up a finger.

"Don't worry about it. I gotta take this."

I purse my lips and give her a curt nod. "Alright. See you Monday then."

She gives a slight wave as she answers the call with a sweet greeting. I make my way out of the shop and blink hard, avoiding the sun.

Fuck. That conversation didn't go as planned. I hope working there isn't the worst fucking idea I've ever had. If it all backfires on me, things will end worse than they did the last time I left, and I'll shatter more than just her heart.

Instead of going home, I stop at Everleigh's boutique.

"Well, how'd it go?" Everleigh asks as she counts money from the cash register.

"I start Monday."

She looks up at me. "Did you see Gemma?"

"*Yep*. Apparently, she had no idea her dad was interviewing me."

She averts her eyes and purses her lips. "Oh, really? I must've forgotten to mention that detail." She closes the register, then hangs the dresses in her hands on a rack.

"Oh, right. Even though you have an impeccable memory and can remember exact conversations from twenty years ago. I'm sure you just...*forgot*."

Everleigh rolls her eyes. "I have selective memory." Even though she's younger, she often tries to keep me in line as though she's *my* big sister.

"Well, tell me how it went." She puts her hands on her hips.

"More awkward than when you tried stealing a box of condoms from the store when you were thirteen." I chuckle at the memory. She was embarrassed the sheriff called and begged me not to tell our grandparents.

"Tyler!" She grabs a balled-up piece of paper and throws it at me. "That was a dare!"

"And you're lucky Father Tim was there shopping and talked the owners out of pressing charges."

Everleigh blushes, then buries her face in her hands before meeting my eyes. "Ah, I almost forgot that part."

"Well, times that by two, and that's how awkward our interaction was. And now I'm going to see her every day." I lean against the wall, crossing my arms over my chest.

"I'm surprised my phone isn't blowing up yet, though she might never talk to me again for not warning her." Everleigh bites into her lower lip, then waves it off. "She'll get over it."

I snort. "She blurted out that she was engaged."

"It's not like you can miss the massive rock on her finger." She moves around the store, and I follow her. She stops and hands me a few shirts. "Make yourself useful and hang these on the back wall."

"I don't work for you." I smirk.

She turns and glares. "You're living in my condo rent-free. Shut up and use your height to hang those up so I don't have to use my extension pole."

I nearly choke. "Your stripper pole?"

"Goddammit, Tyler." Everleigh bursts out laughing, then walks to the corner of the shop. "An *extension* pole. It's a garment hook or hanger retriever for clothes that are high up."

"From now on, I'd go with one of those names instead."

"You haven't changed a bit." She hands me the pole.

"What's that mean?" I'm more different than she'll ever realize.

"Means you're still my annoying big brother." She points at the wall. "Now put them up there for me, would ya?" She grins, then pats my arm before walking away.

Once I'm done figuring out which shirt goes where and how to balance the hangers properly on this stupid retriever pole, I do exactly what she asked. When I'm finished, I find Everleigh on the other side of the store.

"Gemma said they picked a date for the wedding. When is it?"

"March thirteenth."

Only seven months away.

"They were engaged a long time before setting one."

Everleigh nods. "Mm-hmm. He proposed early on, like he wanted to claim her and for everyone to know she was his but wasn't in a rush to actually get married."

"Why do you think that is?" I watch as she organizes a shelf of candles.

"Honestly…" She looks over her shoulder at me and frowns. "I think she likes the idea of loving him and having the picture-perfect life, but in reality, she's second-guessing if it's the right thing to do. Gemma loves her cottage, and I know it's been eating at her to give it up, which is why she won't move in with him."

"They don't live together?"

"Nope. He's been asking for months, and she's adamant about waiting."

Interesting.

"So why's she with him?"

Everleigh goes back to organizing some bracelets by the counter, and I follow her as she walks and talks.

"I have a few theories, but Gemma denies them all."

"Which are?"

She finally stops and turns, folding her arms over her chest as she studies me. "Why do you care so much? I thought you moved on."

"I'll always care for her well-being, even if I'm not in her life, Ev. All I've ever wanted is for Gemma to be happy, and if this guy doesn't make her happy…"

"She tries to be." She shrugs, and her face falls. "Jerry really likes him and the idea of them getting married."

"Really? Her dad approves?"

"Oh, totally. He's over the fucking moon about them finally setting a date. Robert will be able to take care of her financially, and she'll always have what she needs. Growing up, they didn't have much, and Jerry knows she won't have to worry when they start a family. It makes him happy as Pops eatin' warm apple pie, and Gemma wants nothing more than to make her dad happy."

"Do you think that's why she's marrying him? To appease Jerry?"

Everleigh goes behind the counter. "I'm not sure, but even if it was, Gemma wouldn't tell me. I'm only speculating from what I see and hear. She's not super open about their relationship, but then again, Gemma has always been private." She gives me a look, and I read between the lines. Gemma didn't share every detail of our relationship, but Everleigh knew enough to threaten me when I left.

"Wow…" I brush a hand through my hair, trying to process everything.

"Yep. Well, as much as I'm *enjoying* this brotherly chat, I need to get back to work and open the store."

"Yeah, I gotta run some errands anyway."

"What kind of errands?"

"I need to get a checking account, go to the post office and change my address, update my license, and get some new work clothes and shoes."

She rounds the counter and gives me a hug. "Proud of you."

I wrap my arms around her. "For what?"

"For coming back home and starting over. I understand things have been hard for you and know being here won't be easy. I'm proud you came back. I missed you. Our grandparents did too."

She pushes back, and I smile.

"I know. I missed you guys too," I admit, then walk toward the door. Before I make it outside, she calls my name, and I turn.

"Can you walk Sassy when you get home?"

Sassy is an American Eskimo dog with way too much energy who also hates me. "Seriously?"

"Please? She loves you!"

"That's what you call love?" I ask. Everleigh nods eagerly, and I open the door, then wave before walking out.

I wonder if what Everleigh said is true. Why would Gemma marry a man she wasn't head over heels in love with? Did she really wait *years* for me?

I think back to one of the letters she wrote her last year of high school. We both knew I'd be returning home soon.

Dear Tyler,

Senior prom is only a week away, but Everleigh and I decided to do a photoshoot yesterday with our dresses and practice our makeup and hair. Since these letters take so long to get to you, I got a few printed so I could show you.

I hope you like them.

Everleigh is going with a guy from our chem class, and although a few people asked me, I turned them all down. I wish you could be my date. The only person who could make it a night to remember forever is you. You know me better than anyone, which is crazy, considering we haven't seen each other face-to-face in almost four years, but I feel so close to you. There's literally nothing I haven't told you. Some of the things I haven't even told Everleigh or Katie, and they're my best friends.

I guess it's safe to say you could ruin me if you wanted. I've told you all my secrets.

But I know you well enough to know you'd never do that to me.

As weird as it sounds, I always imagined I'd lose my virginity on prom night. It's super cliché, but it seems so romantic. Spend the day getting ready for the magical event, take pictures, go to a fancy dinner, dance for hours, then experience sex for the first time. It'd be the best night of my entire life.

Oh, well.

Promise me things won't be awkward between us when you come home in a couple of months. I've dreamed about the first time we see each other again, and honestly, thinking about it makes me nervous. I told Everleigh we've been writing to each other for years, but she has no idea how much or what we talk about. I have a feeling she knows I've had a crush on you since seventh grade.

I'll write you again after prom to tell you how it went.
See you soon,
Gemma

The photos she added inside that letter had every part of my body on alert. My head felt dizzy from staring at them for so long. Gemma wasn't a *kid* anymore, and while I knew that, the pictures proved it. Though she didn't fully admit it, I could read between the lines. I wished like hell I would've been able to get home sooner, but I still had six weeks left.

Her letters went from sweet and innocent to deep and emotional over the course of those four years. Gemma had always been on the shy side, but she wasn't afraid to express how she felt in her letters. Writing her was therapeutic, and I think she wrote me to deal with the teenage emotions she had during high school. It helped me to open up too and allowed me to work on feelings I had about my childhood. I felt comfortable sharing my life with her, how I was handling the military, and my fears of what I'd do after I was done.

In the few letters she sent me after that day, she became even more honest. She admitted that she couldn't wait to see me, how she hoped we'd spend some time together, and that she wished I'd be her *first*. She was waiting for me.

I could no longer deny I'd fallen for Gemma Reid. Slowly, the words we shared changed everything, and they were no longer a quick check-in or about town gossip. I spilled my heart to her in my final letter, and the anticipation of seeing her was so strong that I hardly recognized myself.

CHAPTER FOUR

GEMMA

Last night, after I had dinner with Robert, I went home and slept like total shit. I kept tossing and turning, thinking about Tyler and his piercing gaze. There's a tug-of-war inside me when I wake up, and I'm so annoyed that neither my dad nor Everleigh mentioned anything about him working at the garage. Yesterday, Tyler glided across the floor as if he was a ghost from my past coming to haunt me. And he is. Glancing at the clock, I realize I need to move my ass so I'm not late. It's one of Dad's biggest pet peeves.

As soon as I unlock the lobby door, we're slammed with customers. I inhale a donut when things finally slow down and replay the conversation Tyler and I had yesterday. My nerves got the best of me, and I felt like I was a teenage girl again. I shake my head and swallow, grabbing a bottle of water from the break room.

I drink it down, hoping it cools off my insides that are hot like an inferno. When my dad walks in to grab a soda, I take the opportunity to nonchalantly mention it since he hasn't yet.

"So...Tyler Blackwood." I casually look at him as he pops the tab of the soda and takes a long swig.

"Yeah. Could use the help. You think he'll be good?"

My breath hitches, but he doesn't notice. "Why didn't you ask me *before* you hired him?" I glance over and force a smile. "I mean, I am the office manager." A title I have earned and am quite proud of.

Dad lets out a chuckle and grins. "You know I was thinkin' about your brother, and how hard it's gonna be for him when he gets out of prison. Tyler's in the same situation, with his record, so I thought I'd give him a chance. He's a hard worker and seems disciplined enough to handle the responsibility, especially with his military experience. Y'all hung out together, so he can't be too bad. And back in the day, he helped me a few times over the summer when I needed a hand."

I lift my eyebrow, still annoyed he didn't give me a heads-up.

"Plus, your old man ain't gettin' any younger. It'll be nice to have some help, but if it makes you feel any better, I told him it was a trial run." He finishes his drink, then throws the can in the garbage. "You're not mad, are ya?"

"No, no. I was just curious. Hopefully, he works out for you." I understand where my dad's coming from because when Noah's released, he'll need all the help he can get. It's a small town, and gossip travels faster than lightning around here. Most won't see my brother or Tyler for who they are, but rather as convicts. It's a stigma that'll follow them around for the rest of their lives. I pray someone offers Noah the same opportunity if he decides to come home when he's released. He calls me twice a month, always asks about Katie and Dad, my job, and other town gossip. I don't visit much—he doesn't like us to see him like that—but when we do, it's better than nothing. I miss him so much and can't wait until he's released. Though I know it won't be easy for him, he deserves the chance to start over.

Noah might've made a tragic mistake, but he's not a murderer. My brother has the kindest, most honest heart, and I don't care what the assholes at the grocery store mutter under their breaths when I walk in. Over the years, it's gotten better, but the wounds aren't fully healed, especially Katie's.

Dad always talks about paying it forward and treating people the way you want to be treated. It's one of his core values, one that Noah and I were taught growing up. While Tyler needs this job, it won't make seeing him every day any easier. There are a lot of hard feelings and buried emotions when it comes to him, and it was easy to forget what happened when he wasn't in town. Now, he'll only be feet away from me; a constant reminder I wasn't enough to make him stay.

My heart races thinking about it.

ONLY HIM

I glance up at the clock and notice I'm late to a lunch date with Robert. Dad pulls out his sandwich and sits at the little table, and I give him a quick squeeze and tell him I'll be back in an hour. That's one good thing about working here. Dad doesn't care if I go out during the day. I have leniency, and pretty much can do whatever I want, though I never leave him hanging. It's a cushy job, and I get paid well. My dad always wants the best for his kids, but he makes me earn it too. Handouts don't and won't ever exist around here.

As I drive across town, my mind spins. Mindlessly, I drive to one of the only fine dining restaurants in town.

Before I get out, I check myself in the mirror and notice how frazzled I look. I tuck my wild hair behind my ears and pull some lipstick from my purse to add some color to my lips. After a few deep breaths, I walk into the restaurant with a smile planted as I search for him.

As soon as Robert sees me, his hazel eyes light up, and he stands. I quickly realize we're not dining alone since a couple of other men are seated at the table. Once I reach him, Robert leans in and gives me a quick kiss on the cheek. Before sitting, he whispers in my ear how pretty I look. Then being the doting fiancée that I am, I smile at all the men at the table and sit next to Robert.

His hard work and determination are admirable. Business is booming right now, and he works himself to the bone. While I understand why he's always on the go, this typically means we don't get to spend as much time together as we'd like. The moments we do have, I want to treasure and not share him with other people, but I make exceptions.

I should be used to this by now, though, because it happens so often. I'm lucky to have found a loving man who wants to make me happy. Most people assume that since we're fifteen years apart, I'm only with him because of his wealth. Being with Robert has nothing to do with his money or businesses. Though he's every woman's cliché of the perfect man—tall, dark, and handsome—I wanted a relationship based on mutual love and respect. I don't care if he can buy me the world. Large diamond rings, mansions, and fancy cars don't matter to me.

"So this is your beautiful fiancée," a man says, then continues, "I'm Stanley."

Robert wraps his arm around me, pulls me close, then properly introduces everyone. Afterward, we order, and I consider getting a glass of wine to relieve the tension. Though my dad wouldn't mind, I try not to go to work buzzed.

As I sip my water, I play out everything that'll happen during this predictable lunch. They're always exactly the same as if we're all reading from a script. Robert laughs when he's supposed to, and I join him like *I'm* supposed to. I can tell they've been talking about this for a while when Robert reminds him other buyers are interested. By the time we finish eating, Stanley finally makes a decision and wants to close on a few acres of land on the outskirts of town. Robert is thrilled about sealing the deal and hands his credit card to the waitress to pay for everyone. They plan to meet at Robert's office in an hour to sign the contract and make it official.

When we get up and say our goodbyes, Robert lingers behind with me as the men leave. He looks at me with bright blue eyes and grins.

"See, sweetie, you're my lucky charm."

I laugh because this isn't the first time he's said that, and I wonder if he really believes it. Perhaps it's why he invites me to these meetings even though I'd rather just spend time alone with him.

Robert and I walk outside hand in hand as he leads me to my car. Before I open the door, he pulls me into his arms and places a chaste kiss on my lips.

"Thank you, beautiful," he murmurs, sliding his arm around my waist.

"For what?"

"For coming to lunch. Agreeing to marry me. Loving me." He nuzzles his lips into my neck, and I can smell the mixture of his soap and cologne. "I miss you so damn much."

"You saw me last night." I chuckle, but I've missed him too.

"Yes, but I hate waking up without you next to me. I hate that my girl won't move in so we can start our life. You should think about it, Gemma. I keep asking because I'm not a patient man. I want you now." He flashes a boyish grin that almost always gets him his way.

He slides his lips across mine, and I sink into him. When we break apart, I let out a dreamy sigh.

"I just want to wake up together every day to be special after we're married," I remind him.

"It's so old-fashioned to wait until marriage, though. There's plenty of room for you in my house. And plenty of room for you in my bed."

He mentions this so much that there's no way I'll be able to keep squirming out of it. So I tell him the truth. "I'm not ready to leave my house yet."

The mood turns serious, but Robert brushes it off like he always does. In another week, he'll bring it up again, hoping I've changed my mind and won't say no, but I will. Then we'll go our separate ways, and he'll be full of disappointment while I harbor all the guilt.

"I'm a greedy man when it comes to you, Gemma. I want to spend all my time with you, and it wounds me that I can't. But I don't want to force you into something you don't want right now." He places his soft lips on my knuckles, and that's when the shame swells inside me.

"There's no need to rush when we have forever," I say sweetly, and he nods. Sometimes, I feel like he's trying too hard, and he shouldn't. Is it insecurity, maybe? Before I can continue to reassure him, his cell rings, and he tells me he has to take the call. Another client. More property sold. And just like that, he gives me a quick peck and rushes to his car.

I drive back to the garage with too many thoughts streaming through my mind, which make me anxious. After I walk back into the shop and tell my dad I've returned, I grab my phone and text Everleigh since I forgot to last night.

Gemma: Please tell me you didn't know your brother would interview for a job at the garage.

The text bubbles pop up then disappear before she finally responds.

Everleigh: I might've known, but I wasn't sure your dad would hire him. That was all Jerry!

I send her an eye roll emoji because she's so fucking sneaky and then tuck my phone in my pocket when Dad comes in and says my name. He hates it when people are on their phones during work hours, and I've gotten my fair share of scowls for bringing it out.

"Wanna join me out here and chat?" he asks, but his demanding tone leaves no room for a discussion.

"I need you to show Tyler around on Monday. Explain how we do things here. I'll be pullin' the engines in two Jeeps that day, so it'd be nice if you could help him out on his first day."

I keep my reaction neutral and nod. "Sure, I'll tell him how anal you are about oil spills and how dirty rags need to be put in the hamper after every shift. Oh, and I'll demand he stay off his phone because it might give you an ulcer."

Dad smiles and laughs. "That's my girl."

Noah and I grew up helping Dad in the garage. Not many women can change their own oil, pull a radiator, and rebuild an engine. It got to a point where we needed a trusted person to handle the finances and set up appointments without fucking it up, so after I got my associates degree from the local community college, I decided to do exactly that.

Working closely with Tyler sounds like a nightmare, but I'll suck it up for my father's sake because he desperately needs the help.

The rest of the day passes quickly, and I lock up once the floor is swept and my desk is organized.

Once I'm home, I pour a glass of wine and soak in the bathtub. It's peaceful and quiet, but as much as I try to relax, it's no use. My mind is too loud with thoughts.

My phone buzzes in the living room, a reminder that it's time to get out. After I wrap a towel around my head and body, I see several missed group text messages.

Everleigh: Okay, girls. I need to use your pretty faces again.

I instantly smile. Though I'm still kinda annoyed she didn't give me a heads-up about Tyler, it's obvious she means well and wants the best for him. Everleigh owns Ever After, a cute boutique around the corner from my dad's shop. It's full of accessories, graphic T-shirts, and fashionable clothing for grown-up millennials. She's worked hard to grow her social media presence, and any time a new shipment arrives, Everleigh asks us to model them.

> **Katie: When? Do I have time to lose five pounds before you put my picture on the internet again?**
>
> **Everleigh: Tomorrow night around 6:30ish? All the new stuff that just arrived is so adorable that I want to get pictures posted as soon as possible. Plus, I'll provide unlimited wine ;)**

A chuckle escapes me as I finish my glass. Everleigh knows the way to our hearts.

> **Gemma: You said the magic word. Wine and I'm in.**
>
> **Everleigh: I knew that'd work!**
>
> **Katie: Fine, fine. Let me see if I can find a sitter. I need a girls' night anyway!**
>
> **Gemma: I guess that means I need to freshen up my hair and makeup beforehand?**
>
> **Everleigh: Unless you want to look like a hot mess monster on my website and social media, I'd say yes.**

I think about the schedule for tomorrow. Considering it's a Friday, there'll be mostly oil changes and state inspections. I'll bring my makeup case and hairspray with me so I can touch up my face and hair before going to Everleigh's shop. It'll probably take a couple of hours, considering we fool around a lot when the three of us get together. I'm already exhausted thinking about it, but I'm excited to hang out with them after the week I've had. Plus, it helps her get more business. When people see the clothes and accessories on bodies rather than mannequins, they immediately want it.

Shit. I usually spend the night at Robert's Friday and Saturday nights, but I'm sure he won't mind if I cancel this one time. Heat rushes to my face, and I'm not sure if it's the wine or the fact that I'd rather be with my friends.

I sit on the couch as I text the girls, and we chat about how the last time we got together for a photoshoot. We drank too much, then stumbled to Everleigh's house for more drinking and girl time. Katie was up early to pick up Owen from her parents', but I slept like a brick on her couch.

Once my glass is empty, I notice the sun is setting and decide to text Robert since I hadn't heard from him since lunch.

Gemma: Hey babe, wanna come over and watch a movie with me? I'll even let you pick this time! No chick flicks, I promise.

We take turns picking and go between action movies and rom-coms. I happen to like them both. When we first started dating, we'd gone through our list of favorite childhood movies. Since he's fifteen years older than me, there were quite a few titles I'd never seen before.

Robert: Sorry, darling. Wish I could, but I'm still at the office finishing up some schematics, and I'm hungry and exhausted. It's been a long day. I'll be heading home within the hour, and you can meet me at the house, or you know, move in with me ;)

The blood drains from my face as I read his message and feel as if he punched me in the gut again. No matter what I do or say, he won't stop until I admit defeat and move in.

I send Everleigh a message outside our group text.

Gemma: Robert is getting pushier about me moving in. I tell him I'm not ready, but it's not enough for him to stop asking, and things get more awkward every time I tell him no.

Everleigh: Stay strong. Enjoy your freedom while you can, because once you move in with him, you'll lose it all.

I chuckle at her response. It's so like her, too. She's independent and fierce, always has been.

Gemma: Sometimes, I wonder if you're a bad influence or not.

Everleigh: Oh, I absolutely am.

CHAPTER FIVE

TYLER

EVERLEIGH DRIVES me to Mimi and Pop's house before she opens the boutique Friday morning. I need to borrow Mimi's Cadillac so I can run errands today. Yesterday, I submitted an address change form at the post office, opened a checking account, and made a list of items I still need to buy. I have some money from before I got arrested, but it won't last long.

"Send my love to Mimi, okay?" Everleigh tells me when she pulls into the driveway and parks.

"I will."

"If she baked *anything*, promise to sneak me a pocketful." She chuckles, and I shake my head before getting out of the car. As she backs out of the driveway, she lays on the horn, causing me to jump. She speeds off, and I'm sure she's probably laughing her ass off.

Even though it's not even eight yet, they're early risers. I'm sure my grandmother has already drunk a pot of coffee and called a handful of friends all while Pops tinkers in his workshop in the backyard. As soon as I walk in, I'm surrounded with childhood memories. The smell of cookies wafts through the living room, and I hear Mimi chatting on the phone in the kitchen. When I enter, she immediately grins and waves me over.

"Susan," she interrupts. "Susan, I gotta let you go, honey. Tyler just walked in."

Seconds later, she ends the call. It's hard not to smile when I'm

ONLY HIM

around my grandmother. She stands and pulls me into a tight embrace.

"I was wonderin' when you were gonna come see me again. Didn't wanna have to beg."

"Oh, Mimi, you know I had that interview a couple of days ago and then had errands to run yesterday."

Her eyes light up, and I can tell she's waiting for the news. I eye the cookies on the plate on the table and snatch one. A chuckle escapes me as I think about Everleigh wanting some as I eat half of it in one bite.

"You gonna leave a woman waiting?" she finally asks.

"I start Monday," I tell her around another mouthful.

She looks relieved, but I'm sure she already knew. Nothing gets past her. Rumors wrapped in sprinkles of truth fly around here like mosquitos in the summer.

"Good, good. Jerry wouldn't have been able to handle my wrath if he *didn't* hire you," she says matter-of-factly. Grandma can be scary, especially when she gets her entire knitting club together to wreak havoc on shady people. They're equivalent to a mob in Lawton Ridge.

Mimi checks the time, then turns to me. "You hungry? Want me to make you some breakfast before you go?"

I shake my head. "Nah, that's okay. Hopefully, it won't take too long to update my license."

She snorts. "Are you kidding me? You obviously haven't been to the DMV here in ages. It's an unorganized disaster. People line up at six in the morning and wait all day to be seen. Let me make you something, I insist."

"I drank a protein shake for breakfast."

"Then I'll make you a sandwich for later." She opens the fridge and pulls out some chopped rotisserie chicken and mayo. Mimi makes the fattest sandwich I've ever seen. It won't fit even in a sandwich bag, so she places it in a gallon Ziploc, then stuffs cookies in another one before handing me a giant glass of sweet tea.

"Better get going if you want to make it out of there before dark."

After I take her gifts, she pulls her keys from her purse, then hands them to me. Before I go, I kiss her on the cheek and tell her I'll be back as soon as I can.

On the way across town, I can't get Gemma off my mind. She looked at me like she wanted to murder me, and as far as I know, she might. Even though I begged her to come with me, I knew it was best to leave on my own. I needed to protect her from the emotional baggage I bear. Considering I'm a felon now, it seems like it was the right decision after all.

After I arrived at the DMV, I realize Mimi wasn't joking. There are no empty spaces in the lot, so I parallel park on the street, then walk inside and grab a ticket. Every seat is taken.

Hours pass, and I eat my sandwich and cookies, grateful Mimi packed me a lunch. I swear sloths are working the counter. An hour before close, my number is finally called, and I take my photo. By the time I leave, I'm annoyed as hell I spent my entire day waiting there.

When I show up to Mimi's just after five with two empty Ziploc bags, she flashes me a smirk. The "told you so" is implied, and I just shake my head with a grin. She offers to drive me home, but I tell her I want to walk. After she sees my face and how frustrated I am, she doesn't argue.

"Please make sure you call me when you make it home. Love you, kiddo."

"I will, Mimi. Love you too," I say as I walk out the door.

On the way home, I call Liam. He's two hours behind me, so I hope he's home, but he usually answers unless he's doing a stakeout.

"Tyler! I was just thinking about you. How are things going?"

I told him about my interview yesterday, but we didn't chat long. "Fine, I guess." I let out a huff.

"Uh-oh, what's wrong?"

I talk about my shitty day, and how I'm so fucking sweaty I can barely stand it. The humidity here is smothering compared to Las Vegas. I continue, explaining how stressed I am, and how I'm still paranoid as fuck. It's gonna take a little while for me to get settled and feel back to *normal*.

"I guess I'm just second-guessing coming here," I admit. "Everything feels wrong, like I'm living in the twilight zone or something. It's more awkward than I thought it'd be, and I already feel like the town outcast."

"I'm sure it's not that bad. You're just not used to being in public. Give it time."

I let out a laugh. "It's this place and these people. While I waited at the DMV, everyone looked at me like I was a chained-up dog ready to bite one of them because I was in prison."

Liam laughs, but he's not laughing at me. "Shoulda got your rabies shots before going home. On a serious note, I bet it's just in your head. I remember when all that stuff was going down with Victoria, I swear everyone was watching me. Even older ladies in the grocery store. I trusted no one. I think when you go through a lot of shit, it fucks with your head. And you've had your fair share. Honestly, they can fuck off. You're doing the best you can, and you're a good guy, Tyler."

A small smile meets my lips. "You're right. It's put me in a shitty mood, though."

"Probably the heat. Just remember you didn't do time because you're a criminal. You went to prison because Victoria is a vindictive bitch. You wanted away from the O'Learys and leaving gave you the freedom to move on from your past. I'll always be grateful for you, and if you change your mind, my home is always available to you. Maddie would be overjoyed if you came back."

"Means a lot, man." My voice trails off as I think about Victoria and all the hatred I have for that woman. I have over five years' worth of pent-up rage waiting for her. If she knows what's best, she'll leave me the fuck alone and forget I ever existed. "I wish I could find a way to get her back without getting my ass back behind bars," I admit. "She'd deserve it."

"Wait, huh? What are you talking about?" He sounds alarmed and shocked. But she ruined my life.

"Victoria. I want to get even."

Liam lets out a calm breath. "Awful idea, Tyler. You need to find a gym and work out your aggression before you do anything stupid. She won't stop if this starts again. She lives for drama and has an endless supply of money to make anything illegal she does go away."

I take everything Liam says into account, but it doesn't release my pent-up anger. While letting it go is the responsible thing to do, I don't know if I'll be able to.

"You're right. I should find a place to work out. I miss boxing. The fighting I did behind bars wasn't for fun."

Liam clears his throat. "I'm sorry."

"No, no, you shouldn't be. I made a choice, and I wouldn't trade it for the world, but being in a place like that changes you. And I'm not sure it was for the better. Either way, I'd do it all again for you and Maddie in a heartbeat."

"Thanks, man. I appreciate it. I wish things were different. I wish none of this had happened. It's something I live with every day, and sometimes, the guilt is a lot to deal with. I'm fully aware of how my shit affected your life. I just hope it doesn't ruin your future."

Now, I feel like a steaming pile of shit because this call wasn't intended to put Liam on the spot or bring him down.

"I never had a brother, Liam, and you're the closest thing to one I've ever had, and I'd do anything for you. You're my chosen family. Don't feel remorse over a damn thing because without all that, who's to say you'd have Maddie right now. It was the catalyst that brought you together, so no fucking regrets."

Liam chuckles. "I should probably get back to the gym too. I think I've gained thirty pounds during Maddie's second pregnancy with all her junk food cravings."

His words cause me to snort. "Not a terrible idea. Get rid of your baby belly. There's only one here, and I haven't stepped inside since before I left for the military, but I'll go check it out tomorrow. Honestly, it probably still looks the same."

"Well, go find you a bar and have a beer for old times' sake."

When Everleigh's condo comes into view, that becomes a better idea. "I think I might."

"Hell, have two."

I quickly ask him about Maddie and how she's managing so close to her due date, and by the time I unlock the front door, we end the call. Once I'm inside, I grab some clothes and go to the bathroom to happily wash off this shitty day. Before I make it there, Sassy is on my heels, barking like I'm an intruder.

"Sassy, no!" I try to make my tone as commanding as possible, but she gives zero fucks about it and tries to nip at my ankles. "Sassy," I say in a sweet tone. "Wanna treat?"

She growls, and I repeat the magic word, raising my pitch and walking into the kitchen to grab her doggy biscuits. As soon as Sassy sees the bag, she sits and wags her tail.

"Of course," I mumble and throw a handful down before heading back to the bathroom.

Ever since my release, I've taken my time in the shower. You don't realize how much privacy is taken for granted until it's snatched away. All freedoms revoked, along with your dignity. Once I finish, I wait for the water to go cold, then dry off and get dressed. Sassy still barks at me as though I'm a stranger, and I hope she gets used to me soon. Before Everleigh even asks me to walk her, I grab her leash, and we take off down the street. Those ten minutes with her give me time to get lost in my thoughts.

Once we're back, I remove the leash, and she drinks from her water bowl until it's empty, so I refill it. Taking Liam's advice, I grab my wallet and walk the few blocks to The Ridge Pub. It's close enough not to need a ride home, which is convenient. Everleigh's place is in the perfect location. It's close to her business and the downtown square, which is the most popular place in town. Thankfully, my job is within walking distance too. So as long as the weather stays nice, it won't be a problem making it on time.

After a quick five-minute walk, I enter the pub, then sit at the bar. I look over the menu, realizing just how hungry I am. The bartender comes back, and I notice it's a guy I went to high school with, but he pretends not to recognize me. Or maybe he doesn't. It's been over a decade.

"Whatcha having?"

"Bud, tall. Shot of tequila. And a double cheeseburger with fries."

He nods, and after entering in my order, he returns with the tequila and beer. I take the shot, hoping it loosens me up some. Greg, or maybe his name is Craig, picks up the empty glass, and I order another. I'm two shots and a beer in by the time he brings me my burger.

Food is another thing I took for granted before I knew better. Between mush and mystery meat, I could barely choke it down.

When I'm halfway done eating, I see Everleigh, Gemma, and Katie walk past the large glass windows, then open the door.

I keep my head down so they don't notice me. But damn, I can't help but glance at Gemma. Yesterday, Everleigh told me they were doing a photoshoot with some of her new inventory. The three of them look fierce as hell, but Gemma steals the show with her loose curls and dark makeup.

I watch through the bar mirror as they find a table, giving me the perfect view of them.

After I finish eating, I order another beer and notice Donald McDouche walking toward their table. The guy was a total asshole in high school, and even now, he looks like a grown-up twelve-year-old.

He leans against the table, and he offers to buy them all drinks while obviously checking them out, though none of them are showing any interest.

Everleigh isn't having it and rolls her eyes, then asks him to go away, but he doesn't get the blatant rejection. When he continues to bother them to the point they all look uncomfortable and annoyed, I grab my drink and walk over.

I'm not sure whose eyes are wider—the douchebag's or the girls'.

Everything goes silent as I look at Donald. By the way he swallows hard, he knows exactly who I am. "Can I help you with something?" I ask.

"I was just offering to buy these ladies a round," he slurs.

"And they said no, so you can move on." I wave my hand in the air, eyeing the space behind him.

"They can speak for themselves."

I look at Everleigh, and she smirks. "We did...twice. So here's a third: you can fuck off."

Grinning, I hold out my hand with the beer in it. "Well, there you go. Fuck off."

Donald hisses, then walks away with his dick tucked between his legs.

I suck in a deep breath, hyper aware that Gemma is staring at me.

"And my brother saves the day! Reminds me of when you threatened the seventh-grade bully who kept throwing spitballs at me." Everleigh laughs.

Chuckling, I nod. "You good now?"

"I think we can handle ourselves," Everleigh says, then takes a sip of her drink.

"Alright, good." I turn to walk away.

Gemma speaks up. "You should join us."

I look at her like she's lost her mind. "Join you?"

"Well yeah, unless you have other plans." Her voice lowers.

"Yes, come sit!" Everleigh scoots over and pats the empty seat next to her.

"As it gets later, the creepier the guys get. It'll be nice having you scare them off for us," Katie says.

"I'd be intruding. You're obviously having a girls' night."

"Don't be stupid." Everleigh smacks the seat again, demanding me with her scowl.

"C'mon, sit." Gemma gives me a sweet smile, and that's when I know I'm fucked.

It's easy to be a disappointment when I'm so far away, but when she's staring at me with such a deep intensity, it's hard as hell to say no.

CHAPTER SIX

GEMMA

Tyler looks at me, and my breath hitches. For a moment, I think he's going to walk away, but then he sits down in front of me next to Everleigh. Though he continues to avoid eye contact, I'm well aware of how close he really is. I can't help but notice how his shirt hugs him in all the right places. When he reaches for his beer, his biceps peek from under his sleeves, and I force myself to look away.

For just ten minutes, I wish we could talk about our past. Unfortunately, that won't be happening any time soon. Considering he's pretending I'm invisible right now, I'm not sure that'll ever happen. Maybe he's forgotten it all, but I haven't. The pain he caused still runs deep, but maybe now that he's back, I'll finally get some closure. At least that's what I'm hoping for, so I can move on for good.

The silence draws on, and my cheeks heat as I finish my margarita. Having him here with us is suddenly awkward, and I try to think of something to talk about, but my mind goes blank. Maybe I *shouldn't* have spoken up and invited him to join us, but once the words were out of my mouth, there was no going back.

"So..." Everleigh looks at us with a mischievous grin. "How about a round of whiskey?"

"The hard stuff, huh?" Tyler chuckles, then empties his mug in a big gulp.

"Only for my favorite people in the world," she sing-songs. It's gonna take the hard stuff for me to get through tonight.

Everleigh calls the waitress over and orders double shots for all of us. When they come, Everleigh holds hers up. "To my amazing brother, Tyler. For kicking ass and taking names." She looks around the table, then we clink our glasses together, and the liquid burns going down. When the server returns to clear the table, I order another margarita with an extra shot of tequila.

I think the only way I can be this close to Tyler is if I'm inebriated. I just hope I don't say anything stupid, like the other day in the lobby when I told him I'd waited years for him. There was no denying the embarrassment I felt after.

The more hours that pass, the drunker we get, except for Tyler. He's switched to drinking water and doesn't join in on our conversation but rather just listens.

Everleigh is two shots away from reliving our early twenties, and I can't stop laughing at everything she says. Katie has the giggles too, and I don't even remember what was so funny when we order another round.

"And look how sexy they look in these new dresses," Everleigh beams, swiping through her photos and showing Tyler the pictures.

"I mean, look at Gemma in that summer dress. She looks like she should be on the cover of *Vogue*, not modeling my clothes in small-town Alabama."

I shake my head, not wanting the attention. Though she's made Katie and me mini celebrities with her customers.

"And Katie. Jesus, girl, you're a MILF if I ever saw one. Still don't know why a man hasn't made an honest woman out of her yet." Everleigh talks loud when she's drunk, and right now, the whole bar can hear her.

Tyler laughs as he shushes her. "Looks like you found the perfect people to guilt into helping you."

This makes Katie and me snort.

"First comes guilt, second comes threats. It's easier to just give in right away," I admit.

"So, what you're saying is, Everleigh hasn't changed one bit since I left?"

"Are you kidding me? Not much has changed around here at

all," I say, smiling. "Everleigh's the same smartass she's always been."

Tyler looks at me. "You have."

My lips fall open, and it's like everything around us disappears. "No, I haven't."

Then I replay what's happened since he's been gone, and I realize he's right. I'm *not* the same naïve eighteen-year-old girl who thought he could rope the moon.

He arches a challenging brow. "Sure about that?"

Nervously, I shrug. "Well, maybe a little."

Everleigh butts in. "We're all more mature and doing pretty good in life. Katie has a son. I have a business. And Gemma has a fiancé."

"And I have a record! Yay me!" Tyler adds with a sarcastic edge in his voice.

I'm relieved when more alcohol arrives, but I'm at the point where I can't feel my lips. I stand to go to the restroom, and the room rocks sideways. Regardless, I continue forward, and that's when it's confirmed that I'm trashed. At least the edge is gone, though it's starting to mess with my emotions and thoughts, which can't be a good thing for me right now.

When I look in the mirror, I smile. My hair and makeup are perfect, and I look hot as hell. Confidence doesn't strike me much because I'm often insecure about my weight. Over the years, people have made various comments about how thin I am, asked if I had an eating disorder, and have even suggested I need to eat a cheeseburger or two. I've heard it most of my life and still continue to struggle with body image so damn much even as an adult. I've tried to accept my petite size, but it's hard for me to gain weight. But right now, none of that matters, because Everleigh put me in a dress that accentuates my waist and shows the perfect amount of cleavage for a quick peek. She could be a personal stylist for any body type, and it's one of the reasons Ever After does so well.

When I go back to the table, I glance at my cell and wonder why Robert hasn't texted me. He was totally okay with me canceling tonight because he's exhausted. He must've gone straight to bed after work. I blink again and notice it's nearly one in the morning. My eyes go wide because it feels like we just got here, but that seems to happen every time I hang out with the girls.

At nearly the same time, Katie notices how late it is too. "I should probably get going." She yawns. The booze must've worn off because she stopped drinking hours ago. "I'll need to get Owen from my parents after breakfast in the morning. He has a birthday party to go to, and I still have to wrap the gift."

"You okay to drive?" Tyler asks, and she nods.

"I wouldn't be if I tried to keep up with these two monsters," she teases.

Everleigh leans over the table and gives me a high five, laughing. My head feels woozy, and I wish I would've passed on that last one. Or maybe stopped three drinks ago.

We say goodbye to Katie as she gets up and makes her way out. Everleigh finishes her drink and slaps some cash on the table.

"I should probably get going too." Everleigh slurs her words as she shoves her phone in her bag. She turns to Tyler. "Before you ask, I'll be fine to walk. This isn't Vegas."

Then he glances at me. "You're in no shape to drive."

I can't even argue with that. I look for my keys in my purse and can't seem to find them.

"Why don't you drive her home, Tyler?" Everleigh suggests, and I could kill her.

"I think I should," he confirms with a nod. I can't stop staring at his bottom lip, and the way his tongue swipes across it. I swallow hard and try to look away, but he's so damn mesmerizing.

"Okay," I tell him. It's better than calling my dad this late or waking Robert. This would be the least inconvenient solution. Also, it might be nice to get Tyler alone without eyes on us.

He stands and lets Everleigh out of the booth. "My car is at the boutique," I remind her. "Guess we're walking some of the way with you after all."

Just as we're moving past the bar, a guy turns around with a beer in his hand. He's not paying attention, and seconds later, he bumps into me. The liquid runs down my dress, and I yelp at the coldness.

"Are you serious?" My dress soaks it in, and he apologizes, but I groan and keep walking.

Everleigh leans in, looping my arm with hers. "Surprised Tyler didn't kick that guy's ass for doing that."

"Shut up," I say playfully as she nudges me. She's aware of how I felt about Tyler and what happened between us by the end of it. While I don't know what she's shared with him about me over the years, I'm sure it's enough to keep him informed.

Though it's late, it's still humid as hell, which doesn't help how sticky I already feel from the beer I'm wearing. I walk beside Everleigh as she chats about posting our photos early next week. Tyler walks behind us, and I swear I can feel his eyes burning a hole in the back of my head.

"Good night, you two," Everleigh sing-songs when the storefront comes into view. She waves her fingers with a teasing smirk. "I'll text you tomorrow!"

I chuckle at her obnoxiousness. Her house isn't too far so she'll make it home fine. "Goodbye!"

Once I find my keys, I hand them to Tyler with a shaky hand. The nervous tension returns when Everleigh is out of sight, and it's just the two of us. Guess there's no amount of whiskey or tequila that can hide it.

"Here, let me help you before you break an ankle." Tyler unlocks, then opens the door for me. It's the first time we've been this close, and I can smell the faint hint of his cologne and soap. Memories flood in from years ago, but I push them away and climb inside. He cranks the car and grins when it rumbles to life.

"What?"

"I've always wanted to drive one of these." When I graduated from college, my dad fully restored a 1967 Ford Mustang for me and painted it jet black.

I lean my head against the seat. "Just be careful, she wants to go ninety all the time."

"Noted. So am I taking you to your fiancé's house or…"

"No, you're taking me home."

"Tell me where that is." His voice is velvety smooth like chocolate.

"It's where it's always been." I chuckle. "The house behind my dad's."

The same place he took my virginity and where we spent endless nights having sex.

"The Snow White cottage?" he asks, pulling out onto the road.

"Yep. Remember when we used to hang out there after I graduated?"

I immediately clamp my mouth shut, but it's too late. The alcohol makes me blurt out those words. Bringing up our past has been on the tip of my tongue all night. The summer I spent with Tyler often feels like a lifetime away, but also seems like it was yesterday.

"How could I forget? It was the best summer I've ever had here." He finally glances over at me, and I'm thankful it's dark so he can't see the heat rising to my cheeks.

We stay silent, listening to the radio until Tyler pulls into the driveway. After getting out of the car, we walk around the house to the cottage. He follows me, and when I turn to look at him, I nearly trip and bust my ass.

The only thing that saves me is Tyler's quick reflexes. For a second, the world momentarily shook on its axis, but he caught me before I embarrassed myself. I look up into his brown eyes and suck in a breath. For a moment, it feels like we're suspended in time as we stare intently at each other. He swallows, and his mouth opens, and I notice his heartbeat pulsing in his neck.

"You okay?" he asks, sounding more confident than he looks.

I shake out of his trance. "Nearly twisted my ankle, but I'll live. These damn shoes. This is why I hate wearing heels, but Everleigh insisted." I bend over to take them off, then walk barefoot the rest of the way.

"You gotta come inside and check the place out. Might shock you compared to the last time you saw it. It took Dad and me an entire summer to renovate and add a kitchen. One reason I'm not looking forward to leaving. Too many memories." I don't know why I mentioned that last part.

He hands over my keys, and I unlock the door. Thankfully, I cleaned up a couple of days ago, so there are no bras or leggings thrown around.

Tyler walks in with a smile that nearly touches his eyes. It's so genuine and contagious, I'm grinning wide as I watch his expression. He looks impressed as he glances around with his arms crossed over his broad chest.

"Wow, you did an amazing job, Gemma. This is…*perfect*. Cozy. And so you."

He studies my mother's paintings on the walls, steps around my quaint kitchen, and runs his fingertip across the marble island that my dad built.

As I watch him take it all in, the sticky clothes start to irritate me and become uncomfortable. I remove my dress and let out a sigh of relief. Next, I pull my hair up into a high bun, then grab a bottle of water from the fridge.

"Wait, how are you getting home?" The realization that he doesn't have a car hits me.

"Walking," he says from behind me.

My eyes widen as I turn around. "In the dark? That's *way* too far."

A laugh escapes him, and it's something I didn't realize I missed until it echoes against the walls. "I lived in Vegas, Gemma. I'm not scared of walking at night here. Aside from the stray cats and crickets, the only terrifying thing in this town is how fast the gossip mills run."

I snort at the truth in his words as I go to the living room and plop down on the sofa. "You could always stay." I pat the throw pillow with an old Mustang on it. A gift my dad got me one Christmas.

"Where? The couch?" He arches a brow at how small it is, which causes me to laugh. His long legs would probably hang over the edge. Immediately, I'm brought back in time and remember what it felt like to be wrapped up in his arms and how it made me feel so tiny.

"Yeah, why not? It's pretty damn comfy." The room spins, and I blink hard until it stops.

When I look up at him, I notice he's staring down at the ring on my finger. The light makes it sparkle and brings unnecessary attention to it. A lump forms in my throat, and the urge to change the subject hits me hard.

"Damn. Where are my manners?" I stand and go back to the kitchen. "Want something to drink? I have bottled water, Diet Coke, sweet tea…"

He chews his bottom lip as he shakes his head, then lowers his eyes down my body.

Tyler clears his throat. "Might want to put on some clothes?"

My body is on fire with embarrassment as I remember I'm only in my bra and panties.

Stupid, stupid, stupid. "Shit. I'm sorry, hold on…" Blushing, I turn and hurry to my bedroom.

I wasn't thinking straight, and the wet dress and alcohol flowing through my veins didn't help. I feel like the emperor when he realizes he's walked around in his birthday suit and want to smack myself for being so dumb.

When I return in shorts and a T-shirt, he's standing against the island. "Better?" I chuckle to ease the tension, then step in front of him. "Please don't walk home." The thought of him being out this late has me concerned. He might not get mugged, but too many stupid people are driving around this time of night, and that scares me.

Tyler takes me by surprise when he gently places his hands on my shoulders. It's the first time he's touched me, causing an internal freak-out of emotions. His hands are warm against my skin, and the scent of his cologne is more prevalent this close to him. "Gemma, don't worry about me. I've dealt with plenty of shady people throughout the years. I promise I'll be careful."

I lick my lips and stare at his features—something I never thought I'd see again. "Earlier, you said I'd changed. But one thing that hasn't is how much I worry about you." I meet his eyes and feel as if I'm floating as our gaze locks. The electricity streaming between us nearly has me losing my breath.

"Don't," he says, then grabs a piece of my hair and tucks it behind my ear. My entire body shivers as his finger brushes across my cheek. "But you should drink more water and sleep off your impending hangover." He smirks and places his soft lips on my forehead, then backs away.

I immediately notice the space he's created between us, and I'm confused as I feel the loss of his warmth, smell, and closeness. *What the hell am I doing?*

"Okay," I agree, though I really want him to stay and talk to me until the sun comes up like old times. There's so much about his life I don't know, and instead of asking Everleigh, I want him to tell me everything I missed. However, I doubt he ever will. He's more private than I remember and has built a wall so high I'll never be able to scale it. At times, his motions are almost robotic as if he's forgotten how to be human.

"Do you want me to tell you when I get home?" he asks, rubbing a hand over his trimmed jawline.

"Yes, please," I say without hesitation. "Do you need my number?"

One side of Tyler's mouth tilts up as he grabs his phone from his back pocket. He hands it over to me, and I program my name before giving it back.

"I'll text you when I'm safe and sound." He flashes me a wink, and those stupid butterflies reappear. "Good night, Gemma." The hoarse way he says my name nearly makes my panties combust. Though he looks like there's something more he wants to say, and he lingers for a second, he stays silent before moving toward the door.

I follow him outside, and the glow of the porch light illuminates his face as he lifts his hand and waves.

"Be careful," I say one last time before he's out of sight.

I'm embarrassed for even asking him to stay the night. Instead of inviting him in, I should've just thanked him at the door and went to bed with my dignity intact.

Once back inside the cottage, I go into the bathroom and wash the makeup off my face. I lie in bed and replay every look we exchanged with guilt streaming through me as I think about how unfair that was to Robert. Though it was harmless, and I had real concern for him walking this late, I know everything about it was inappropriate. I don't know why him being back is affecting me so much after all this time, but I can't stop wondering where we'd be if he had stayed. Probably married with a few kids and that what-ifs are what caused so many of my sleepless nights. Finally, my phone dings with a text from Tyler.

Tyler: Made it in one piece :)

Then he attached a selfie of him and Sassy looking straight up adorable, and my mind spins out of control all over again. But knowing he made it safely allows me to drift off without worry.

CHAPTER SEVEN

TYLER

The sun hasn't risen yet, but I wake up anyway and make coffee. Thankfully, Sassy is sleeping in Everleigh's room, or she'd be begging to go out or barking for attention, and it's too early for either.

As I'm waiting for the drip to stop, I think back to Friday night at the pub and taking Gemma home afterward.

One thing's for certain, it was awkward as hell between us. I'm constantly stuck wondering what I should say and how much I should share. We're not friends and haven't been for a long time. I'm sure she hasn't forgiven me, either, but I can't deny the way she still affects me.

As we sat on the couch, I could smell her fruity shampoo. It's so familiar and brought me back to a time when I was allowed to touch and kiss her. However, her engagement ring—or rather, *rock*—was the reminder I needed that things can never go back to how they were.

She'll be married soon and one hundred percent off-limits. My heart pounded in my chest as too many unspoken words and stolen glances lingered between us. It was better that I left before either of us acted on whatever the fuck was bubbling under the surface. I'm sure her fiancé wouldn't appreciate a convict being in his woman's house at nearly two in the morning. I'd almost bet money he wouldn't like me sleeping on her couch, either. So, to avoid any trouble, I got the hell out. I needed some fresh air to clear my head anyway, and she needed to sober up.

The following day, I finally joined the gym and am happy I have a place to go blow off some steam. I hope to make a friend or two outside my sister's circle and work.

When I was in prison, I worked out as much as I could, but I missed putting on gloves and training people how to box like I did before shit hit the fan. The ring always felt like home. Though this gym doesn't have one, it has a small area with punching bags that'll work for now. Those thoughts have me reminiscing about how boxing helped Mason and Liam work through their issues. If it can help them, then it can undoubtedly help me. I want to get back to the life I had before the O'Learys entered it.

It's Monday morning, and I've been on edge all weekend about seeing Gemma today. Instead of dwelling on it, I pour some coffee into a travel mug and change into my workout clothes. I'll drink it on the way to the gym. When I step outside, I'm surprised it's not blazing hot yet. I spend an hour working out, then go home, shower, and get ready for work.

Now that my mind is clear, I'm hoping I'll be able to focus, but it'll be hard, considering I'll be around Gemma. She throws me off more than I realized she would.

Just as I'm leaving, Everleigh wakes up and wishes me good luck on my first day. I keep replaying how Gemma begged me to stay over and how she admitted she still worries about me. I think about it while I walk the few blocks to work. I check the time and know Jerry will be happy how punctual I am.

I suck in a few deep breaths as I walk into the waiting area. Gemma is busy on the computer, but when she looks up at me, she blushes, then lowers her eyes and tries to hide her reaction.

She's embarrassed about being a tipsy hot mess Friday night, but I thought it was kinda adorable. Drunk Gemma is fun and easygoing and not so reserved once the alcohol hits her system. But now, we're back to where we were when I arrived here on Wednesday last week —awkward tension.

The silence pierces my ears.

Thankfully, Jerry walks in and greets me in his booming fatherly voice. I turn to him and smile as he picks up a donut.

"I have to pull some engines this mornin', so I thought Gemma could show you around the place and give you a rundown of shop rules. We can meet up after lunch, and I'll get you started on your first project," he explains.

"Okay, sounds great."

Jerry grabs a cup of coffee, then goes back to the garage. Once Gemma and I are alone again, all the air in the room seems to evaporate.

She finishes typing something, then stops and looks at me. "Well, this is the lobby where customers wait, over there is the customer bathroom, and next to it, is the break room and fridge—employees only, though." Gemma grins, though she tries to hide it.

I chuckle at her smart-ass tone. "Yep. Figured that much out."

Gemma walks out from behind the counter and takes me into the garage. It's much smaller than I remember it being. She explains where all the tools are kept, and her dad's hard rules.

"My dad runs a tight ship. He's fired people for being lazy and late," she warns, and I make a mental note, so I don't disappoint him. "Make sure to clean up after yourself. Messy shop, unhappy Pops."

After the grand tour, she takes me into the small office that smells like engine oil and Old Spice. She turns and stares at me. At first, she hesitates, then just comes out and says what's on her mind. Something I know isn't always easy for her.

"Can we forget about Friday? I'm absolutely humiliated by my behavior."

I lean my shoulder against the frame of the door and cross my arms over my chest. Smirking, I shake my head. "No way. Forget seeing you down in your underwear, begging me to sleep on your couch? It's been on repeat in my head all weekend."

She groans. "When you say it like that, it sounds much worse than what really happened, though, it's still pretty bad."

"Whiskey is your kryptonite. But I kinda like that about you, Gemma. You weren't so uptight."

"I'm *not* uptight, Tyler."

The way she says my name has me swallowing hard. She's trying so hard to convince me, but it's not gonna work.

I grin. "No?" I tuck my hands in my pockets and shrug. "Okay, well maybe we both are. You more than me, though," I tease.

She glares at me, and I laugh. Gemma grabs a book from the desk, then changes the subject. She sits and flips it open.

"This is the schedule book where we write the appointments. It's old-school, but Dad prefers not to have to get on the computer for anything, so I save it electronically but also write it in here. If you ever wonder what's planned for the week, it's in here." She taps her finger on the pages. Her handwriting is as meticulous as I remember it.

I lean over and look at the calendar. She tilts her head, aware of how close I am. Though I pretend I don't notice how her breasts rise and fall with each of her breaths, I do.

"Awesome, seems straightforward," I say, and my breath brushes against her skin. Goose bumps form on her arms, and I take a step back, needing space. Those old emotions threaten to come to the surface, but I force them away.

"Great." She stands and walks out of the office. Before following her, I regain my composure, then meet her back in the waiting room. Only three chairs sit against the wall in front of the counter that's big enough to hold a computer, keyboard, and for a person to write a check. Yes, a check, because they're so damn old-fashioned here. Mimi still refuses to get a debit card.

"That's pretty much all I have for you, and there's still a few hours before lunch." She doesn't look up at me as she types.

"What do I do then? Your dad isn't meeting with me until after lunch."

"Not sure. Wash the windows? Sweep the floor? Clean the bathroom?"

Though she's messing with me, the windows *are* filthy. Instead of sitting around, I decide to make myself useful.

"Alright, where are the cleaning supplies?"

"I wasn't serious."

"Yeah, but look at them. I can take care of it and anything else you need, then meet your dad after lunch."

For the first time since the office, she meets my eyes again. Her gaze nearly paralyzes me in place, and I wonder if she feels it too.

"Under the sink in the break room. Extra rags are in the supply closet."

I nod and get to work. I find a bucket, soap, and spare towels. After filling it with scalding water, I grab my supplies and go outside. I'm drenched with sweat after washing one window from top to bottom. It's the distraction I need, and I lose myself in these damn windows.

I try not to let my thoughts wander too much, and each time Gemma pops into my head, I glance at her. After all this time, it's hard to believe she's only feet away. I notice her mannerisms are still the same. When she's concentrating hard, she bites her bottom lip and tilts her head. I used to find it so adorable when I'd tell her about the military because she just didn't fully understand it. She used to be a crossword junkie and still taps her pen against the paper when she's lost in thought. It takes me over two hours to clean the glass, and it's so clean when I look inside that I can see Gemma staring at me.

When I catch her, she glances away.

Boundaries, I remind myself. She's fucking engaged to a man who can give her everything she's ever wanted. What do I have to offer other than a fucked-up past and a pile of baggage?

I tackle the restroom next and don't leave until it fucking sparkles. Anything to take me away from being in the lobby right now. When it's lunchtime, I put away the supplies, then let Gemma know I'm going on my break. She tells me I have an hour, which is plenty of time to rinse off the sweat at home and change clothes. I'll have to hurry so I have time to grab something to eat before I have to return.

After I quickly clean up, I stop by the pub and grab a cheeseburger since it's on the way to the garage. After I scarf down my food in four big bites, I rush back. When I walk in, Gemma ignores my existence like I'm an annoying mosquito. Avoiding me is for the best, or at least that's what I tell myself so we don't get too friendly. It won't give those old feelings the opportunity to return. Her future path is set, and I'll be damned if I ruin that or give her fiancé any reason to be jealous, so staying away is for the best.

Going out to the shop, I find Jerry happily sipping on a milkshake. There's an old malt shop on the corner of Main where all the older people like to visit. I totally forgot about that place until just now.

"Ready to get started?" he asks.

I nod. "Sure am."

He takes me over to the lift where a car is already in the air. "This one needs an oil change and tire rotation." He peeks his head out the door where the small side parking lot is full. "And so do those six. I'll be workin' on these Jeep engines for the rest of the week, so if you can take care of all the service items, that'd help me out a ton."

"No problem. Sounds easy enough," I answer confidently.

"Good, but if you have any issues or questions, just ask."

"Will do." Though it's bitch work, I don't mind. I'm happy to do it. As I grab the tools and filters I'll need, Jerry calls my name.

"Yeah?" I spin around and face him.

"Good job with the windows. I can actually see my reflection in them now," he tells me with a belly laugh.

"Thank you, sir." I smile, then continue.

For the rest of the day, I spend my time carefully changing out oil filters and tightening and loosening bolts and lug nuts. When I finish each car and truck, I give Gemma the keys after I've parked them out front for pick up. Reid's Garage is the only place in town that services vehicles and has been for twenty years. People refuse to drive over and support the chain stores. It's another reason Everleigh's boutique has done so well. The citizens shop local as much as possible.

By closing time, I'm exhausted. My arms are sore from moving heavy tires around, and my clothes are drenched with sweat and grease. While there's a big box fan and all the doors were open, the humidity is still torturous.

I go inside after finishing the oil change on the last car for the day, walk past Gemma at the counter, and grab some water from the dispenser. Just as Gemma goes to lock the door, an older clean-cut man walks in carrying an oversized bouquet of pink and white roses.

Instantly, I know exactly who he is.

The way he carries himself tells me he thinks he's hot shit. It's almost comical how smug he looks, but I keep my opinions to myself. I would've never pictured Gemma with someone like him, and I'm curious what she actually sees in him.

I shouldn't watch them, but I can't help it. I notice the surprised look on Gemma's face as he hands her the flowers, and she sheepishly grins with a quiet, "Thank you." Mr. Egomaniac places his arm around her and pulls her in for a kiss. While she returns the affection, her shoulders squeeze together before she pulls away. It's so obvious he's trying to show off for whatever reason. Instead of witnessing their public display of affection, I turn my back to them and drink my water.

"What's the special occasion?" Gemma asks.

"I'm taking you to a fancy lobster dinner at Cajun Seafood tonight."

"Really?" Her voice goes up a notch.

"I'm meeting a client and would love to introduce him to my future wife," he explains. *And there it is*...butter her up with flowers and the mention of a nice dinner just to look good in front of other uptight men.

When I turn to walk to the break room, I notice the grin on her face falters, but she puts it back on, forcing it. God, he's a moron. And this act, *fuck*. It's disgusting.

She's smart enough to see it, but then again, maybe she's not the same girl I fell in love with all those years ago. He's using her to show how much of a family man he is while also putting her on display like she's some kind of trophy. I finish my water, and Jerry comes in with a wide smile.

"You did well today and were an enormous help," Jerry says. "I think we might get caught up before the end of next week. Thanks for workin' so hard."

"Well, thank you again for the opportunity. I appreciate it more than I can explain."

After we exchange our goodbyes, I decide to leave. There's no way I'm sticking around to watch the Gemma and fiancé shitshow. Before I can walk past the counter, her man stops me, sizing me up.

"Who's this?" he asks Gemma, but he's giving me a threatening glare.

"I'm Tyler," I answer for her, reaching out to shake his hand. He gives me a million-dollar smile that's fake as fuck and squeezes my hand as hard as he can. It's a warning, and I give him the same pressure.

"He's my dad's new employee," Gemma tells him. "So he doesn't get behind over the summer."

"I'm Robert, Gemma's future husband."

I swallow down a laugh at how obnoxious he is. "Congrats. Well, I gotta go. Nice meeting you," I say dryly and get the fuck out of there.

My adrenaline spikes as I walk outside past the clean windows and notice he's talking to Gemma with his arms raised. Intimidation isn't a good look for him, especially since he seems like the type of guy who doesn't take no for an answer.

Instead of going home, I stop by Everleigh's boutique. The front door is locked, so I tap lightly, and when she sees me, she rushes to let me in.

"Hey!" She gives me a side hug before re-locking the door. "How was your first day?"

I laugh with a shrug. "It was work. Got filthy and hustled."

Everleigh walks around and straightens up racks and refolds shirts that have been picked up and crumpled by customers. I admire what she's been able to accomplish with her store. It's cozy and hip, a place she would've killed someone to walk through when she was a teen. She offers a number of appealing items—T-shirts, jewelry, dresses, jeans, and even novelty items like coffee mugs and tumblers. All with witty sayings that reflect her personality.

"Was Gemma weird today?" she blurts out. "I mean, with you being there, did she seem like it bothered her?"

"Nah. Not until her *future husband* walked in," I repeat it the same way Robert had.

Everleigh lets out a hearty laugh. "He tries too hard sometimes."

"No shit." I roll my eyes.

"He means well, but he's very concerned about his reputation."

"I noticed." Compared to most townspeople, he sticks out like a sore thumb in his expensive suit and George Clooney haircut.

"He's not Gemma's type at all. I mean, he's a good-looking guy, but he's too old for her."

That makes me snort because I thought the same thing. "How old is he anyway?"

"Like forty-five or something. Gemma told me he uses Touch of

Gray hair dye." She chuckles. "But you didn't hear that from me." She puts a finger over her lips.

"Seriously?" I'd laugh if I didn't have so many questions, but I also don't bother asking. Based on the little information Everleigh told me, the feeling I had when he first walked into the shop was valid.

I'm already convinced she's not as in love with him as she claims. She's settling.

But the real question is *why*?

CHAPTER EIGHT

GEMMA

I UNDERSTAND how important it is to Robert that I join him at his business dinner, but I hate that it's not just the two of us. Though I smiled through our whole conversation, Tyler looked as if he could see straight through me. After working all day, the last thing I want to do is entertain strangers, but I go anyway.

When we walk in, I expect us to be meeting one or two people, but it's an entire table filled with men in suits. This annoys me more than anything, but I keep the smile planted. Something I became really good at after my mom passed away. As long as I pretended I was happy, no one asked questions, not even Noah or my dad. While this is a different situation, it still oddly feels just as fake.

We have a nice lobster dinner and fluffy rolls with honey butter just as Robert promised. Several people ask how we met and about the wedding, and I feel like a giant spotlight is on me with every question. Considering I'm an introvert, this makes me anxious.

Once dinner is over, they shake hands over their done deals. We say our goodbyes, and I'm nearly gasping for air when I walk outside. Robert smiles proudly.

"Another done deal all because of you, baby," he says with a pep in his step. I know this was a big one, an entire subdivision for development.

I shrug uncomfortably. "I can't take the credit for it. That was all you."

He pulls me close, and I smell the faint hint of his cologne.

"So, you gonna tell me about this Tyler guy?"

When his name leaves Robert's mouth, my heart rate increases. There's a hint of something else in his tone, almost as if he's trying to appear casual but definitely isn't. The threatening way he looked at Tyler earlier wasn't lost on me, either.

We get in his truck, and he drives me back to the shop where my car is parked. "He's Everleigh's brother and just moved back to town."

"Yeah? So you two know each other?" he asks, but I don't want to discuss this.

"Yeah, he's only four years older, plus it's a small town." I shrug, annoyed that he's making me feel like I'm under his microscope.

"Ahh. That makes sense now. Did you two ever…?"

"Robert." I stop the conversation before it even starts. Though I don't want to be a liar about my past, the minute he finds out Tyler and I dated, he'll lose his shit. It was a decade ago and shouldn't matter, but Robert's a little possessive when it comes to what's his. There doesn't need to be any more tension between us than there already is. "We're not friends. My dad offered him a job because Tyler was just released from prison and needed something to get back on his feet. He's on a trial run right now to see how it goes."

Thankfully, he pulls up to my car and parks, and I desperately want to jump out of the SUV. I'm so damn annoyed, not necessarily by what he asked, but *how* he asked. I already know he thinks he's better than Tyler because of his past, and I hate how judgmental Robert can be, so the less he knows about him, the better.

"Trust me, I was more than surprised when he walked into the shop and my dad hired him, but he's a good worker, and it's what my father needs."

Robert turns to me. "I'm not trying to interrogate you, darling. I just want to be aware of who you're spending your days with and make sure you're safe. You're the love of my life, and I'd never get over it if something happened to you."

"I appreciate that, babe. But I'm working at the garage, not having a bachelorette party with strippers all day."

He leans forward and gently kisses me, his lips tasting like wine. "I know that."

"Maybe we can have a date night tomorrow? Just the two of us?" I suggest, hoping it'll ease him about our relationship.

"Not sure. Tomorrow's gonna be busy for me, but I'll double-check my schedule and let you know as soon as I can."

I give him a smile, though I'm nearly fuming inside. "Okay then." Reaching for the door handle, I add, "Good night."

"Love you," he says before I step out.

"Love you too."

He waits until I'm inside my car and it's cranked before he pulls away.

I'm so damn annoyed while I drive home that by the time I walk into my door, I'm raging pissed. It's been a long time since I've been this irritated with Robert. Sure, his constant parading of me in front of his clients has gotten old, but I'm used to that by now. However, asking me about Tyler as if there was something between us was uncalled for. He acted like Tyler getting hired was some ploy so we could hang out all day.

I go straight to the bathroom and start the water, but before I can get undressed, I get a call from Everleigh.

"Hey, whatcha doing right now?" she asks as I turn off the faucet.

It's barely eight, but I'm exhausted and have to be up early for work tomorrow. "I was getting ready to soak in the tub."

"Okay, what are you doing after that?"

I can already tell she's up to something.

"Going to bed."

"Instead of taking a bath, you should come over. I asked Katie, but she just put Owen to bed. I need help choosing which pictures of you two to post because I'm second-guessing which ones will get the most attention. I really love them all, but I need another perspective. There are too many to email to you, so would you mind coming over and helping me pick? Pretty please?" she begs.

Groaning, I look at the bubble bath and wait for her to tell me she's joking. "You're serious?"

"As serious as a heatstroke. I need your expert opinion! I want to get some of them posted tomorrow and start moving this new inventory. Plus, you always choose the best ones."

I chuckle at the way she always wears me down with her compliments. However, being around her would help clear my mind and distract me from my own thoughts. "Fine, but you better have a glass of wine waiting for me when I get there."

"Yay!" she squeals. "Red or white?"

"Surprise me," I say. I tell her I'll be right over, and we say our goodbyes. I throw my hair into a high ponytail, change into yoga pants and a tank top, then drive over.

When I show up, Everleigh swings the door open, holding a glass of wine. I snort as she hands it to me before my feet even cross the entrance.

"You're gonna make some guy super happy one day if this is the kind of treatment you provide," I say, then take a sip. "Oh, wow. The good stuff. You're really trying to butter me up."

I follow her into the living room, and she furrows her brows when she looks at me. "You okay?"

I shrug, not wanting to bring her mood down with mine. "I'll tell you later." Waving her off, I sit on the couch.

"Okay, you better." Everleigh goes to the kitchen, then returns moments later with a huge bowl of fresh popcorn drizzled with butter. She hands it over to me, then grabs her fancy camera. Once we're both settled and comfortable on the sofa, Everleigh scrolls through the photos.

"Oh my God, you took two thousand pictures?" I glance at her as she stuffs her face and nods.

"This is why I couldn't decide!"

Shaking my head, I watch as she goes through them. "They're all so good. If the boutique doesn't work out, you should be a photographer."

"Are you flirtin' with me already?" She flips her hair.

"You wish." I laugh. "Oh, I love this one of Katie where she's looking off in the distance."

Everleigh moves closer. "Yes, me too. She looks gorgeous. Every woman in a hundred-mile radius is gonna want this outfit. And look at you in that red skirt, you little sexy firecracker." She waggles her brows.

"That *is* a good one," a deep voice says from behind us, and every cell in my body comes alive.

Everleigh and I both jump as Tyler straightens up and chuckles. Everleigh grabs a pillow and tosses it at him but completely misses.

"I'm sad I wasn't invited to the slumber party." He smirks and walks into the kitchen. That's when I notice he's not wearing a shirt and see his joggers hanging off his hips. Immediately, I chug my wine, though the image of his ripped body and the way the muscles cascade down his back are now imprinted into my memory. *Fuck.*

"Well, you're the one who didn't want to look at two thousand pictures with me," Everleigh counters. "You snooze, you lose."

My mouth falls open. "So I was your *third* choice? I'm offended!"

She snorts and winks. "Third time's the charm, baby."

Tyler returns to the living room, sipping a beer. I avoid looking at him because I don't think I'll be able to pick my jaw off the floor before he notices.

"Welp," he says. "I'll leave you two hens to it."

"Mm-hmm." Everleigh continues to scroll through the pictures.

When I look up, he's staring at me with so much intent that I stop breathing. Tyler blinks, breaking our contact.

"Good night," I say, but it comes out in a whisper.

"Night," he says, then leaves the room, taking all the air with him. If Everleigh notices my reaction, she doesn't say anything, and for that, I'm grateful.

"How about this one?" she asks, bringing me back to reality. It's one of Katie and me laughing our asses off at something Everleigh said without a doubt.

"Yes, I love that one! It's perfect and looks so natural. The only thing it's missing is you in there with us."

"I have the satisfaction of knowing this picture was taken when I was talking about butt stuff."

Cabernet nearly shoots out of my nose, but I manage to choke it back down. "Jesus, give a girl some warning."

"I can't help that we're like twelve-year-old boys when it comes to that." She giggles.

"Oh, for sure." I point out a few more that she should definitely use. By the time we get through half of them, she has a notebook page full of image numbers. Hanging out with her was just what I needed tonight.

"So, you gonna tell me what had your panties bunched in a big old knot when you showed up, or am I'm gonna have to beat it out of you?"

I roll my eyes and huff. I swear this glass of wine is never-ending because I need more alcohol in my system to discuss this. "Robert."

She doesn't make a face or react, but just listens to me as I explain my frustrations and insecurities. As I talk, Everleigh grabs an empty glass and the bottle, then returns to the couch. She refills mine and pours her some too.

"And I understand he wants me to be involved in his work, but you're well aware of how I feel about a big crowd. Especially when they put me at the center of attention. I want to throw up."

"You *hate* it. Always have."

"Right! It makes me anxious, and I always have to answer the same questions over and over. It's just, I dunno, it makes me feel weird—like I'm a prop in his business deals," I admit.

"Like you're playing a part."

"Right, like an actress showing up to a movie set whose character is married to the rich and famous, living a glamorous lifestyle."

Everleigh glances down at the big ass ring on my finger, then shrugs before sucking down half of her glass. "If the ring fits, though, right?"

Groaning, I lean my head against the couch. "I wanted a simple life with a husband and a couple of kids. Though I knew how important Robert's career was before we got engaged, entertaining people has become an every week occurrence now."

"He's definitely driven. But aside from that, when's the last time you two did it?" she blurts out.

I close my eyes, trying to remember, but it's been too long. "Weeks. Fuck, maybe months. He's been so busy with clients, contracts, golfing—and that doesn't include my schedule. By the time we're actually alone, we're both exhausted. I know it's stupid to think this, considering he's the one who's eager to have me live with him, but sometimes, I don't feel like a priority to him."

The realization has me burning from the inside out, and I feel smothered by my thoughts. The only thing that saves me from drowning is Everleigh placing her hand on mine.

"Gemma. Are you *absolutely*, without a doubt, positively sure you want to marry him? It's not too late to change your mind. Everyone would understand."

I pause, not sure how to respond. No one has really questioned me about our relationship, and everyone has been supportive. Even my dad is caught in Robert's web.

"Well…" I swallow hard, trying to find my words.

"You're hesitating." She arches a brow.

"I don't know." I shrug, lowering my eyes as I hold back tears. "Things have been off between us, and maybe they have been for a while, but I'm just now seeing it. He's pushy about me moving in with him, and since we don't get to see each other much, he thinks living together will give us more quality time."

"And what do you think? Will moving in with him change that? Or will he still be too exhausted to spend alone time like he claims? Do you see things getting better once you're married, or will you feel stuck?"

I empty my glass, wishing the alcohol would hit my system faster. "I really don't know."

"Listen, I just want you to be happy. You're my best friend, Gemma. I don't doubt that you love him, but I don't know if you're *in love* with him or just the idea of it. Maybe you need a vacation because all the stress of the wedding is catching up to you. It happens!" Everleigh grabs the bottle and pours more into my glass.

But does it? Is this stress, or is there an underlying issue?

"I wouldn't say no to a vacation," I say, grinning. "Mimosas by the beach, suntanning, and the ocean breeze. Hell, let's plan a girls' trip. No boys allowed." *Especially no ex-lovers.*

"Sign me up for that!" Everleigh gives me a high five. "Well, my best guess is that you're just having wedding day nerves. What do you think?"

I shrug with a frown. "How can it be nerves when it's so far away?" I don't even have much to do since Robert hired a wedding planner.

"It's still a huge fucking change. And it's a forever contract. Hell, I'm nervous just thinking about it, and I'm the most eligible bachelorette in Lawton Ridge. I'll probably be single with four dogs by the time I'm forty."

Her exaggeration makes me snort. "No, there's Old Lady Annette and her thirteen cats. Speaking of, where's Sassy?"

Everleigh is full-on laughing, the kind that makes her nose scrunch. "Annette was promiscuous back in the day, though. I heard stories of her breaking three different men's hearts at once. Guess she realized she was too good for them. But if I ever get that many dogs, trust me when I say it's a cry for help." She gulps her wine. "Oh, Sassy's sleeping on my bed. She was tired and put herself to bed."

"Well, there's no denying her name fits." I chuckle, which feels good, considering the conversation we're having.

"It sure does." The room grows quiet except for the sound of Everleigh chewing popcorn.

"Robert met Tyler today," I say. I don't know what possesses me to even bring it up, but I need to get it off my chest.

Her eyebrow pops up, and she repositions herself with a smirk. "And?"

"And Robert asked if there had been anything between us in the past."

"Oh, God." She grins. "What'd you say?"

I bury my face in my hands and exhale, then look at her. "Well, I cut him off before he could fully ask, but I knew where he was going with it. So I didn't technically lie, but I just didn't tell him the truth."

"Why not? Everyone has past relationships. He can't get mad about that."

"Because I think he'd be jealous and insecure about us working together. How fucking stupid is that, though? I mean, come on…" I turn my hand around, show her the ring, and she grins.

"That's hilarious."

I tilt my head at her. "No! It was awkward."

"Well, maybe it's time to come clean about your previous relationships. It's not like he didn't date a decade before you were even legal."

I roll my eyes. "He's not *that* old."

"At least men get better looking with age while women have to put on under eye cream and slather ourselves in lotion to look young. Hell, if Leonardo DiCaprio showed up at my door, I'd give him the time of his life, and nothing would be off-limits. I'd let him draw me like a French girl any day of the year." She releases a dreamy sigh, and I laugh at her *Titanic* reference.

"Point taken."

"At least tell me the sex is mind-blowing. Like if he's the best you've ever had, I'll forgive his old man traditional values."

I think about it. Sadly, I barely remember the last time we had sex.

Her mouth falls open when I take too long to respond.

"If it was monumental, you would've immediately answered with a fat, cheesy grin." She frowns. "It's mediocre at best, isn't it?"

Heat meets my cheeks, and I hate the pitiful look she gives me. "I seriously can't get anything past you, can I?"

"Are you kiddin' me? We used to exchange diaries, remember? I especially loved your middle school entries about my brother." She giggles.

"That was *your* idea!" I remind her, blushing at the memory.

"Yeah, and I learned a lot about you that summer. And you learned a lot about me too."

I nod as I remember reading about how much she missed having her mother in her life. We connected, and it's a bond that's never been broken.

"Well, I'm not sure what to say, but sorry. You're too young to be compromising hot as fuck sex. You deserve someone who's not so vanilla—some hair-pulling, ass-smacking, throat-squeezing sex—Neapolitan would be more your style."

"Jesus." I chuckle at her descriptive version, but she's not wrong. That sounds hot as hell. "You're right. But I'm pretty vanilla too."

"Maybe you are, but at least you have sprinkles. If a man offered to tie you up or handcuff you to the headboard, you wouldn't say no. Amiright?"

She lifts an eyebrow at me, and I smirk.

"Regardless, it's not that I'm some relationship expert or anything because you know how many men are knocking on *my* door." She holds up her hand showing a big fat zero with her fingers. "But if the work lunches and dinners are too much, you should tell him, along with the other concerns you have. Honesty is the best policy. Unless it's about dick size. You don't want to inflate their ego."

I snort. "You're right, but I feel guilty telling him I don't want to go to these client outings. Like I'm not being supportive, especially when he calls me his *lucky charm*. He gets so excited when he closes a deal with me there."

Everleigh finishes her wine. "Welp, seems like you've got some decisions to make, my friend." Her words are sincere, and there's so much truth in them that it nearly slices me to the bone.

"I do," I agree softly.

For the next hour, we go through the rest of the pictures, and Everleigh's list to post nearly doubles. But at least we narrowed it down to the top fifty.

"Looks like I have enough for the next couple of months, too." I'm so proud of her for making her dreams come true. When we were teenagers, there were no local clothing stores for women under sixty, so she made it her mission to have a store for women of all ages and sizes.

After my buzz has worn off and the yawning begins, I decide to go home. I'm going to be exhausted at work tomorrow, but it'll be totally worth it. Tonight was just what I needed.

On the way back to the cottage, I can't stop thinking about our conversation. She made so many valid points. Robert and I do need to talk, but where do I even start? I hate confrontation, and the last thing I want is to hurt his feelings. Things have always been simple between us, and I thought I was okay with that, but I'm starting to realize I may have just accepted that without considering what I truly want.

I want a person who's as obsessed with me as I am him.

Someone who craves alone time together.

A man who listens and understands my needs just the way I do for them.

As I walk through the door, I kick off my shoes, strip out of my clothes, and take a quick shower. After I'm clean, I slip on a T-shirt and panties, then climb into bed.

When I close my eyes, I expect to see Robert, but I don't.

I see a shirtless Tyler and fall asleep with him on my mind.

CHAPTER NINE

TYLER

Though I'd like to say working around Gemma is getting easier, it would be a lie straight from the pits of hell. I've tried my best to keep our conversations short and stay out of the lobby as much as possible. Sometimes when I'm grabbing water or in the break room, I hear her humming with the radio. In the past, I'd tease her about it, but after I left, it was one thing I missed the most. Perhaps I should wear earbuds to drown it out before it completely fucks with my head how much I enjoy hearing it again.

Helping Jerry in the shop the past week has been enjoyable. He works his ass off to make an honest living, and at times, he runs circles around me. More than once, he's shown his gratitude for my help, but it's nothing compared to how I feel for him giving me this chance. We're no longer on a trial basis because I've arrived before Gemma each day and haven't fucked off on my phone once. It's a steady, secure income—something I never had in Vegas. Sure, I'd trained people, but sometimes, my clients would quit or move. I lived that hustle life, doing what I could to make ends meet. I loved living in the city, enjoyed the desert air, and had no intention of ever coming back. But here I am.

People have a simpler way of living here. There aren't bars on every corner, gangs that run the streets, or robberies happening every day. The biggest gamble people take here is buying out of season fruit at the grocery store. Not that I'm complaining about my new simple life, but I wonder how long I'll last before craving my old reckless lifestyle.

Though I've been at work for eight hours already, it feels like I just walked in. There's always something more to do and no time to be idle, so the days pass by quickly. My mind stays busy with tasks instead of thoughts. Too often when I'm alone, I replay everything that happened with Victoria. It's at those times when the urge for revenge runs through me like poison, and I want her to pay for what she did. I want her to know what it was like to spend five years in prison. Drugs and weapons are not my forte. Even though I didn't have a record, money can buy anything when the court system is corrupt as fuck. I admit, I have a chip on my shoulder, and I'm not sure anything can repair it.

After I clock out, my gaze drifts to Gemma. She notices, and her lips fall open to say something, but then her dad walks in. Instead of sticking around for a potentially awkward conversation, I head out.

Needing to blow off some pent-up aggression, I quickly walk home, change into workout clothes, and then go to the gym. It still smells the same as it did when I was a teen because getting buff to impress the ladies at school was the thing to do. Now, as I look around at all the kids in here, I laugh at the memory.

Old carpet covers the floors, and the walls have wood paneling. It's looked this way over the past few decades. Sam, the owner, is getting older and moving a lot slower. He's here every morning at five to open the doors, and then his granddaughter closes at nine p.m. I wonder what his plans are with the place when he decides to retire. I'd love to eventually be in a position to buy it, but that might be a pipe dream.

A few meat heads are lifting weights in front of the mirror. I hold back my laughter and walk to the area for kickboxing. Grabbing a set of gloves, I put them on, then pound my fists together.

I feel alive the moment I put them on, then take my frustrations out on the bags in fifteen-minute sprints. I punch and swing as hard as I fucking can, then I switch positions to stay light on my feet. It's a relief to just let it out of my system and burn off the extra energy after working. Every once in a while, I throw in a few kicks, ducking and imagining Victoria's sneer on the other side. It doesn't take long before I'm exhausted, but I don't stop until I've worked out for a full hour. Even though I'm completely worn down, I feel more calm with a sense of clarity.

As I head home, the sun hangs lazily in the sky over the old buildings in the town square. The warm breeze brushes against my sweaty skin, cooling me down even quicker. When I walk inside the house, Sassy sprints toward me, wagging her tail, so I quickly take her outside. We've been taking regular walks, and she can't seem to get enough of me now. I bend down and pet her before grabbing some clothes and jumping in the shower. The stream falls over my body, and I think about my life. It feels like I'm living in an alternate universe. When my skin prunes, I get out and put on some joggers and a T-shirt, then place a frozen lasagna in the oven. It'll take an hour, but Everleigh will be home by then, so it works out perfectly.

After grabbing a beer, I sit on the couch with Sassy, turn on the TV, and flip through the channels. Some survival show where the contestants run around naked catches my attention, and I'm oddly intrigued. Eventually, the timer goes off, and minutes later, Everleigh walks through the door, grinning as she smells the food. We load up our plates and settle in to eat in the living room.

"This is so good," she says around a mouthful. "I only had time to eat a shitty protein bar for lunch, so I was starving. After I posted those pictures of Katie and Gemma, I sold out of those outfits in nearly three hours and had to order more before I left." The bracelets on her wrist jingle as she brushes her hair out of her eyes, and though she's smiling, she looks exhausted.

"That's great. Just wait until you post the others. Bet you sell out every time."

"I hope so! This summer is gonna be insane. Sure you don't need a second job on the weekends?" She waggles her brows. "Put your height to good use and help me out around the shop?"

I nearly choke on my food and snort. "Yeah, right. From prison to chic."

Her eyes widen as if I just gave her the best idea ever.

"No," I say firmly before she can say another word about it.

"Come on, Tyler. You'd be the perfect eye candy." She leans over and rolls up my sleeve, then squeezes my sore biceps. "I could dress you up like I did when we were kids, and you'd be a nice attraction piece for all the single ladies."

I roll my eyes. "You're too much. You can't use your psychology techniques on me to get what you want like you do your friends."

"Fine." With a scoff, she goes back to her food.

"While I appreciate you wanting to hire me, I think man candy is the last thing you need in your boutique. I tend to make ladies uncomfortable," I remind her.

She lifts an eyebrow. "Speaking of that…"

"Don't wanna talk about it."

She doesn't continue with whatever relationship advice she was going to give me, so I focus on the TV as we finish eating. Once she's cleaned her plate, I carry them into the kitchen, and after I rinse them, I put them in the dishwasher. When I'm done, I realize I left my phone in my gym shorts and go to grab it. I see three missed calls from a Las Vegas area code, which is alarming, and then I notice there's a voicemail too.

I check it as my heart hammers in my chest. Whatever it is can't be good.

"Hey, Tyler. It's Eric. We used to work for Victoria O'Leary together. I need to talk to you as soon as possible." He lingers, then lets out a breath. "It's *important*."

The message ends, and I play it again. There's an edginess in his voice, and the confident air he used to have is gone. Eric was an asshole, and I couldn't stand him. I stuff my phone in my pocket, my head spinning with reasons as to why he'd be calling me. However, it doesn't matter because my mind is already made.

I'm not calling him back. Fuck that, and fuck him. I don't want to be a part of whatever he's gotten himself into. I bury the thoughts and go back to the living room.

"What's wrong?" Everleigh asks, muting the TV.

I shake my head. "It's nothing."

"You look like you've seen a ghost."

"Nah. What were we talking about before?" I can't remember because the only thing that's in my head right now is Eric's alarming voice. Whatever he wants feels like a trap, and I don't want anything to do with the family ever again.

"Gemma," she says. "We were talking about Gemma."

I chuckle. "*No,* we weren't."

I'd actually remember that.

"Well, I was *going* to talk about Gemma. You said women act uncomfortable around you, so I just thought I'd ask how things are at the shop with you two working together."

Sucking in a deep breath, I grin. "She pretends I'm not there, so it's going as expected."

"Not surprising. What about Jerry? I'm sure he's happy you're there."

"He's a good boss. Doesn't micromanage. Gives me tasks and lets me figure it out without hovering. It's a godsend of a position in this godforsaken town." I throw her a wink.

"If it doesn't work out, you can always come work for me," she sing-songs.

I roll my eyes. "Shut up and keep dreamin'."

"Don't worry, I will."

"But seriously, it's nice to feel like I have a purpose again and something else to focus on."

"Any more surprise visits from Gemma's fiancé?" Everleigh asks, and I stiffen. Though the blood seems to move quicker through my veins, I keep my breath steady, not wanting her to notice the slightest change in my behavior. I overcompensate and put my feet up on the coffee table as if I'm uninterested.

"Nope." I shrug, keeping my opinions about the guy to myself because they wouldn't be very nice.

"I only ask because Gemma mentioned you two met at the garage the other day."

"Yep," I confirm.

"Between you and me, I don't think Gemma's ready to marry the guy. She's my best friend, so I'll support her no matter what, but I'm wondering if she'll go through with it or not."

Stay. Calm. "Wow, that's pretty bad, Ev," I say, keeping my eyes on the TV.

"I know, I know, but seriously! They've been engaged for eighteen months and just recently set a date. If you're madly in love with someone, you don't wait that long unless there's a good reason —like a death in the family, or someone's sick, or you're saving up money—and those are definitely not the reasons." My throat tightens as she rambles on. I feel bad talking about Gemma like this, but it seems my sister needs to vent to someone, so I let her continue. "She's stalling. At first, I thought it was nerves, and some of it still might be, but there are other issues now." Everleigh drinks half the glass of wine she must've poured when I was in the bathroom. In about five minutes, she's going to have loose lips and tell me everything I already suspected.

"Gemma's a grown ass woman and can make her own decisions. Marriage used to be a big deal to her, so I doubt she'd jump into a relationship just to do it," I tell her, though I'm not convinced either after meeting the guy.

Everleigh finishes her drink, then leans back against the couch and looks at me. I can feel her eyes peeling back my flesh as though she's ready to open me up and dissect my thoughts.

"Do you still have feelings for her? Like you used to?" She narrows her eyes as if she already knows my answer.

"What's it matter? Even if I do, it wouldn't change anything. She's planning a wedding, and I won't ruin that. After fucking up her life enough already, I promised myself I'd stay away."

Everleigh grins. "You didn't say no."

"I didn't say yes, either," I counter. "I'm Switzerland with my answer, completely neutral," I say.

"Oh bullshit." She scowls. "You've been an opinionated badass my whole life. You aren't fooling me."

"Nope, I mean it. She can marry the Prince of England for all I care, and I wouldn't say a thing."

Everleigh snorts. "That's not dramatic at all. Plus, how would she meet a prince in small-town Alabama?"

"I don't know, you tell me. You're the one who watches all those Lifetime and Hallmark movies."

She laughs with a nod, then her lips fall into a frown. "Well, I'm just frustrated with the whole thing, even more now that Gemma's told me some more personal details." I don't want to know, but she continues before I can ask her to stop. "When a man is too tired to have sex with someone as hot as Gemma and throws her to the side like she's some play toy, there's an issue."

Well, I didn't expect *that*. What the fuck? So Robert's old *and* unable to satisfy her?

"When a man tries to buy my best friend's love instead of showing it, I know something's wrong. What's even more annoying is I can't be the one to save her. She has to save herself and admit he's all wrong for her, but I feel like she's already too tangled up with him. The whole town knows they're engaged. She'd rather go through with the wedding than disappoint her father."

"Well, then let her make that decision because she's the one who has to live with it," I say although I'm boiling inside. Gemma pretends everything is picture-perfect on the outside, but according to what she's telling my sister, it's all fake.

Everleigh shakes her head. "It's not supposed to be like this for her, though."

"There's nothing you can do except be there for her and support whatever she decides," I say firmly, though I'm screaming the exact opposite on the inside. I want to shake some goddamn sense into her and help her realize she doesn't love him the way she once loved me. She's jeopardizing her own happiness to make others happy.

"I will be," she concedes. "I'm just frustrated and annoyed."

"And drunk," I add.

"Maybe a tad tipsy but not drunk yet," she says with a hiccup, and I shake my head with a laugh. She shared more about Gemma with me than I think she was supposed to, but I'm glad she did. Though I want to stay out of it, I'm not so sure it's possible anymore.

Sassy jumps on the couch and lays her head on my lap. "This is ridiculous. You go from wanting to bite my legs off to claiming them as yours."

"She likes you." Everleigh reaches over and pets her head, then uses baby talk. "Because she's such a *good girl, yes she is, aren't you*?"

"Yeah, she's precious," I deadpan. "She scratches on the bedroom door until I let her in so she can sleep with me."

"It seems like she's training *you* just fine." Everleigh bends down and kisses Sassy's head. "Such a smart dog."

"Har har. Now all I need to do is teach her to fetch me a beer from the fridge, and then she'll be the perfect companion."

"I wouldn't bet your money on that."

We continue watching TV until neither of us can stop yawning. I've been getting up early to work out, and if I'm frustrated in the afternoons, I go back for round two. Plus, being on my feet all day doing manual labor is exhausting.

"I think I'm gonna go to bed," I tell her, standing and stretching my arms over my head.

Everleigh agrees with another yawn. "Same. Good night."

I walk toward my room, but before I can open the door, Everleigh calls out my name. When I turn around, I see Sassy's on my heels. "I'm glad you came back, brother. I've missed you a lot."

"I missed you too," I reply with a smile.

Once Sassy's in my room, she jumps on my bed like it's hers. Deciding I need to talk to Liam, I pull out my phone.

Tyler: Call me as soon as you can.

I climb under the covers and listen to the message again. Ten minutes later, my phone rings. "Hey."

"Hi, man. What's up?" Liam asks. "How're things going?"

"I got a call from Eric."

"From who?" he asks.

"Eric. The other bodyguard Victoria had hired to watch Maddie at the cabin with me," I explain, keeping my voice low so Everleigh can't overhear through the thin walls.

There's a thick silence between us, and I can tell Liam is on the move. Probably walking somewhere else to give us more privacy so he doesn't alarm Maddie. She's incredibly observant, especially when you don't want her to be. I think she and Everleigh would be good friends if they lived closer.

"What did he want?" Liam's concerned voice finally comes through.

"Just said to call him back and that it's important. I could definitely hear a tense edge in his voice, though. I don't know, it just feels a bit too coincidental that he's calling me shortly after I got released."

"Yeah, sounds fishy as hell," Liam agrees.

"That's definitely my thought too. I don't trust him, and it seems like a trap. I don't even know how he got my goddamn number. I just want to forget it all, but then reminders like this pop up, and—" I shake my head, unable to finish.

"It's behind you. You're in Alabama moving on with your life. Don't let one phone call deter that."

I chuckle. "I feel like I'm living in the *Groundhog Day* movie. I go to the gym, then work for eight hours, maybe work out again after, and then go home. Shower, eat, watch TV, then go to sleep. *Rinse, wash, repeat.* I'm totally living the life." My blatant sarcasm causes Liam to chuckle. "But at least I get to choose what I want to do every day, and I'm not behind bars, so I'm grateful for that. Guess it could be worse, right?"

"Exactly, which means anything that has to do with Victoria needs to just stay in Vegas, away from you and me. I don't know what Eric wants, but whatever it is, nothing good will come of it."

"I agree." Eric and I definitely weren't on *good terms.* Though I can't help but wonder what he wants. Either way, I don't want anything to do with that situation. I've already paid my price.

"Anyway. How's Maddie doing?" I ask

"Miserable. Ready to push the baby out. Still craving weird-ass food. Yesterday was pickles and vanilla ice cream. I almost threw up."

"That's hilarious." I laugh.

"Oh, after our talk last time, I rejoined the gym. Gotta take off the thirty pounds I put on during Maddie's pregnancy," he says with a chuckle. "Thought you'd be proud."

"Yeah? That's awesome, man. I could write you up some workouts and email them to you, if you want," I offer.

"I was totally gonna ask but didn't want to put more on your plate. But yeah, I'd like that," Liam says. "It's just not the same without you here pushing and yelling at me to stop being a pussy."

His admission makes me chuckle. "I mean, put me on speakerphone while you're there, and I'll do just that for ya."

"Thanks for the offer." He snorts. "It still won't be the same without ya."

"Yeah, I miss you too, man."

Liam laughs. "Now, don't go getting all mushy on me."

"Ha! Tell Maddie I asked about her."

"I will. Take care of yourself, Tyler."

"Don't worry. I'm not gonna do anything stupid," I tell him.

After Liam and I end the call, I stare up at the ceiling with Sassy sleeping next to me.

If Eric has my number, then they know exactly where I am. I just want to be left alone. While I've never been one to run from my problems, if they show up here, they'll be the ones who find trouble.

CHAPTER TEN

GEMMA

I WAKE up with the sun beaming on my face. It'll be another hot day, but luckily, I won't be in the office sweating my ass off. Daddy sometimes goes into the garage on Saturdays to catch up on maintenance, sign for special deliveries, or to clean, but I take the weekends off.

Turning, I notice Robert's side of the bed is empty and the sheets are cool. He never sleeps in with me and is typically drinking coffee in his home office by the time I get up.

"Morning," I say when I find him refilling his mug with coffee in the kitchen. He's already showered and dressed while I'm in comfy shorts and a T-shirt. His black hair is combed, and he's freshly shaved. Robert never stops working, and on a typical day, he wears slacks and a button-up shirt, or a suit if he has a business meeting. His motto is to dress for success because he never knows who he'll meet that day. While I admire his drive, constantly having to be on my A game when we leave the house is exhausting. I'd love to just lounge around for an afternoon and watch old eighties movies, but he never has time for that.

"Good morning, darling." He walks toward me and presses a kiss to my forehead. "How'd you sleep?" Robert takes a seat at the kitchen table, and I pour myself a cup of coffee and add creamer before sitting across from him.

"I slept fine. How about you?" I hold the warm mug in my hands.

"Great." He smiles at me before grabbing the newspaper and giving it his full attention.

I normally sleep over at his house on the weekends, though I wish he'd stay at mine every once in a while. Although he insists I keep my things here, I don't and still pack a bag. He's almost become militant about me moving in, but I haven't caved yet. I'm biding my time, which is quickly running out, because soon, we'll be married.

"Did you eat breakfast yet?" I look around, noticing the counters are spotless.

"No, I was waiting for you."

I blow on my coffee before taking a sip. "What are you hungry for?"

"Something light. I have a lunch meeting with Greg Klein at one. Eggs and toast would be great," he says without looking up at me.

Biting into my lower lip, I swallow down the words that will inevitably start an argument. I wasn't aware he had a work meeting scheduled, and I was hoping he'd spend the day with me, but I shouldn't be surprised. He'll do his thing, I'll do mine, and then we'll meet up for dinner like usual.

"Sure." I move behind the large marble island, then grab a pan and the ingredients from the fridge. As I prepare our food, I contemplate texting Katie to see if she's busy this afternoon. Everleigh's working at the boutique until six, and while I could go visit her, Saturdays are the busiest, and I don't want to get in the way.

Once Robert's breakfast is done, I set his plate in front of him with a smile.

"Could you get me a glass of orange juice, darling?"

"Of course."

After he's settled, I prepare my food. By the time I join him, he's nearly done eating.

"You should skip the toast," he states without hesitation, flipping to a different section in the paper as I dip it into the yolk.

I blink hard, freezing before I take a bite. "What do you mean?"

"Do you think you'll be wedding-ready by March?"

I clear my throat before setting my food down on the plate. "I thought Winnie was coordinating—"

"Not *that*. Your body. Will you be ready to wear a dress and be photographed? Our wedding photos will be posted all over the internet." He finally makes eye contact with me, and I know he's serious.

"You think I need to lose weight beforehand?" My shaky voice gives away my nervousness, but I can't help it. I'm a size four, sometimes a six when I'm bloated, but I've been petite my entire life. In fact, I've struggled so fucking hard to gain, and it's something I've been self-conscious about since I was a scrawny teenager. I hit puberty late, and I didn't get hips or boobs until I was nearly twenty. Not exactly a magnet for attracting guys when girls my age were rocking double D's and had perfect asses.

"Doesn't every bride-to-be stress about being in tip-top shape for their big day? I assumed you'd go on some crazed diet to ensure you'd look your absolute best. It'll be the event of the year and so many eyes will be on you."

I'm not sure how I should take his assumption, considering I've hardly mentioned the wedding, and I have *never* talked about dieting. If anything, I'd like to be at least ten pounds heavier beforehand so I can fill out the bodice. "Well, to answer your question–yes, my body is *ready*," I say between clenched teeth, offended. "Most dresses have to be altered after their purchase to fit properly."

"When do you think you'll go try some on? I'd love to join you. We can make a day out of it."

Narrowing my brows, I dive back into my food that's getting cold. "That's breaking tradition."

"Can't the groom have an opinion on his bride's gown?"

"You should think I'm beautiful in whatever I pick."

He flashes a small grin. "Of course I will."

"I haven't had time to look, but I suppose since we set the date, I could. I'll try to schedule something with Katie and Everleigh soon."

"In that case, why wait until March? Find a dress next weekend and let's move up the date."

I nearly choke on the toast I just shoved into my mouth but quickly recover before he notices. "Move it? March only gives us seven months as it is."

"Yes, but we've been engaged for a year and a half. Invites haven't been sent yet. I'm tired of waiting to make you my wife." He reaches across the table and takes my hand, then squeezes. "The sooner we get married, the sooner we can have children."

"Children?" We've talked about starting a family but not right away. I was thinking we'd have one kid since Robert is in his mid-forties, but he works so much that he hardly spends time with me, let alone any children we may have.

"I'd like three, maybe four." He says it so casually I feel like I'm in a dream or maybe a nightmare. Perhaps we should've talked about this sooner, but he's laying so much on me at once I feel like the walls are closing in.

"Excuse me." I take my plate and stand. "I'm going to shower and get ready for the day."

As I rinse my dish, Robert comes up behind me and brushes the hair off my neck, then moves it to one shoulder while he massages my muscles.

"Darling, you're tense," he whispers, then places a sweet kiss on my cheek. "The longer we ride out this engagement, the more stressed you'll be. I'll call Winnie and have her reschedule everything for November. We'll have a beautiful fall wedding."

My eyes widen, and I swallow hard. *November?* "That's only three months away. Most venues book out at least a year in advance." It was a miracle we managed to get our dream location for the date we picked. If I remember correctly, they were booked through the rest of the year.

Robert rubs his hands down my arms, then squeezes. "With enough money, I can secure any venue in town. Don't worry. I understand you were in love with the place we chose, but I've already looked into a few others, and they'd be honored to host it for us."

"You did that without consulting me?" I tilt my head, feeling blindsided.

"Just made a couple of phone calls so we had options."

"Surely, that's not enough time to figure out all the details. The decorations, the flowers, the invites, my dress."

"Sweetheart..." His voice lowers as he spins me around and tilts up my chin. "That's why I hired a wedding planner. Let *her* worry about it. Just tell her what you want, and she'll get it for you. There's no budget when it comes to giving my bride what she wants."

What I *want* is not to rush into walking down the aisle. I thought I had at least seven more months to prepare. My father loves Robert and the idea of us getting married so much he lights up anytime it's mentioned. I know Daddy wants the absolute best for me, and I want nothing more than to make him happy and proud.

I inhale a deep breath. "Can I think about it?"

"Sure, dear. But not too long because I need to tell Winnie."

I smile and nod as he leans in and kisses my cheek. "I won't."

After Robert walks out of the kitchen, I finish rinsing the other dishes, then load the dishwasher. I try to imagine myself living here and this being my home. I'd cook, clean, and raise our beautiful kids while trying to be the perfect wife for Robert.

Right now, it's decorated for a man, not a family. It's clean and modern, but it doesn't feel homey. Certainly not like my cottage where I have pictures, candles, and throw pillows scattered on the furniture. He hired an interior designer after he built this house but never added any personality to it.

If we get married in three months, everything will change. I've barely wrapped my head around the date we set for next year and pushing it up sounds more stressful than waiting. Robert's kind, and it's obvious he has my best interests at heart. And while I love him, I've also been questioning if I'm *in* love with him. Though I've dated in the past, Robert was the first serious relationship I've had and the first guy I told I loved after Tyler left. I have strong feelings for him, and I care, but I wonder if that's enough.

How do you know if what you're feeling is love, lust, or infatuation?

Can you ever know for sure?

After I finished getting ready, I send Katie a text to see if she could hang out or rather, talk me off the ledge, and she was all for it. I stopped by the liquor store for margarita ingredients, then made my way there.

"Hey!" she greets as she whips open the door, then pulls me in for a hug. "You look so cute."

"So do you, sexy mama." I step inside and follow her to the kitchen. "I brought the goods."

"Thank God, because honestly, I'm at my wits' end. If I don't drink some tequila, I might lose my shit." She plugs in the blender and grabs the ice while I unload the bags.

"Why? What's going on?"

"Owen," she says flatly. "He's been acting out more than usual, and by the time I pick him up from my parents' after work, I'm exhausted, and he's found his second wind."

"Why do you think he's acting out?" I pour the margarita mix and tequila into the blender.

"Well, I imagine it's preteen hormones."

"Already? He's only nine."

"I think so. He's asked about his daddy since he was four. However, I get the feeling he's bitter or envious he doesn't have one and his friends do. He's at that age where he needs a father figure, and nothing I say or do is good enough."

"Oh no." I frown.

After Gabe, her husband and my cousin, died and my brother, Noah, went to prison for the accidental homicide, her entire world was rocked. So was my family's. In fact, the whole town was shocked. That was almost ten years ago, and she's still picking up the pieces. Owen wasn't born yet and has never met his father. Though Gabe wasn't a great husband, I think he would've been an amazing father. When he wasn't drinking, he was a fun cousin to be around and always made me laugh. I miss him at times and wonder how different our lives would be if he were still alive.

"Yeah, so welcome to my pity party." She starts the blender, and I grab two glasses. Once it's done, she pours the liquid, giving us the same amount. "Your turn." Katie smirks, then leads me to the patio where Owen's playing with a friend on the trampoline.

"I have nothing to complain about, really." I set my drink down and settle on the lounge chair with my legs stretched out. "It's wedding jitters, I'm sure."

"Already?" she asks, getting comfy in the chair next to me. "I thought the date wasn't until March."

"Robert wants to move it to November," I explain.

She nearly spits out her margarita but quickly covers her mouth. "November? *Why*?"

I laugh at her shocked expression. "He thinks we've waited long enough and wants to make me his wife so we can move in together and start making babies. He was raised with traditional values, and the men and women in his family get married quickly and raise a family."

"Whoa…that's a lot to process." She blinks, taking another sip. "What'd you say?"

"I told him I needed time to think about it. He put me on the spot. I haven't even fully processed that we only have seven months left, so I was caught off guard."

"Well, money isn't the issue. That man will buy you anything you want," she says with a grin. "So what's holding you back?"

I shrug, not sure how to explain the mixed feelings I'm having. I adore his parents, and I know they love Robert and me together. I met them early in our relationship and his mother, Christine, gushed over all the grandchildren we'd give her. We try and meet them once a month for brunch on Sundays and she fills me in on all the gossip in her elite circle. After a while, she felt like the mother-figure I've been without for over twenty years. She'd be devastated if we split up, and truthfully, I would too. She's the epitome of beauty and wealth, but she has a big heart and always invites me to her country club parties to socialize with their friends. Even though I get along well with his family, it can't be the reason we rush to the altar if it doesn't feel right.

"How'd you know you were in love with Gabe?"

She smiles briefly before the corners of her lips fall. "I just did. I was pretty damn smitten by him, but at first, it was high school puppy love. That first summer we spent together was like something you'd read in a Nicholas Sparks novel. We wanted to be around each other constantly. Day or night, no matter what, and our feelings blossomed so fast. He made me laugh a lot and looked at me like I was his whole world. Gabe was the first and only man I've ever loved. He could do no wrong, and as time passed, I was blinded to the issues we were having. Then we got married, and I got pregnant, and—"

"Yeah, I know," I say softly and grab her hand when she doesn't continue because that story doesn't end happily.

"You get butterflies in the beginning, and then after a while, you fall into a comfortable routine. Happens to all relationships." She takes a long swig of her drink. "I'm sure you two are just in a lull, and once the big day gets closer, you'll be itching to walk down the aisle."

I hope so because right now it feels like I'm settling for the kind of love that doesn't excite me. On the other hand, Robert can take care of me the way my father wants. Robert isn't a bad guy, but I wouldn't be his only love. He'd be more married to his job than me. Hell, he already is.

"Yeah, probably." Tipping my head back, I empty my glass.

"Speaking of Robert, do you think he'd be able to help me find some property?"

"You're looking to buy a house?"

"Yep, I think it's time. Owen needs a bigger yard and bedroom, and I need more space for me. But I need something in a decent neighborhood that I can afford, so I'm thinking it'll have to be a fixer-upper. I thought maybe Robert would know of something or know someone who might."

"Wait, wait, wait." I hold up my hand, amused. "You, Katie Walker, are going to remodel a house? I added way too much tequila."

She chuckles and sticks out her tongue. "I've been watching plenty of tutorials online and remodeling TV shows, thank you very much. I might not be an expert, but I can follow directions, and well, if I completely fuck it up, I can call a contractor."

Her Southern accent gets thicker as she drinks more, and I laugh. I'm guilty of it too. "I'm trying to imagine you in overalls with a tool belt, and I'm sorry, but I can't."

"Well, try harder, babe, because it's happening. I'll be tearing down walls, repairing floors, and installing sinks. Hell, I might get my own reality TV show by the end of it. Single mom renovates an old home. It has a certain ring to it, doesn't it?"

"I think the booze has gone straight to your head." Laughing, I grab our empty glasses, then head inside for refills.

"Make mine a double!" she calls from outside.

After I make another batch, I go back outside and hand hers over. "Take it easy now. It's still the afternoon."

"Oh, but it's five o'clock somewhere."

"I'll cheer to that."

We hang out, gossip, and listen to music while watching Owen play. I realize how much I've missed just talking to a friend over drinks.

"Hey, Mom." Owen rushes over, nearly out of breath.

I smile at his cute dimples and messy dark hair. He looks more like Gabe the older he gets. Though he'll never be able to meet him, I know his father would be proud of him.

"What, babe?" Katie asks, narrowing her eyes.

"Can Austin and I ride bikes to the park?"

Katie puts a hand above her eyes to block out the sun as she ponders it. "Alright, but wear your helmet."

"*Mom.*" He groans with an eye roll. "I'm too old to wear that."

"Oh, really? You're too old to get hit by a truck and get your brain smashed? I didn't realize there was an age limit for that..."

"Fine, whatever." He walks off with Austin behind him, and I laugh as soon as he's out of view. The park isn't too far, but Katie's always been protective of her son. Considering what she's gone through, I don't blame her.

"You have your hands full. That's for sure," I tease, taking a big gulp.

"Hence why we're drinking margaritas." She finishes her second one. "But seriously, he's a good kid. I wish the circumstances were different, and he had a dad, or even a male figure in his life to hang out with."

Before I can think twice about it, I blurt out, "What about Tyler?"

"You want me to marry Tyler so he can have a dad?"

My eyes widen as I take in how tipsy Katie is, and then I burst out laughing. "No! I meant he could be Owen's friend or whatever.

I'm sure Tyler wouldn't mind playing basketball or football with him. Like the Big Brothers program, except he's not a stranger."

"I know Tyler from *high school*. I don't know Tyler *after prison*. He just moved back. Plus, I don't want the first real conversation we have to be about him hanging out with my son."

"Yeah, he's definitely…changed."

Turning toward me, she studies my face. "How are things going with him at the shop? Things seemed tense at the bar last weekend."

I swallow hard and lick my lips. "It's…*interesting*. After I made a fool of myself when he took me home, I can barely look at him," I admit with shame.

"Whoa, what? You better spill the tea. *Wait!* We need another round."

"No, no, no…"

"Yes! C'mon. Let's get out of the sun before we turn into lobsters. Then I wanna hear *all* about it."

Oh God. I groan and follow her into the house where I recap that night and blush at how embarrassing it was.

"Wow…" She smirks as we sit on the couch with our third glass of margaritas. "I can't believe you stripped down to your bra and panties. What do you think would've happened if he'd stayed the night?"

My cheeks heat at the number of times I've thought of that same thing over the past week. "I should've never asked…" I shake my head, unable to finish. "Anyway, now it's awkward, and I'm an idiot."

"No, you're not. I'm sure him being here is confusing, considering you've had feelings for him since you were a teenager. Even more now that you see him every day at work."

I nod with a frown. "I feel like a piece of shit. I'm engaged to another man, but still think about Tyler, even after he broke my heart. After all the years I waited for him, there's still that *what-if* in the back of my mind that I can't let go."

Katie leans over and wraps her arm around me, pulling me in for a hug. "Only you know what your heart is feeling, and only you can decide what you want. Follow your gut because if I had done that ten years ago, *everything* would be different."

CHAPTER ELEVEN

TYLER

It's officially my second week of working at Reid's Garage, and I enjoy the solitude when I'm focused on a task. I've always been good with my hands and figuring out how to fix things, but lately, I've been distracted. My head's still spinning with thoughts of Gemma. I can't stop thinking about how she flirted with me after I took her home last Friday. It doesn't help that I hear her sweet humming all day at work.

She walks around the shop and into the break room, avoiding my gaze. I'm starting to get used to it even though I wish she'd just forget about it so we can move on from the awkward tension.

Today's the second day in a row she's worn a tight pencil skirt and low-cut blouse to work. I'm pretty sure she's trying to kill me or at the very least give me blue balls.

"Tyler," Jerry calls as I wash the grease off my hands. He walks over to me, then slaps a hand on my shoulder. "You have lunch plans today?"

"No, sir." I grab a towel and dry off.

"Good. Come with me to the Main Street Deli. We can chat and eat."

"Sounds good."

Jerry and I walk a couple of blocks to the deli, and as soon as we enter, we're greeted by the owner.

"Hey, Belinda!" Jerry waves. "Remember Tyler Blackwood?"

"I sure do. Heard you were back. Welcome home."

I give her a head nod. "Thanks."

"Sit wherever y'all want. I'll be right there to take your order."

"This place hasn't changed." I chuckle as I look around. I haven't been inside since before the summer I left.

"That's not true," Belinda says, pulling out her notepad and pen. "Fresh paint and new tables."

"It all looks great. I bet the food is just as amazing, too."

Jerry laughs. "Of course it is! Speakin' of which, I'll take my regular and a Diet Coke."

Quickly glancing over the menu, I order a turkey melt and a water.

"You got it. Be back in a jiffy with your drinks."

"I know it's only been a week, but what do you think about workin' at the shop so far? Any concerns or things you wanna discuss?" Jerry asks after Belinda walks away.

"Honestly, I like it. Keeps my mind busy, and I like fixing things."

"Everleigh said you were a boxing trainer in Vegas?"

"I was. Trained in Sacramento, too. I really miss it."

"Did you check out the gym here?"

"I did last Saturday. It's been a good stress reliever." I grin. "Plus, there's nothing else to do on the weekends since my sister works at her boutique, and I don't really have any friends here."

"Nonsense! We gotta change that."

I chuckle, and we continue chatting until Belinda delivers our food. It's as delicious as I remember, and I'm relieved things aren't awkward with Jerry.

Once we finish eating and pay, we head back to the garage.

"How was lunch?" Gemma asks sweetly as soon as we walk in. She stands, glancing back and forth between her father and me. If she's trying to act unaffected by us spending time together, she's doing a shit job.

"Delicious as always." Jerry pats his beer belly. "Belinda told me to say hello, by the way."

Gemma smiles at him, then lowers her eyes to avoid mine.

"I had a great idea," Jerry says before we get back to work.

"What's that, Daddy?"

"You and Robert should plan a double date with Tyler. Help him get back out there and meet some friends." Jerry grins wide as if he's proud he suggested it.

"Uh, I don't think that's a good idea." Gemma fidgets with the hem of her shirt, and I cock my head at her hesitancy.

"Why not?" Jerry pats me on the back. "He's a good-lookin' guy. Tall and muscular. Women like that, or so I'm told." He chuckles at his own joke.

"Yeah, why not?" I cross my arms over my chest. She finally meets my gaze, and I flash her a smirk, knowing she has no excuses. Jerry knows we briefly dated after I returned from the Army but isn't aware of the repressed feelings we still have for each other. Gemma pretends they don't exist and has convinced herself to marry Robert, but I see through her façade.

"I'm not sure who I'd invite." Gemma shrugs.

"How 'bout Katie? I mentioned it when I saw her yesterday, and she seemed excited. Plus, she's single, has a good job at the bank, and Tyler said he likes kids. I bet they'd really hit it off!" Jerry waves his hand around. "Set it up, Gemma. I think Katie would love to get to know Tyler better. Maybe they'll be the next couple to get engaged in Lawton Ridge."

Gemma swallows hard, licking her lips. Amusement floods through me as I watch her panic, but she forces a smile. "Sure, Daddy. I'll ask her when she's free."

"Perfect!" Jerry grins, then walks around me and opens the door to the shop. As soon as it closes, I step toward Gemma as she moves behind the counter.

I tap my knuckles against the wood. "You sure you'd be okay with that?"

"Of course. Why wouldn't I?"

"Most people who hang out together are friends. Not sure we classify as such."

"We can be friends. We're co-workers, so we might as well be."

Arching a brow, I study her features and notice her lying tells. "Might as well be, huh?"

Her shoulders slump. "That's not what I meant. We're going to see each other a lot, so it'd be easier if we were friends. That way it's not weird between us."

"Does it feel weird for you, Gemma? Seeing me again? Working with me?"

Her tongue flicks out as she licks her lips, then sucks them between her teeth. "A little, but I'll get used to it."

"You think Richard would be okay with us having dinner?"

"*Robert*," she corrects. "And it'd be a double date, so I'm sure it'd be fine. You might even find you two have something in common."

I bark out a loud laugh, then rest my arms on the counter and lean in closer. "The only thing we have in common is we've both seen ya naked." I flash her a wink, then walk toward the shop door before she can say another world.

For the rest of the afternoon, I stay by Jerry's side, and we knock out several projects, finishing everything that was on the schedule for the day. Gemma pops in and out, relaying messages to her dad and asking questions about scheduling. When she walks back into the office humming, the sound goes straight to my dick and fucks with my head for the rest of my shift.

"Good night, Gemma," I say as I walk toward the exit. She's behind the counter, still avoiding eye contact. I stop and look at her before opening the door. "Don't forget to set up that double date. I'm available Saturday."

She finally looks up at me with a fake smile. "Sure, I'll get right on that."

With a smirk, I turn around, then leave. I know I'm getting to her as much as she gets to me.

As I walk home, I check my notifications and see Eric left another voicemail. My heart pounds hard in my chest when he mentions Victoria, begging me to call him back. As much as I don't want to deal with the O'Learys or Eric, I doubt he'll leave me alone until I return his call. So I decide to get it over with and hit his number.

"Tyler?" he answers.

"Yeah, it's me."

Eric releases a breath. "We gotta talk."

"What do you want?" I have little patience already.

"I need you to come to Vegas and do a character witness deposition of Victoria O'Leary."

"That'd be a death sentence for me," I argue. "I literally got out of prison two weeks ago because she set me up."

"Man, I know. I wouldn't be asking if it wasn't crucial."

"What'd she do?" I ask, preparing for the worst. "*Specifically*. You didn't tell me in your message."

Victoria's gotten away with a ton of shady shit, including shooting her brother in cold blood without serving any time.

"She caught me talking to the police and instead of letting me explain, she cornered me and my girlfriend, Amara, and demanded I prove my loyalty. She held a gun to my head, then told me to choose who'd get shot. Myself or Amara. I stepped closer and said me."

Eric chokes up, and my stomach clenches at how his story ends.

"Amara burst out into tears, and I tried to calm her. I grabbed her hand and squeezed as the cold metal rested on my temple. Victoria looked at me with emotionless eyes, released the safety, then turned the gun on Amara and shot her without a beat of hesitancy."

"Fuck," I hiss between my teeth. Shaking my head, I swallow hard as bile burns my throat. "I'm so sorry, Eric."

"That's only a part of it. She had one of her bodyguards beat the shit out of me, which landed me in ICU for three weeks. Fractured ribs, bruises, broken jaw, and a punctured lung. She stood by and watched with a sneer like it was the best entertainment she'd ever seen."

"She's fucking sick. So why didn't they arrest her?"

"There's not enough evidence to hold her. The FBI has a mile-long file of shit related to the O'Learys, but Victoria, specifically, uses other people to do her dirty work. I explained she shot Amara and was told without proof, it's my word against hers. The gun is long gone by now, and the bullets are not traceable. The guy who kicked my ass has a solid alibi of where he was that night. But I didn't give up. I brought the investigator a mountain of evidence from other crimes she'd committed or arranged, and their tune changed. They're finally ready to prosecute her with corruption and money laundering. While it's not the first-degree murder charge she deserves, it's better than nothing. If they try to indict her for something without evidence, her lawyers will cry circumstantial evidence and the opportunity will disappear."

"So how will my statement help?"

"Getting as many character witnesses to tell the truth about what they saw or heard her do will help prove repeat behavior. There's already ten on board, but I need more. You got involved for the sake of your friend and have a firsthand account of all the shady shit she did in that short amount of time. It's better than nothing. I need you."

I want to help him, I really do, but this whole thing could cause a shitstorm of problems I don't want or need. Moving to Alabama was meant to help me get a fresh start away from Vegas and all the terrible things that happened five years ago. Going back would allow all of it back into my life.

"How long do I have to decide?"

"As soon as possible. If you agree to do it, the prosecutor will put you on the witness list, and they'll schedule your deposition. The defense will cross-examine you as well."

"Yeah, that's the part I'm worried about. They're fucking assholes when it comes to that shit."

"Trust me, I get it, but I'm done hiding. Victoria needs to pay, even if I have to die trying."

"Give me some time to think about it, okay? I'll let you know as soon as I can."

"Thanks, I really appreciate it, Tyler. I know we didn't end on good terms, but I'd like to change that. Working for Victoria is the worst decision I ever made, and I wish I could take it all back."

"I'll call you soon."

We hang up just as I arrive home. I'm immediately welcomed by Sassy, who barks at me relentlessly. Deciding I need to call Liam and give him an update, I grab the leash and take Sassy on a walk.

"Hey, man," Liam answers in an upbeat tone. "How's it going?"

"Eric left me another voicemail, and I called him back this time."

"Really? Tell me everything."

I repeat our conversation and voice my concerns.

"Wow. Just...*wow*."

"We knew she was a fucking savage, but what she did to Eric was plain ruthless. She deserves more than just prison time," I say.

"Honestly, I'd call Serena and get her suggestions. If you decide to do it, I'd have her go as your council, so the defense won't ask questions that'll get you in trouble instead."

"That's probably a good idea, but I haven't talked to her in years. I feel bad calling her to ask for a favor."

"Trust me, she won't mind. I bet she'd love to hear from you. She actually asked about you before you got out."

"Send me her number," I tell him.

"Will do. I'll text it right now."

"Thanks, Liam. Appreciate it."

"I got you. Let me know what she says, okay?"

"I'll message you as soon as we're done."

We say goodbye, and then I call Serena. I'm nervous as hell as the phone rings.

"Hello?"

"Hi, Serena. It's Tyler Blackwood."

There's a beat of silence at first. "Tyler? Oh my God!"

Her ecstatic energy brings a smile to my face. "Yeah, it's me. Been a while. How are you?"

"I've thought about you a lot over the years."

"Same here."

Serena was my lawyer and represented me when Victoria planted drugs and illegal guns in my truck. While Serena did everything she could, it wouldn't have mattered because Victoria had already sabotaged the outcome. I know she felt bad, but there was nothing more she could do.

"So tell me, how's life? What's new?"

I chuckle at her eagerness and give a quick update.

"I'm glad, Tyler. You deserve good things."

"How's your little guy?" I ask. She was a single mom the last time we talked.

"Not so little anymore! He's six and going into first grade this year."

"Wow, time flies, huh?"

"Yes, it does." She lingers for a moment. "I have a feeling you didn't call to shoot the shit. What's going on?"

"It's Victoria," I tell her with a rushed breath.

"What the fuck is that bitch up to now? Is she trying to pin something else on you?"

"Not exactly," I say and pause briefly before telling her about Eric and Amara.

"Oh my God," she whispers. "That woman is worse than the devil himself."

"What do you think I should do? Will this somehow backfire on me? Will she know I did a deposition?" Sassy finishes sniffing around a fire hydrant, then we continue down the sidewalk.

"It's possible. Your name will be on the witness sheet, but whether she sees it or not, I can't say. More than likely, she'll use the family money to buy her way out of it."

"I want to help Eric if I can, and if I can help fuck her life up the same way she did mine, that'd be a nice bonus."

"I agree, but without specific details, it's hard to give a green light on this. Can you have him set up a conference call with you, me, and the prosecutor? That way we can ask more questions before you make a decision."

"Yeah, I'll ask him as soon as I get home."

"Great, just text me what he says. I'll do whatever I can to help."

"You were always a great friend even though we hardly knew each other. I really appreciate it, Serena."

"What you did for Liam and Maddie is admirable, so I was happy to help, even if I feel like I didn't." She chuckles.

We wrap up the call a few minutes later, and after Sassy does her business, I walk her back. Once we're inside, I refill her water and food, then text Eric. Less than ten minutes later, he responds.

Eric: I'll set it up and get back with you on the date and time.

Tyler: Sounds good. Thanks.

I text Serena, then grab some clothes and go to the bathroom to rinse off the day's sweat. As I stand with the stream beating against my back, I lower my head and suck in a deep breath. I can't believe after five years, I'm being brought back into Victoria's corrupt life. If she finds out I'm helping Eric and the prosecution's case, she'll come for me.

And if she does, she won't just plant drugs and guns.

She'll make sure to end me for good.

CHAPTER TWELVE

GEMMA

I wake up Saturday morning, relieved to be off work and not have to face Tyler—or rather, find ways to avoid him—but then I remember our "double date" is tonight, and I'm annoyed all over again.

I hated putting Katie on the spot, but surprisingly, she didn't mind. Plus, she expected it after she ran into my dad in town. I told her about my conflicted feelings when he returned and explained there was no closure when things fell apart. However, she asked me if it was okay to go on a date with Tyler or if it'd be too weird for me. I played it off like it was no big deal—though I already know it's going to be awkward as hell—so now the four of us will be meeting for drinks tonight.

Once I'm out of bed and showered, Daddy and I walk to Main Street for the farmers' market. It's held every Saturday during the summer and is one of my favorite things to do on the weekends with my dad when I'm not staying with Robert. All the shops open their doors and put extra tables outside for easy shopping. Everleigh always does a sale, which is when I usually grab a couple of extra things.

"What a beautiful day," Dad says as we cross the intersection. "I wish you and Robert were getting married this month. The weather is beautiful."

"It's humid and miserable," I argue.

"Nah. It's perfect."

I smile at his eagerness. He can't wait to walk me down the aisle, wear a tux, and give his father-of-the-bride speech. Being his only daughter, I thought he'd be sad to give me away, but considering I'm thirty years old, he's probably thinking it's about damn time. Dad's mentioned more than once that he can't wait for grandkids, and though I want to be a mom someday, I'm not ready yet. I don't feel prepared for any of this.

"I'm gonna go say hi to Everleigh," I tell him as he stops to buy a few vegetables.

"Oh, I'll come with you."

I wait until he's done, and then we walk to the boutique together. My breath hitches when I see Tyler inside talking to Katie, smiling wide. Owen's there too, totally intrigued by Tyler. I stare at the three of them and see the potential my father noticed. They *could* be a cute little family. Tyler seems great with kids, and Owen would love having a man in his life that he could eventually call dad.

"Gemma!" Everleigh squeals as she rushes around the counter, then pulls me in for a hug.

"Hey! Just stopped in to check on you. Looks like you already have company, though."

"Yeah, Katie and Owen were saying hi when Tyler came in to bring me something I *forgot* at the house." She waggles her brows and grins wide. She definitely planned this run-in.

"Oh, gotcha. Well, Dad and I were doing some shopping."

"Tyler!" My dad steps over toward him and slaps him on the back. "You kids excited for tonight?"

He's reminded me every day since Tuesday to plan the double date, so yesterday, I finally did just to get him off my back. But seeing Tyler and Katie together is making me regret it. When the two of them smile at each other, my temperature rises, and I just want to disappear.

I love Katie and want her to be happy—she deserves it after the hell she's been through—but Tyler and I have a history. If I told Katie it made me feel uneasy, she'd back away and understand, especially since she knows all about our past. But I don't want to be *that* person.

I'll never be the type of woman who can't have a guy but doesn't want anyone else to have him either. It's not fair to either of them since I'm marrying Robert.

"Yeah, definitely! Owen's gonna have a sleepover at my parents' tonight, so I'll have the whole evening," Katie says happily.

I lock my arms behind my back and try to act normal. By the tone of her voice, she's implying she'll have time after the date to be with Tyler. The hard pounding of my heart tells me I'm losing control of my emotions.

Stupid, stupid, stupid.

I *cannot* be jealous. I'm engaged, planning a wedding, and moving out. Robert and I are in love, and we're going to have a happy life together. A blast from the past won't change that.

It can't. Or at least that's what I'm trying to convince myself.

"Where are y'all goin' tonight?" Daddy asks.

"The pub," I tell him. "For some drinks and pool."

"The pub?" My dad scrunches his face. "For a *date*?"

"Daddy, it's a relaxed get-to-know-you kinda thing. Nothing serious."

"We'll save the wining and dining for our first official date," Tyler chimes in, flicking his eyes to mine with a devilish look. He knows exactly what he's doing, hoping to get a reaction from me in front of everyone. Over the past two weeks, I've noticed he enjoys doing that. Tyler tests me during every conversation we have, and I don't know if it's because he enjoys the chase or he loves to watch me squirm. Either way, it grates on my last nerve.

"Ah, that's my boy." My dad chuckles.

"Where's Robert?" Tyler asks smugly.

"He's working." I glare at him.

"Must suck that he works so much." The corner of his lips perks up. "You sure he'll make it tonight?"

"Yes. He'll be there."

"Great. Looking forward to it." Tyler smirks, then turns to Katie. "I have to run, but I'll see you later."

"Yep, can't wait." She beams.

Tyler waves to everyone as he walks toward the open door, and when I glance over my shoulder at him, he flashes me a wink, then chuckles.

Asshole.

"Hey." Katie pulls me aside. "Everything okay?"

I tilt my head and furrow my brows. "Yeah, why?"

"You seem off. I just want to make sure this date won't be too much or awkward with Robert and Tyler together."

Too much is the understatement of the century.

"It'll be totally fine. You two will be chatting mostly anyway, and Robert and I will shoot pool or play darts to give y'all some privacy." I smile wide, hoping to convince her, though I genuinely want her to have a good time.

"Okay, because it's not too late to cancel if you've changed your mind. I just thought with your history and everything—"

"Katie." I suck in a breath. "I'm engaged to Robert. Tyler and I dated years ago for three months. It's ancient history at this point."

"Alright, as long as you're not uncomfortable because I could see myself liking him after we get to know each other a little better."

My jaw nearly snaps off as my heart pounds rapidly in my chest. "Really?"

"Well, based on what I've seen or know about him. I wouldn't normally introduce a man to Owen so soon, but the moment Tyler started talking about football, Owen lit up."

"Then I hope it works out, Katie. Honestly. Tyler's a nice guy."

The moment Robert and I walk into the pub, I immediately need a drink. Tyler and Katie are already in a booth with theirs. We're only a few minutes late, but it looks like they've been here a while.

"Hey," I greet when we walk up.

"Hey!" Katie stands and wraps her arms around me. "We were just talking about you."

"Hopefully all good," I tease, unable to look at Tyler.

"Of course. It's always good," Tyler says, and when I glance at him, I instantly regret it. His brown eyes are warm and inviting, and I hate that they send chills down my body.

"Pinot Noir, darling?" Robert grasps my shoulders and squeezes lightly.

Though Tyler isn't watching us, I see him tighten his grip on the neck of his beer and grin at the wine Robert suggested. Wine won't get me drunk enough to get through this night, getting sick tomorrow be damned.

"No, I'd like a Jack and Coke and four shots of vodka to get this night started!"

Robert tilts his head, studying me, and I give him a sweet smile. "It's been a *long* week."

"Of course, sweetheart. Be right back." He presses his lips to my cheek, and I smile before he walks off.

"Here, I'll sit next to Tyler so you and Robert can sit together." Katie moves and scoots close to him. He rests his arm on the back of the booth, and she happily notices.

Those drinks need to get here stat.

Katie and Tyler continue chatting while I wait for Robert to return. They talk about high school and his time in the military. It's not hard to eavesdrop, but as soon as Robert sits down next to me with our drinks, they stop.

"Shots!" I say, passing around the vodka. The four of us take them, and I slam my glass on the table before grabbing my Jack and Coke.

"Whoa." Katie chuckles. "Save room for the margaritas."

"Oh, you know I will." I wink.

After a while, Robert and I excuse ourselves to play a round of pool. When we first started dating, he taught me all the rules and always kicks my ass. Tonight, I don't care about winning, I just want to let loose.

"You're actually getting better," he teases.

"Or maybe you're getting worse?" I mock.

"I *highly* doubt that." He wraps his arms around my waist and pulls me into his chest.

"You could be a gentleman and let me win once in a while." I smile up at him, the alcohol streaming through my veins, and cup his face. Our lips crash together roughly, but before things get too heated, he puts space between us.

"Gemma, we're in public in a bar," he hisses and releases me, then walks around the pool table to call his shot. He doesn't like PDA because it's not "professional," but why can't he relax for just one night? It's not like I'm some random chick. I'm his fiancée.

Needing a refill, I head to the bar and order two strawberry margaritas, then bring one back to Katie, who's laughing at something Tyler said. She thanks me, then I return to Robert and grab my pool stick.

Fuck it. I'm bored and don't care about this game and purposely sink his ball into the pocket. "Whoopsies." I shrug, then take down a quarter of my drink, wanting it to take hold quicker.

"Good thing you excel at other things," Robert says, then takes his turn until he clears the table. His tone isn't harsh but rather condescending.

Robert continues drinking Grey Goose and Perrier as I sip my margarita. Once our game is over, we go back to the booth and catch up with Katie and Tyler.

"We were just gonna play a round of darts," Katie tells me as she stands. "Should we play teams?"

I bite down on my lower lip and hesitate before Robert answers. "I'm in. But darling, maybe you should sit this one out?"

Turning, I look at Robert and see he's serious. *What the hell?* "I'm fine. I think I can throw a dart."

He shrugs casually. "Alright, let's play then."

We grab the darts and set our drinks on a high top table. Katie goes first, and I watch Tyler stand close to her, whispering in her ear and giving her pointers. She does as he says and throws a bull's-eye on the first try.

Her arms go up, and she squeals, then Tyler gives her a high-five. I go next and line up my shot with Robert on my right and Tyler on my left. Either the alcohol is hitting me harder or I'm imagining things, but the air is so tense I can almost feel the thickness against my hand as I throw the dart.

I don't hit the center, but I don't miss either, so I call that a win. I throw two more, then move so Tyler can take his turn. As we pass, his arm brushes mine. When he's in place, he glances over at me, smirking.

Tyler narrows in on the target and hits the inner circle perfectly with his second dart. Katie squeals, and they give each other a hug. As he prepares to throw his third, Robert clears his throat and steps closer. "So Tyler. What'd you do to get yourself five years in prison?"

My head nearly explodes at his bluntness. I snap my attention to him and glare. "Robert!" I hiss, wishing he'd stop.

Tyler acts unfazed and continues playing, hitting the ring outside the center.

"Nah, it's okay. I figured he'd ask eventually since we work together every day, *all* day." The corner of Tyler's lips tilts up in a smug, cocky grin.

Robert continues drinking, then scoops the darts off the table and gets ready to play.

"I got caught up with a mafia family," Tyler says as Robert puffs his chest out and flicks his wrist forward. The dart lands on the edge of the board.

Robert faces Tyler who acts unaffected, but I feel as if I'm dying inside. Without content, this story sounds worse than it is. "The official charges were for having illegal guns and tons of drugs."

Tyler lets him gnaw on that piece of information for a minute. Katie and I exchange looks, and I can tell she's just as uncomfortable as I am.

"I was set up by the mob boss's daughter for betraying her. After my friend put a gun to her boyfriend's head, she decided to cough up some cash and pay the judge to give me a lesser sentence." Tyler glowers.

Robert turns and looks at me incredulously. I lower my gaze, knowing he'll say something to me later.

"You're lucky your sister talked Jerry into hiring you. If it were up to me, a criminal wouldn't be anywhere near that garage." Robert's crass words have my heart racing. *What the fuck?*

"Well, fortunately that's not up to you," Tyler retorts, staring at Robert while taking a swig of beer.

"He's not a criminal. He was framed," I explain.

Robert glares at me with disapproval in his expression as if he's my goddamn father. "Did you not hear the part where he worked for a mafia family? He's far from innocent."

I swallow hard, the tension nearly smothering me. "Well, you don't know the whole story," I say.

"Why are you defending him? He's probably murdered people and robbed people."

Heat rushes to my cheeks as his words fuel my anger. *"What?* Don't be insane! You're making him sound like a monster when you don't even know him."

"Gemma." Tyler says my name gently, and there's too much rage burning inside me as I stare at Robert, but Tyler continues as our gazes lock. "It's okay. You don't have to argue on my behalf." His eyes soften, and I feel awful about all of this.

Katie sucks in a deep breath as Tyler turns back to Robert.

"Not that it's any of your business, but I was undercover to help out my friend. When his girlfriend was kidnapped, I infiltrated the mob and got hired as a bodyguard so I could help her escape. The mafia princess got even with me for betraying her. And I *don't* fucking regret it."

I smile but then quickly suppress it so Robert doesn't catch me. He'll never admit he was wrong for jumping to conclusions because in Robert's world, he's *always* right. He doesn't say another word as he slams the darts on the table, then walks to the bar. I'm so infuriated and humiliated, but I can't even hide it because my face is red hot.

"I'm so sorry," I say to Tyler and Katie. "He doesn't usually drink this much and—"

Tyler wraps an arm around Katie but keeps his eyes locked on me. "Nothing I can't handle. Been dealing with assholes like him for most of my life." He shrugs. A small part of me hoped they would've gotten along.

"He's not usually an asshole," I say. "The stress from work is getting to him."

By the way his jaw clenches, I know Tyler doesn't believe me. I'm making excuses for Robert when he should be the one apologizing to everyone.

"Well, anyway…" I wipe my palms down my dress. "You two have fun. We're gonna head out."

I give Katie a hug, and she squeezes me tight. Her demeanor changes, and she becomes more upbeat than she was just moments ago. I flash her a smile in return, and whisper in her ear, "Hope you guys hit it off."

"Thank you."

I pull away from her, then turn. "Good night, Tyler."

"Night, Gemma."

My throat tightens, and I force away tears as I meet up with Robert and tell him I want to go. He roughly grabs my hand and jerks me out of the pub.

I'm at a complete loss. I don't know how to deal with the conflicting feelings in my head. Tyler blew back into my life like a tornado, and now everything's upside down and messy. A part of me wishes things would go back to how they were before he arrived, but another part of me knows that's a complete fucking lie.

CHAPTER THIRTEEN
TYLER

I watch Robert pull Gemma through the bar, then possessively drag her out the door. My jaw tightens as I replay the last ten minutes. Robert was a dick to embarrass Gemma like that in a public place while also making Katie uncomfortable. I'm not pissed he put me on the spot, but I wasn't going to stand that and be compliant either. I know I got under his skin, and now we're even. He didn't expect my response and got pissed that his fiancée took up for me.

Honestly, I'm surprised she did. It's obvious that Gemma's more conflicted about marrying Robert than I originally thought. I'm not trying to make things harder for her, and I actually try to stay out of her way as much as possible. Maybe she was content before I arrived, but I see it clear as day that she's not one-hundred percent positive she wants to marry him.

"Is he always that rude?" I ask Katie after they leave.

"He's got a hard exterior, but he treats Gemma like a queen. Always buying her expensive things, spoils her like crazy, and constantly begs her to move in with him. He's also open about starting a family and wanting kids right away, too. Wouldn't surprise me if she ended up being a stay-at-home wife and mom. Robert's *very* traditional."

"Buying someone stuff doesn't always mean treating them well," I counter, grabbing my almost empty beer. "Does she want all that?"

"I'm not sure, but when she gets pregnant, she'll stay home with the baby. He's been very pushy about that, so I'm not sure she'll have a choice."

There's no doubt Robert Hawkley could give her a dream life, but I don't understand what she sees in him as a person. Is it all about wealth and status? Gemma isn't that superficial, but then again, there's a lot I don't know about her anymore.

"Wanna grab another drink?" I offer, needing to escape this conversation.

"Sure. Just one more, though."

"So I have to be transparent with you," I tell her after we grab some beers and sit in the booth. At the last minute, we decided to order fries to help soak up the alcohol. My stomach is in knots over what I'm about to say. "I know Jerry had good intentions telling Gemma to plan a double date, but I don't want to lead you on. While I think you're beautiful and a lot of fun, I don't think—"

"You don't even have to finish." She pats my hand. My shoulders relax when she nods. "I'm sure Jerry's heart was in the right place, but I've realized I'm not in the right mindset to be dating right now. Owen's my priority at the moment. Plus, I'm trying to buy a house and stay focused at work because I want a promotion."

"Whew, okay." I chuckle. "I was nervous, considering I haven't gone on a date in...well, since before I went to prison."

"Really? No fan mail in prison or conjugal visits?" Katie smirks before taking a sip.

"Oh, there's always stalker mail, but dating has been the last thing on my mind."

"How long exactly?" She narrows her eyes, resting her arms on the table.

"How long has it been since I've dated or had sex?"

"Well, now that you brought it up, both."

I laugh at her boldness. "Let's just say, it's been a *very* long time since I've dated or had sex. It's been well over five years."

"Me too. Sometimes I think I'm okay with being alone. I'm set in my ways, and raising Owen is a full-time job on its own. Then I remember what it felt like to have a partner, someone to come home to after a long shift at work. That's what I miss the most —companionship."

I frown, vaguely remembering what happened between her

husband and Noah. Though I wasn't living in Lawton Ridge at the time, Everleigh told me all about it and how distraught she was. Katie lost her husband and her best friend at the same time.

"From what I've heard, you've done an amazing job raising Owen and being on your own. Whoever you end up with will be a very lucky man."

"That might be a while...it's slim pickings in this town. My options range from the jobless just graduated college guys who get their parents to co-sign loans for them or the old church-goer widowers. There's literally no in-between."

I bark out a laugh. "Well, let's weigh the pros and cons here..." I hold out my hands and rock them back and forth. "The younger guys are active enough to play and keep up with Owen. The flip side is you'll probably have to teach them how to be an adult and do things like balancing a bank account, saving money, and paying bills on time."

Katie throws a fry at me, chuckling. "Wow, thanks. If I wanted to take care of a man-child, I'd just get pregnant again and teach one from birth."

"Pros of dating an old guy is getting a senior discount at restaurants." I shrug, reaching for a couple of fries before shoving them into my mouth. "Plus, Viagra means you can go all night long. Personally, older sounds better, so you should start going to church."

"You give out the *best* advice! It's a wonder you're single!"

We're both laughing when the waitress asks if we'd like refills. We pass and finish our basket of fries.

"I wrote Noah in prison," she says softly, looking down. "For years, actually."

"Did he write back?"

"Never. Doesn't let me visit him either."

I tilt my head, studying her sad expression. I can tell how much it hurts her. "Do you know why?"

Katie shrugs as she quickly brushes a tear off her cheek. "No. I wish I did, though. Everleigh and Gemma think I'm holding out for his return, but the minute I see him, I plan to cuss his ass out, then slap him."

"Has anyone else talked to him? Maybe they can ask—"

"Only Jerry and Gemma. He says it's complicated."

I furrow my brows, trying to think of a reasonable explanation as to why Noah would push his best friend away. Gemma swears Noah's been in love with Katie for years, even before Gabe asked her out.

"He's probably embarrassed and distraught over what happened and can't face you."

"I thought that too, but it's been years now! I haven't seen or talked to him since the day of the accident. I never got to say goodbye."

"Prison's an ugly place, and I'm sure he doesn't want you to see him like that."

"Why can't he just lift a damn pen and write me back?"

"Because he's a coward?" I guess. "I wish I had a better answer for you."

Defeated, she shrugs and leans against the booth. "I only want answers from him, but it seems like it won't ever happen. I was heartbroken over losing Gabe even though he was cheating, but not having Noah in my life broke me in other ways."

"I hope for your sake he comes back and fixes his mistakes. I'll tell you, though, life after prison isn't easy. Especially with how long he'll be in there." Noah got twelve years, but Gemma told me it's looking more like ten with his good behavior.

"I'm not welcoming him back with open arms, if that's your suggestion."

I chuckle at the way she scoffs. "Nope. Not at all. He's got a lot of explaining to do and not only to you either."

Katie smiles and finally releases a soft laugh. "Thanks, Tyler. I really appreciate you talking to me."

"What are awkward first dates for?" I beam, and we finish off the rest of the fries.

"Good mornin'," I greet Gemma Monday morning with a wide grin when I walk inside the lobby.

She looks up at me from the computer. "Morning. My dad's looking for you."

"Uh-oh. Am I in trouble?" I pretend to pout, then walk over to fill a cup with coffee.

"Doubtful. He adores you."

Stepping toward her, I lean one arm against the counter. "And you?"

"What? No!" Her forehead creases. "I mean, wait…do I what?"

Before I can respond, Jerry enters the lobby in a chipper mood. "Tyler! Good to see ya, son." He cheerfully pats my shoulder, then gets himself a cup of coffee, too. "Hope you've recovered from your hot date because we have a jam-packed day."

"Yes, sir." I chuckle, then flash Gemma a wink who then narrows her eyes. "A little sore, but nothing I can't handle."

I don't mention it's from working out all weekend and bruising my knuckles on the punching bag, but neither of them needs to know that. It's clear Gemma has no idea that Katie and I decided to just be friends, or her nostrils wouldn't be flaring with jealousy.

"Good, good." Jerry walks past me with his coffee in hand. "If you and Katie get real hot and heavy, y'all might even beat Gemma and Robert to the altar with how long they've been waiting."

I nearly choke on the hot liquid as Gemma's cheeks burn red.

Jerry chuckles as he opens the shop door. "See ya out there."

"Since we had a double date, maybe we should have a double wedding too? Whatcha think?" I rest an elbow on the counter.

"Why are you enjoying this so much?"

"Enjoying life? Could be the fact that I'm no longer behind bars. What's not to enjoy, Gemma?"

She rolls her eyes with a huff. "I don't have time for your childish games, so go do your job so I can do mine."

I stand tall and salute her. "Yes, ma'am."

Smirking at her displeased groan, I enter the shop and start my first assignment.

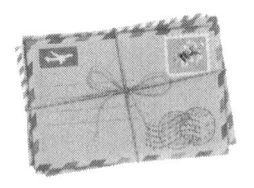

"You're a fuckin' asshole," Gemma snaps the moment we're alone in the break room. She marched inside as soon as I grabbed my lunch from the fridge.

"Excuse me?"

"I just spoke to Katie, who told me exactly how your date ended."

"Did she now?" I muse. "Did she explain it thoroughly enough, or would you like a demonstration?"

She crosses her arms over her chest, glaring. "Cut the shit, Tyler. I know y'all decided to just be friends and shared a basket of fries."

"Best damn fries in town." I set down my food and take a seat.

Gemma slams her palm on the table. "Why do you insist on driving me crazy?"

"How am I driving you crazy exactly? I'm sitting here, trying to eat. So either join me or go back to your fiancé."

"Is that what your damn problem is? You left, and *years* later, I finally moved on and found a man who loves me. Now you're hell-bent on…what exactly?" She throws up her arms, flustered. "Making me jealous? What was I supposed to do, wait for you forever? You barrel back into town and—"

"And what?" I snap. Pushing to my feet, I walk until I'm standing directly in front of her. "I'm not trying to make you jealous. Katie and I decided to be only friends, but I never said otherwise because you didn't ask. But if you're second-guessing your loyalty to your fiancé, then that's on you and was happening way before I came back. So, think about that instead of accusing me of being the problem."

"I never said you were the problem…" she whispers.

"So there's a problem?" I ask, and she lowers her eyes. "Does he always act like he did Saturday night?"

She swallows hard before licking her lips. "No. I mean, not really.

He doesn't have a bad temper, but he'd been drinking and was frustrated."

I step back slightly and cross my arms to stop myself from reaching out and touching her. "Over what?"

Gemma shakes her head and attempts to walk away, but I grab her arm and gently pull her back. "Tell me."

"He wants to move the wedding to November instead of March."

I swallow hard as the vein in my throat threatens to burst. "How come?"

"He thinks we've been engaged long enough and doesn't want to wait anymore."

Closing the gap between us, I tilt her chin up until her eyes lock with mine. "And what do *you* want?"

"I thought I knew, but now I'm second-guessing myself." Her voice sounds so broken that I'm tempted to lower my mouth to hers and take away the pain. But I know that'd only cause more harm than good.

"Follow your heart, Gemma. You can't go wrong then. Whatever your gut is telling you, believe it." Cupping her face, I press a gentle kiss to her forehead.

Then I do the hardest thing I've done in years and walk away so I don't do anything stupid.

Slowly but surely, Gemma's weaving herself back into my heart as if no time ever separated us, except she's not mine to have anymore. I gave her up, and now we're both paying the price of the heartache.

After work, Gemma's nowhere to be found, which is a good thing. With what happened during lunch, we both need the reminder that she's engaged to another man.

Even worse, I don't have time to lose myself working out because

I have a conference call with Serena, Eric, and the prosecutor to discuss the deposition. Serena agreed to be on the call to help me make an educated decision.

When I'm finished showering, my phone dings with a text from Serena.

Serena: Ready? They're supposed to call in ten minutes.

Tyler: Ready as I'll ever be.

Serena: Good. Let me do the talking so you don't unintentionally spill any information he doesn't need, just to be safe.

Tyler: Got it.

Then I send her a zipped-lip emoji, and she sends a laughing one in return.

Thankfully, Everleigh isn't home, so I can have some privacy. I don't want her knowing the details of what's going on just yet.

Right on time, I get on the call and introduce myself and Serena to the prosecutor. Eric chimes in and re-explains the situation for Serena's sake and the prosecutor confirms everything he says. As Serena asks questions, I stay quiet and listen. She knows more about the risks of agreeing to this than I do and drills them for thirty minutes straight. They answer everything without hesitation.

"When would you need me to come there?" I ask. I might need to request a day or two off work to fly there and back.

"These things take time, so about a month. I'd like to get a few more on board before we commit to a date, but as soon as I find out, I'll send you the final paperwork if you're in," the prosecutor explains.

"Alright, I should be able to do that. Gives me enough time to tell my boss. How long do I have to decide?"

"We'll need to know as soon as possible, but if you and Serena need to discuss, then I'd just ask that you let me or Eric know within forty-eight hours."

"Alright, I can do that."

"Please understand that this is a long process, and it's going to be a while before everything is in motion, but this is one step toward justice," he explains.

"I'll never stop fighting for justice for Amara," Eric grinds out. "So you'd really be helping me out."

"I understand, man. I'll let you know soon."

Once the conference call is over, Serena calls me and tells me her thoughts. She explains the cons—getting involved with anything that has to do with the O'Learys again could always lead to backlash —and the pros—helping that bitch get what she finally deserves.

"It's settled then," I confirm. "I'm gonna text Eric and tell him I'm in."

CHAPTER FOURTEEN

GEMMA

This morning, Robert invited me to have dinner at his house tonight. Ever since I agreed, I've been a nervous wreck. On the way to his house after work, I grow more anxious, but I don't know why. We spoke a little yesterday about what happened Saturday night and mostly cleared the air, though if my pounding heart is any indication, some lingering tension remains between us. It doesn't help that Tyler and I had a weird moment today. My head is still spinning from it all.

When I walk through the front door, I find Robert in the kitchen, preparing lemon pepper chicken and roasted potatoes. Over his shoulder, he gives me a smile, but it looks forced. Maybe it's just me, though, because I've been restless the past two nights.

"Hi, darling. Dinner's almost ready. Can you pour the wine?" he asks as I set my things down.

"Sure. Which kind do you want?" I ask. Robert's a wine snob, and I never pick the one that pairs correctly with our food.

After grabbing the white wine he requests, I set the table, then take a seat to wait. As soon as it's all ready, he brings my plate and glass of Sauvignon Blanc, then kisses my head.

"Eat up, sweetheart."

"Thank you. This looks delicious."

Robert's a great cook. In fact, he's good at everything he does, or at least, it seems that way. I don't think he's bad at anything. He always gets what he wants and works hard to make sure it stays that way. It can be intimidating because compared to him, I always feel as though I'm lacking.

We make small talk while we eat but don't chat about anything in particular. His responses are quick and to the point, which is odd, considering he loves to talk in depth about work. I can tell something is off, but I'm not sure if I should bring it up.

After our plates are empty, I thank him again for cooking, then I clear the table. I rinse the dishes and soak the pans, then Robert mentions we should watch a movie as I suggested last Thursday.

As I snuggle against him while a war movie plays, he wraps his arm around me and squeezes me closer to his body. "So, I was thinking it's time for you to quit your job."

When I look at him, a lump forms in my throat. He's dead serious.

"What did you say?"

"There's no reason for you to work, Gemma. I'll be taking care of you."

My mouth falls open, and I'm almost at a loss for words. "Robert, I can't just *quit* my job. I work for my *family's* business."

His eyes harden. "Then your dad needs to fire Tyler. He's the one who hired him after all."

I tilt my head at him and realize this isn't about him wanting to provide for his future wife. It's something different.

Furrowing my brows, I look at the man in front of me and wonder when the hell he changed. Or maybe I'm the one who has? Perhaps he's been this way all along, and I've been blind to it.

"What does Tyler have to do with anything?" I ask. And why did he wait two days to bring this up? He apologized for his behavior yesterday, and now tonight it's like our conversation never happened.

Robert stands, then turns on the lights. His face is red as he begins pacing the living room. Adrenaline rushes through me as I watch him getting worked up, more than I've ever seen.

"Tyler is dangerous!" he shouts. "I don't want my future wife around a criminal. I don't give two fucks if he claims he was 'set up.' How can you or anyone trust a convict like him?"

I glare at him as he continues raising his voice. He's yelling at me like I'm a child, and I'm two seconds away from grabbing my keys and bolting.

"On top of his shady drug dealing past, I don't like the way he fucking looks at you—like you're a piece of meat and drooling over you. You are *mine*, Gemma. You. Are. Mine!" He picks up a picture frame and whips it across the room. The glass shatters against the wall, making me jump.

"Robert, stop! You're scaring me," I tell him. I see the crazed look in his eyes, and it makes me want to crawl out of my skin. "Tyler is just trying to get his life back on track. He's not a threat to anyone."

"Bullshit! I have lost all respect for your father. He's useless."

Hearing him talk about my dad makes me snap. No one gets to talk shit about my family, especially not him.

"Are you fucking kidding me?" I stand and speak louder, meeting his level of rage. "You're not going to talk about my dad like that. He did Tyler a favor because that's the kind of man my father is. I didn't even know Tyler was applying for the job, so you're making it out to be something it's not, which is seriously pathetic. You need to grow up, Robert. Not everything is about you!" Weeks of pent-up stress and frustration blow through me as he works my last nerve.

Robert snarls at me, stepping closer with darkness in his eyes. "Why are you defending Tyler *again*?" He studies me with a harsh expression. "Are you sleeping with him?"

My jaw nearly falls to the floor, and I'm in such shock that I slightly lose my words, and then the anger begins to boil over. His accusation is a slap in the face, and I shake my head, seeing red. "How dare you! How fucking dare you!"

"Well?" He waits with his arms crossed over this chest as if my reaction wasn't enough of an answer.

I walk out of the living room to the kitchen island, then grab my purse. I'm not wasting another minute on this ridiculous conversation. As soon as I turn to walk out, Robert grabs my wrist and pulls me back.

"You're not leaving," he demands.

"I don't know how you have the audacity to look me in the eyes and ask if I've slept with another man. How can you even think that? I've been one-hundred percent loyal to you and our relationship the entire time. I agreed to marry you, for god's sake!"

"What am I supposed to think when you're dead set on defending him and your father's choice to hire him? You're supposed to be on my side." He jerks me closer to him. "Not some loser convict who's probably going to steal the rug out from under you both. He's gonna screw you guys over big time, and y'all will come crying to me to fix it."

"Have you lost your goddamn mind?" I hiss. Tyler would never do that, *ever*, to anyone.

"It makes perfect sense that you're fucking him behind my back. I saw the way you two looked at each other as if y'all were hiding a secret. Do you know how embarrassing it was when you stood up for him in the bar? You should've kept your damn mouth shut."

I forcefully escape from his grasp, and my wrist throbs from how tight he was holding me. There's no point in even trying to talk to him right now. He's completely out of line.

"I'm leaving. We can talk again when you can be rational."

"We need to move the wedding up. I'm tired of waiting. So decide if you want to marry me or if you want to keep fucking that drug dealer behind my back. But don't think for a second I'm letting you go that easy. He'll be a dead man before I let him take my fiancée."

My mouth falls open, and I'm so furious, tears well in my eyes at his threats. It's been a long time since I've angry-cried. He glares at me, and all I can do is shake my head before I spin around and walk out the door. Surprisingly, he doesn't try to stop me this time.

When I get into my car, I let out a guttural groan, and tears spill down my cheek. I can't believe that just happened. Robert has never spoken to me that way, and aside from this past weekend, he's never acted so rude to another person. Swallowing hard, I try to regain my composure, then back out of the driveway. Dad always taught me not to get behind the wheel when I'm upset, but I can't stay inside that house while Robert's temper spikes.

On my way home, I decide to call Everleigh because I need someone to talk to before I go crazy, and she's always a great listener.

"Hey," I quickly say as soon as she answers.

"Uh-oh." She pauses, hearing my sniffles. "What's wrong?"

"Robert and I had a huge fight, like the biggest we've ever had." The music in the background tells me she's still at the boutique.

She typically doesn't leave until dark during the summer, and every Monday, she has a mystery sale to move old inventory. "Shit, babe. I'm sorry. If you give me like ten to fifteen minutes, I'll be home. And don't worry, Tyler's busy so he won't be there."

Just the sound of his name has my heart thumping harder, and while I want to know what he's doing, it's not my business nor should I want to ask.

"Okay, deal," I tell her and take the backroads to give her time to get home. Considering Robert lives on the outskirts of town, I arrive well after Everleigh. She opens the door before I can even knock and immediately wraps me in a hug.

"Come in. I gotta let Sassy out real quick." I watch as the dog follows her to the back door, and Everleigh lets her out. Moments later, they both return, and we walk to the kitchen.

"I picked up margarita mix because they're your favorite."

"You're the best." I grin, taking a seat at the breakfast bar. "Make mine a double."

"Already on it." She winks and begins mixing it all together.

Once they're finished, she sits down on the stool next to me. "You hungry?"

I shake my head. "Robert cooked before our big blowout."

"Alright, well since I don't have to offer you a gourmet meal, I'm eating a sandwich quickly before the alcohol goes right to my head."

I giggle, knowing how true that is. Everleigh isn't a lightweight, but she doesn't tend to eat a lot when she's busy at work all day. The booze would most definitely get her drunk faster on an empty stomach. Everleigh grabs the ingredients, then lays it all out on a plate in front of me. I stare in disgust as she piles pickles, olives, and mustard on top of the turkey.

"Don't judge me." She points at me with the butter knife and chuckles. "So tell me what happened. From the beginning."

"Well, there was the awkward double date from hell, he apologized yesterday, then he invited me over for dinner tonight. Something felt off, but I wasn't sure what it was until he just unleashed on me out of the blue."

"What'd he say?"

"That I needed to quit my job and how Tyler is bad news, so he doesn't want me around him."

Everleigh nearly drops her sandwich on the floor as her eyes widen in shock. Sassy's eagerly waiting at her feet for any spare crumbs. Everleigh sets it on the plate and stares at me. "What the fuck?"

"Exactly! Completely pulled the rug out from under me. I've never seen Robert this mad before. There was no reasoning with him, so I just got the hell out of there."

She huffs. "What's wrong with him?"

I look down at the two-carat diamond ring on my finger. Right now, it feels more like a symbol of prison than love. It's not supposed to be like this.

"He said Tyler is a criminal and that he no longer respects my dad for hiring him." I force my eyes closed as the anger builds again.

"Fuck him," she snaps. "My brother may have gone to prison, but he's not a *criminal*. It's jackasses like Robert who believe all those dumbass rumors instead of his side of the story. That's a part of the reason Tyler didn't want to come home in the first place. I've seen the way people look at him. It's ridiculous."

"I know." My voice is nearly a whisper. "I'm sorry."

"What're you gonna do?" Everleigh picks up her sandwich, and Sassy walks away, defeated.

"What do you mean?"

"Are you gonna quit? Robert doesn't seem like the type who's just going to let you go to work if he doesn't agree."

I grit my teeth. "I'm *not* quitting. He acts like I'm just supposed to blindly agree with whatever he says, but I'm putting my foot down on this. Then he bitched me out for standing up for Tyler at the bar when Robert was commenting on why he went to prison."

She lifts an eyebrow. "Sounds like he's jealous and threatened, maybe even worried that Tyler's going to steal you away from him." An evil grin spreads across her face.

"That's dumb." I sip my margarita that's so strong it tastes like pure tequila.

"Is it, though?" she questions.

Considering where Tyler and I stand at the moment, it seems like a non-issue. Has everyone lost their minds? "Yeah, it is. So was Robert asking me if I'm sleeping with Tyler behind his back."

This makes Everleigh snort. "Flirting…maybe. Anything else, I don't see that happening."

"We don't flirt. We hardly speak to each other. He said he saw the way Tyler and I looked at each other, which is crazy. What does that even mean?"

Everleigh gets up and grabs a bag of chips. "It sounds like he's insecure that you won't move in with him, so he's looking for a fight. Probably hoping it'll get you to change your mind. But I mean, I kinda get it. My brother's good-looking, closer to your age than him, and has a lot to offer any woman. Plus, most people associate him with being mysterious because he's typically on the quiet side and keeps to himself. With that being said, I don't think Tyler's looking at you any differently than how he always has." I lay my head on the bar top and let out a groan. "This is so confusing."

"What is?" she asks.

I lift my head and look at her, then follow her to the couch. "Everything. Tyler working at the garage. Robert demanding I quit and marry him ASAP, which he brought up again. Knowing my dad couldn't run the shop without me nor do I want him to. He'd be heartbroken if I left and so would I. I don't want to have to choose between Robert and my dad, but if it comes to that, my family will always come first. *Always*."

"As it should. Him saying that about your dad makes me so fucking mad. Out of everyone in your life, he's been Team Robert since day one."

"He's Team Tyler too," I say. As the words leave my mouth, the door swings open, and Tyler enters, wearing a T-shirt with the sleeves cut off. It shows off his muscular biceps and the shorts that hang low on his hips leave nothing to the imagination.

"Who's Team Tyler?" he asks with a boyish grin. He's drenched with sweat, and I assume he's been at the gym.

Sassy perks up, and her tail wags when she sees him. He walks over, pets her head, then looks at me. "Well?"

My words are stuck in my throat. "My dad," I croak out.

My body is burning from the inside out.

Tyler chuckles. "I'm Team Jerry. He's a good guy. Really appreciate everything he's done for me." The room falls silent. "Anyway, I'm gonna jump in the shower."

When he walks away, I can smell the hint of his cologne mixed with sweat. I watch until he's out of sight, then turn to see Everleigh grinning.

"What?"

She shakes her head with a wide smile.

"You better tell me!" I let out a huff.

"If Robert saw you look at Tyler the way I just did, I can understand why he's pissed. That's all." She shrugs.

My mouth falls open. "Like what? I don't know what you're talkin' about."

Everleigh glances at me. "Are you sure, like one-million percent sure, that you want to marry Robert? And I'm only asking because you're my best friend, and I love you. You deserve to be happy."

"I'd be lying if I said I wasn't nervous about marrying him. I do have doubts, especially now that he's being extra pushy about moving the date. On top of it, leaving my mother's cabin so quickly feels wrong. And now he wants me to quit my job just because he doesn't like one of the employees? It feels like a lot of change at once that I'm not ready for, and instead of giving me time and space, he's become more demanding and pushier."

"If that's any indication of how things are now, it won't get easier being married, Gemma." She keeps her voice low, and I hope Tyler can't hear our conversation over the water running.

"That's what concerns me the most. What if I learn too late that he's super possessive, or he gives me an ultimatum that forces me to quit working at the garage? I'll work there until I physically can't, or he decides he wants to retire and sells the place, but he's already told me it's mine. It's literally my family's legacy in this town. My grandfather and father both spent their entire lives there. I'm shocked Robert has the audacity to even demand it. A part of me wonders if he's doing this so I'll tell my dad to fire him instead, then Robert gets what he wants either way."

She lets out a calm breath. "Sounds like he's manipulating you. On top of that, he's controlling. I don't remember you guys ever fighting this much before."

"The only thing we argued about mostly was how much he worked, wanting to spend more time with him, and him wanting to set a date and moving in together. Now it's like he wants to argue about everything until I agree with him."

"And we both know you can't keep going back and forth like that. Random question, but how does Robert feel about me?" she asks.

"What do you mean?"

"Well, does he know my brother lives here? I'm kinda thinking not because if so, he'd probably tell you to stop hanging out with me. He's too jealous not to. I just don't want his insecurities to come between us, Gemma. It would break my heart. You're my best friend in the whole world."

Her words have me smiling. "You're family, Everleigh. I'd tell him to fuck off." Though I don't know if Robert realizes Tyler lives here or not. He hasn't asked, and I've never told him, though it only makes sense, considering Tyler needs help getting back on his feet.

She laughs. "Yeah, right."

"I would, trust me. No one will ever come between my dad and me or you and me. It's like he wants to take me away from everyone who means anything to me so he can have me all to himself. But even if he had all my time, he's too busy to give me any of his. I think he means well, and he has a big heart. It's what made me fall for him in the first place. But something's different with him lately, and I have a feeling it's not going to get better if we can't work through all these issues before the wedding. I'm not getting married just to get a divorce."

"I don't think anyone plans for that but imagine how much more difficult it'd be to get out when you have kids. Women stay with their abusive husbands because they don't want their kids growing up in a broken home."

"Robert would never hit me," I say confidently.

"If he's manipulating you, Gemma, then he's *emotionally* abusing you. It's not a stretch to think things could turn to verbal and physical abuse too."

Her words make me sick to my stomach because she's right. While I could never see Robert hurting me, he's definitely hurt me in other ways.

The water stops, and I can almost hear blood pumping through my veins. The bathroom door opens, and I catch a glimpse of Tyler with wet hair and a towel wrapped low around his waist, showing off his ripped body. I hurry and turn away before I get caught.

"Well, you need to talk to him."

"Who?" I ask, my mind on someone else.

"Robert," she clarifies. "Put your foot down now so he knows where you stand. Make it crystal clear how you feel about his behavior and that you aren't quitting just because he's uncomfortable with who else works there. He should trust you no matter what anyway."

I nod, knowing it's what I have to do. If we're going to be together, there needs to be mutual respect. Robert and I have a good time when it's just the two of us alone, but those moments are few and far between lately.

"If you still want to marry him, try to work things out so you two can get back to a happy place. Perhaps he needs to work on his own issues first if he's acting this way about my brother. What happens when another single man moves to town? Is he gonna think you're screwing him, too?"

I snort, then look around, hoping Tyler isn't eavesdropping. "We barely speak to each other at work, and when we do, it's quick and to the point. Tyler and I are a non-issue. I don't even know why he's built it up into his head to be more."

"Tell Robert that, not me, and if he can't accept your decision, then drop his ass like a bad habit. I mean, is it too much to ask for my brother to marry my best friend so then you can officially be my sister? Then you two can have a million babies and make me the happiest auntie in the world."

"Yes," I hear Tyler say from behind the couch, which makes me tense. "It's entirely too much to ask."

He sounds pissed, and his voice comes out like a growl. "Everleigh, you're gonna have to stop with this shit. Gemma's engaged. She's getting married. End of story."

I can't read her expression as she looks at him with her head tilted. It's as if she's aware of something I'm not, but I can't ask her while Tyler is close.

"Yeah, well, her fiancé told her to quit working at the garage because of you and—"

"Everleigh," I interrupt.

"What? Why?" Tyler snaps, glaring.

"It's nothing. Don't worry about it," I rush out, then give Everleigh a death stare.

"I'm sorry," she whispers. "Tequila made me do it."

I shake my head. "Stupid margaritas. Stupid Robert. Stupid *everything*. I'm just having a shitty day."

Tyler sits in the recliner across from us. I look up at him and swallow hard, needing air or an escape.

"Be right back." I excuse myself and walk to the bathroom. I can't think clearly with him near, especially with alcohol in my system, and everything that happened with Robert tonight just makes it worse.

When did things get so complicated?

CHAPTER FIFTEEN

TYLER

When Gemma disappears down the hallway, Everleigh looks over at me.

"She and Robert got into a huge fight tonight. I'm just trying to calm her down."

"Over me?" I shake my head in disbelief.

"Well...*sorta*."

My hands ball into fists. "He has nothing to worry about. I'm sure it's because of what happened Saturday night. He nearly dragged her out of the place after she spoke up for me when he ran his mouth about why I was in prison."

"He's jealous and intimidated, so he gave her an ultimatum. She's pretty upset about all of it."

"And she has every right to be. She deserves better than him," I whisper-hiss. Men like Robert think they can buy anything they want and treat women like property.

When the bathroom door opens, I get up and walk to my room. Gemma passes me in the hallway, and we briefly make eye contact. Before she gets too far, I gently grab her elbow, and she looks up at me. Her chest rises and falls with shallow breaths.

"You okay?" I ask, keeping my tone soft even though I'm seething inside.

She nods. "I'll be fine," she claims, her voice just above a whisper.

I drop my hand, and we share a moment before she walks away.

Her silence speaks louder than her words could as I stared at her. Gemma's been crying, and she's not herself. Once in my room, I sit on the edge of my bed and brush my hands over my face.

Maybe coming back home was a mistake after all. The last thing I ever wanted to do was affect Gemma's relationship or screw things up for her. It's one reason I've kept my distance. While I want to tune out everything they're saying, I can't. They continue talking about the fight, and this time, they are loud enough that I can hear every word. It's so hard for me to keep my opinions to myself, but I'm going to try really fucking hard because this isn't my business.

Robert acts like I'm trying to swoop in and steal his woman, but there's nothing between us except our past.

When I hear Gemma talk about her dad and what Robert said, I'm half-tempted to tell her to call him so we can fight this out like men. Jerry's kindhearted and doesn't deserve the belittling. He knows the truth about me and so does Gemma.

Fuck Robert. When I first met him, I got a bad vibe. Now, I know it was warranted.

I shouldn't be listening.

I should leave, go for a walk, try to blow off the steam that's somehow returned, but I don't.

"Let me see," Everleigh says. "Wow, he grabbed you hard."

What the fuck? He touched her.

I stand and pace the room. It's not my place to get involved, but if he lays a hand on her again, I will break every one of his fingers. Maybe Gemma isn't mine, but I won't allow Robert—or *anyone*—to hurt her.

"You should stay over tonight," Everleigh suggests. "There's no reason to be alone, plus you've been drinking. Just get up a little early and run home for a shower before work."

"That's a good idea. Might as well fill my glass to the top then." Gemma laughs.

I hear Everleigh's feet pad against the floor. A cabinet opens and closes, then moments later, the blender starts. After a few minutes, it's silent, and I imagine them on the couch with strong margaritas so they can continue their conversation.

What I appreciate about Everleigh is she asks the right questions, the ones that make you think past your own biases so you can figure shit out for yourself—even to her closest friends.

I lie down with my arms crossed behind my head and stare at the ceiling for over thirty minutes. When my stomach growls, I decide to make myself something to eat since I haven't eaten dinner.

As soon as my door opens, their conversation stops, which I'm grateful for. Too much anger streamed through me as I listened to how Robert treated Gemma.

"You two hungry?" I ask, glancing at the clock and noticing it's almost nine.

Everleigh laughs. "I'm always hungry if you're cooking."

I look at Gemma. "How about you?"

Her cup is empty, and her cheeks are a rosy red. "Sure. I mean, I already ate earlier, but..."

Everleigh elbows her. "He doesn't care about that. I always eat twice when Tyler offers to make something."

"Seriously?" I laugh at her confession. I had no idea, though I shouldn't be that surprised.

"Well, yeah. It's the only reason I agreed to let you live here rent-free. Your food is like Grandma's, and I could eat it every single day."

That has me chuckling. I plan to prepare extra so she has some to take to work tomorrow. "What are you in the mood for? Wait, let me guess...*pasta*."

"Bingo! Pasta for every meal. I swear, there's bound to be Italian somewhere in our bloodline," Everleigh says, but then changes the subject, considering we don't know much about our father.

I take out the ingredients and place them on the counter, ready to get to work. I boil the noodles while I chop the chicken and whip up the homemade sauce. It doesn't take long before the aroma from the spices and garlic bread in the oven fills the kitchen. My mouth waters in anticipation as I fill our bowls full of chicken Alfredo.

"Second dinner is served," I call out, then place the dishes in front of them. We sit and wait for the steam to clear before digging in.

Gemma moans, and that sweet sound has me adjusting myself as memories of our time together resurface. I meet her eyes, and she blushes before quickly looking away.

"How's business going?" I ask my sister.

Everleigh immediately perks up and gets super excited to chat about the boutique. "The mystery sale today went amazing. Next week, I think I'm gonna try an online pre-order campaign. Drum up excitement for a few of the new summer items and give everyone a chance to buy what they want. Some of my customers were pissed today that I sold out of the skirt Gemma had on for the shoot."

She continues chatting about her ideas, and Gemma throws in different suggestions, but I can't seem to pay attention to either of them. My mind wanders too much as I think about Robert grabbing Gemma. I glance down at her wrist and notice a small bruise has formed where he dug his fingers into her skin. I suck in a deep breath and try to pay attention to Everleigh, adding something to the conversation so she doesn't notice I was lost in my head again.

"It would be smart to order fall stuff now, too. You know all these women are gonna be dressing like Hans Solo with their leggings and boots as soon as the temp drops to sixty-five."

Gemma snorts. "You're right, and I'm totally guilty of it."

Her laughter causes my lips to turn up.

"Oh my God. I wear the same thing, so that's an amazing idea. Get ahead of the rush. First cold front that comes, my regulars beg for cardigans and buffalo plaid, too."

"Now, you're thinking like a business owner. Don't forget the pumpkin spice candles." I flash a wink at Gemma, who nearly chokes on her pasta from laughing so hard.

"I love fall candles!" Gemma gushes. I know she does. She talked about stocking up on them in one of her letters.

"Ready to come work with me on the weekends now?" Everleigh mocks.

Gemma tilts her head at Everleigh. "You offered Tyler a job?"

A roar of laughter fills the room. "I've been trying to talk him into it. Might be able to find him a girlfriend or something. Plus, I think he'd help me sell more clothes being Mr. Eye Candy."

I shake my head. "You're relentless with this. It's not happening."

Gemma's grin falters. I narrow my eyes at my sister, knowing she's trying to gauge Gemma's reaction. I'm not stupid and can see straight through it. Plus, after the way Gemma acted about Katie and me, I know it makes her uncomfortable.

"I don't need a girlfriend," I say around a mouthful.

"Why not?" Everleigh questions. "I'm sure you don't want to be single for the rest of your life. Plus, I want to be an auntie someday."

I fill my mouth full of garlic bread, giving myself time to think about my next words.

"I won't be. I'll eventually find someone, but that doesn't mean I'm searching. I'm a firm believer that you find the right person for you when you least expect it. In layman's terms, I'm not searching for love."

Everleigh lifts her almost empty glass. "Cheers to being alone forever."

Gemma doesn't join her toast, so I do, just to appease Everleigh. I can't leave her hanging. The room grows silent as we eat, but Everleigh speaks up, keeping the conversation moving.

"When are you available to model again?" she asks Gemma.

"Whenever you want," she tells her. "It was a lot of fun."

"I'm gonna hold you to that. I'll need to get with Katie too, and we can make it a night. It'll be a blast when the fall clothes come in."

Once our bowls are empty, I stand to clean the kitchen. Everleigh and Gemma continue chatting as I rinse the dishes, then load the dishwasher. A moment later, Everleigh returns with a spare blanket and pillows for Gemma.

Everleigh yawns and tells Gemma good night. Before walking to her room, Everleigh flashes me a smirk, and I know she's up to something. Once she's gone, it's just Gemma and me, and the awkward tension nearly chokes me.

"Will you watch a movie with me?" she asks, and I look at the clock and see it's past ten.

"Yeah, sure," I say, knowing I shouldn't, but I can't say no to her. After the day she's had, I don't want her to be alone either. We sit on the couch, and I hand her the remote. "You choose."

"Really?" Gemma acts surprised.

"Why not? It was your idea." I glance over at her, and she seems to be thinking about something else before she flips through the channels.

She settles on *You've Got Mail* with Tom Hanks and Meg Ryan from the 90s. "This okay?"

"It's perfect," I say, not really caring as long as I get to spend time with her. I shouldn't get excited to see her and be close to her, but I can't help it. She's only a few inches away, and by the way she tenses, I think she notices too.

I finally laugh and shake my head.

"What?" She looks at me.

"It feels like old times when we'd stay up late and watch a movie together on your couch. I'd supply the booze and hope your dad didn't burst into the cottage and catch us." I chuckle and watch as she tucks loose strands of hair behind her ear.

She nods. "Yeah, it is kinda like that, isn't it? Except now we don't have to sneak in the alcohol." She hiccups and covers her mouth with a giggle, which makes me smile. "Too much tequila. Everleigh makes them strong."

"Adulting at its finest."

We get to the part in the movie where Meg Ryan goes to the bookstore that's going to ruin her business, and Gemma puts her hand over her heart as she intently watches the scene unfold. Though I'm certain she's seen this, her reactions are cute. Honestly, she's more interesting than this movie, but I force myself to focus on the screen. Even if it's hard as hell.

She repeats the lines, and I snort. Why does she have to be so fucking adorable? It makes keeping her at a distance so damn hard— harder than I ever thought was possible.

When Gemma bites her bottom lip, I'm tempted to pull her into my arms and kiss the fuck out of her. Kiss her worries away. Tell her she doesn't have to marry that douchebag if she doesn't want to, that she *shouldn't*. But I don't want to send her mixed signals. While I wish she were mine, I'd inevitably fuck it up *again*. She's too good for Robert, but if I'm being honest, she's too good for me, too.

Gemma would do anything for anyone, and she loves with every part of her being. Robert wanting her to quit her job because of me nearly has a blood vessel bursting, but I bury the anger and keep my feelings to myself. Something I've perfected over the years.

It's obvious Gemma isn't having "cold feet." The woman has always gone after what she wants. Considering everything that's happened over the past few weeks with her and Robert, it's obvious there's more to this. She has to ultimately make the final decision, but I don't want it to be because of me. I want her to call off the wedding because she realizes she won't be happy with him. I'm well-aware that Robert has a lot of money, but I also know material possessions don't buy love. Nothing can.

"Gemma," I say as she leans her head against the couch. We're so close. *Too close*. I can smell her shampoo every time she brushes loose strands of hair out of her face. "He didn't lay his hands on you, did he?"

I shouldn't be asking. I shouldn't get involved, but I care about her—sometimes too fucking much. She tucks her lips into her mouth and looks up at me with big green eyes. "He was trying to make me stay, Tyler. He wasn't trying to hurt me."

"You're positive about that?" I ask. I've heard women say that before, but I'm trying to give her the benefit of the doubt.

"Yes. I wouldn't put up with it otherwise. He's not like that," she reassures.

"Alright, good," I say. "If you need boxing lessons and want to learn how to take someone down in ten seconds flat, just say the word."

She laughs. "Did you forget who my brother is?"

The thought of Noah brings the mood to a somber place.

"Nah. But I also know you've gotten rusty at kicking dudes in the balls. Though…" I grin. "When you were younger, you were a goddamn pro."

Her head falls back with laughter. "I was a little shit, wasn't I?"

"Everyone knew not to mess with you, Katie, or Everleigh because y'all were a bunch of little scrappers. Or because I threatened to kick anyone's ass who messed with my little sister and her friends." I chuckle thinking about it.

"I didn't take anyone's crap back then, and trust me when I say I'm not going to take it now. I'm okay, Tyler. But thank you. If I'm ever not okay, I'll mention it."

"Is that a promise?" I push.

"Yes." She turns back to the movie and squeezes my arm. "Oh, this is my favorite part."

Tom Hanks walks past the coffee shop and sees Meg Ryan inside, then goes in and pretends not to be the man on the other end of their messenger conversation.

"This would never happen nowadays," I say, very aware of how close she is to me now.

"It could, especially with all the dating apps and stuff. What about forums? Reddit is popular. I think it's possible. Now shush." She smirks, then winks at me.

Is she flirting? Gemma shifts, and her knee touches mine. The heat from her skin nearly burns a hole through my skin, but I don't move. I wonder if she feels the strong tug of electricity that's pulling us together, or if I'm just imagining it. Perhaps it's never left us. Not even time could change what we have, regardless if we're too fucking stubborn to admit it. We should be able to hang out together as friends, despite our past, or the fact she's moved on. However, my biggest concern is that eventually, it'll all come to a head. Both of us will be powerless to deny our attraction, but it'll be too late.

I tell myself I'm imagining everything, knowing I can't act on it, but when I see her pulse thumping in her neck, there's no way it's not real. Needing to distance myself for a moment, I stand and grab a bottle of water.

"Want one?" I hold it up, and she nods.

I hand it to her, making sure to create more space between us when I sit, though I think she notices.

We continue watching the movie in silence. Gemma's nearly in tears when Tom Hanks shows up at the end with his dog, Brinkley. She lets out an aww when they kiss, and it makes me smile.

Once the credits roll, she yawns, which quickly makes me, too.

"Damn, you gotta stop that," I say with a chuckle, yawning again.

"Sorry, I can't help it," she says around another one, and we both laugh. It's getting late, and we both have to be up early for work in the morning.

"Thanks for hanging out with me," she says, adjusting the pillow on the couch and grabbing the quilt Everleigh threw over the back.

"Anytime." I smile and wonder how many nights Robert has denied spending time with her. Probably happens more often than not. What a dumbass. He clearly doesn't know what he's missing, or perhaps he just doesn't care.

"You should take my bed," I suggest. "It's nice and comfy, and the only thing you have to deal with is Sassy waking you up around three a.m. to go outside."

Gemma giggles. "No way, I couldn't."

"Yes way, you can. You're the guest of the evening. Might as well get a good night's rest."

She shakes her head, and I'm sure I won't be able to convince her to trade with me, but I try anyway.

"I'm perfectly fine. I've passed out after too many drinks on this couch more times than I can count. I sink into it just like a cloud." She lies back and shows me.

"Have you always been this stubborn?" I ask firmly, but I'm grinning at how cute she looks.

"Ever since I was a teen," she throws back.

When our eyes meet for a moment, many unspoken words stream between us. I imagine walking over to her and sliding my lips against hers, tasting her tongue and the leftover margarita. I want to tell her how goddamn beautiful and perfect she is as I swoop my arms under her body and carry her to my bed. I'd slowly undress her, making sure to take in every smooth inch of her. I'd feather kisses along the softness of her skin and—

Fuck. Before I completely lose myself, I shake my head and push those thoughts away.

"What?" Her question pulls me from the fantasy of it all.

"Nothing. Just exhausted."

She sits up. "Liar! Now you have to tell me."

I grab my bottle of water off the coffee table. "I don't think so. That's a trap just waiting to happen."

She snorts. "A trap? Okay, maybe I don't want to know, but it was something."

Gemma carefully watches me, and I lift an eyebrow at her. "It *was* something, but I'll keep it to myself. I am a gentleman, after all."

I walk closer, adjust the blanket over her body, then brush a loose strand of hair from her face before placing a kiss on her forehead.

"Good night, Gemma. My bed's waiting for you if you change your mind," I say.

She swallows hard with wide eyes.

"No. *Shit.* That totally came out wrong. I mean, if you want to *trade.*" I nervously laugh, and she does too, but I also notice the blush on her cheeks. "Okay, good night!"

I walk to my room, replaying my own stupidity. Apparently, I forget to think straight around her, and I'm afraid one of these days it's really going to catch up to me

CHAPTER SIXTEEN

TYLER

I HARDLY SLEEP, tossing and turning all night as images of Gemma's tears burn in my mind. Hanging out and watching a movie with her after Everleigh went to bed was probably a bad idea, but I don't regret it. I hated seeing her so upset, and it makes me want to track Robert down and speak to him with my fists. If spending two hours with her was enough to put her in a better mood, then I'd do it all over again. Hearing her laughter and seeing her smile was worth the awkward tension.

At five a.m., I give up trying to sleep and can't stop thinking about one of the letters she sent me. She was sixteen and obsessing over romantic comedies.

Dear Tyler,

Do y'all get to watch movies over there? If so, you NEED to see 13 Going on 30 *with Jennifer Garner. It's my absolute new favorite movie, and if I don't fall in love the way she does, then I don't ever want to. Just kidding (kinda!).*

But seriously! Jenna's best friend, Matty, is basically in love with her, and while she's having this horrible middle school party, she starts wishing she was thirty instead of thirteen. Matty builds her a dollhouse and sprinkles it with "magic dust." As she's wishing to be 30, the dust goes everywhere, and her wish comes true. When she wakes up the next day, she realizes her wish was granted. The kicker is she doesn't remember any part of her life since the party and has to go through the next several weeks trying to figure it out. She grew up as one of the catty popular girls and ditches Matty basically. And since she doesn't know anything about her adult life, she has to catch up and ends up finding him. She doesn't realize they stopped being friends and guess what? HE'S ENGAGED! (I legit screamed!!!)

They rekindle their friendship while she's discovering who she is and doesn't like the person she's become. At the end, he's about to walk down the aisle and returns the dollhouse he made for her. She leaves in tears (and at this point, I'm SOBBING) and closes her eyes to make another wish, and the magic dust on the dollhouse blows in the wind. Then, she's 13 again and kisses Matty! She gets a redo, and it ends in a big fat happily ever after!

I know it sounds cheesy, but it's seriously the best, and I've put it on repeat. Then Everleigh and I decided to have a girls' night, and we chose A Walk to Remember. *Though we bet each other we wouldn't, we cried through the second half.*

So, in case you've ever wondered what happens at sleepovers, we watch sappy romance movies and stuff our faces with junk food while trying not to cry but failing miserably.

Maybe look up the soundtrack for A Walk to Remember *if you have time to check it out. It's such a good album.*

The Notebook *is on our list for next weekend, and I'm going to be an emotional mess, guaranteed. I'll update you in my next letter :)*

Until then, please be safe!

Love, Gemma

Though I had no plans to watch either of those movies, hearing her gush over them had me curious. I was able to listen to the soundtrack like she recommended, then found them on Netflix. In my next letter, I explained I saw them all, and that I thought she deserved to have someone like Matty or Landon in her life. I hoped she'd get to experience love in the same way and feel all the raw emotions they did, even if I personally felt like it was an unrealistic expectation. But she deserved and still deserves everything she wishes for.

As promised, she sent me a follow-up letter gushing over *The*

Notebook. How she and my sister used an entire box of tissues and put it on repeat three times in a row. Hearing from her always brought a smile to my face along with laughter during the hard times. Everleigh and I kept in touch too, but not as much as Gemma and I did. Sometimes, there wasn't anything new going on, but it didn't stop us from talking. Not being face-to-face helped us open up as the years passed, and we became more comfortable. It's crazy to think about how much we shared and how quickly our relationship vanished after I left Alabama.

Sometimes, I wonder what would've happened if I had stayed, but I undoubtedly would've felt suffocated. Between my absent father and my alcoholic mother, I wanted to be where no one knew of my past or upbringing. I needed and wanted a new start away from it all. But if I could change anything, I wouldn't have cut Gemma out of my life and would've made an effort to come home and visit more. I hurt a lot of people by avoiding Lawton Ridge, but I'm back now and hope to make up for it.

Finally, at six a.m., I roll out of the bed and decide to make breakfast for the girls since I'm wide-awake. Though a small part of me hopes Gemma will tell Robert off, the other part doesn't want me to be the reason she's second-guessing her relationship. I know Robert's been pushing her to move up the wedding date, but she's clearly not ready. I bet their problems started before I even arrived. If she's not in a rush, she's ignoring some underlying issues.

"Good mornin'," I say when Gemma and Everleigh walk into the kitchen thirty minutes later. "Coffee and breakfast are ready."

Everleigh comes closer, then puts her palm to my forehead.

"What're you doing?" I look at her as though she's lost her mind.

"Checkin' to see if you have a fever."

I snort before swatting her away. "Can't a big brother make breakfast for y'all? I used to cook all the time, remember?"

"Depends. Does it come with a side of tequila?" Gemma opens the cabinet, grabs a mug, then fills it before adding creamer and stirring it.

"Thought you'd still be stuffed from all the margaritas you had?" Everleigh teases as she empties the rest of the coffee.

"Har har." Gemma groans. "I'm gonna need something to get through this day."

"Me too. Maybe we can call in sick," I taunt.

Gemma chuckles. "That wouldn't be suspicious at all. My dad wouldn't know how to handle the phone."

"Well, you might have to train someone if you plan to leave," Everleigh says, grabbing a plate, then scooping scrambled eggs and potatoes onto it.

I study Gemma's expression. She frowns, then shrugs. "Not happenin'."

The three of us sit at the kitchen table and chat. Everleigh finishes, then pops up with a giddy smile. "I'm gonna shower so I can get to work a little early." She punches my shoulder and laughs.

I playfully rub the spot. "That's all ya got? Wuss. Gotta put your weight into it."

"Next time you hog all the hot water like you did yesterday morning, it'll be much worse. I swear, you take the longest showers. I have long hair to wash and legs to shave. What the hell do you do in there?"

"What do you think?" I waggle my brows, and Gemma nearly chokes on her food, quickly recovering as she takes a sip of her coffee.

"Ew, *gross*! You're my brother." She gags.

"That's how I felt when I found your little clit massager in there the other day. Perhaps put it away after you're done?"

Everleigh gasps, her cheeks burning red. "That's it. I hate you. Move out."

Gemma and I laugh hysterically. "Never. You're stuck with me, sis." I smirk wide as she huffs and storms down the hallway.

"That was mean." Gemma chuckles.

"Siblings, remember? I have years of catching up to do. Next will be hiding her bra and panties in the freezer."

"Oh my God…" She laughs again, and the sound makes up for the restless night's sleep. I could get used to hearing it every morning, but too bad she pretends I don't exist when we're at the garage. She stands, taking her empty plate to the sink. "Thanks for last night. I feel so much better this morning."

"No need to thank me. It was fun even though I'll miss your commentary about it later." I grin, and it takes her a minute to catch on to what I'm referring to.

"I was obsessed with movies in high school and recapped them for you, didn't I?"

I stand as well, setting my dish on the counter. "If I remember correctly, twenty-six. Some multiple times, though."

"What can I say? I'm a hopeless romantic."

"I didn't mind. Though some things you suggested I see were questionable."

"That's early 2000s rom-coms for ya." She spins around, and we're face-to-face. Her chest rises and falls at the realization of how close we are.

"I will say, though, that I got a lot of heat for watching *Bring It On*."

"Another classic." Gemma snickers. "Two decades later and I can still recite every line."

"It's a shame I was never able to get you to try a Jack Nicholson movie. Now, he's a badass actor."

"Most of the stuff he's in is ancient," she counters. "And I'm ninety-nine percent positive they don't involve romance of any kind." She folds her arms over her chest and blinks at me.

"No, but you need to expand your portfolio. Perhaps we should plan a movie marathon with all *my* favorites." I place a hand to my chest and lock eyes with her. "*One Flew Over the Cuckoo's Nest* and *The Shining*. Those two *definitely* need to happen. Then we'll make our way up to his more recent films."

"How many has he been in?"

"Like fifty or sixty. So a lot."

"Damn. It could take months to get through everything."

"Well, good thing I'm not going anywhere this time."

"Really? You're staying in town?" she asks as if she hadn't expected me to, but I don't blame her.

"Yep. Ready to put down roots and eventually get my own place. Starting over from almost nothing will take me a while, though. A large portion of the money I had saved before prison went to my lawyer, Serena, and paying off my lease."

"I'm sorry to hear that, Tyler." She reaches out and touches my arm. The simple act sends heat throughout my entire body. "But if anyone can do this and be successful, it's you. I have no doubt about it."

"Just another bump in the road. Nothing I can't handle… hopefully." I flash her a wink and pat her hand that's still pressed to my skin.

She blinks hard as if just realizing she was touching me and quickly removes it. I step back to place space between us and watch as her eyes lower as if she's stopping herself from speaking.

"Gemma…" I whisper, and she finally raises her head until our gazes lock. Thick air flows between us, and I want to say so much but can't.

Before I can get another word out, her phone rings, and the connection between us is lost. She rushes toward the kitchen table and grabs it.

"It's Robert," she says.

I clear my throat and walk toward the hallway. "I'll give you some privacy." I gotta get ready for work anyway, though I'd be content staying here with her all day.

She gives me a little smile before answering.

"Hi," she says without emotion.

I stand in the hallway where she can't see me, and even though I shouldn't eavesdrop, I do.

"That's because I'm at Everleigh's," she says. "No, he's not here."

My brows shoot up. He asked her if I was here, and I can't figure out why he feels so damn threatened by me. Perhaps this is a sign that rushing to get married is the wrong answer. Though I'm not a relationship expert so it's not like anyone would listen anyway.

"I have to go home and get ready for work so I'm not late. Can we talk tonight instead?" She pauses briefly, then tells him goodbye.

I shuffle down the hallway and notice the bathroom door is still closed. The water isn't running so hopefully that means Everleigh's almost done. I wait in my room, and when a knock echoes, I open the door and see Gemma.

"Just wanted to let you know I was heading out and will see you at work. Unless you want a ride?"

I brush a hand through my hair, trying to read her, but it feels impossible right now. "No, you don't have to make a special trip for me. I'll be fine. I walk every day." I shrug. "But thanks."

"Sure." She smiles gently. "See you in a bit then." Gemma turns and starts walking, but I quickly stop her.

"Gemma," I say her name with urgency, and she quickly spins around. "Do you love him?"

She tilts her head, furrowing her brows as she stares at me. There's a long pause before she swallows and straightens. "Of course. We're getting married."

I close the gap between us and rest my hands on her shoulders. I want to ask her if she's *in* love with him as much as she claims to be or if it's the idea of being in love that she wants. But I don't. "Then I hope he makes you as happy as you deserve, the way Noah made Allie happy. In a true love kind of way. Don't settle for anything less, okay?"

Her breath hitches at my reference to *The Notebook*, which has my heart racing at what she must be thinking. Before either of us can stay another word, Everleigh lets me know from her room that she's out of the bathroom. I drop my arms and flash Gemma a small smile before walking away.

Gemma and I hardly spoke all day. Though we were busy trying to keep up with our workload, I could still feel the tension, especially when I asked if she loved Robert. I made things awkward again, but I'm not sure it'll ever not be that way between us. Shortly after I leave for the day, Liam calls me back.

Last night, after the gym, I texted him with some concerns I had. I swore someone followed me home, but I figured I was just being paranoid now that I agreed to do the deposition. I hardly doubt it's been documented yet, but Victoria tends to find out shit.

"Hey, man. I was starting to think you were avoiding me."

"No way. Been dealing with a lot of shit here, but I wanted to check in from your message." He sounds breathless as though he's been running or something.

"Nah, it's nothing. I'm fine, but are you? Sounds like you're gasping for air."

"I've been running after Tyler for an hour, trying to get him to take a bath. He thinks we're playing hide-and-seek, so he keeps hiding."

I chuckle, envisioning Liam chasing his little toddler around the house. "Sounds fun."

"Nah, fuck it. I give up. I'll just spray him with a hose."

"You will *not*!" Maddie screeches in the background. "Get your son in that bathtub now!"

While I'm laughing, I also feel a rush of sadness. I miss them both so much. "Damn, her hormones are next level. She's scary as hell."

"You have no fucking idea," he whispers. "I think they've doubled this time around."

I snort, turning on the street that leads to the gym. "Sorry I'm not there to witness it."

"Yeah, right. But since I don't have a lot of time, I'm gonna get straight to the point. I'm worried about you. Are you sure you should go to Vegas?" Liam's voice is full of concern. "Victoria's gonna find out one way or another. She might send her guards after you as soon as she finds out you're involved with this case. I seriously wouldn't put anything past her at this point. She's a monster, and you don't wanna be at the end of her wrath. Are you absolutely sure you wanna do this?"

"I have nothing to lose at this point…" I say without hesitation. If she tries to retaliate, she'll come after *me* this time. The only way I'll ever move on is to keep living my life without worry. Since I can't do anything about Victoria framing me, the least I can do is help take her down for another crime she's committed. "It's the only revenge I'll get. If she's having me followed, it's just a scare tactic, and it's not gonna work this time. I refuse to let her get away with another murder. I'm not letting her have that kind of power over me."

"I understand what you're saying, Tyler, but she's dangerous. I just know you wanted a fresh start and not to get mixed up into the same old shit as before."

"It's one deposition," I remind him. "But if the opportunity presented itself to take her out for good, I can't promise that I wouldn't take it."

"Tyler..." He groans.

"I have to do this, Liam. She doesn't get to run my life anymore. If she wants to come after me, then I'll do whatever it takes to protect myself and the ones I love."

"Please be careful. Don't go to Vegas alone."

"Serena and Eric will be there. I'm flying in, doing the deposition, then flying home. It's not for another few weeks, so don't get your panties in a bunch."

He sighs, defeated. "Alright, if you must do this, then at least promise me you'll be careful. If you think you're being followed, call the police."

"You mean Sheriff Todd? He's all we have in this small town," I say with a chuckle. "He's fat and can't run to save his life."

"God. Don't tell me that."

"Liam, I'll be fine, I *promise*. If I think I'm being followed, I'll just go up to the SUV and confront them."

"Goddammit, Tyler."

I laugh at my best friend's frustration. "I'm kidding, relax. You know me. I'd be pulling them out by their collars and kicking their asses."

"I'm gonna go find my child before I jump on a plane to kick *your* ass."

"You wish!"

"Let me talk to him." I hear Maddie's booming voice in the background. Liam passes the phone, and she clears her throat. "Tyler James Blackwood."

"That's not my middle name," I sing-song, but she continues.

"I know you're six-feet-something and two hundred pounds of pure muscle, but for the love of God, don't put yourself in danger."

"For the record, I'm six-five and a hundred and seventy-five pounds. Well, maybe one eighty after eating all the Southern food down here."

"Not the point, Tyler!"

I chuckle at her annoyance. Maddie's always been dramatic and loud, but it's why I love her.

"Then what *is* your point, Mads?"

"You're a big guy, and you like to fight, but I'm asking you not to, okay? If you see one of her bodyguards, don't instigate the situation. Just quietly walk away."

I snort loudly, shaking my head at her motherly tone.

"I'm being serious. You have a criminal record now, which means you can't just go around kicking people's asses. It'll be easy to throw you back in prison. Though I'd probably see you more if you were, but I don't want to see you in that position again. I want better for you because you deserve to have the life you want, Tyler. Don't make me worry."

I hear the sincerity in her tone and wish I could reach through the phone and give her a big hug.

"Okay, Mads. I'll be careful and not cause any mischief. I promise."

She exhales a deep breath. "Thank you. Now I can sleep tonight."

Chuckling, I say, "Somehow, I doubt thoughts of me were the reason you've been awake."

"No, it's your nephew who's playing hopscotch on my bladder all night long and giving me the worst heartburn of my life. Seriously, I think this kid is gonna come out with a full head of hair."

Her exaggeration has me cracking up. I imagine their baby coming out looking like Steven Tyler and double over.

"Laugh all you want, assface, but just remember someday your wife is going to be pregnant with your child, and I'm gonna tell her to put you through hell."

"You wouldn't dare. You love me," I muse, opening the gym door. There's hardly anyone inside, but I still don't want to be rude and talk on the phone. "Alright listen, I'm gonna work out for a bit, so I gotta let ya go."

"Fine." She scoffs. "Even though you left me, I still love you like a brother. Please be careful."

"I will, and I know. I love you like a pain in the ass sister, too."

CHAPTER SEVENTEEN
GEMMA

IT'S BEEN a week since Robert and I had our big fight, and after an apology and three dozen roses, he's back to acting the way he was before his meltdown. Robert doesn't like unresolved issues, and although he apologized for blowing up about Tyler and my dad, I'm not certain it was genuine. I'm also not convinced he won't bring it up again. He continues to talk about moving the wedding date, and although I'm hesitant, he's convinced I'll change my mind.

I love Robert, and when we started dating, things felt like a fairy tale. Now it feels like we're together for convenience, and I need to figure out why that is before I agree to marry him in three months. He'll have to commit to spending more quality time with me before that happens.

"Gemma, darlin', you look wonderful." Robert walks into the bathroom as I finish getting ready for the Labor Day parade that's in a few hours. I'm dolled up in a 1950s A-line dress and apron. I look absolutely ridiculous with my hair flipped out, but the costume goes with Robert's tiny home float to promote his company.

"You don't think it's over the top and too flashy?" I ask self-consciously.

Robert grips my waist, pulling me closer. "No, you look perfect. Very fitting for the part."

"And what part is that?"

"Being my wife and the mother of my children," he states confidently. "You're a natural."

I scrunch my nose. "I don't know about that." Stepping back, he drops his hands, and I grab the hairspray off the counter. "I'll be ready in a couple of minutes."

Things with Robert still feel off, and I know it's my own conflicting thoughts causing it. I'm the one who's changed. Seeing Tyler again after all these years still affects me when I thought it wouldn't. I believed I was ready to move on and jump headfirst into a relationship.

I don't want to be hung up on someone who can't reciprocate my feelings, and I've struggled with the battle daily since he returned. Avoiding Tyler is impossible, and it'll only get worse as we keep tap-dancing around each other.

No matter how hard I've tried to forget, our history and past can't be erased. I don't think I ever got over him or let go of the hope that we'd end up together again.

As I finish spraying my hair, I think back to my junior year in high school when I finally found the courage to admit my feelings. I wrote the letter and was nervous for two weeks while I waited for his response.

Dear Gemma,

After reading your letter, I'll admit it took me a few days to decide how to respond. When I read that you were developing "more than friendship" feelings for me, I was partially caught off guard but also happy as hell. I have to be careful about what and how I say this because you're still under eighteen. But since you're probably wearing out your bedroom carpet from pacing, I'll give you some comfort in letting you know that it's not one-sided.

I'm not quite sure how to explain it, but I look forward to every letter you send me and always get nervous writing you one back. I didn't date in high school, and I'm worried I won't be good at it. My home life and childhood were messed up, which was a part of the reason I had to get out of town, but you've heard all about that already.

I've been gone for three years, and the only thing I look forward to when I return is seeing you again. I'm scared I'll break your heart, but you make me want to at least try. I can't promise anything, Gemma, so please don't get your hopes up.

But for what it's worth, you're the first person I think of when I wake up and the last when I go to bed.

Love, Tyler

That letter had me happy crying for days.

Everleigh knew I had a crush on Tyler, but I didn't tell her the feelings were mutual until a couple of months before he returned. She wasn't surprised, considering the way I'd talked about him, and having her blessing lifted a huge weight off my shoulders.

After getting stuck in a little traffic, Robert and I arrive at the float with smiles on our faces. The parade route isn't too long, and we'll do a big loop around downtown. I told Robert to buy ridiculous amounts of candy for the kids because it was my favorite part when I was younger. As I look around, it seems like the whole town has already started setting up lawn chairs on Main Street to watch.

Robert's dressed in his usual suit and tie, and he slicked back his hair with gel to match my 1950s attire. On the outside, we look like the perfect happy couple, but I'm screaming on the inside. My chest is tight, and I feel like the breath has been knocked out of me.

"Darlin', are you alright?" Robert asks as I try to suck in air.

I inhale and force out a smile. "Yeah, just nerves."

He rubs a soothing hand down my back and brushes a few strands of hair off my face. "Don't be nervous, honey."

Robert helps me onto the float before coming to stand next to me. One of his employees is driving the truck, and soon, we're moving into position.

"Are you sure you're okay?"

"I think I ate something weird, but I'm sure it's nothing," I tell him with a smile. Nausea rolls through me, and I question whether I'm getting sick, or if it's something else.

We make it down the first block, handing out full-size candy bars and dollar bills. Robert makes sure his float stands out not just by the way it's decorated but also by the extravagant things we pass out.

I start to feel better and wave to the crowd of people cheering loudly and kids squealing over their candy. Soon, we're in front of

Everleigh's boutique, and the parade stops so the high school cheerleaders can perform a routine.

"Gemma!" Everleigh and Katie scream my name as Owen waves at us. I wave back, then notice Tyler.

Robert wraps an arm around my waist, pulling me flush against him. He's playing the doting husband role with expertise, and I wonder if this is what it'll be like once we're actually married.

"Aunt Gemma!" Owen calls out.

"Come get some candy," Robert tells him, holding out three full-size Hershey bars.

He runs up, and Robert kneels so he can hand them over. "Thanks, Robert."

"Wait, I got something else for you." He reaches for his wallet, then pulls out a twenty-dollar bill. I release a tight sigh, knowing how this will look to Tyler. Of course, Katie will tell Owen to return the cash, but Robert will refuse it.

"Wow, thank you!" Owen beams as he walks back to his mom.

"You're welcome, buddy!" Robert waves again and makes his way over to me.

"That was very nice," I tell him. "He's going to talk about that for days, maybe weeks."

"Just wanted to help the kid out. I know Katie isn't making that much money at the bank."

I'm taken aback by his rude comment. Katie might not be loaded with a hefty savings account, but she's done damn well, considering her situation.

"Actually, I think she makes great money, and if that's the only reason—"

"Gemma, not now. Smile, for Christ's sake. Everyone can see you."

My lips move into a frown as I glare at the man in front of me with disgust. I glance over at my friends and see Tyler watching us. His arms are crossed over his chest as he narrows his eyes with a shake of his head. There's no way he could've heard what Robert said, but he undoubtedly sees how tense I am.

Between the disastrous double date and the fight with Robert, then my talk with Tyler afterward, my mind is a fucking mess. Robert's true colors have always been right in front of me, and for whatever reason, I've turned a blind eye. I wanted to please my dad and make him proud, but it's not his fault I ignored the red flags. I know Robert isn't a bad man, but he might not be the man for me. His intentions have always been very clear—he wants a wife, someone who will stay home with his children and have dinner ready when he comes home.

When the parade ends, we're out of candy and money. All the children were so ecstatic over Robert's gifts and how generous he was. Right now, I'm feeling too claustrophobic, and I think I need some space from Robert. Once we get home and I change, I'll explain I need to do some laundry and clean before work tomorrow. Hopefully, it will give me the ability to clear my head.

"I wish you'd stay," he says, repeating the words he always says when I leave. "Or move in."

My jaw tenses at his constant pushing. "I'll see you tomorrow, I'm sure," I deflect, not in the mood to have the same conversation again.

He tells me he loves me, and though I repeat the words to him before closing the door behind me, it's the first time in our relationship when I've second-guessed if I still do.

Tyler arrives at work the next day with a mumbled *good morning* and barely looks in my direction as he goes into the garage instead of making small talk. Over the past week, he'd make himself a cup of coffee or refill his tumbler and chat with me before starting with his first project. However, today he looks at me with an annoyed or pissed-off expression, though I'm not sure why.

Last night, I had hoped taking a hot bath would help me relax, but it only allowed me to overthink everything. For the first time in a year and a half, I cried about missing my mom. Before that, it was when Robert proposed, and I had wished more than anything she was here to celebrate with us. But now I'd do anything to talk to her about how I feel so she could guide and tell me what to do.

Although I don't remember a lot about her, I feel the emptiness and ache in my chest from her not being here. Katie and Everleigh give great advice and tell me to do what feels right, but I still need and miss my mom. She had life experience that I'll never learn from and stories I'll never hear. After years of being married, having kids and a family, Mom would know what's best and could give me the advice I need.

My father leaves work early to drive out of town for a custom part, but Tyler stays in the garage even after I lock the lobby. We hardly spoke when we were in the break room earlier. I asked him what he thought of the Labor Day parade, and he responded with, "It was eye-opening."

Instead of asking him what he meant by that, I nodded and left the room. I don't know how to fix the tension that swarms between us. The friendship, or whatever it is, gives me whiplash. One moment things are fine, and the next, it's awkward.

After work, I don't immediately go home and stop by the store to pick up some groceries. Robert texted me earlier and said he had a work meeting and wouldn't be able to stop by tonight but told me to be at his house so he could see me. Instead of agreeing, like usual, I declined and tell him I'm cooking dinner for my dad. We still haven't talked about what happened yesterday at the parade because the moment I speak up about his behavior and the pressure he's putting on me, it'll blow up and turn into another huge fight. Perhaps it needs to happen, but I don't have the energy to deal with that right now.

As I load my bags into the back of my car, I notice a black SUV sitting across the street. I focus on it, trying to read the license plate, and swear it was parked near the garage today. It could be a coincidence, but my paranoia has me convinced Robert's having me followed. There's no other reason someone would park outside where I work for hours and then conveniently be at the store when I am.

Witnessing his temper at the double date and listening to his demands about firing Tyler or quitting already doesn't sit well with me. But if he has the audacity to hire someone to follow and watch me throughout the day, I'm going to be at a level of pissed off he's never seen.

As I drive home, I watch in my rearview mirror. They stay far enough back not to be obvious but close enough that I notice I'm being followed. Before making any false accusations, I decide to turn down a random street, and when they do too, my stomach clenches.

What the actual fuck?

Does he really think I'm going to cheat on him? Or that Tyler and I are hooking up in the work bathroom with my father nearby? Every time Robert says something negative, I second-guess marrying him, wondering if I truly know the man I'm going to spend forever with.

I turn again, and the SUV tails me, which confirms my suspicions. Whoever Robert hired more than likely already has my address, so I decide to end this and go home. Hopefully, once this asshole sees I'm not being joined by anyone, he'll leave.

As soon as I pull into my driveway, I grab my three grocery bags and rush inside the cottage. I peek out the window and see the SUV park across the street.

"Seriously?" I mutter as my blood pressure rises. "This is an invasion of privacy."

Grabbing my phone from my bag, I call Robert, and I'm sent straight to voicemail. Growing angrier by the second, I call back. Voicemail again. He's at a dinner meeting, and the fact that he'd rather ignore my calls than interrupt his mealtime pisses me off.

Gemma: Call me as soon as you can. It's important.

He reads it seconds later, but it takes him a few minutes to respond.

Robert: Are you okay? I'm with a client.

Gemma: If you really cared, you would've answered my calls. It could've been an emergency.

Robert: I'll be done in an hour, maybe two. Meet me at my house, and we'll talk then.

I roll my eyes and toss my phone on the counter without bothering to reply. That's always his answer. We'll "talk" when it's convenient for *him*.

Wanting to get a better look, I sneak around the side of my dad's house and look toward the street, trying my best to stay hidden. I watch a man in a suit get out of the SUV. For a moment, I think he's coming to my dad's front door, but then another man exits from the passenger side, and they scope out the place. One of them has a camera around his neck and the other has binoculars. My adrenaline rushes through my body so quickly, my hands shake. I tuck my lips into my mouth and rush back to the cottage. My heart pounds hard in my chest, and I swear I hear leaves crunching in the backyard. I'm so fucking scared; I close my blinds and curtains, then lock the doors, hoping they leave.

This is insane. They saw me leave the grocery store with bags in my hands. I'm alone, but it's not good enough for them. I'm sure they're hoping to catch me in the act to provide Robert the proof that doesn't exist. Whoever they are, they looked like professionals, but I'm not sure what they're after.

Gemma: You crossed a line. Call off your private investigators!

Robert: I have no idea what you're talking about. What private investigators?

Gemma: The ones you hired to follow me.

Robert: Why would I hire people to follow you? You aren't making any sense.

I swallow hard, unsure if he's being honest or not. Robert isn't a liar, but he's a pro at getting what he wants. If this is a scare tactic so I'll agree to move in with him, I'm going to unleash my wrath. Perhaps it's a stretch to think that's why they're following me, but there's literally no other reason. Maybe he hopes I'll be too nervous to live alone, and it'll push me to move up the wedding date.

If that's the case, I'll cancel the whole thing, including our relationship.

Panic rushes through me as I think about these men being outside my house. With my dad being away, I can't call him for help, but I wouldn't want to worry him either. I text Everleigh and Katie, but neither of them responds as I put away the rest of the things I bought at the store. Another twenty minutes go by when I decide to take another look outside. The SUV's finally gone.

I release a deep breath, relief flooding through me, but it doesn't stop the anxiety from taking over. My heart races, and I double-check to make sure all my windows and doors are locked. I can't settle down, and after no one returns my texts or calls, I break down and reach out to Tyler.

Gemma: I'm sorry to bother you, but I'm kinda freaking out. Would you mind coming over? Someone followed me tonight, and I'm scared.

His response comes immediately.

Tyler: Stay in your house. I'll be there in less than ten minutes.

Gemma: Thank you.

I pace around the house while I wait, and when there's a knock on the door, I jump. I'm worked up more than I realized.

"Gemma, it's Tyler," he calls out with another knock.

I unlock the deadbolt and turn the knob, then release a sigh as soon as I see him.

"Hey," he says rushed, pushing me back into the house and locking the door. He turns around, and his eyes roam down my body. "Are you okay?"

I nod, feeling my insides tremble. "Yes, just weirded out."

"Tell me what happened," he says. We walk the few feet into the kitchen while I explain everything from noticing the SUV at work to being followed home. Then I tell him how I saw two men get out and walk around the yard.

"Fuck," he curses under his breath, brushing a hand through his hair.

"It's probably nothing. I'm fine, just worked up."

My entire body is cold, and I can't seem to stop shivering. I don't admit that I think Robert's behind it because he'll judge me even more, and I can't deal with Tyler pitying me.

He studies me briefly before closing the gap between us, then wraps his arms around me. "You're shaking. You aren't fine."

I give in to the part of me that wants to feel his touch again and relax against his chest. He tenses, but as soon as I rest my head on his chest, he softens.

"Gemma."

Leaning back, our gazes lock, and there's something behind the fire in his eyes. Tyler's jaw locks as he stares intently at me. He lowers his hands and slides his tongue across his lower lip.

"Yeah?"

"Why'd you ask me to come tonight?"

I blink hard, a thousand thoughts fluttering through my head. "I told you why. Someone followed—"

"Where's your fiancé?" he interrupts, harshly.

"He's in a meeting with a client."

"Did you tell him what happened?"

I swallow hard, shaking my head. "I called a couple of times, and after they went to voicemail, he texted and asked if I was okay."

"Why didn't you explain what was going on?"

I lower my eyes, hesitant to spill the truth, but it comes out anyway. "Because I knew he wouldn't come. He told me to go to his house, and he'd meet me there in a couple of hours."

The intensity in Tyler's eyes have butterflies swarming in my stomach, and I hate that he still has this effect on me. I shouldn't still feel this way twelve years after he broke my heart.

Tyler scratches his fingers along his scruffy jawline, and I find myself wondering if it's soft or rough. Probably rough, like his hands. The hands that have touched every inch of my body, the fingers that have marked me, the palms that have slapped across my ass.

I choke down the visual and blink away the memories.

"What'd the SUV look like?" he asks.

"Black. Tinted windows. Big, like an Escalade. Alabama plates."

"And you saw two men?"

"Yes. Both in suits. Tall. One had a camera, and the other had binoculars."

He nods as if he's not surprised, which is perplexing.

"I think they're private investigators," I admit.

Tyler clears his throat before rounding my little kitchen table and opens the fridge. "Could be."

He rummages around and pulls out items.

"What are you doing?"

"Gonna cook you some dinner and help get your mind off everything." He spins around and flashes me a sincere smile. "I mean, if that's okay. If I remember correctly, you love homemade chili and anything spicy."

I smile, and those stupid flutters return. "Alright, on one condition."

"What's that?" He tilts his head with an amused expression.

"You tell me about Vegas. The *real* story."

CHAPTER EIGHTEEN
TYLER

The real story.

Only Liam and Maddie know what really happened, and it's not a story I repeat. Gemma knows I was set up and was saving my friends, but that's it. I've never talked about getting involved with the O'Learys and the terrible things I witnessed, but then again, Victoria isn't someone I enjoy discussing. Considering the deposition is soon, it has me concerned that she's responsible for having Gemma followed. I keep it to myself because I don't want her to live in fear. It makes no sense for someone to be tailing her because Victoria's guards are usually more strategic than that. Though she might be trying to use scare tactics from the beginning because Victoria's bat-shit fucking crazy.

"What exactly do you wanna know?" I ask, avoiding her gaze while I move around her quaint kitchen and set the ingredients on the counter. The other day, I felt like I was being watched too, and now I'm wondering if this is a coincidence.

"The events that led up to you getting arrested, and what it was like behind bars."

I narrow my eyes as I look at her.

"Shit, sorry. You probably don't want to discuss prison."

Not particularly, but if it'll keep her mind off those assholes following her, I'll tell her what I can. We used to chat for hours between ripping off each other's clothes. She'd want to know about the Army, and I'd tell her stories of the trouble my friends and I would get into during leave.

"It's okay, I just haven't really talked about it with anyone except Liam. Not even Everleigh knows all the details."

"She only told me a little if I brought it up, but after a while, I stopped asking."

"Why?" She tilts her head at me as I continue. "Why'd you stop?"

She shrugs with a faint blush. "Once I met Robert, I thought it was inappropriate. I didn't want Everleigh thinking I was still hung up on you while I was dating another man."

I arch a brow. "Were you still hung up on me?"

A small smile meets her lips. "I thought I was because I never had closure so I could properly move on. I tried to forget about you. But once I heard what happened, I asked Everleigh about you because I wanted to be there for her, too."

"I'm truly sorry about that." I frown at the sadness in her eyes. The day I left without her was one of the worst days of my life. "I appreciate you asking about me and being a support system for my sister. I know she took it hard."

"Your grandparents did too."

Guilt hits me hard as I think back to five years ago when Everleigh told me how they reacted to the news. I had done exactly what I tried to avoid—disappointed them.

"I didn't do it," I say, keeping my hands busy as I cut an onion. Something I've repeated so many damn times since I was charged.

"Everleigh told me."

"Did you believe her?"

"Of course. And I believe you too. Regardless of how much time had passed, I knew you'd never be involved with illegal guns and drugs."

"I didn't deserve to go to prison for crimes I didn't commit, but I was involved with some shady people. I never wanted to be a part of that lifestyle, but I did what I needed to help my friends."

As I make the chili, I tell her about Liam and his arranged marriage to the mob princess. I talk about the day I got sentenced and the realization that nothing would be the same again. Then I admit to keeping her letters and having most of them memorized word for word.

"You do? Really?"

"Why do you sound so surprised?" I wash my hands, then dry them. When the chili boils, I turn the heat down to a low simmer.

"I don't know…" she murmurs softly. "I guess I just thought you forgot about me after all this time, and—"

"*Forgot*?" I raise my brows. "Are you insane? You're all I've thought about for *years*."

Her cheeks turn bright red. Gemma lowers her eyes as if she's embarrassed we're talking about this.

"Gemma." I step closer, tilting her chin up to look at me. "I could *never* forget you."

She stares at me, then licks her lips.

"You were my first love. I didn't leave because I didn't want you. I was twenty-two and thought the grass was greener on the other side. I had a desire to see what else the world had to offer, but don't think it was ever easy for me to be without you. My heart was breaking while I simultaneously broke yours."

Tears well in her eyes, but she holds it back. "Then why didn't you come back? You just cut off all communication with no warning. I was devastated."

"I knew it'd only be harder if we kept in touch. I felt like if I visited, I'd never leave, and I'd be here forever."

"And would that have been so bad?"

"At the time, yes. I didn't want to feel trapped. I was scared to death of ending up like my mother or worse, my father. I was convinced the only way to break the mold was to leave Lawton Ridge and stay away."

"I wish you would've given me the chance to show you how wrong you were. You would've never ended up like them." She shakes her head when tears stream down her cheeks.

Closing the gap between us, I brush the pads of my thumbs under her eyes.

"Don't cry, Gem. We can't rewrite the past."

She relaxes against my touch. As I cup her face, I lean in and press a kiss to her forehead.

"It's not the first time I've cried over you," she says with a laugh.

"I think I was so hung up on you because you were my first...well, my first *everything*. Guess it's true what they say."

"What's that?"

"No matter how much time goes by, you never really get over your first love. They'll always have a place in your heart, whether you want them there or not."

"Sounds about right..." I mutter. "Never felt that way about anyone again."

Gemma's head snaps up. "You didn't?"

I look down at her, second-guessing if we should be this close or if I should even be admitting these things, but I can't keep them hidden from her anymore. For years, I've held back how much Gemma meant to me and how much I missed her. I've wished my stupid head would forget it all, but it's impossible when my heart still aches for her.

My thumb brushes over her bottom lip, removing it from between her teeth. "No. I don't think finding love like we had is in the cards for me."

"Why would you think that?" she asks softly, almost bracing herself for my response.

Grabbing a loose strand of her hair, I slowly tuck it behind her ear, and an electric spark jolts between us.

"No woman compares to you," I say honestly, then add, "No woman ever will."

"Tyler..." she whispers on a strangled cry.

I cup her face, bringing our foreheads together. Gemma fists my shirt with her fingers, then wraps her arms around my waist. It's the closest we've been since I've been home, and though it's wrong, it's never felt more right.

Our heavy breathing fills the silence, and there's a plethora of raw emotions lingering between us. I'm waiting for her to tell me what to do—back off, leave, stay—and I'll do whatever she asks.

"What do you want, Gemma?" I'm trying to read her, but it's impossible.

"Kiss me." Her words are so soft that I'm positive I misheard her. When I don't move, she pulls back slightly allowing our gazes to lock. "I *want* to remember. Remind me?" she pleads.

How can I tell her no? How do I deny the woman I'm still in love with? I can't.

I slide one hand around the base of her neck and cup her face with the other. We're so close. Our lips aren't touching, but I can feel her ragged breathing against my skin.

"Are you sure?"

She gently nods, and before either of us can change our minds, I claim her lips, crashing our mouths together in a hot, needy kiss. My tongue swipes inside, the heat of her breath hitting me with full force. Gemma clings to me, grabbing my shirt and sliding her fingers underneath. Her nails claw down my back, and I gasp out a growl.

"Fuck," I hiss, lowering my hands down her body until I cup her ass. Her arms loop around my neck, and I lift her body until her legs wrap around me. As our tongues dance together, we quickly lose control. We're on the front lines, fighting this war of desire, both surrendering and wanting more.

Walking with Gemma in my arms, I manage to find her loveseat, and we sit. She straddles my lap, and as her back arches, Gemma grinds her hips against me. The fire burning between us is so hot, neither of us can stop to put it out.

"Goddamn, baby," I mutter, moving inside her shirt and cupping her breast.

Pulling back slightly, she grabs the hem of her blouse, then removes it. Without a word, I do the same. Gemma's beautiful, there's no doubt about that, but when she's this ravenous, she's fucking breathtaking.

I undo her bra in one swift motion, which leaves her gasping. Haven't done that in years, but apparently, I haven't forgotten. My cock is so hard in my jeans that it's becoming painful, and with Gemma rocking against me, it's not making it any easier.

"Touch me," she begs.

I move my lips to her neck as my fingers pinch her nipple. I gently suck as her eyes roll in the back of her head. Gemma arches her back as she moans and digs her nails into my shoulders.

"Christ," I growl, then drag my tongue along her collarbone. "Your skin's so soft, baby. I still remember the way you taste."

"Mmm…" she hums with a smile as she fights with my zipper but loses.

I smirk and pull her skirt above her waist. "I bet if I rubbed between your legs, you'd be wet for me right now. Am I right?" Sliding my palm up her thigh, I rub over her panties and feel her arousal. "Fuck, I am."

Gemma's so goddamn responsive, it makes me wonder if her fiancé knows how to give the pleasure she damn well deserves. He probably has to take a boner pill just to get hard, or maybe she has to murmur dollar figures to turn him on. Considering he'd rather be at a business meeting than comforting his woman, my guess is he doesn't do shit when it comes to satisfying her.

Once I slide her panties to the side, I brush over her pussy, and she immediately coats my finger. Though my dick is fucking aching to be inside her, I'm not going to rush this, even though it's torture.

"Don't tease me…" she says with a small chuckle, moving against my touch.

Jesus, she needs it bad.

I push two fingers inside, and she gasps, throwing her head back as she grinds harder against me. Keeping my other hand steady on her hip, I hold her tightly as she rocks up and down.

"Yes, just like that, baby. Take what you need from me."

Gemma squeezes my shoulders and presses her mouth to mine in a desperate kiss. It feels incredible to taste her again and feel her unraveling around me. It's been years, but I haven't forgotten how amazing things were between us.

Sliding her tongue between my lips, she moans when I rub her clit with the pad of my thumb. At this rate, it won't be long before she falls over the edge. She pants and moans as I finger fuck her.

"Oh my God," she breathes out, melting against me. Her head falls back again, and I slide my teeth across her bare throat. I suck on her soft skin as I increase the pressure on her clit.

"Your cunt is so perfect, Gemma. Goddamn, I've missed this," I whisper hoarsely in her ear. "Come on my fingers, baby. I know you're close."

I pinch her nipple as I nibble on the shell of her ear, and seconds later, her pussy tightens, and she screams out with satisfaction. Her nails dig into my shoulders as she rides out her release, and it's the sexiest thing I've ever seen.

Once her body relaxes against me, I bring my fingers to my mouth and taste them.

"Mmm…so fucking delicious." I smirk, licking my lips. "I've missed that."

Gemma's head snaps to mine as her green eyes widen in horror. For a moment, I think she sees something behind me, but then I notice panic and realization in them.

"Oh, shit. Oh my God. *Shit, shit, shit,*" she mutters as she fights to push off me and lowers her skirt when she stands. She grabs her shirt off the floor and pulls it on, her breathing rapid and harsh.

I'm so thrown off by her reaction that I'm not sure what to do besides wait for her to toss me out or explain. "Gemma…" I say gently, trying to adjust my hard-on so I can stand.

Her hand covers her mouth as she stares at me in shock, shaking her head before speaking. "I-I'm so sorry…I can't, *we* can't…I wasn't thinking clearly. That shouldn't have happened."

Well, that's like a nice cold bucket of ice water to the face. Though I can't say I regret it. Fuck Robert and his perfect fiancé façade. If he loved her the way he claims, he'd be here right now instead of me. He would've dropped everything to make sure his woman was safe.

"Gemma, please stop freaking out…" I finally get to my feet, and she steps away, putting space between us.

"You have to go. Please, go." She walks over to her kitchen island. "I'm so sorry, I shouldn't have let it go that far."

"You asked me to kiss you…" I remind her.

"I know, and I shouldn't have."

"I wasn't complaining."

She swallows hard and licks her lips, the ones I just kissed. Gemma is having a complete meltdown, and all I want to do is pull her into my arms and comfort her, but I don't. I keep my feet planted.

"What just happened was wrong, Tyler."

I want to ask her why it felt so right then. But instead, I shrug, not buying her words. I see through them. While she wants to do the right thing, even she knows deep inside that being with *him* is wrong. All the red flags are proof. How can she not see what we have, *could* have, would be the real thing?

"Well, I call bullshit."

"What?"

"I said, I call bullshit. You knew exactly what you were doing when you asked me to kiss you. You think you love him, but you still have feelings for me."

"Tyler, please. Don't."

Gemma's nearly in tears, and I hate upsetting her. I know the love and desire we had all those years ago is still there just by the way her body reacted to my touch. It's frustrating to see her lie to herself and pretend the spark isn't there. The past twenty minutes was all the proof I needed.

"Make sure to stir the chili," I say, scooping my shirt off the floor.

"Wait, what?" She nearly stutters over her words, and I point at the pot behind her.

"The chili. It'll be ready soon. Stir it so the seasonings mix and don't stick to the bottom of the pot."

I yank my shirt over my head and grab my keys. "Make sure to lock up behind me."

Then I pull open the door, briefly waiting to see if Gemma says something, and when she doesn't, I shake my head and leave.

When I leave, I look up and down the street, seeing if I notice anything suspicious or the SUV she described, but I don't. Fucking lucky too because I'm in a shitty mood. I would've had no problem pulling those assholes out of the car and giving them a piece of my mind with my fists. I'm halfway to the condo when the sky opens up and unleashes on me.

Fucking great.

I'm drenched by the time I make it inside, and Everleigh gasps when I enter.

"God, what happened to you?"

I glare at her as I kick off my shoes, then go to the bathroom. Immediately, I strip out of my wet clothes and hop in the shower. My heart pounds and races with adrenaline. The need to punch someone or something weighs heavily on me, but I grip my cock and punish myself instead.

Gemma *isn't* mine.

I don't deserve her.

Even twelve years ago, I knew I didn't, but I still had her. I've fucked up a lot in my life, but giving her up is my biggest regret. Tasting her again and knowing it can't ever happen again might kill me. I'm so fucked. I should've walked away when she asked me to kiss her, well before her lips touched mine.

I shake my head.

I should've bent her over and given her a dozen reasons she'll always be *mine* and not his.

My thoughts jostle as I roughly stroke my shaft and grunt to images of Gemma's mouth falling open as she came by my touch.

You can't rewrite the past, I told her.

You were my first love.

Being alone with her is equivalent to playing with fire and then getting pissed when I get burned.

I should know better.

Gemma's pure and sweet and shouldn't get wrapped up with a guy like me who has more baggage than an airport. Even if Robert is a phony fuck, he can give her things I never could. A life she deserves.

My balls tighten as my hand squeezes hard, and I hiss through the orgasm as the memories of her flood my mind. I'm never going to get over her.

I toss and turn all damn night, fighting with the urge to text her or keep my distance. Deciding on the latter, I give up trying to sleep and get out of bed at four a.m. Grabbing my workout clothes, I change and brush my teeth, then head outside for a run. This pent-up rage isn't going anywhere, so I have to work it off.

After an hour, I head to the gym, stretch, then I give the punching bag hell. After another hour, I feel better, but my frustration is still there.

A guy who's at least ten years younger watches me, and I wonder if he's on Victoria's payroll.

"Do you think you could teach me to box like that?" he asks. I realize he can't be more than a few years out of high school.

"Sure. What do you wanna know?"

"How to kick ass and take names," he says with a grin. "My name is Luke."

'"Tyler." I give him a pair of gloves and go over some basics. As I guide him on proper form, I hold the bag in place for him while he practices. The kid has some power behind his punch and reminds me of myself when I was his age. Eager to learn. For the forty-five minutes, I instruct him, and I actually forget about being pissed as a rush of happiness surges through me. I loved training and teaching people how to box, and this brings me right back to coaching Mason and Liam. When I moved to Vegas, I taught at an elite gym, and after working with him, I realize how much I miss it.

"You're so good. Thank you," Luke says before grabbing a towel. "Will you come back tomorrow?"

I nod with a smile. "Yeah, I'll be here."

He waves as he walks to the locker room, and the owner approaches me.

Shit, is he gonna be pissed I was training?

"Tyler, hey."

"Hi. Good morning."

"You lookin' for a job?" he asks, taking me by surprise. "Could use another trainer."

"Depends. Are the hours flexible?"

"You can make your own. How's that?"

My brows rise. "Really? I already work a full-time job, but how about evenings and weekends? Maybe a couple of mornings?" Hell, I'd work night and day if it'd take my mind off Gemma and the dirty thoughts that surround her.

Sam smirks, then holds out his hand. I take it, and we shake. "See you tomorrow then."

Well, that was unexpected. The gym is small, but it's the only one in town, so it stays busy. I don't even bother to ask him what the pay is because at this point, I'd do it for free if it meant keeping me busy.

"That looked like the easiest job interview I've ever seen." A girl pops up out of nowhere. I've seen her here a few times. Her brunette hair is longer in the front but shorter on the sides. Tattoos cover both of her arms, which I find fascinating. She's wearing a tank that shows off how muscular she is, which means she must lift weights a lot.

I chuckle at her words and nod. "I guess so."

"I'm Ruby." She gives me her hand.

"Tyler," I reply.

"I work the front counter," she clarifies. "I guess that means we'll be seeing each other a lot."

"I guess you're right." I smirk, walking backward toward the door. "See ya tomorrow?"

Ruby smiles, showing off her bright, straight teeth. "Six sharp."

By the time I make it home, I have thirty minutes to shower and get ready for work. Though I wasn't expecting to be out that long this morning, I feel a million times better and am glad I did. I should be exhausted, but I'm running on pure adrenaline. I got a second job, plus I made a new friend. It might not be a shitty day after all.

By the time I walk into the shop, Gemma's already working. She meets my eyes for a split second, then looks back at her computer. Neither of us says a word as I make my way to the garage and close the door behind me. I don't bother grabbing coffee or a pastry even though I really should've after my morning, but I'll manage until my lunch break.

Jerry keeps me busy all morning, but by noon, I'm drained from a lack of sleep. I'm losing energy, and he notices, asking me if I'm okay. I admit I didn't get any rest and got up early to work out. I worry about disappointing him, but he understands.

"Go home, son. I can clean up," he tells me at three, a couple of hours before my shift is supposed to end.

"You're sure?" I feel guilty about leaving him to do the rest.

"Of course. I managed without help for years." He barks out a hefty laugh.

"I owe you one, Jerry." I take off my gloves, then wash my hands before waving goodbye. As I open the door, I immediately regret not walking out the back exit.

Fucking Robert.

They continue talking as I make my way to the coffee table. He's

ONLY HIM

not even being quiet as he asks her about last night, and my spine straightens as I listen to her response.

"It was nothing, just a false alarm. I thought someone was following me."

What the fuck? Why would she lie about that?

"Are you sure? I can get the sheriff to investigate this and stake out your place for a few nights. He owes me a helluva favor anyway."

I roll my eyes. Of course, he does. Probably throws his money at everything and everyone in this town.

"No, no," Gemma insists. "That's not necessary."

Once I grab the last donut and fill my cup with coffee, I stalk toward the door. Before I can walk out, Gemma calls my name, holding me in place.

"Are you leaving?"

"Jerry said I could."

Robert mutters something under his breath, and I hear her tell him to be quiet.

"Oh, okay. See you tomorrow then."

She glares at Robert when he mumbles something else.

"Is there a problem?" I step inside, letting the door hit my back.

"No, it's nothing. Enjoy your afternoon," Gemma quickly says before Robert can get a word out.

I know the asshole hates me, considering the way he tried to bombard me at the pub a few weeks ago, but if he has something to say, then he can man up and say it to my face.

"What's the issue then?" My feet move forward as my exhaustion and anger catch up to me.

Robert faces me. "My issue is that you're working with my wife, and you have a criminal record," he finally speaks louder so I can understand him.

"She's not your wife *yet*," I spit out.

"Gemma will be very soon," he states proudly. "But it won't matter because she won't be working here much longer, so it won't be a problem."

Oh, there's gonna be a big motherfucking problem if he thinks he can mold her into whatever the hell he wants.

I wait for Gemma to argue, to say she's not going to be a Stepford wife, and stand up for herself or something. But she stays silent and bows her head.

"So, it's gonna be like that." I tighten my lips and nod. "Alright, then."

I slam my hand against the door, and when it whips open, I walk out without glancing back.

CHAPTER NINETEEN

GEMMA

I'M SO happy it's Saturday because the past three days at work have been absolute torture. I can't believe I asked Tyler to kiss me and then lost control with him. I can't even blame my bad decisions on being drunk. Of course, I remembered what kissing him felt like, but for some reason, I wanted the reminder. I *needed* the reminder. It was just as good as it was all those years ago, too. I was brought back to being two ravenous kids hungry and desperate for each other. As soon as my body unraveled and I came down from my high, realization hit and so did the guilt. Cheating was something I never thought I'd do, but I did, and my emotions overwhelmed me as the remorse settled in.

Tyler was so pissed and hurt. He had every right to be, considering I led him on, but it's no secret I'm engaged. I'm so damn confused. Feeling his mouth pressed against mine and allowing the moment to consume me felt so right even though I knew it was wrong. I'm not sure how Robert would react or what he'd do if he found out. He already hates and judges Tyler, and after their awkward standoff in the lobby, I know it wouldn't be good. I wish I could forget it happened, but that's been impossible.

I've never felt a stream of electricity like that with anyone else, only Tyler. And I'd thought after all these years, it'd have dissipated, but it's only gotten stronger.

Ever since the "incident," we've avoided each other like an STD.

The only conversations we've had have been related to work and to the point. He avoids eye contact, and if I walk into a room, he leaves. At first, I expected it, but now it's driving me insane. All week I've thought about confronting him so we can finally clear the air, but I can't do it at work. I don't want my dad to get suspicious, and it's better if it stays between the two of us.

Instead of pacing around my house all day, I grab my keys, determined to talk to him. I check the clock and see it's just past noon. Showing up unannounced is rude, but since Everleigh's working, it means Tyler will be alone.

My heart pounds rapidly as I drive there. I haven't figured out what I'm going to say when I see him, but I'm hoping the words just fall out so we can get past the awkwardness. Above it all, I owe him an apology and hope he accepts it. I never should've crossed the line. If we were two different people, there's no doubt the night would've ended in my bed. A part of me wishes it would have, but the other part is glad it didn't. It's nearly impossible to ignore the chemistry between us and pretend the constant tug of emotions isn't there.

When I turn the corner and see Everleigh's place, my courage begins to wane, but I have to do this. I pull into the driveway and see a car parked on the street in front of her condo that I don't recognize. Ever since those two men followed me, I've been hyperaware of my surroundings. After I turn off the engine, I tighten my ponytail, then walk to the door.

I find my words and suck in a deep breath, hoping this ends well. We need to find common ground again and move on with our lives. After I press the doorbell, Sassy barks, but I don't hear anything else.

Growing impatient, I ring it again just as the door swings open.

Tyler stands in front of me with only a towel wrapped low around his waist. Water drips down his chest using his muscles as a path to his happy trail. I bite down on my lower lip, not prepared to get a show before we talked.

"Gemma," he snaps. "Everleigh isn't here. She's at the boutique."

I tilt my head at him. "Right, but I actually came here to talk to you."

He doesn't budge and continues to stand while keeping the door cracked. "Okay, go ahead."

"Don't you want to get dressed first?"

I'm tempted to push past him and let myself inside since he didn't offer.

"I'm kinda busy. Will this be a long conversation?"

With every passing second, I grow more frustrated. He's not being his typical self and isn't acting like the Tyler I know. He's acting like I'm the biggest inconvenience of his life, and honestly, I don't like this side of him.

"I want to talk about what happened between us the other night. So you want me to stand right here and have that conversation? Or do you want to invite me inside where we can have some privacy?"

He shrugs but doesn't say anything.

Fine then.

"We need to get back to normal. My dad asked what's going on because he noticed things have changed between us. I don't want him to get suspicious, so can we act like we're friends at least? For the sake of working together every day?" I hate how desperate my voice comes out but talking to him and being this close to him when he looks like that makes me anxious.

Tyler crosses his arms over his chest. "It was nothing more than a heated kiss and a *mistake*, Gemma. That's it. You're engaged, and like you said, it never should've happened, so let's pretend it didn't. It meant nothing to me anyway, so you can go back to planning the wedding of your dreams."

Excuse me? My blood boils as my adrenaline spikes. "It meant nothing to you?"

I'm not sure what I wanted or expected him to say, but it wasn't that. If he's saying that to hurt me, it's working.

"That's what I said. You. Are. Engaged." He stresses every word.

"I am. But that doesn't mean you have to lie, Tyler. I felt something, and you fucking did too."

"Sorry, I didn't," he says calmly. "It'd been a long time since I touched a woman, so perhaps you got the wrong signals."

My breaths are shallow as my anger rises, and when I open my mouth, I see a gorgeous brunette walking down the hallway wearing nothing but a towel.

She smiles wide as I look her up and down. She rocks a short pixie cut, sleeves of tattoos on both arms, and bright blue eyes. The woman looks like she fell off the pages of a fitness magazine as she saunters toward us. She oozes confidence, and the closer she comes, the smaller I feel. My heart stops when Tyler turns and smiles suggestively at her. It's not hard for me to put all the pieces together since they're both wearing towels.

Fuck, I'm an idiot.

"I'm sorry. I didn't realize you had company."

Tyler grips the side of the door as though he's ready to slam it in my face. "It's fine. Do you need anything else, or are we done here?"

"I guess we're done."

The woman moves beside Tyler, and we make eye contact. Her perfect smile has my jealousy burning me alive.

"Hey, I'm Ruby." She holds out her hand, and I reluctantly take it.

"Gemma. I'm Tyler's sister's best friend."

"Nice to meet you! From what Tyler's told me, Everleigh is awesome."

I swallow hard at how sweet she's being and know I won't be able to hate her for having a crappy personality. "She is." Blinking hard, I stare at how radiantly beautiful Ruby is. "How'd you meet Tyler?" The words blurt out, and I mentally slap my forehead.

"The gym," she says, which makes sense by how toned her arms and legs are. It's obvious they have working out in common.

"Alright then," Tyler interrupts. "Ruby and I have plans, so I'll see you Monday," Tyler tells me before shutting the door in my face. I walk to my car more frustrated than I was when I arrived. My mind is reeling, and I don't know why my emotions are bouncing around like a ping-pong ball. As I back out of the driveway, angry tears stream down my face. I'm pissed at myself, and my confusion isn't helping.

When I get home, I sit and turn on the TV, but I'm not paying attention to it. I replay everything when Tyler came over that night. Is it possible that I exaggerated what happened? That I felt something he didn't, and he was just going through the motions?

There's no way.

His body responded just as quickly as mine. Did he say it meant nothing because he's dating Ruby? I flipped out right after he gave me the best orgasm I've had in years, then told him it was a mistake. I asked him to forget it and leave. Perhaps I should be happy that he moved on.

Even if he is dating someone, it shouldn't matter. I'm fucking engaged.

Leaning my head back on the cushion, I close my eyes and slowly inhale. I feel absolutely ridiculous for going over there. If I could take it all back, I would. If I hadn't lost control and gave myself to him, I wouldn't feel so damn guilty and confused.

It's never felt that way with Robert, not even in the beginning. And it's supposed to, right? I'm supposed to feel like I'm floating on cloud nine with fireworks as I succumb to him. Admittedly, there have been numerous times when Robert couldn't make me come during foreplay or sex. With Tyler, my panties were drenched before he even touched me. Though it's wrong, Tyler touching me like that is what I fantasize about when I'm alone. He's always known my body better than I do and still has every inch of me memorized. When we were together in the past, we shared more than just a physical attraction. We've always had a deep emotional connection, and it made the sex even better. Though we've changed, the chemistry between us hasn't.

I'm a blubbering mess, and I need to calm the hell down. It's not too early to drink, is it? Fuck it. I go ahead and have a glass of wine that soon turns into three, and before long, the whole bottle's gone. With heavy eyes, I lie on the couch and watch the Hallmark channel until I fall asleep. Hours pass and I'm woken by a text message from Everleigh.

Everleigh: Any plans tonight?

Gemma: No. I've already drunk a bottle of wine.

Everleigh: Girl. It's only 4 p.m. What's going on?

I want to spill all my secrets. I want to tell her so fucking bad because she's my best friend, but I don't even know how to start the conversation. She's already doubted Robert so much that this would only add fuel to the fire. Not to mention, I cheated with her brother.

Gemma: I'm just…I dunno. Questioning everything again.

Everleigh doesn't reply for a little while, but she's also in the process of closing the boutique.

Everleigh: Want to hang out and talk about it?

Gemma: I'd rather drink myself stupid and go to bed.

Everleigh: Adulting at its finest.

I want to ask her if she knows if Tyler's dating someone or that there was a woman at her house, but I don't want to start anything.

Gemma: I'm a hot mess.

Everleigh: What did Robert do now?

Honestly, I haven't talked or texted him all day. It's proof that he'd rather do other things than be with me. I didn't sleep over last night like usual since he had a late business meeting, and I didn't want to be at his house alone. Normally, it wouldn't bother me that there's been no communication, but it's like the filthy curtain covering our relationship has been removed, and I'm noticing all the things I don't like.

Gemma: Nothing. He hasn't done anything.

The alcohol is swimming, and I type out another message.

Gemma: It's Tyler. I thought I'd be okay being around him, but I was wrong.

Everleigh: Do you want me to talk to him?

Gemma: No! Absolutely not. Please don't. I don't need things to be any more awkward between us. It's just…I don't know. I'm dumb.

Everleigh sends me an eye-roll emoji.

Everleigh: Dumb? Or you realized there's still something between you and my brother?

I suck in a deep breath and frown.

Gemma: There can't be, though.

Everleigh: You're right. Robert already hates him. And he kinda has that serial killer vibe, so it's probably best you keep them away from each other.

Gemma: Gee, thanks. Now I'm marrying a future murderer. Great!

I lock my phone and stare at the TV. After ten minutes, it dings twice. I have a text from Everleigh and one from Robert. When I see his name, I expect to feel some sort of excitement, but all that remains is a suffocating feeling of dread.

It's not supposed to be like this.

I think back to Dad telling me how in love he was with my mom and how they never wasted a single moment together. Then I think about Robert, and how he puts me on a pedestal but only when it's convenient for him. Perhaps some women would be into that, but it makes me feel like a prize he's won and wants to show me off like a trophy.

I check Everleigh's message first.

Everleigh: I'll keep my mouth shut and won't talk to Tyler, but if you want me to say something to him, I will. Although I'll always be Team Gyler getting married and having all the babies, I've always got your back.

She sends a winky emoji, and I laugh at the ridiculous couple nickname.

Gemma: You're TERRIBLE!

Next, I open Robert's message.

Robert: Have you made a decision about moving in? I really would've loved having you next to me this morning when I woke up since you didn't come over last night.

Here we go again. I'm not even surprised at this point. He refuses to listen to me or validate my feelings. I set my phone down on the table and open another bottle of wine. Once my glass is full, I go outside for some fresh air and sit in one of the patio chairs under the small awning. It's the middle of September, and even though the humidity hasn't completely vanished, at least there's a cool breeze.

The evening silence draws on as I hear the faint sounds of birds and crickets chirping. The sky is a bright pink and purple with the sun sitting lazily in the sky. I take another drink just as my dad walks outside whistling.

"Hey, sweetie," he says before glancing down at my wine glass, then back at me.

"Hey, Dad. How's it goin'?"

"I'm good. You okay?" He takes the empty seat next to me.

"Fine, just peachy," I lie.

Dad glances at me. "Before your mother and I got married, she suggested we run away together and elope."

I snort at his random comment. "What?"

"Yeah, she couldn't wait to get married and wanted to start our lives together right away. Plus, planning the wedding with her mother's input was stressful. She always joked that it's what caused her first gray hair."

I smile thinking about it. "Well, Grandma is super particular."

"*Everything* became an argument. Chocolate or strawberry cake. Red or white roses. Inside or outside ceremony. I didn't care as long as we were married at the end of the day. Whatever she wanted was good enough for me." He grins as he reminisces. I know he misses her every single day, and I do too. They were soul mates.

"But you didn't elope, did you?" I ask, wondering if they got married before the date we celebrate as their anniversary.

"No, but she nearly had me convinced when she complained about her mom wanting her to wear her wedding gown. It was awful looking." He leans back and looks up at the fluffy clouds in the distance just as the cicadas start.

"That's funny."

Dad chuckles. "I guess my point is, if you're nervous or stressed about this wedding stuff, I understand. It can drive a woman crazy. Your mother, who loved tradition, was ready to throw in the towel and book us a flight to Vegas."

My heart aches that he thinks my bad mood is because of the wedding.

"Robert wants to move up the wedding to November," I tell him for the first time. "That means we'd be getting married in two months."

"Wow. That's coming up. But what do you want?"

I shrug. "It feels too soon. I'm not sure if I'm ready for all those changes right now. I think I need more time," I admit.

"Oh, Gemma." He pats my hand. "Out of my two kids, you were always the critical thinker and people pleaser. But sweetheart, you have to follow your heart. It always knows the right thing to do before your head does. So if it's telling you to wait, then wait, but if not, it wouldn't hurt to move the date. I wished your mother and I had because we would've gotten more time to be married. But the invitations were already sent, and RSVPs were coming in. Robert's the perfect guy for you, and he wants to make you happy, which I know he can for the rest of your lives. I'm positive he'll do whatever you want."

Dad twists the dagger that's been lodged in my heart since that night with Tyler. Dad really likes Robert, but I'm no longer confident he's the right man for me. Can he truly make me happy for the rest of my life when it feels like he wants to control it?

"Dad, I have a question for you."

"Go on."

"Did you still get butterflies from Mom after all those years of being together?"

HIs lips tilt up into a toothy grin. "Yes. I never once stopped feeling that spark when I was with her. Even when our arms would brush, I'd get goose bumps. I think that's how you know it's real, pumpkin. When you wake up in the morning or when you go to bed, that's the person you think about. And it's who you want to spend all your time with."

I listen to his words and take them all in, realizing I've not felt that way about Robert in a long time. He proposed so quickly into our relationship, and I said yes but haven't taken the time to really think any of this through until now.

When I woke up this morning, the only person on my mind was Tyler. I feel like such a piece of shit, and unfortunately, this conversation hasn't helped. But I don't give my insecurities away and keep sipping my wine, trying to enjoy this time with my father.

"Man, I miss your mom so much," he admits, and I suck in a deep breath, the air feeling thin in my lungs.

"Me too," I say, wishing she were here right now.

The mood turns somber, and I finish my drink. When Dad stands, I do too, and he pulls me into a hug.

"Marriage is supposed to be the happiest time of your life, sweetie. Don't let all the small things ruin this moment."

I squeeze him tight, wishing I could tell him everything but keep it buried deep inside. Maybe one day, he'll know the truth, but that's not going to be today.

"Love you, Dad."

"Love you too," he says before turning and walking inside the house.

I go into the cottage and grab my cell phone to see another text from Robert. Maybe this is all in my head, and I'm creating issues that aren't there? Maybe I need to give him another chance to prove himself?

Unlocking my phone, I read his message.

Robert: I know I'm being pushy, baby. I just think about you all the time and miss you so much. Want to come over tonight?

I look up at the clock and realize how tipsy I actually am, but I could sober up in a few hours.

Gemma: Sorry, I was chatting with my dad. I'd like that a lot. What time?

The best thing I can do is get Tyler out of my mind and replace all those thoughts with Robert. He's going to be my future husband,

and I can't allow what happened between Tyler and me to ruin my plans.

Robert suggests I come over around seven, and I tell him I'll be there.

At least he's trying. I should too. Relationships are full of ups and downs. Robert wants to marry me more than anything, so the least I can do is give it my all to see if that's what I want too.

Tyler's reaction today might be the closure I've so desperately needed, and since he felt nothing, maybe I'll finally be able to move on without him.

CHAPTER TWENTY

TYLER

It's been a week since Gemma came over to talk about what happened between us. I was purposely rude and short because I need to keep her away, regardless of how much it fucking hurts. The disappointment on her face when I told her I felt nothing was something I won't forget for the rest of my life. Though, I'm not sure what she wanted me to say. If I admitted that it meant more to me than I led on and that I think she should dump her douchebag fiancé, it would've caused more problems.

So, I rejected her before she could ultimately deny me. Plus, that's what she wants anyway—to pretend nothing happened. Must be so goddamn nice to easily forget something so goddamn beautiful. Regardless, that moment will forever live in my memory.

We lost control. I could've said no, but when it comes to Gemma, I'm weak as fuck. Maybe it was a mistake, but I don't regret it. Right now, she's doing enough of that for the both of us. Gemma already told me how she felt afterward before I stormed out, and I didn't need to hear her say it again. I didn't need or want the reminder that she's not mine, even if for that moment I had her and she had me. That night, she would've undoubtedly given herself to me, allowed me to make love to her until the sun rose.

I saw the need in her eyes. I heard the desire in her breathless pants. She wanted me, and no matter how wrong she thinks it was, she didn't stop. Instead, she fucked my fingers like she hadn't been touched in a decade, and considering who her fiancé is, it doesn't surprise me.

I woke up early this morning and trained two people, lifted some weights, then went home and showered. I'm in a good mood as I walk to work. It's Friday, and I'm happy I'll get a break from seeing Gemma this weekend, but then again, I love watching her squirm. She has an attitude and is treating me the same way she has all week—like a major inconvenience she'd rather not deal with.

After I grabbed a pastry, filled my coffee, and stood in the lobby, she huffed and puffed while typing loudly.

I think at this point she wishes I'd just quit, just like her future hubby wants, but it ain't happening. Every time she steals a glance my way, I'm curious if I remind her that she willingly cheated on Robert. I wonder if she thinks about how she grinded against my cock, how I tasted her release on my fingers, and how she begged for more. She may not belong to me, but her body says otherwise. I try to push the thoughts away, but they always return.

How the fuck am I going to get over her?

"Just got a call from one of my part suppliers, and he's not gonna be able to deliver the parts I need until after close. I have to meet a long-time customer about a car that won't start. Kinda disappointed because it was all supposed to be here this mornin'. Don't feel obligated to say yes, but do you mind waitin' around for it to make sure it's what we need?" Jerry asks between eating bites of a chocolate frosted donut. He let me leave early last week because I was so exhausted, so I owe him, plus he doesn't ask for much.

"Sure, I don't mind," I say as I replace an air filter in a car.

Jerry smiles, then pats me on the back. "Thanks. Appreciate ya, son."

After I'm done changing the oil in three vehicles and add refrigerant to another, I glance at the clock and see it's lunchtime. When I walk into the lobby, there's a dozen roses on the counter. I lift an eyebrow at her, shake my head, then leave and go to the deli on the corner. Belinda sets a sweet tea down on the table, and I order a hoagie. Once my food is set in front of me, my phone goes off, and I see a text from Liam.

Liam: Maddie's water broke early this morning! Baby should be here today!

Tyler: Awesome, man! Keep me updated!

I finish eating, then go back to the garage and immediately busy myself. I try to keep my mind focused on the tasks at hand, only taking breaks for water. It's miserably hot, and I'm sweating nonstop. When I walk into the lobby, I hear Gemma humming and wonder how I'll be able to move on.

When five o'clock finally hits, Jerry cleans up and thanks me again for staying late. I put all my tools up because he hates a messy shop. After I'm done, I walk inside and go into the break room where Gemma is sitting at the small table texting. Once she realizes I'm in there, she locks her phone, then gets up and walks away. I grab a bottle of water and nearly finish it in one gulp as I follow her to the lobby.

"Do you want me to lock up?" I ask since I'm staying late. I'm sure she has a hot date to get ready for, considering she stays at Robert's house every weekend—well, when it's convenient for him—plus, he sent more roses today.

"I'm more than capable," she snaps.

"Okay, well your dad asked me to wait for some parts for the Chevy he's rebuilding. Supposed to be here around seven," I explain.

She narrows her eyes at me, and her annoyance is obvious. "Seriously? He asked me to stay so I could pay the guy." She lets out a sigh. "Great."

A smirk hits my lips, and I almost wonder if Jerry planned this. He's asked Gemma what was going on between us, and he's not stupid. The thought makes me laugh as I sit in one of the chairs and pull out my phone and text Liam for an update on Maddie.

Tyler: Any news?

Liam: No baby yet. Doctor says it will probably be a few more hours. I'm pacing around like a crazy person, and Maddie is as calm as can be.

Tyler: It's because she thrives under pressure. You better tell me when Tobias is finally here!

Liam: Will do!

An hour passes and neither of us have said a word to each other. The air is thick, and I can smell the stench of those flowers. Must suck to have to overcompensate so much. Right now would be a perfect time to discuss what happened, but I don't know how to bring it up or what I'd say. She's already said what she had to say.

I think back to when she saw Ruby at the house and realized I wasn't alone. Gemma looked crushed as hell. Her face turned bright red, and I could see her pulse racing in her neck. That level of jealousy is dangerous, but it also sends so many damn mixed signals. It was adorable to see her get so worked up, which is why I continued the act. This way, she'll continue with her plans, marry the douchebag, and become the woman he's determined to mold her into—someone I won't even recognize.

It's nearly six when Gemma gets a call from the supplier. I try to focus on my phone but can't when she's so worked up and aggravated.

"Eight o'clock? Wow. Guess I don't have any other choice. No, don't reschedule for tomorrow. I'll cancel my dinner plans. We needed those parts this morning," she barks, then continues, "I'll be here, just hurry up."

After she hangs up, she picks up her cell and starts typing furiously. I'm sure she's telling Robert she won't be able to entertain his clients tonight with her phony smile and fake interest in their pathetic lives. The thought makes me snort.

"They're running late," she tells me, but I already gathered as much.

Minutes later, her phone rings, and she walks to the break room for some privacy, but she's not far enough away for that.

"There's absolutely nothing I can do, Robert. I have to wait for them to arrive. No, my dad had other obligations and asked me to stay. That is not happening, so you're just going to have to deal with it. This is my job, and I have obligations, just as you do with yours," she tells him firmly, and I love this stern side of her. It's as if she's grown a backbone finally and isn't afraid to tell Robert no. Sounds like he's not appreciating it as much, though. "Okay then. Bye."

Oddly enough, there was no exchange of "I love you" at the end. Though I'm smiling at her toughness, when she enters the lobby, I wipe it off, not wanting her to realize I heard every word. I close my eyes, lean my head against the wall, and wish I could take a nap. It's been a long ass day already.

At seven, my stomach growls, and I swear Gemma heard it because she looks up at me.

"Are you hungry?" She stands, and her soft eyes meet mine.

"Yeah, I could use a bite to eat," I admit.

Gemma comes around the counter and hands me a paper menu from the pub. I smell the faint hint of her soap and perfume, and all I want to do is kiss and taste her sweet lips again. The skirt she's wearing shows off the perfect amount of thigh, the same ones that were straddling me almost two weeks ago.

"I'll order us something and go get it. My treat for agreeing to stay. I'm sure you had plans tonight." And I swear I hear her mutter Ruby's name under her breath as she walks back to her chair, which causes me to smirk.

I lower my voice. "Gemma."

She swallows hard, her gaze focused on my lips. Heat streams between us, but I try to pretend it doesn't. She said what happened was wrong, but ignoring what we have somehow seems worse.

"I insist. I'm using the company card anyway." A nervous laugh escapes her. It's the first time I've heard that sound in a while, and I wonder what's up with the change of heart. Sometimes, it's night and day with her. One minute, she's cold as ice, and the next, she's blazing hot, and it's making my head spin.

"Alright. I'll take a double cheeseburger with onion rings. Do they do to-go whiskey?" I tease.

"Wish they did," she says, and I'm wondering if it is because she needs alcohol to be around me. Wouldn't be the first time. "Dad keeps a small bottle in the bottom drawer of the office."

"Really?" I chuckle. "That's badass. Always liked your dad, but now I think I might love him."

"Maybe we'll crack it open while we eat." She calls the pub and places our order. Fifteen minutes pass before she leaves to go pick it up.

Moments later, my phone rings, and I'm ecstatic when I see it's a FaceTime call from Maddie. Liam must've forgotten to text me, but I completely understand. I can't imagine how fucking excited he is that his baby boy is here.

I answer with a smile. The room is dark, and she looks exhausted but also full of energy.

"Hi," she whispers. "There's someone new here."

I'm so fucking happy for them that I nearly combust.

"Really? Let me see!" She turns the camera around so I can see him sleeping peacefully on her chest. He's so lucky because he's going to have the best parents in the world. "He's beautiful, Mads."

Maddie moves the camera and points it back to herself. "Thank you. I wish you were still here." She pushes out her bottom lip and pouts.

I laugh and realize I was so caught up in the conversation I didn't hear the door swing open.

"Hey, Ty–" Gemma says from behind me and stops. "Oh, sorry, didn't realize you were on the phone."

I turn to face her. "It's fine. I'll be off in a minute."

She nods and walks to the break room carrying our bags of food. Once she's out of sight, I look back at the screen where Maddie's eyebrows are lifted. She's waiting for an explanation. "Excuse me, who is that?"

I roll my eyes at her. "It's not what you think. Her dad is my new boss."

Her voice is nearly a whisper. "Gemma?"

I nod once.

"Oh. Em. Gee!" I turn down the volume because she's on speaker. "The plot thickens."

Brushing my fingers through my hair, I groan. "There's no plot. We're...friends."

She snorts and nods because she doesn't believe a word I'm saying. Hell, I'm not either, but I'm not going into that story right now. "Yeah, I remember when Liam said that for years, too. Good luck with that." She gives me her infamous smirk.

I tilt my head at her, hoping Gemma can't hear this conversation. "For someone who just gave birth, you're awfully energized."

"Don't change the subject," she teases. "When are you gonna ask her out?"

"Jesus." I blow out a breath, wishing she'd stop. "I gotta go, Mads."

"You liar! You're just trying to get rid of me."

I throw her a boyish grin. "I'd never."

"I want details, you hear me? Text me all the juiciness." She points her finger at me.

Scrunching my nose, I shake my head. She's just as bad as Everleigh. "I think you've confused me with one of your gossipy girlfriends again."

With narrowed eyes, she tries to persuade me, but it's not going to work. "Liam and I won't be able to have sex for six weeks. I need your dating life to hold me over."

"Maddie, I didn't enjoy hearing you guys in the next room for three weeks, so I most definitely don't enjoy hearing you talk about it." It's as bad as finding my sister's clit massager.

"Geez, you're so dramatic."

In the break room, I can hear the plastic bags rustling and the fridge closing.

"If you want a girl to gossip with, I'll give you my sister's number," I mock, but regret it the moment I say it.

"Really?" She perks up. "Good. She'll tell me all the details of your love life."

"Shit. I really shot myself in the foot by saying that. Never mind. My sister doesn't have a phone."

"I gave birth today, but I wasn't born today. So nice try," she retorts

Seconds later, I hear Liam and nearly jump. "Quit hassling the man."

"What are you doing here? Where's Tyler?" Maddie panics as Liam comes into view and presses a kiss to her forehead.

"Relax. My dad is sleeping over. I didn't want you two to be alone."

The way they look at each other is something I desperately wish I had. "Aww," I sing-song. "You two are disgustingly adorable."

"Dude." Liam moves closer. "How are things down in the South?"

We talk often, but he likes to ask these basic questions when Maddie is around, just so the conversation doesn't move to Victoria.

"Fuckin' hot, that's what. Especially in the garage." I groan, still wearing my sweaty clothes from today. I can't wait to go home and take a damn shower.

"Hey, no bad language around the baby!" The moment the words leave Maddie's mouth, she chuckles.

"How are the new jobs going?" Liam asks. I told him last week about getting hired at the gym.

"Not bad. Keeps my mind occupied, which I like, and off other things." I don't mention what those other things are, but nothing gets past Maddie.

"Like Gemma…" she whispers and grins.

"No, like the mafia princess who put me in prison," I say sternly, but she was right. Gemma is always on my mind too. I just can't admit that with her so close. But considering I'm going to Vegas this weekend for my deposition on Monday, it's hard not to think about Victoria.

"Tyler, you better not be thinking what I think you are," Liam states firmly.

I shrug, fully aware my food is getting cold in the next room. "I really do have to go, though."

"We love you!" Maddie tells me. "Please call me soon. You know I'll be bored on maternity leave!"

"I will, Mads. Don't worry," I promise with a sincere smile.

After we say our goodbyes, I hang up, take a deep breath, then enter the break room. Gemma really did pull the whiskey from her dad's bottom drawer and opened it.

"I'm sorry, I didn't wait," she tells me around a mouthful. I move closer to her and brush my thumb across her cheek, wiping away the extra mayo on her face.

She swallows down her food and grabs a napkin. "I'm a hot mess."

"What else is new?" I laugh and sit across from her. "Thanks for dinner."

"Welcome," she says, then hands me the whiskey. I take a huge swig, then hand it back to her, and she takes one too. As I take my food out of my bag and cut my burger, she grabs two plastic cups, and we empty the bottle of whiskey between us. While it takes the edge off, it's not enough to get me drunk. It's dangerous for her to be around me when she drinks because when her inhibitions are down, we do stupid things. But I promised myself that I'd try harder to keep her at arm's length.

A part of me expects we'll discuss what happened, but Gemma never brings it up and neither do I. We eat in silence, only the sounds of our breathing filling the space. When we're almost done, she speaks up.

"Everleigh's fall sale did great this week," she tells me. "Sold out of all the Hans Solo costumes."

I chuckle, thinking back to the beginning of the summer when I suggested she order all the leggings, vests, and boots. "I heard. She's doing so well."

"She is. I'm really proud of her for following her dreams."

I meet her eyes. "What about your dreams?"

"I'm living my dreams right now." She grins, but I wonder if it's genuine.

"Yeah?"

With a nod, she gulps down the whiskey. "Yep. Working at the garage. Getting married to a good man. Living in an amazing town with amazing friends. I can't really complain."

"I'm happy for you," I say, grabbing my cup and finishing mine. By the smile on her face, she hopes she's convinced me, but her façade is crystal clear. I can see she's playing a role, just as Robert wants her to. A part of me wants to shake her awake and force her to stop fooling herself and everyone around her, but I don't. It's obvious she wouldn't leave him for me with everything he offers her.

Once we're finished eating, I pick up our empty containers and take the trash to the dumpster out back. When I get to the side of the garage, the delivery truck backs into place. Gemma comes through the door and takes inventory as I check to make sure everything is correct. After thirty minutes, the driver is paid, parts are stocked on the shelf, and it's finally time to go.

Gemma grabs her purse and locks up. "I guess that's it."

"Yeah," I say. "Let me walk you to your car."

She nods as we head outside. "Okay. I'm parked right up the street because the side lot was so full this morning."

We move in silence toward her car that's lit by a streetlight. I look around, checking for any vehicles I don't recognize, but it all looks normal. When we turn the corner, Ruby seems to magically appear with a huge smile.

"Tyler! I was hoping I'd find you," she says, pulling me in for a hug, then kisses my cheek. Ruby pulls back with a wide grin, then looks directly at Gemma who tenses.

"Wanna get a drink?" she asks, meeting my eyes.

I look down at the time on my phone and see it's just past nine, which means she just got off work. "Yeah, I'd love that."

Gemma scowls when Ruby latches onto my bicep.

"Wanna join us?" she asks Gemma sweetly.

"No, I can't. Y'all have fun, though." She glances at me, and I study her reaction. Jealousy. Regret. Maybe both. "Thanks again for helping. Good night, Tyler."

"Good night," I respond and watch her cross the street. Ruby and I wait until Gemma drives off before heading to the pub. It actually cracks me the fuck up that she's so damn jealous when the ball has always been in her court.

Once Ruby and I are inside, we order a beer at the bar and talk about our day. Then she blurts out, "Are you absolutely positive she's not into girls?"

I let out a bark of a laugh because this isn't the first time she's brought up my sister. "Everleigh? I'm positive, which is a good thing because I'm sure you'd ruin her."

"Damn right, I would. But I saw the way she was looking at me when we met last weekend, and the other day when I picked you up. She was totally giving me the sexy bedroom eyes," Ruby waggles her eyebrows, then chuckles. "She *definitely* liked what she saw." She swirls her tongue against her top lip.

"You're such a little shit." I shake my head and take a sip of my beer. "Pretty sure she's sworn off dating for life."

"Oh, I'd be delighted to help change her mind. I bet she'd be game for a threesome, too. I was totally gettin' a kinky vibe from her."

"I think I might throw up. That's my sister, so stop putting nasty images in my head." I shudder, glaring at her, which causes her to snort-laugh.

"Alright fine, you big pussy. What about Gemma then? Think I could steal her away from that needle-dick she's engaged to?"

"Don't even start," I warn.

"Oh, c'mon. You know I'm just giving you shit. She is beautiful, though. I wouldn't mind exploring her body with my tongue and—"

"I'm gonna kick your ass, Ruby," I threaten.

"Well, if you'd put on some gloves and meet me in the ring, we'd see about that. Pretty sure I could take you." She flexes, then winks.

I grin, shaking my head at her confidence. "Oh, Ruby. What am I gonna do with you?"

"Well, my ex-girlfriend enjoyed slapping my ass and twisting my nipples, so if you wanna punish me…"

"God help me, I'm gonna need more alcohol." I groan as she sticks out her tongue.

Though we give each other shit, I'm so fucking happy I have at least one friend I can hang out with who's not connected to my sister in Lawton Ridge.

All week, I've been trying to forget about my upcoming trip to Vegas and pushed it to the back of my mind. I tried to keep my mind busy and not to think about Gemma or the deposition. Everleigh agreed to drive me to the airport for my flight on Sunday, but not before she bombarded me with a million questions. I refused to admit what's going on or that I hope to serve a slice of justice pie to the woman who nearly ruined my life. The less details she knows, the better. Not worrying her more than I already have and keeping her safe are my only priorities.

On the way to the airport Sunday morning, my blood felt like it was boiling in my veins, but I stayed calm so I didn't alarm my sister. Everleigh continued to question me, but I didn't cave even though she threatened me with bodily harm. Of course, I laughed, considering I'm twice her size and she'd cry about breaking a nail before hurting me. Before I got out of the car, I gave her a hug and told her not to be late picking me up Tuesday night. She agreed and demanded I be careful.

My flight to Nevada was boring and so was the Uber ride to the hotel. Viewing the bright lights and tall hotels on The Strip brought back a lot of memories. While I'd love to go out and revisit my old stomping grounds, it's not safe for me here.

Monday comes quick and waking up in Vegas for the first time in half a decade is odd. I've been away too long for this to feel like home. Now, it just seems like a nightmare I can't wake from.

After I have a cup of shitty hotel coffee and get ready for the day, I text Serena and tell her I'm heading to the lawyer's office. I'm meeting her, along with Eric and the prosecutors in the next thirty minutes, and I'm a ball of nerves.

Serena's a godsend for coming with me today. Otherwise, I'd be without representation and up shit creek. When I see her, I smile at the familiar face. She looks exactly the way she did when we first met all those years ago. Professional and like she's ready to kick some ass. As we wait for the deposition to start, she walks me through what I should expect, reminding me to be truthful but to also watch what I say. We wait outside the conference room as she coaches me, and I feel as if I'm preparing for the fight of my life, and maybe I am, considering Victoria is involved.

When I catch sight of Eric and his lawyers coming down the hallway, I know it's showtime. Reality hits me like a ton of bricks when we enter the room and memories from five years ago resurface.

I'm asked to take a seat and introductions take place. One of the lawyers gives a briefing and explains the next steps. The prosecution will ask me questions first, and then the defense will be allowed to if they wish. I loosen the collar that feels like it's choking me as sweat beads on my forehead.

I look at Serena, and our gazes meet. She gives me the same look she did years ago, one that reminds me to stay calm and that this'll all be over soon. Once I catch my breath, everything begins.

My heart rapidly beats in my chest as I relive and share details of the past. I don't like to discuss it because it brings back too many bad memories, but I'm here to help, so I push through them. Their questions are bold, and the defense is as nasty as anticipated. Their goal is to make me look like I'm not a credible witness. While I always knew Victoria was a monster, it's only been confirmed by all the countless murders she's committed. I'm sure she's convinced she'll get away with it too.

After an hour, it's finally over, and I release a breath of relief. Vegas holds bad memories for me, and for the first time in my life, I can't wait to get my ass back to Lawton Ridge where I belong.

CHAPTER TWENTY-ONE

GEMMA

My weekend was spent going over wedding details with Winnie, who wouldn't stop calling and texting me. I'm sure Robert paid her double or something because she was relentless and unavoidable. While I haven't made an official decision about moving the date yet, time is running out, and I'll have to decide soon. I'm not sure how much longer he'll wait for my answer, but I think I'm going to tell him I'd feel more comfortable keeping the date as it is. Just thinking about it causes anxiety and unnecessary stress.

Monday morning comes quickly, and I wake up earlier than usual. I spend my extra time drinking coffee and can hear the birds singing outside. As I sit at the kitchen island, I notice the way the early morning sunshine peeks through the kitchen window and splashes across the cottage floor. I try to soak in every detail, fully understanding that living here will eventually be nothing more than a memory. The thought saddens me, but I push it to the side.

After I get dressed, I check the time, then grab my purse. On the way out, my phone buzzes, and I look at it when I climb inside my car.

Robert: Don't forget about letting me know about dinner tonight! Have a great day. Love you!

I smile and am relieved how much better things have been since we had a long discussion the other night. I came clean about my insecurities and what I expect out of our relationship. He apologized again for suggesting I quit my job and for acting so possessive around Tyler. He only wants the best for me and believes deep down he can provide that. Talking without an audience or interruption was a relief, and I think we're finally on the same page.

Yesterday, he explained he has a meeting planned with a new female client tonight at Fancie's Restaurant and asked me to go so no one speculated he was cheating. While I would never jump to that conclusion, I respect that he told me. Marriage needs to be about compromise and doing things that make Robert happy, even if it makes me uncomfortable. As long as there's give and take, our relationship will be stronger. The bottom line is, I'm trying because I deserve to be happy.

The drive to the garage isn't anything special. By the time I arrive, Dad's already started his task list for the day.

"Morning!" Dad yells when I walk into the garage. I can only see his legs poking out from under a car.

"Need anything?" I move closer, looking around to see if Tyler is here yet.

"Nah, I'm good," he says, and I hear him tightening something.

"Alrighty. Donuts should be here any minute."

"Sounds good. I'll come grab one soon."

I go back into the lobby and power on the computer. Right on time, Mrs. Wright enters with a box of donuts and bear claws. We talk about the weather and the cold front that's supposed to move through this weekend before she's on her way.

After I make a cup of coffee, Mrs. Zelda comes in with the keys to her Camaro, and before long, the lobby is full of customers who didn't have appointments. Once I've gotten them all taken care of, I go back to the garage and notice Tyler isn't around.

"Dad, we just had six cars pull up for oil changes. Is Tyler here?"

He turns and looks at me. "No. Said he needed off."

"For what?" I ask as he wipes his greasy hands on a cloth.

"Not quite sure. He mentioned needin' to leave town for something important and would be back on Wednesday. I told him it was fine." He tilts his head at me when my nostrils flare. "You okay?"

Frustrated doesn't explain how I feel right now. "That would've been great information to have before I told everyone their vehicles would be ready for pick up this afternoon."

He waves it off like it's not a big deal. "It'll be alright. I handled all of this before Tyler started helping out, and I can do it again for two days."

My eyes soften. "I know, Daddy. I just don't want you to overwork yourself. That's all."

"It keeps me young, sweetie. Everyone's vehicles will be ready before close. And if not, go home and change during lunch and help me out. I mean, if you still remember how to remove an oil pan and change a filter." He gives me a hefty laugh.

This has me snorting. "Dad, I could do it in my sleep."

"That's my girl," he says, then gets back to what he was doing because there's no extra time for chitchat. "If people don't want to wait, tell them to come back later this week."

I nod and return to the lobby where my mind races. Tyler never mentioned going out of town, and a small part of me thinks he's planning to leave Lawton Ridge again, regardless if he said he wasn't. Deep inside, I feel as if I've pushed him away, and the guilt comes in full force, but so does the jealousy. Seeing him with that woman again is slowly eating away at me. All weekend, I've tried to ignore how happy Ruby looked when she saw him or how her voice changed an octave. I shouldn't care that the man I first loved is moving on with his life because I have. Right?

When I get a little break, I text Everleigh and ask if she'd like to grab a quick lunch. She's been so busy at the boutique with all the fall sales and decorating for Halloween that it's been hard to get together, but she agrees to meet me. As soon as noon rolls around, Dad and I leave the garage at the same time and go our separate ways. It takes me a couple of minutes to walk to the deli where Everleigh is happily waiting in a booth by the big windows. She waves at me with her million-dollar smile, and I hurry inside. Once I sit, we order our chicken ranch wraps and sweet teas.

"So, what's new?" She grins, raising her eyebrows. It's the first time we've been face-to-face since I slept over after Robert and I had that big fight three weeks ago.

I bite my lip. "Nothing much. Did wedding shit all weekend. Winnie is like a cracked-out wedding junkie," I tell her.

"Really? Need any help deciding on anything? Like who your maid of honor will be?" She waggles her brows, and I laugh at her obvious tone. I don't want to have to pick between her and Katie, so I've pushed it off.

I shake my head. "Nah. I just randomly picked things. Honestly, Robert would be better off doing all this, considering he's so meticulous about the colors, cake, and the song for our first dance." I quickly change the subject, hoping she takes the bait. "How's the boutique?"

She grabs a pack of crackers from the caddy and opens them. "Great. Super busy. You sure you don't want a weekend job?" she asks around a mouthful, probably hoping I'll say yes this time. "I can't even guilt Tyler into helping me anymore since he got a job at the gym."

My cheeks heat at the mention of Tyler and how I had no idea he was employed there, too. No wonder he's not having any problems moving on from our heated make-out session.

Swallowing hard, I push the images of that night out of my head. "Girl, you should put an ad in the paper. I'm sure you'd have a handful of teenagers dying to be at your beck and call for an employee discount," I tease. "I wish I had the time, but between the garage and wedding planning, there'd be no extra time." I groan.

She playfully rolls her eyes. "I guess that's a good enough reason, but if you change your mind, hit me up," she sing-songs.

As I think about my next words, my heart begins to race. "Tyler didn't show up today. Is…everything okay?" I can't help the hesitation in my voice.

"I think so. All he told me was he had something to do in Vegas. I drove him to the airport yesterday afternoon, and I'll pick him up late Tuesday night. He didn't give me much info, regardless of how hard I tried. Honestly, I thought you were aware because he said he was approved to be off work. Sorry, I would've mentioned it otherwise." She narrows her eyes. "It's suspicious that no one knows what he's doing in Vegas, right?"

"It is," I say with a nod. I think about him leaving again and moving back to Sin City, but then I think about Ruby. Would he leave her too?

"What?" She watches me, noticing my mood change.

I force a smile and try not to act too curious. "Does Tyler have a girlfriend?"

Everleigh is in stitches over my question, but I don't think it's that funny. "A girlfriend?" She snorts. It's obvious she has no idea about Ruby, but I won't be the one to tell her because it's not my business to do so.

"He's never had a girlfriend—other than you, of course—and he probably won't start now. It's not in our blood to be in relationships." There's a sadness in her tone when she talks, and I figure it's because of how they grew up. The only healthy marriage they witnessed was their grandparents'. Everleigh shows me her ringless finger and wiggles her hand.

"I suppose. Though, if it's any consolation, any man would be lucky to be with you. Assuming he could wrangle you down." I laugh, and she throws a piece of her cracker at me.

"Yeah, yeah, whatever. What do you know that you're not telling me?" she asks as our food is set in front of us, and we thank the waitress.

I lower my eyes, looking at the plate. "Nothing at all."

"You're such a bad liar!" she scolds, and I meet her stare. "Is my brother dating someone?" She arches a brow, waiting for me to answer.

One thing is for certain—Everleigh won't let this die and will probably confront Tyler as soon as he's home. Tucking my lips inside my mouth, I pretend as if I'm zipping them up and tossing the key.

"Did you forget who you're talkin' to? You can't change the subject that easily, she continues, then takes a big bite of her wrap, but I've lost my appetite. "Who is she?"

"No idea. I don't know anything about it, but thought you would if it was serious," I confirm, which isn't a lie. I don't dare tell her how pretty the woman is and how she's perfect for Tyler—fit with tattoos, bright eyes, and high cheekbones. Instead, I keep those details to myself because just thinking about her causes my blood to boil. Compared to her, I'm homely, the girl next door type. Ruby seems like she could give Tyler the best night of his life, and as much as I shouldn't care and tell myself I don't, there's no denying the fact that I do.

I pick at my food, eating half of it as she talks about the shop and the new inventory she ordered. I'm happy she fills the silence because I don't have much to say.

After we're done eating, she hurries and grabs the check before I can, then takes care of it.

"No fair! You never let me pay." I pretend to pout but smile and thank her. We exchange a hug, and before I turn and walk toward the garage, she looks at me.

"Everything okay between you and Tyler?"

Though a cool breeze is blowing against my cheeks, I feel like I'm on fire.

"Yeah, why?" I press, wondering if he said something about me.

She shakes her head. "Just wondering. You've both been…weird lately."

I force a laugh. "No idea what you're talking about. Everything about Tyler and me working together is weird."

Waving her hand, she chuckles. "I guess you're right. If you get bored tonight or tomorrow, come over! We can have a girls' night since my brother's gone. We can get drunk watching nineties rom-coms and eating Ben & Jerry's."

I grin, remembering I have to decide if I'm going to dinner with Robert tonight. "Maybe tomorrow."

"Deal!" she tells me, and we go our separate ways. "Hope you sell out of everything today!" I shout over my shoulder.

She chuckles, giving me a thumbs-up.

The rest of the day at the garage is busy as hell. Robert texts me again about tonight, and I decide to join him. Apparently, I need to dress nice because the client we're meeting is extremely high profile. I read between the lines of his message and know he wants to impress her. A few minutes later, he calls me.

"Hey, darling. What're you up to?"

I smile at his genuine tone. "Just working my ass off. It's been a Monday from hell."

He chuckles. "Hope I'm not bothering you."

"You're not," I say, as I make a fresh pot of coffee because I'm hitting my afternoon slump.

"Oh, I wanted to ask if you could write Winnie a check? She's ordering some things for the wedding, and I'm about an hour and a half away from the house."

"Yeah, sure. Not a problem. Can I do it when I get off at five?"

"That's perfect. The checkbook is in the top drawer of my desk. Write it for five thousand, put it in an envelope, and place it in the mailbox. She said she'd run by after she got done with a client. I won't have time to make it home before I pick you up for dinner."

"Will do," I tell him.

"I miss you and am so happy you're coming tonight," he admits. "Can't wait to see you."

"I know, baby, me too. Only a few more hours," I remind him.

"Will you stay the night with me afterward?" he nearly begs. "I know it's not the weekend, but I bought you something from that lingerie shop you like. Thought you could model it for me."

A smile touches my lips. It means a lot to see him actually trying to spend more time with me. "Yeah, I'd love that."

"Thank you for everything. I gotta go. Don't forget about taking care of that for Winnie. Love you!"

"Love you too, Robert." I end the call, then get back to work. The rest of the day passes by in a blink. Just as Dad promised, all the vehicles are ready to be picked up before close. He looks and sounds exhausted. We lock up and say our goodbyes.

When I pull out of the parking lot, I head over to Robert's house and turn off the security alarm, then walk into his office. When I agreed to marry him, he added me to his bank account, though I never use his money for anything.

I sit at his oversized oak desk and open the top drawer. Once I find his checkbook, I write it out for the amount he said, then scribble the information in the registry. Afterward, I notice a handful of payments for three thousand dollars that are all dated within the last month. They're not written out to anyone in particular, so I flip to the carbon copies to see if there's more information. I sit there confused because the name is blank and only has the dollar amount and his signature on them.

Sucking in a deep breath, I close the checkbook and place it back in the top drawer. It doesn't close properly, so I reach my hand in and pull out several wads of crumpled paper. Instinctively, I smooth them out and notice they're handwritten receipts.

The moment I read the company name, my heart drops.

I can't breathe and nearly gasp for air when I realize they're for a private investigator.

With shaky hands and adrenaline rushing through me, I put them where they were, hidden and wadded up behind the stack of files. I grab Winnie's payment, stuff it in an envelope, and try to calm down.

After I place it in the mailbox, I get the fuck out of there. I'm so angry that I'm nearly in tears, and I can't think straight. Maybe it was for something else, but I know for a fact I was being followed, and hell, maybe I still am. That means Robert was gaslighting me when he said he didn't know what I was talking about and made me feel like I was going crazy.

I have a feeling he knew exactly what was going on, and that's why he didn't come to my rescue. It makes me sick that he'd do this to me.

How do I even bring this up after we agreed to put more effort into our relationship? This will undoubtedly change everything. I've lost complete trust in him and faith in our future. If I hadn't already agreed to go with him tonight, we'd be discussing it right away.

On the way home, I think about the check registry, and the timeline of when they were written matches when I first saw the SUV parked outside of the garage.

I park in my driveway and allow myself a few minutes. My paranoia is in overdrive, wondering what they must've seen. Did they see Tyler come to my house the night they were there? Does Robert have pictures of him leaving? Is he following me because he thinks I'm cheating? A million thoughts and questions hit me, but I won't get answers until after dinner.

Though I technically crossed a line with Tyler, I stopped it before it went too far and have felt guilty about it ever since. Regardless, it doesn't justify Robert hiring someone to follow me and invade my privacy.

As I enter the cottage, while losing my goddamn mind, I get a text from Robert. I've already agreed to join him tonight, and I'll have to make sure I play the perfect part so he doesn't get suspicious. Afterward, when we go back to his house, I'll confront him. I guess he didn't remember what evidence he left in the drawer when he asked me to write Winnie a check. Or maybe he thought I was too stupid to find it.

Robert: I'll be at your house around seven. Don't forget to pack a bag :)

I feel sick.

This gives me an hour to shower, get ready, and settle down. I don't want to do this, *any* of this. But I'll do it tonight, so I get ready anyway. I slip on a black form-fitting dress and apply some makeup, but my stomach is in tight knots. Right on time, a knock taps on my door, and I open to see him. He's all smiles as he looks at me from head to toe, then leans forward and kisses me. It feels dirty and wrong, and I try not to tense. There's bound to be an explanation for this, right?

"You look gorgeous, Gemma. Are you ready?"

"Mm-hmm. Let me grab my duffel." I force out a smile and grab my bag.

Robert takes it from me, and we walk to his car hand in hand. He presses a soft kiss on my knuckles before opening the door and ushering me inside.

On the way to the restaurant, he talks about how huge this contract will be. His client wants to buy a hundred acres of land on the outskirts of town to fund a new upscale subdivision. He talks about her idea of million-dollar mansions built around a large pond. She also wants to get into other business ventures and possibly have a strip mall built close to downtown, which would give his company consistent business for years. It'd be his biggest contract to date, and he reminds me how great this would be for *us*. I try to act excited, but I'm not feeling anything but dread. Too many questions are soaring through my head about the wedding and our relationship.

Regardless that I'm dying inside, I try to keep the conversation moving. "How does she have so much money?"

"Her family is extremely rich, like generations of wealth, and she wants to expand her investments to small towns where she can capitalize. Getting her to sign with me would be a game changer for my company." He turns and looks at me, grabbing my hand. "It's why I brought my lucky charm."

With everything I have, I hold back a groan and the urge to throw up. After parking, we walk inside with our fingers interlocked. The lights are dim, and the waiters are all wearing black ties and slacks. It's a five-star restaurant where all the drinks are served in crystal glasses, and every table has an expensive bottle of wine on it. This is the type of place you'd take someone to propose.

A smile fills his face, and I swear I see dollar signs in his eyes as he looks across the room. He waves to someone and then pulls me close before walking toward her. Even from a distance, the woman is gorgeous with her platinum blond hair and smoky eyes. She stands to greet us once we're within arm's length. I notice her skintight pearl-colored dress that probably costs thousands, and her designer heels are at least five inches tall. With her perfectly plump lips, high cheekbones, and contoured face, she could easily be a Kardashian cousin. This woman oozes elitism, and I know Robert is drooling over that fact.

She looks me up and down and smirks.

"Hey, so glad you could make it," Robert says, taking her hand in his. "I managed to bring my beautiful fiancée with me after all," he tells her, sliding his arm around my waist.

"It's so nice to finally meet you, Gemma," she says kindly, shaking my hand next.

"You too," I reply, then we all take our seats.

"Robert has told me so much about his future wife, I feel like I already know you." She chuckles as she taps her long nails on the table. "He talks nonstop about the two of you and how you're getting married before the end of the year at the little white church on the hill. Congrats! It sounds like it'll be a beautiful wedding."

I look over at Robert, narrowing my eyes in confusion. Nothing has been set in stone yet. What the hell is she talking about?

He leans over and kisses my cheek with a bright smile. "Surprise, sweetie! I finalized everything over the weekend."

"What?" I wish we didn't have company. Why would he spring this on me? No wonder Winnie needed to be paid right away, and she was all over my ass to pick out all the details. All the pieces are finally clicking together, which has me fuming inside.

He flashes me a wink. "Can't wait to make you my wife, darling. We'll talk about it later. Tonight, we have some serious business to discuss." He gives me a smile and another kiss. "Oh, I almost forgot to introduce you two."

My blood boils, and I can't focus as Robert speaks.

"Gemma. This is Ms. O'Leary."

A devilish smile meets her lips. She holds out her dainty hand, and that's when I notice the gigantic diamond on her left ring finger. "It's really nice to *officially* meet you. I'm Victoria."

CHAPTER TWENTY-TWO

TYLER

Two grueling hours of being drilled by lawyers over my past wasn't an enjoyable experience, but now it's over. I'm dismissed, and my head pounds when I exit the conference room. I suck in a deep breath and try to calm down while burying the memories of Victoria. As I stand in the hallway, Eric walks up to me.

He holds out his hand, and when I take it, he pulls me into a tight hug.

"Thank you, man. I know how hard that must've been to relive all that."

"No problem. I just hope it's enough to help you get the justice you deserve." When I meet his gaze, I notice the dark circles under his eyes. He looks beat down and exhausted. Helping him makes me feel good, but I won't assume anything will come of it, considering who's involved.

"We'll talk soon, okay?" he says before leaving with his lawyer.

"That went well," Serena says, tucking her brown hair behind her ears.

"I guess. Do you wanna grab some lunch?"

She checks the time on her phone. "I actually need to be at the airport in an hour."

"Okay, no problem." I appreciate that she interrupted her busy schedule for me and flew here.

"What are your plans today?" Serena glances at me as we walk toward the elevator.

I shrug. "Nothing much."

"And before your flight tomorrow?"

I shake my head.

"You can say no, but you should come to Sacramento with me, then fly home from there instead. Liam and Maddie came home from the hospital with the new baby yesterday, and I know how much they'd love to see you."

A smile touches my lips at her great idea. "I didn't think about that. Damn, it's like you're a genius lawyer or something with all this amazing logic."

She snorts and rolls her eyes. "I can drop you off at their house. Check if you can get on my flight. It leaves at noon."

We walk outside, and I follow her to the rental car as I contact the airline. Serena drives to my hotel, and by the time she parks, I've already purchased a flight and rescheduled my departure.

"I'll wait here while you grab your things and check out of your room."

"Great," I say, eager to get out of Vegas.

It takes less than ten minutes to pack my small bag and turn in my hotel key. Even Serena is surprised when I return in record time.

"Damn," she mutters. "You're fast."

We chat as we make our way to the airport, and she updates me on life in California, her son, and how busy the law firm is these days. After we get through security, I watch as tourists feed bills into the slot machines, trying their last chance at winning big. After living in this city for so long, I'm still desensitized to the bright lights and noises of the machines. It brings me back to Liam's gambling problem and how it brought Victoria into his life. I can't help but shake my head as we walk toward our gate.

Serena and I grab something to eat while we wait to board. As I stare out at the crowds of people, I replay what happened in that conference room. Then my thoughts quickly move to Gemma. She has no idea what she does to me and may never understand how deeply I care. I never mentioned I'd be missing work today and haven't spoken to her since Friday night, so there's no telling what she thinks about me being gone. I push the thoughts away before Serena notices my silence and asks what's on my mind.

"Liam's gonna be so damn surprised when he opens the door and sees you standing there. I'm excited to witness the shock on his face."

"Can't wait, honestly. Maddie FaceTimed me after he was born, but it's not the same as seeing him in real life."

"You're right. I spoke with them yesterday, and they're both worried sick about you, so it'll be a fun little reunion. Plus, I don't think I would've been able to sleep tonight after hearing those in-depth stories about Victoria and knowing you were in the same city as her." Genuine concern is displayed on her face.

"I didn't care to stay, anyway. The city harbors too many awful memories for me to ever enjoy it these days. I'm relieved to leave early." *And never return if I can help it.*

Our plane arrives, and once we find our seats, it doesn't take long before we're in the air. For the entire two-hour flight, I stare out the window, and my mind wanders back to Gemma and everything that's happened since I returned to Lawton Ridge.

I wish I could pull her into my arms and kiss the hell out of her to show her what she's missing. When Robert treats her like an afterthought, I want to tell her I'd *always* put her first. I might not be rich with a mansion or a successful business, but I'd give her the damn world. Too bad she's engaged and too blind to see how wrong Robert is for her.

Once we land, Serena and I take a shuttle to her car. Within thirty minutes, she's pulling into Liam and Maddie's driveway. Excitement rushes through me as I think about seeing my best friends again.

Before I get out, I turn to Serena, who's smiling wide. "Thanks for everything. You've been such an enormous help. I don't know how I'll ever be able to repay you."

"Liam and Mason helped me through some rough shit over the years. The least I could do is give back to a close friend of theirs. I still regret not being able to fight a corrupt system that landed you in prison in the first place."

"You did everything you could. Short of a few million dollars exchanged under the table, nothing would've been able to get me out of serving those years. I don't regret what I did that got me in there, but I still appreciate how hard you tried to save me."

"Thank you, Tyler. Means a lot." She sucks in a deep breath. "I hope justice is actually served to that bitch. She deserves to rot in hell for the things she's done."

I grunt. "Agreed."

"Now, get out before you make me emotional," she demands playfully. "I can only take so many compliments in one day. Also, knock lightly. Unless you'd like to feel Maddie's wrath, don't you dare wake a sleeping baby."

"Duly noted." I grin, then grab my bag.

Before I get out, Serena tells me she'll call if she hears anything about the case. I thank her once more, then walk toward the house. Taking her advice, I tap lightly on the hard wood. Serena's waiting in the car. I look at her with a shrug. She waves me forward, so I try again, slightly louder.

Seconds later, the door swings open, and Liam's face transforms from shock to joy as he pulls me into a giant hug.

"Holy shit!" he says, and I laugh as he smacks my back.

Serena lowers the window, and shouts, "You're welcome!" Liam grins at her with a wave, then Serena backs out of the driveway before she zooms down the street.

"Maddie's gonna freak the hell out. I'm so happy to see you, man!" He hurries me inside. "She's trying to catch up on sleep. Tyler's taking a nap too, but when they wake up, prepare to be bombarded—by both of them," Liam warns. After I gladly accept his offer for a beer, he rushes to the kitchen and quickly returns with two Bud Lights. I nearly drink it all in three big gulps.

We go into the living room, and as soon as we sit, Maddie walks in with disheveled hair, looking exhausted. Her mouth falls open, and she slaps her cheek. Chuckling, I stand. "I'm really here."

"Tyler! Oh my God! What are you doing here?" she whisper-shouts, closing the gap between us. I pull her into a hug, and she tightens her grip around me.

Almost immediately, she starts crying. "Gah!" She drops her arms before wiping her cheeks. "My hormones are still out of whack." She goes over to Liam and smacks his arm. "You should've woken me up!"

"I've been here for five minutes, Mads. You didn't miss much."

"Jesus," Liam mutters, rubbing his bicep.

Maddie gives him her infamous eye roll. "Quit being a baby. I barely touched you."

"Good to see nothing's changed between you two." I chuckle.

"Don't worry. I'll get even in six weeks when the doctor releases her."

"Releases her from what?" I ask.

"Liam, shut up!" Maddie scolds.

Liam waggles his brows. "Releases her body back to *me*."

"Okay, now I'm making you wait twelve weeks. Keep it up, and I'll triple it." She pouts with her hands on her hips.

"Yeah, right. You jumping me is the reason we even have two kids."

"Ugh," Maddie groans as Liam pulls her into his big arms and kisses her.

"There you two go again, being sickly cute. Please, spare me. I didn't come all this way to witness you making baby number three."

Liam releases Maddie from his hold, and she smirks at me. "Okay, good. The kids are asleep. Tyler is napping in our bed, but you can still meet Tobias."

"I'll be quiet. Lead the way, Mama."

The three of us walk into their room where a bassinet is next to their king-sized bed. Tyler's sprawled out in the middle, sleeping peacefully. When I lean over and see Tobias, I instantly smile.

"Oh, Mads. He's beautiful."

Liam squeezes my shoulder, and I'm overcome with joy for my friends. They look at their sons with so much adoration. One day, I hope I get to experience what they have, but for now, I'll live vicariously through them.

"There's nothing like a sleeping baby," Maddie whispers.

Tyler begins to stir, so Maddie sits on the edge of the mattress and rubs his back. She's such an amazing mother, and her kids are so damn lucky to have them as parents. I would've killed to grow up in a household overflowing with love like theirs.

His eyes pop open, and Liam swoops him up in his arms. Tobias doesn't wake as Maddie watches him in awe. Tyler places his head on his daddy's shoulder, and Maddie grabs the baby monitor. Quietly, she moves past us, and we follow her into the living room.

"I missed you all so much," I say as I sit on the couch.

"Well, it's not too late to move back and live with us." Maddie flashes a knowing grin.

I look at her incredulously, and Liam chuckles, then goes to the kitchen.

Maddie shrugs. "Well, it doesn't hurt to try. How long are you staying?" She glances over at my small bag on the floor.

"I fly out tomorrow afternoon. Have to be back at work on Wednesday morning."

She lifts an eyebrow. "How's Gemma?"

I scoff, shaking my head. "You're relentless."

"What do you expect? You tease me about this mystery woman, and then when I ask, you don't give me any details, only crumbs of information. You're like a vault and should be glad I don't live closer."

"Oh, I am. There's no doubt you'd infiltrate her group of friends just to learn all the Gemma gossip."

"I'm still waiting for you to give me your sister's phone number. We'd be besties, I'm sure of it. Then she'd tell me all I need to know."

"You probably would. Maybe I *should* give you her number. You might like her so much that you'd consider moving to Alabama. You'd love Lawton Ridge. Everyone knows everyone. Plus, you'd go crazy in Everleigh's boutique."

"I'm following her Facebook page," she admits.

My eyes go wide. "Really?"

"Oh yeah. When I googled her name, it popped up. I've already bought like five fall T-shirts online. And a coffee mug. And a candle. And a few bracelets. I'm kinda addicted." She snorts, then lowers her voice. "I'm a lot addicted. Don't tell Liam."

"Damn. Didn't realize you were so basic," I mock, knowing damn well she's the poster child.

She throws a pillow at me. "Basic?"

"Bet you're counting down the days till pumpkin spice season," I say, tossing it back at her. "Tell me I'm wrong."

"Well...*maybe*. But who doesn't love pumpkin spice!"

Tyler runs into the living room and giggles. We both look at him. "Mama funny."

She picks him up, then tickles his tummy. "No, you're funny."

As Tyler's laughter fills the living room, Liam returns. "There you are! Made you lunch, buddy."

Liam takes him from Maddie's arms, then carries him to the kitchen.

Once we're alone, Maddie shoots me a death glare. "You're not leaving this house until you tell me about Gemma."

"What are you gonna do? Keep me hostage?"

"I just might, Tyler Blackwood. Plus, I birthed a tiny human, so the very least you can do is appease me while I suffer with raw nipples and explosive diapers!"

"Ahh, Mads!" I put my palms to my ears as she doubles over with laughter.

I can hear Liam chatting with Tyler about dinosaur chicken nuggets and wish I could trade places with him right now.

"See, don't you feel sorry for me? Now, give me all the details." She pouts, sticking out her lower lip, and even though it's pathetic, it works.

"She's engaged, Mads. Getting married in only a few months," I explain. "There's nothing I can do about that but sit back and watch it all happen."

With a huff, she crosses her arms. "Wrong! You can steal her away and go live up on a hill in your little Southern town and have a handful of babies. Preferably girls so when our kids grow up, they can get married."

I snort. "Trust me when I say my life isn't and won't ever be like one of your Hallmark movies."

"It could be if you weren't so stubborn. Have you met her fiancé yet?"

I nod. "Unfortunately."

"And how does she act around him? Are they all lovey-dovey with gross PDA, or does she act like she can't stand the sight of him?"

Maddie's not going easy on me, but I know avoiding her questions isn't an option, either. "She acts…awkward. I don't know how to explain it. Uncomfortable might be a better way to describe it."

She contemplates my words. "Regularly?"

I think back to the times I've seen Gemma around Robert and nod. "Yeah."

Maddie taps her pointer finger on her lips. "I need your sister's number now. Gonna get this shit figured out."

"Detective Maddie to the rescue." I roll my eyes. "Gemma's too committed at this point to break it off. Even if she doesn't love him—which is the conclusion Everleigh and I have drawn—Gemma's very loyal."

"Just like you," she retorts. "When Sophie dated that psycho, she acted weird too. We'd invite her places, and she'd come up with excuses for why she couldn't. When we did hang out, I could tell my sister was in love with the idea of getting married, but that's about it. Maybe it's kinda the same thing."

"It could be. Apparently, he's jealous of me."

She lets out a hearty laugh. "Of course, he is. Have you seen *you*?"

Before Maddie can say anything else, tiny cries come from the baby monitor. "Feeding time." She gets up. "I'll be right back."

I'm grateful to have some silence to think about how Gemma acts around Robert. She promised she'd tell me if something wasn't right. I just hope she stays true to her word. Liam explained what happened to Sophie and the guy she was engaged to, and how it ended tragically. I refuse to allow that to happen to Gemma. I'd go back to prison if Robert threatened her life because I would stop him. Even if I can't admit it to her, she means too much to me.

Liam returns with Tyler beside him. He's more awake and talking a lot more. When he walks up to me, he has a fire truck in his hand. "Look!"

"Wow, that's cool," I say as he hands it over to me.

"People." He points his little finger at the window, then shoves it in my face so I can see them inside.

"Oh wow. There are!"

Tyler giggles, and I can tell he'll be just as outgoing as Maddie when he's older. "I have more." He runs off, and I can hear his feet pounding against the carpet.

"You've opened a can of worms now," Liam warns me, sitting down next to me. "So how long are you here for?"

"Only a day. My flight leaves tomorrow afternoon."

"Not long enough, but I'm so glad you're here, man. I've missed you," he admits.

"Yeah, me too. I've missed kicking your ass in the gym, too," I taunt, which causes him to snort.

"You wish! But I'm glad I re-joined. Just going before work three times a week has helped me gain some muscle. Need to lose this baby weight." He chuckles, patting his six-pack.

"Proud of you," I say, just as Maddie walks in holding Tobias.

"You wanna hold him?" she asks, stepping closer.

I can't remember the last time I held a baby. Maddie doesn't really give me a choice, though, before she's putting him in my arms. I cradle him as he stirs lightly and can't help smiling at the little guy. He has his entire life ahead of him, and I put a little wish up in the universe that the world is kinder to him than it was to me. With parents like his, though, I have no doubt he'll get the love and support he needs to thrive in life.

I watch Tobias with a grin, and when I look up, Maddie and Liam are smiling at us.

"Yep, now it's your turn to have a few mini-yous," she declares. "Make me an auntie."

"Don't get any ideas, Mads. It takes two people to make babies," I say softly. "Not to mention, it helps if you're dating or married."

"Don't tell her that. She'll be setting you up on blind dates in Lawton Ridge. The power of the internet," Liam says.

"Now that's an idea!" Maddie beams. "Need to get you on a dating app, STAT."

I roll my eyes, trying to ignore her, but it's so damn hard when she's steadily talking shit.

Tyler comes back with a bag full of trucks and smacks them down on my leg.

"Gotta be careful around your brother, sweetie. Don't get too close." Maddie walks over and places his toys on the couch next to me instead.

After a few more minutes, Maddie takes Tobias, and Tyler zeros in on me. He climbs on the sofa and takes out each truck, stacking them on my legs until I'm covered. It's the cutest thing I've ever seen, and it makes me wish we lived closer. I plan to visit more, though, especially since Maddie and Liam are determined to pop out kids every couple of years.

I'm so damn thankful Serena suggested I surprise them with a visit. For the rest of the afternoon, we hang out and catch up. I play with Tyler and keep him occupied so Maddie and Liam can tend to the baby.

When dinnertime comes around, I volunteer to cook. Maddie demands I make Cajun chicken pasta, so I do. Once we're done eating and Tyler's tucked into bed, Liam grabs a couple of beers, and we sit out on the patio until after the sun goes down. We talk about old times, and I realize even more how much I've missed his company. I go to bed with a smile on my face, which is a stark difference from only twenty-four hours ago.

The next morning, I wake up and make breakfast—biscuits, country gravy, sausage, and eggs. Maddie's in love with it all and demands I stay, which sounds just like my sister.

After Liam and I clean the kitchen, I realize it's almost time for me to go to the airport. Just mentioning I need to go has Maddie emotional. Once I'm packed, I give her a hug goodbye, and she squeezes me tight.

"You better come back and visit us!"

"I will," I promise.

"And bring Gemma with you," she adds when we break apart.

"Sure. I'll make sure her fiancé comes too. It'll be a big ole threesome," I mock.

"We better get on the road," Liam interrupts.

I give Tyler a high five, then Liam and I leave. There's no traffic, so we arrive at the airport earlier than expected.

As I grab my bag from the back seat, Liam speaks up, "Our house is always open to you, Tyler. Don't be a stranger."

"I won't. But hey, when Tobias is a little older, y'all come visit me so I can show you around. Wouldn't suggest coming in the summer, though, unless you wanna have a heatstroke." I chuckle at the memories of Liam telling me stories of Maddie being pregnant all summer and how miserable she was.

"Yeah, maybe someday. I'll miss you, bro," Liam tells me as I step out of his SUV.

"You too. We'll keep in touch," I vow, then walk inside.

Goodbyes are always the hardest, especially when I'm leaving people I love, which is probably why I try to avoid saying them. Before I board, I text Everleigh and remind her when my flight lands. While I hate to leave my friends in Sacramento, I'm happy to be going back to Lawton Ridge—a sentiment I never thought I'd feel.

CHAPTER TWENTY-THREE

GEMMA

When I climb into Robert's car, my skin feels like it's melting off my body. I'm ready to internally combust after Victoria dropped the bomb that our wedding has been moved up. Robert thinks he's so cunning, but I see through this act, and I'm disgusted I fell for it. When Winnie messaged me more than usual this weekend, it should've raised some red flags. I went from talking to her every other week to getting questions every ten minutes. It all makes perfect sense now.

During the drive to his house, Robert goes on and on about how excited he is that Victoria's interested in his company. I don't respond to anything he says and just stare out the window. Instead, I get lost in my thoughts, wishing I was anywhere but here. When we pull into his driveway, he notices I'm not playing the part of the ecstatic fiancée. After client dinners, he loves to have his ego stroked, but I'm not in the mood tonight. Too many revelations have come to light, and I'm questioning our relationship in a way I never have before.

Over the past few months, I've seen glimpses of this side of him, but I always made excuses for his behavior. I'd blame it on his drinking or jealousy, but an underlying issue exists that's bigger than I ever imagined. It's frightening not to truly know who he is, and I hope I haven't been scammed into marrying a man who doesn't exist. Though a part of me should've seen this coming, considering how pushy he's been. I'm so stupid for falling for his manipulative ways.

"What's wrong, darling?" he asks as he yanks my weekend bag from the back seat. Without waiting for my response, because it's not as if he cares anyway, he gets out of the car. I grab my purse, then follow him to the front door. I need to figure out how to bring up the receipt I found for the private investigator and list my other grievances, but it won't be easy. The last time I complained, he listened, but then nothing changed.

Once we're inside the house and the door closes behind me, my emotions nearly boil over.

"How could you move the date of the wedding without consulting me first?" I finally blurt out. "That completely blindsided me tonight. It was disrespectful for me to have to find out from a stranger instead of my fiancé."

Robert sits on the couch and slips off his shoes. "For weeks, I've asked you about it, and you've been indecisive. I understand you've been under a lot of pressure, which I assume is because you work with a criminal, so I'll give you some slack. I can't imagine how stressful that is for you, not knowing if it's safe or if you're being robbed blind. But I digress. Instead of adding more to your plate, I made the decision for *us*, something I'll be doing *a lot* of when we're married."

My mouth falls open at his pitiful attempt to throw jabs at me, but he doesn't seem to notice or care. I refuse to entertain him or argue about any of this because we have much bigger issues at hand. I'm well aware that Robert will continue to throw this in my face until I bend to his will, but quitting the garage isn't up for negotiation, and I've made that crystal clear.

"The last thing I want is for the happiest day of your entire life —*our wedding*—to cause any anguish, Gemma. I thought if I moved the date and took care of the major things, you wouldn't have to worry about it. And you said so yourself, you'll be ready, so I took care of your dress and veil as well. Everything's in place. Winnie's paid and so is the venue. Invitations are going out soon."

"My wedding dress?" My blood is pumping so hard, I think I can hear my heartbeat echoing in my head. I'm tempted to pinch myself to make sure I'm not living in some weird nightmare because this can't be real. He's officially crossed the line, and he is delusional if he thinks I'm going along with this.

I want to slap the smug look off his face. Robert tilts his head and smiles, but it's not kind nor inviting. Instead, it's menacing, and his eyes are cold. It's like the curtain has been pulled back, and the man behind it all is evil.

"Of course, Gemma. I'm sure you haven't planned anything with Everleigh and Katie like you said."

"Well, not yet but—"

"I knew you hadn't, so I did it for you. I'm sure they're both too busy trying to support themselves since they don't have men to provide for them. So, I felt this was a better alternative, considering your mother is no longer here, and you have no one else of importance in your life." He stares at me, and I feel as if I'm suffocating. Mentioning my mother is just so goddamn cruel. I've voiced my dread of not having her with me on such a monumental day. *Bastard.*

"It wasn't your decision to make," I seethe.

"Well, I figured it was best for you. I even found a tailor to adjust my mother's wedding dress to fit you based on some clothes you left here. Only the absolute best for my bride!" he proudly boasts.

My expression doesn't change, which causes his helpful husband persona to quickly fade.

"You can thank me *now*," he snaps.

I finally catch my breath from the whiplash he's just given me. "You want me to thank you for what you've done? Have you lost your mind?" I walk toward my bag, and Robert rushes to stand. He stalks toward me with annoyance on his face. Wrapping his fingers around my wrist, he jerks me toward the couch and forces me to sit. I can't believe I agreed to marry such a controlling, manipulative man.

"Take me home," I demand, wishing I would've driven myself.

Throwing his head back, he lets out a boom of a laugh as he sits next to me, but instead of it being welcoming, it forces a chill up my spine. "Not fucking happening."

I try to wiggle from his grasp, but he doesn't let go. Instead, he only holds me tighter. My anger rises, and I grit down, holding my tongue as I try to figure out how I'm going to get the hell out of here. My phone is in my purse across the room.

My thoughts are a jumbled mess, but I need to calm down to think clearly.

"The plan was for you to sleep over and stay with me, so you will. I won't be taking you anywhere but to my bedroom. Would you like a drink?"

He gets up, but I don't dare move, too scared to make any sudden movements. Robert goes to the kitchen, then comes back with a scotch on the rocks and settles in the chair in front of me.

Sitting straighter, I plead, "Please take me home. We can discuss this tomorrow after you've had some time to calm down."

He chuckles darkly, then drinks half the glass. "Don't you fucking listen? The answer is no. Quit trying to defy me, Gemma. It's an ugly look for you."

"I can't do this," I tell him, breathlessly. "I can't do *this* anymore."

"*This*, as in what? The wedding is set for November. You will not fucking embarrass me."

"There will be no wedding, Robert. Call it off, immediately." The words tumble out of my mouth, and I can't stop from saying what I want.

Robert charges toward me. Quickly, I run to my purse and manage to pull out my phone. He chases after me and grabs my hair, pulling me back. My scalp burns from the tug, and I scream out in pain before pushing him away. Angry tears stream down my cheeks as I hurry to the kitchen. I pull a knife from the block and point the blade at him. When I cooked last, it was sharp enough to slice through meat with no issue, so I hope he doesn't make me use it.

"Don't you take another step toward me." I hold it tightly in my grasp, my hand shaking from the adrenaline.

He's in a blind rage, so my threats don't faze him. He takes a step, holding out his hands as if he's surrendering, but I'm not fooled. I try to unlock my phone but fumble. If I can text Everleigh with one hand, then maybe she can come get me. Seconds later, Robert rushes after me. The sudden movement startles me, and I drop my phone and the blade.

He grabs me, squeezing my shoulders so hard that I screech. "You need to stop being a selfish bitch, Gemma."

My phone rings, and the high-pitched tone nearly pierces my ears. Everleigh's photo flashes on the screen, and I whisper a little prayer, hoping she won't give up on getting in touch with me. "I need to answer that."

Another dark chuckle escapes him.

I try to push away, and he grabs my dress, ripping the thin material of the sleeve from the hem. I look down, then back at him. "If you think we're getting married, you're crazier than I thought. The wedding is off, Robert. So do what you have to do to cancel everything."

My phone rings again. "Over *your* dead body," he hisses.

"I told Everleigh that I'm staying at your house tonight, so she knows I'm with you. She won't stop calling until I pick up," I force out, needing to place some fear in him. His image means too much, and if Everleigh catches wind of this, the entire town will know what he did to me by the end of the week. My phone buzzes again, and Robert finally lets me go. I eagerly grab it, but he watches my every move as if he's waiting to pounce if I say the wrong thing.

"You better watch what you fucking tell her," he seethes, crossing his arms over his broad chest. His shirt is still tucked into his slacks, and the sneer hasn't vanished from his lips.

"Babe! Everything okay? You sent me a bunch of gibberish in a text," Everleigh asks as soon as I answer.

Robert picks up the knife, and I'm afraid of what he's capable of doing. The light reflects off the blade as he looks at it, then glances at me. The man I agreed to marry isn't who's standing in front of me, trying to force my hand at marriage and threaten me. I try to steady my tone, but I hope to God Everleigh reads between the lines.

"I'm perfectly fine," I say calmly, and Robert nods, giving me his tacit approval. Robert places the knife in the sink and stalks past me, grabbing his scotch and finishing it before pouring another.

Adrenaline rushes through me like a strong wind in a narrow canyon.

"What's wrong?" she asks.

"Everything's great. Dinner was amazing," I say, forcing myself to smile when I speak so at least he thinks I'm trying.

"No, it's not. I can tell by the shakiness in your voice. Where are you? Robert's house?"

I laugh, pretending we're having a much different conversation.

"Of course. We'll do dinner there one night soon after you get off work. The bisque was incredible. The best I've ever had."

"Now I know something is wrong since you're holding a one-sided conversation," she says seriously, and I'm relieved she understands what I'm doing.

"Right, I must've texted by accident when I threw it in my purse." I keep up the act, which pleases the monster who hasn't taken his eyes from me.

"Alright, I'm coming to get you," she reassures. "Something's wrong. I'm bringing my pepper spray." I hear her walking, accompanied by the dangling of her keys. I'm thankful she's so observant even when I don't want her to be. Otherwise, I might not have escaped him tonight.

"Thank you," I say. "Yeah, brunch tomorrow sounds great. Thanks for checking on me."

"I'll be there as soon as I can. Hang tight, okay?" she adds at the end, then lingers for a few seconds. I don't say anything, and my silence speaks louder than my words ever could.

"Great, talk to you later." I end the call.

"*Good girl*," Robert coos. "Now we've got some things to discuss, don't we?"

I check the clock on my phone and hope Everleigh hurries. When she shows up unexpectedly, Robert won't be able to force me to stay. I want to get the hell out of here as quickly as possible before he hurts me again. The way he's acting makes me think he will, if needed.

"Alright." I sit on the edge of the couch, counting down the minutes.

"The wedding will happen, Gemma. You've already committed. You know how I feel about people who back out of contracts, and when you accepted my proposal, you verbally agreed to be my wife. So, it's happening, and things will move forward as discussed."

"Why did you have me followed?" I snap, ignoring his words.

He grins, not at all concerned that I found out. He's practiced the doting husband act so much that he can switch it on and off so easily. That's more terrifying than his words could ever be. "Followed? I'm not sure what you're talking about, sweetheart." He tilts his head back and takes a large gulp of his scotch.

"I saw the receipt in your desk for the private investigator you hired. When I called you all panicked about someone following me, you didn't seem concerned, and it's because you were behind it all along. What's wrong with you? What kind of man hires someone to stalk the woman he supposedly loves and trusts?"

Robert charges toward me. I want to get up and run away, but it's no use. I try to act as if I'm not threatened by his sudden movement and keep a straight face. He doesn't seem to like that reaction either and pushes me down until my back is against the couch. With his strength, he forces my arms over my head and straddles me. His face is inches from mine, and the scotch on his breath smells rotten.

"It's time for us to be honest with each other, isn't it?"

I blink up at him through the tears forming in my eyes.

"I don't fucking trust you," he says roughly, adding more pressure to my wrists. He's heavy and too strong for me to break free.

"Get off me!" I scream. "You're *hurting* me."

He moves his face even closer. "You think I'm stupid? You lied about your past with Tyler. Didn't think I'd find out you two used to be a hot item, huh? I know about it, Gemma. The whole goddamn town does too," he snarls.

"Stop it," I cry out, fighting against his hold and jerking my body. "Robert, stop!"

It doesn't faze him as he squeezes his knees tighter into my ribs. "I knew about you and him before he returned. Then he conveniently started working at the garage, so when I asked, I wanted to hear the truth from your lips. Being my future wife, I thought you'd share everything with me, but you acted like there was nothing to tell. So you left me no choice. I had to ensure my assets were protected."

I snap my eyes, wishing this would end. "What assets?"

"*You.* Gemma. You're my property. I knew it would only be a matter of time before you fucked him. I arranged for you and your little *friend* to be watched for weeks. I have a handful of photos of you two flirting, and it makes me so fucking sick. Everyone sees the way he looks at you, and the way you eye fuck him when he's around you. So goddamn embarrassing," Robert hisses before trying to force his mouth against mine, but I turn my head. I don't want his lips anywhere near me.

"Why are you even with me then?" I wiggle against his hold. "There's no trust between us, so it's time to end it."

"I'll never let you go, Gemma," he growls. "Not unless one of us is dead. Don't you fucking get that by now?" he snaps, his eyes darkening with every word.

"No!" I scream. "It's over."

"It's not. And I'm only gonna tell you this only once, Gemma. You need to be *very* fucking careful. And so should Tyler."

"What's that supposed to mean?" I say, tears spilling down my cheeks.

"Exactly what you think it means." He tsks, sliding his body down mine.

"Get off me!" I'm brought back to being eleven years old when the boys picked on me at recess. Lifting my knee, I plant it right between his legs. Robert grunts, and I push him to the floor. "You cunt," he breathes out, holding his crotch.

I'm breathing hard, my chest heaving as Robert manages to stand.

"Just stop," I beg. "Please, stop." I create space between us, ready to run out the front door. If his neighbors heard us arguing on his perfectly landscaped lawn, Robert would die of a heart attack because the rumors would fly. He'd do anything to avoid being the talk of the town.

"Don't you go anywhere," he orders as if he read my mind. "Sit. Right now." He talks to me as if I'm a child, and I guess in his mind, I am one. Only wanting to temporarily appease him, I do.

Before I can open my mouth to rebut his threats, the doorbell rings followed by rapid knocking. Robert narrows his eyes at me. "What have you fucking done?" he hisses.

Robert moves toward the door, and I take the opportunity to grab my shit. I hear Everleigh ask where I am, and Robert lies that I'm taking a bath. She doesn't believe his bullshit and barges past him. Once Everleigh sees me, she grabs my hand, then pulls me through the house.

"You're not going anywhere!" Robert shouts.

"Fuck off," I throw at him as Everleigh rushes us toward the door.

"If you leave, I promise you'll regret this," he warns as I walk outside. The warm air feels amazing on my skin. The front door slamming behind us startles me, and I'm tempted to look over my shoulder, but Everleigh maintains her fast pace toward her car that she's left running.

She opens the passenger door, and I climb inside. As the adrenaline subsides, I begin to break down, overwhelmed by my emotions. He has no idea how much I regret agreeing to marry him. Everleigh hops in the driver's side, and my body begins to shake. She glances at my torn dress and frowns. Seconds later, she backs out of the driveway. Silence fills the ride to her house, which I'm grateful for.

When we pull into Everleigh's driveway, she turns and looks at me. "I know this is a stupid question, but are you okay?"

I clear my throat and find my inner strength. "I'm not sure," I say honestly. "I'm safe tonight, thanks to you, but I don't know how Robert will retaliate tomorrow."

CHAPTER TWENTY-FOUR

TYLER

Waking up in Lawton Ridge without a target on my back is such a relief. Now that it's starting to feel like home again, I actually miss it when I'm gone. It just sucks that Gemma can hardly stand being around me. Ever since we lost control with each other two weeks ago and she said it was a huge mistake, things between us have been awkward. It doesn't help that her fiancé hates me, and she constantly makes excuses for his behavior. Though my heart says otherwise, keeping my distance is the best decision for us both.

I last saw Gemma five days ago. Just when the tension started to evaporate between us, Ruby showed up, and I saw the jealousy written on Gemma's face. I have no idea what to expect when I see her today, but maybe if I pretend everything's fine, she'll actually talk to me again.

After Everleigh picked me up from the airport last night, I could tell something was wrong. She looked exhausted as if she'd hadn't been sleeping. Of course, my sister was sealed like a vault and claimed it was nothing, but I knew better.

This morning, I skipped the gym and slept in because I am still drained from the weekend. It was awesome seeing Liam and Maddie. Though I'm not sure when I'll visit again, I hope it's sooner than later. When I walk into work, Gemma's behind the counter typing away on the computer.

Immediately, I head toward the coffee and fill a cup.

"You're back," she mutters, but I can't read her expression.

I feel bad for not telling her I'd be gone, but we weren't exactly on speaking terms. Considering I can't forget how sweet she tasted and how tight her pussy squeezed my fingers, it takes all my willpower not to stare at her mouth and replay the memory in my mind.

"I am." I grab some sugar, needing the extra boost. "Ya miss me?"

Smirking, I turn around, and when her bloodshot gaze meets mine, I can tell she's been crying. The dark circles under her eyes are prevalent, and her cheeks are blotchy. While she's still the most beautiful woman I've ever seen, she looks like someone ran over her dog. When I add in how Everleigh was acting last night, I'm concerned.

"Gemma," I murmur and walk toward her. "Are you okay? What happened?" Leaning over the counter, I check her body for marks.

Tears well in her eyes as she shakes her head.

"Did he hit you?" My stomach tightens at the thought of that asshole laying another finger on her.

"No," she whispers, glancing around to make sure Jerry isn't listening.

"Tell me," I demand.

Gemma swallows hard, then bows her head. I watch as she wipes away the tears that unintentionally spill over. "Not here. After work?" When she composes herself and lifts her head, I notice how broken she is.

"Sure. You want me to come over so we can talk in private?"

My blood boils as I imagine what that fucker did to her. I've never seen her this upset, and the urge to find and use him as a human punching bag takes over.

Gemma licks her lips. "You sure that'd be appropriate? Your girlfriend wouldn't mind?"

I arch a brow. "Girlfriend?" This is news to me.

"Ruby," she clarifies. "Or whatever she is to you."

Brushing a hand over my scruffy jaw, I hide the amused smirk behind my fingers. "Yeah, I'm pretty sure she'll be cool with it." It's comical, considering Ruby would be far more interested in her or my sister. Too bad she can't see that Ruby and I are only friends and the only woman I want is sitting in front of me.

Gemma nods. "I should meet you at Everleigh's. It's not safe for you to come to my house."

"Are *you* safe?"

She glances around, focusing on the front windows. "Everleigh knows what's going on, so it'll be better if we talk there."

"Gemma." I lower my voice.

She snaps her eyes to mine as if she's seen a ghost. She goes pale, and terror washes over her face.

"Why isn't it safe?"

"I'll tell you later, but the short story is Robert hired the private investigator who followed me. I don't know if they still are, but I refuse to give Robert any more reasons to come after you."

Pfft. I'd like to see him try.

"You're sure it was him?" I was certain Victoria was behind it, but it makes sense if he feels that threatened by me.

"Positive. I found the receipts."

I tap my knuckles on the counter and try to control the rage building inside me.

"Tyler…" My name comes out as a strained whisper. "He *knows* about us."

I blink hard, my heart racing in my chest. "Knows what?"

We haven't been an *us* in twelve years, and other than the make-out session misstep, we've kept our distance.

"That we dated."

"So?" I shrug. "That was long before you two got together. Why does it matter?"

Gemma cheeks flush as she chews on her bottom lip. "I didn't tell him we had a history when he asked questions about you. Someone must've told him, or he paid to get the information, but it's not as though we were a secret. When I brushed off that you were working at the garage, he hired a PI. He said he didn't trust me and wanted to keep an eye on me. Robert's convinced it was only a matter of time."

"Until what?" I ask, crossing my arms over my chest.

"Until we…" She clears her throat and stands straighter. "Until I was unfaithful to him. I don't think he knows what happened recently, but he's suspicious enough to have us followed."

I roll my eyes at the audacity of this asshole.

"I told him I wanted out," she softly declares almost as if she's afraid to say the words aloud.

Thank God. Her confession has my entire body buzzing. I wish I could round the counter, pull her into my arms, and tell her she's safe with me. But instead, I keep my hands and admissions to myself.

"*Good.* You deserve better, Gemma."

"Yeah," she whispers. "He was pissed. Robert won't let me go without a fight."

"Well, I hope you told him to fuck off because if he harasses you again, I won't be as nice as I was at the bar."

That causes a slight smile to curl her lips. "He doesn't use his fists, Tyler. He throws money at his problems and pays people to do his dirty work."

"Pussy," I mutter, causing Gemma to chuckle. "Alright, well don't eat before you come over. I'll make dinner."

"You don't have to go to any trouble, Tyler," she insists, but she's crazy if she thinks I'm not gonna use this opportunity to cook for her again.

"Cooking for you is never trouble." I flash her a wink.

The front door opens, and when I look over my shoulder, I see it's a customer.

"We better get back to work," she says, smiling at the woman behind me.

"'Kay. See ya later. Holler if you need anything, okay?"

"I will."

A thousand thoughts fill my head as I walk into the shop.

She called off the wedding.

And not because I asked her to.

Robert's a douche and sabotaged himself. I couldn't be happier about it either.

Even if Gemma's single right now, it doesn't mean things will be any easier between us. It's still really complicated. Though I can't stop thinking about the way her body responded when I touched her. It brought back memories of the summer we spent together, memories that saved me during my darkest days. That same spark between us is sizzling just as hot as before, but we're different people now. No matter what, Gemma needs time to heal her broken heart, and I just hope she'll let me help.

As much as I want to swoop her into my arms and claim her as mine, I won't rush anything. I tried staying away, but I'm not wasting this second chance to be with her. When she's ready, I'll be here waiting.

"Mornin'," Jerry says, handing me a sheet of paper. "Glad you're back."

"Me, too." I study the list of everything that needs to be done today. "I'll get right to work."

"Thanks, son. Been hectic without ya here, and it's only gettin' busier."

"Don't worry, we'll catch up." I flash him a smirk, and he smiles. I wonder if Gemma told him about her and Robert.

As I go through my to-do orders, I think about what to make this evening. I never asked her what she thought of the chili I made at her place. Tonight, I'd like to surprise her with something special. Even though we won't be alone and it won't be a date, she deserves it after the past few days she's had.

"Jerry." I walk up to him before my lunch break. "What's Gemma's favorite dish?"

His lips pinch together as he studies me.

Quickly, I add, "She and my sister are having a girls' night, and I offered to cook. So I was wondering if you could help a guy out."

That makes him chuckle, and his shoulders relax. "Shrimp and grits."

Grinning, I nod. "Thanks. I'll see what I can do."

"You can't go wrong with biscuits and gravy, either," he tells me.

"Is her favorite dessert still red velvet cake?"

"Sure is."

Good to know.

"Thanks. Sounds like I'll be putting my cooking skills to the test later," I say with a laugh. It's been a while since I've made seafood.

Jerry steps around me but not without a strong pat on the back. "Just remember she's an engaged woman."

I swallow hard and straighten my stance so he doesn't notice the tension in my shoulders. "I'm well aware."

Without another word, he walks away.

He definitely doesn't know about their current situation, and I won't be the one to disappoint the man. According to Everleigh, Jerry's tremendously supportive of Gemma marrying Robert. When he learns it ended, he'll probably want to point fingers at *someone*.

I head to the break room and pull out my phone to text my sister.

Tyler: Gemma told me she and Robert broke up. She didn't give me all the details. We're gonna talk at your place tonight. That okay?

I set my cell on the table and grab the leftovers I brought. Everleigh made some sort of mystery meat the other day, and I didn't want it to go to waste. I take a sniff and decide to give it a shot.

Moments later, she responds.

Everleigh: That's fine. Just brace yourself, it was a bad situation.

Tyler: What do you mean?

My blood pressure rises.

Everleigh: I picked her up from his house on Monday night, and he didn't want her to go. Told her she'd be sorry if she did.

That motherfucker.

Tyler: Jesus Christ. No wonder she's still upset.

Everleigh: She was in pretty bad shape emotionally yesterday, so I was hoping she'd be a little better today.

Tyler: She said he hired a PI to follow us.

Everleigh: Yep. Robert wasn't even sorry about it.

I don't wish ill will toward many people, but he and Victoria are tied for the top spot.

Tyler: Fucking bullshit. I should've punched his face in when I had the chance.

Everleigh: He's not worth it. I only hope Gemma sticks to her guns and doesn't go back to him.

Tyler: You think she would?

Everleigh: Honestly, I don't know.

That thought puts a bad taste in my mouth before I even get a chance to try my food. The moment I do, my eyes go wide.

"Hey," Gemma says, walking toward me with a bag. "I got a couple of subs from the deli. Want one?"

I swallow down my bite and nearly gag. "Yes, please."

Putting the lid back on the container, Gemma moves it away and chuckles. "Everleigh can't cook."

"I'm realizing this."

She hands me one of the sandwiches.

"That's why she was so willing to let me live with her. She needed a chef in the house."

Gemma grins as she unwraps her food. "She lives off protein bars and smoothies from the cafe."

"Hopefully, we'll all be eating like kings tonight."

She pops a brow. "Really? Whatcha making?"

"It's a surprise. Just come hungry."

"Don't worry, I will. I haven't eaten much over the past couple of days," she admits with a frown.

"Everleigh told me she picked you up from his house. What happened?"

"Is it okay if we don't talk about it right now? I'll tell you everything after work."

"Of course. I'm sorry to bring it up again. What do you wanna chat about?" I ask, then take a large bite of the warm bread and meat.

"Where were you?"

Should've seen that coming. Not that it's a secret, but I want to keep that part of my life as far away from Gemma as possible.

"Vegas," I exhale. "Had some old business to take care of."

"Everleigh told me that much."

I nod, then narrow my eyes at her concerned expression. "What?"

"Nothing." She shakes her head, but I continue watching her, not buying it. "It's just, I was worried. You have a history in Vegas, and it was suspicious when you just up and left."

Studying her sweet features, I grin. "I had something to do for an old friend. That's it." I don't go into detail because I want to put it all behind me. "You have nothing to worry about, I promise."

That causes her to flash me a smile. "Glad to hear that."

The room grows silent as we finish eating. The color has returned to her cheeks, and she doesn't seem as distressed as she was this morning. Though I can tell the shit with Robert still weighs heavily on her.

Wanting to put her in a better mood, I bring something up that will have her laughing.

"Do you remember talking about the movie *13 Going on 30* in one of your letters?"

She chokes but quickly recovers. "Oh my God. How do you remember that? I was like what, fifteen?"

"You were obsessed with the romantic comedies of the early 2000s."

"Still am, mostly." She chuckles with a shrug. "How crazy to think I was dying to be an adult, and now here I am, wishing I could turn back time and be a naïve teenager again."

"It's funny how that works out, isn't it? Always eager to grow up until you realize adults don't have it figured out either."

"I swore my dad knew everything. It wasn't until I was much older that I realized he was just winging it like the rest of us."

"If you could go back to any age and relive it, when would you pick?" I ask, and when she lowers her head, I realize it's a really stupid question.

"You won't like my answer," she states, meeting my eyes.

"Sorry, forget it. I wasn't—"

"As much as I'd like to say falling in love with you was worth the pain of you leaving, I'd be lying if I hadn't wondered what it would've been like to never have fallen for you in the first place. There were years of sadness when I questioned why I wasn't enough for you to stay or come back."

Fuck.

"Gemma," I say softly, reaching for her hand resting on the table. "Nothing I say will take away what I did, but I'm so damn sorry I left the way I did. I had a lot of shit in my life that I needed to figure out, and I couldn't do it here. I wanted you to come with me," I remind her. "But I knew you couldn't. You had your own life to figure out, too."

She nods with sadness in her eyes. "I understand that. I just wish you'd have been able to come home two years ago. Life would be so different now."

Two years ago. Before she met Robert.

"I wish a lot was different, Gemma. However, if I've learned anything in the past five years, it's that we don't get to deal our own cards. We have to take the hand we're dealt and do the best we can with it."

Gemma squeezes my fingers. "I've discovered a lot about myself recently. The reality of some things I don't like, but some, I do. I've never been good at standing up for myself because I'm a people pleaser. Now, I'm learning what my limits are and how I need to set higher standards. The way I allowed Robert to constantly treat me makes me sick. That relationship should've never lasted more than a month."

"So why did it?" I ask, relieved she's realized that she deserves better.

She shrugs, resting her chin in her palm. "He said the right things and did stuff to impress me. Though it's embarrassing to admit, I was desperate for affection. And as pathetic as it sounds, he was the first guy since you who I actually felt *something* for. Stupid me didn't realize it was merely infatuation or lust. That quickly dissolved, but when he proposed, it was expected that I'd accept. Didn't help that it made my dad so damn happy. The happiest I'd seen him in years. Robert fed me the fantasy of being married and living a beautiful life together. It didn't click how manipulative and possessive he was because I was blinded by his promises. I never had a healthy relationship to look up to, so I thought it was normal."

Before I can respond, a whistling Jerry waltzes in, then immediately stops when his eyes land on our hands touching. Quickly, I pull back and turn away from Gemma, but there's no doubt he saw us. There's no denying that he thinks I'm a homewrecker.

"Hi, Daddy," Gemma greets with a smile. "How was lunch with George?"

"Fine," he grumbles, walking to the fridge, then grabbing a diet Coke. "How was yours?"

"Delicious," I interject. "Belinda makes a mean turkey and cheese."

Jerry slams the door and eyes me. "Back to work in fifteen."

"Yes, sir."

The room stays silent until he walks out, and we hear the shop door slam shut.

"Fuck, he's pissed."

"I haven't told him about Robert yet, so he thinks…"

"That I'm trying to seduce you so you'll leave your fiancé."

"Yeah, probably. I'm gonna have to spill the beans soon."

"Well…" I stand, then push in my chair. "Maybe sooner than later since I have to work with him. He's a nice guy and all, but I don't want to have to duck from tools being thrown at my head."

Gemma giggles with a smirk. "Promise. When the time's right, I'll tell him everything."

"Great. I'll wear a hard hat until then." I flash her a wink.

"Just tell him about Ruby and that he has nothing to worry about."

Does she seriously believe I'm with Ruby?

"Good point," I say, though I have no intention of doing that. "See you tonight around seven? Need to stop by the store and hit the shower first."

"Yep, see you then."

I throw my trash away, then brave the next four hours with a man who thinks I'm trying to steal his daughter away from her future husband.

This should be very interesting.

CHAPTER TWENTY-FIVE
GEMMA

The rest of the shift passes in a blink, and I can breathe again knowing Tyler's safely back in town. Though it's not my business, I'm not completely convinced he's staying in Lawton Ridge for good. A small voice in the back of my mind says it's only a matter of time until he leaves again. I wasn't enough for him then, so what makes me enough now? *Nothing.* He's explained himself several times, but it still hurts. I force away the self-deprecating thoughts and go home to take a shower before dinner.

For the past two days, I've felt like a hollow version of myself. When I replay what happened with Robert, it still seems like a nightmare. Because of his threats, my paranoia has been in overdrive. He's always been a man of his word, so I'm waiting for him to retaliate because he doesn't like not getting his way.

Once I'm inside my cottage, I release a deep breath, thankful nothing happened on my drive home. I hate how much power Robert's words have over me and knowing what he's capable of doing to me. Undoubtedly, he's planning something. He won't go down willingly.

I take a quick shower, then blow-dry my hair and put on some light makeup. My eyes are swollen from crying, and when I look in the mirror, I barely recognize my reflection. No man should ever make a woman feel so broken, and I hate that I've allowed him to.

Tyler said to come over around seven, so I try to keep my mind busy and tidy up in the meantime. My mind wanders as I think back to Monday and how I should've canceled dinner after I found that receipt. After everything, I should've predicted he'd react badly, so why did I put myself in that situation? Everleigh always joked that Robert seemed a little off, but now I wonder if she wasn't kidding.

I put a load of clothes in the washer, then fold the ones I left in the dryer yesterday. Once there's nothing else for me to do around the house, I leave. Arriving a little early will give Tyler and me the opportunity to have some privacy before Everleigh comes home.

My mouth goes dry when I see a black Suburban in my rearview mirror speeding around the cars behind me. Immediately, I press on the gas, trying to lose them.

"Fuck," I whisper under my breath when the light turns red. My heart rate quickens as I grab the steering wheel with white knuckles. The SUV stops next to me, and I keep my face forward until my curiosity gets the best of me. Looking over, I make eye contact with a woman who has fire red hair and a vehicle full of kids. I let out a relieved laugh because my fear created a totally different scenario.

During lunch yesterday, two dozen pink and yellow roses were delivered to the shop in a crystal vase. Even before reading the card, I knew they were from Robert. Anytime we have a fight, he sends me flowers and gifts. It's his way of showing or rather *buying* my love, and I used to fall for it too. I'd accept his apologies and excuses. *Not anymore.*

As soon as my father left to grab food, I opened the note. It simply stated the wedding would happen whether I liked it or not. Immediately, I grabbed the expensive vase and flowers, stormed outside, then threw them in the dumpster. Though I hated trashing something so pretty, what they represented made me sick to my stomach. The pungent smell of them stayed in my nose until I got home. It didn't take long for Robert to text me, asking why I got rid of them.

I should block his number, but it wouldn't stop him from finding ways to torment me.

I demanded he stop watching me and fucking leave me alone. The wedding isn't happening, and I won't change my mind. So, naturally, after yesterday's incident, my senses are in overdrive.

The light turns green, and I suck in a deep breath, shaking my head at myself. When I arrive at Everleigh's, I grow more anxious. I'm already on edge, but knowing I'm about to spill everything to Tyler makes it worse. Hopefully, wine joins this conversation because I need something to help take off the ledge. I get out of the car, check the street for anything out of the ordinary, then walk up the sidewalk.

Tyler opens the door wearing a sweet grin.

"Right on time," he kindly says, but I know I'm early. Once inside, I smell the hearty aroma of the spices. I sit at the bar as Tyler hurries to the stove.

"It's almost ready," he says, looking over his shoulder at me. When he moves around, I can't help but notice how his shirt hugs his muscles.

"What'd you cook?" I ask.

"Shrimp and grits."

"It's my favorite. You remembered?" I ask, surprised.

He chuckles, and the sound is inviting and warm. "I actually asked your dad."

"Great. He's really gonna think something's going on between us, especially after lunch today." I sigh, not sure how to bring up the conversation with my dad.

"Yeah, he made sure to remind me that you were engaged. Talk about awkward." Tyler stirs the shrimp and sauce.

"How mortifying. I'm so sorry." I cover my face.

"It's not a big deal."

Tyler pulls out the grit patties he roasted from the oven, covers them with foil, then sets them on the stovetop. The way he moves so comfortably in the kitchen is mesmerizing, and I'm thankful he pulls me away from my thoughts, even if it's briefly.

"Want something to drink?" he asks, pulling two wine glasses from the cabinet before I answer. "Everleigh's wine subscription box was delivered today, so there are a ton of choices. She won't mind." He winks.

After what happened on Monday and how she came to my rescue, I'm sure she wouldn't. Hell, she'd tell me to open two bottles. I choose a chardonnay, not sure if it pairs with our dinner, but not caring either. Unlike Robert, Tyler doesn't say shit about my choice. Instead, he happily unscrews the cork and fills our glasses.

When I'm around Tyler, I'm happier. There's no acting a part or being judged, and I can just be myself without those worries. Tyler makes me feel human again, and I appreciate the normalcy for once.

I take a sip of wine. "This is really good."

"Just wait until you try dinner. Once the shrimp is done, we can start eating, so it shouldn't be too much longer. Hopefully, Everleigh isn't late either." Tyler places a lid on the skillet as it simmers, then sits next to me. This conversation is happening, and there's no going back now.

"So…" he says, lingering. "I understand what happened with Robert isn't gonna be easy to repeat, so if you—"

I shake my head, not wanting him to continue. "I'm okay talking about it. I trust you, Tyler. I always have."

He smiles as he lifts his wine glass, and I tap mine against his before taking a big gulp. I explain each detail from the beginning from finding the receipt in Robert's desk to having his client congratulate us on getting married before the end of the year.

"Wait. He moved the wedding date without telling you?" Tyler asks, stunned.

"Yep. I didn't even know what to say, so I just sat through dinner in shock."

"And he just thought you'd go along with it?" he asks, standing to go to stir the roux, but then he comes right back.

"In his perfect world, he really did."

Next, I mention the wedding dress and invitations. With flared nostrils, his face distorts. My emotions are all over the place as I speak, so Tyler grabs my hand and squeezes. It's a friendly gesture, but it sets my body on fire.

"I was scared. No telling what would've happened if Everleigh hadn't come to get me. I've never seen him act that way before and handle me so aggressively. Thankfully, Everleigh called after getting a gibberish text message and knew something was wrong when I was finally able to answer her call. I was a mess when she brought me here." All she kept saying was how much she wanted to kick his ass and how sorry she was that it happened. The only person who should've been apologizing that night was Robert. After my tears dried up, we watched Hallmark until I couldn't keep my eyes open anymore. Friends like her are worth their weight in gold, and I'll never be able to repay her for rescuing me from that dangerous situation.

Tyler huffs, and his jaw tightens. "What he did to you isn't okay, Gemma."

His eyes pierce through me, and the only thing that pulls us away is Everleigh bursting through the door. She bolts toward me, wrapping me in a big hug. "I'm so glad you're here. Oh my God." She moves her nose around like a drug-sniffing dog. "What is that delicious smell?"

"Our dinner," Tyler responds.

Everleigh looks at me and releases an offended gasp. "He never cooks like this for me."

I beam and shrug. "I feel special."

Tyler plates our food and sets them in front of us. It's picture perfect with the garnish on top. The aromas make my mouth water, and I didn't realize how hungry I was until I take a bite. The grits nearly melt in my mouth, and the shrimp and sauce are cooked perfectly.

"Whoever you end up with is in for a treat," Everleigh says around a mouthful.

"I'm sure Ruby is happy she found a man who can cook," I say, trying to keep my voice level so they can't hear the jealousy in my tone.

Everleigh snorts, and her eyes go wide. "Wait, what? You think Tyler's dating Ruby?" Everleigh nearly doubles over with laughter. Tyler joins in, but at least has the decency to try to hide it as he shoves food in his mouth.

Embarrassment washes over me as I watch their reactions. "Well, yeah? They're always together." Not to mention the scene I almost walked into the day I came over to talk to him, and they were both only wearing towels. I'm lost as I look between them. "What's so funny?"

Tyler smirks. "Because I'm not really Ruby's cup of tea, if you catch my drift. Everleigh would be, though."

Furrowing my brows, I let his words sink in as it finally hits me. My cheeks heat as I replay the way I've acted every time she was around, and the stupid things I've said to him regarding their relationship. "Now, I feel really stupid," I admit. "Why didn't you tell me when I called her your girlfriend!" I scold Tyler, but he just shrugs with a smirk. "Well, at least it wasn't out of the realm of possibilities. She's gorgeous and into working out like you are."

"The Blackwoods don't date, Gemma," Tyler states. "I mean, take Everleigh, for example, who spends her nights alone drinking. And well, my history is bleak."

"Hey!" Everleigh grimaces. "That's not fair. There aren't any decent single guys in this damn town." She pops a shrimp in her mouth. "But there *are* single women." She waggles her brows, taunting Tyler as he groans.

"Great, so you're in on Ruby's joke too." He rolls his eyes, sipping his wine. "Can we not have your sexless life be the topic of conversation tonight?"

Everleigh snorts. "As long as yours isn't either."

They glance my way, and just like that, the attention is back on me. "Or mine." I chuckle.

"So what's your plan?" Everleigh asks. "Has Robert contacted you since yesterday?"

"Yesterday?" Tyler snaps his eyes to mine. I hadn't gotten that far in the story.

"He sent me flowers. I threw them away, and he texted me afterward and asked me why."

"What the fuck? He's watching you again?" Tyler asks, setting his fork down. "You need to get a restraining order against him, Gemma. He's gone too far, and who knows what else he'll do. I don't like the idea of him watching you, especially at work," Tyler admits, sounding more tense than before.

I shake my head. "That's not the solution to *this* problem. It's a lot of paperwork and court orders, and even if I tried to get a temporary one, he's padded everyone's pockets already. The judge, the sheriff… hell, he's probably paid off the whole town. The corruption runs really deep," I explain.

"After seeing how crazed he was the other night, I'm afraid it would only cause more issues," Everleigh adds.

We eat in silence for a few minutes, all of us deep in thought. "You have to do something," Tyler finally speaks up. "Robert doesn't seem like the kind of guy who's gonna give up on getting what he wants, and you can't be the type of woman to give in to his demands."

"He's not. Trust me when I say I won't be crawling back to him. I've been thinking about it, and I dunno if this will work, but if I tell everyone the wedding is off, no one would expect us to be together. People will start talking, which is exactly what he doesn't want, and the gossip will spread. Once it gets back to him, maybe then he'll finally stop and move on. He's too concerned about his reputation to retaliate once it's public knowledge. If anything happened to me, every single person would point the finger at him. It's kind of like an insurance policy if he came after me."

"You should text the wedding planner yourself and tell her it's no longer happening," she suggests. "I bet he's still moving forward with everything, based on the note attached to those flowers."

Tyler sits and listens to us go back and forth with different scenarios. "That's not a bad idea. Telling people would make it official."

I take a few more bites until my plate is clean. Sitting back, I suck in a deep breath, feeling full.

"You want more? I made extra," Tyler offers with a smile.

I smile at the sweet thought. "No, thanks. I'm stuffed to the brim and not sure where I'd put it." Meeting his gaze, I blush at the way he's studying me. "Thank you so much for dinner. It was amazing. The wine tasted good, too. The company is even better."

Everleigh's done eating too and helps clean Tyler's mess in the kitchen.

"Gemma, maybe you should come over every night for the rest of eternity so Tyler will make dinner like this on the regular."

He chuckles. "Nice try."

Tyler and I exchange a look, and for a brief second, that familiar electricity streams through me. I think he feels it too because his Adam's apple bobs in his throat. Too many unspoken words flow between us, and I force myself to turn and focus my attention on Everleigh.

"Where's Sassy?" she finally asks.

"I took her for a walk when I got home from work, and after she devoured her food, she went to bed. She's in your room," he says.

"Ahh, okay. Gonna go check on my baby now." Everleigh shoots me a wink when Tyler looks away, then walks down the hallway, leaving us to ourselves.

"You're pretty rude for not telling me the truth about you and Ruby," I reiterate.

"You should've asked if you weren't sure." We walk to the living room and sit on the couch.

"It wasn't my business to ask or get involved," I admit with a shrug. "But it wasn't that hard to assume when I saw her in here wearing only a towel."

"We took separate showers after working out together," he explains with a shit-eating grin. "I obviously didn't know you were gonna show up, but it was adorable to watch you get jealous," he mocks.

"Jealous?" I squeal as my internal temperature rises.

"Yep, I think that's what we call it these days. You thought we were sleeping together, and it bothered you." He flashes me a sexy smirk, and I groan, mortified that he could see that.

"Guess I'm more transparent than I thought." There's no denying how it made me feel when I saw Tyler with her. Even if I was engaged at the time, it didn't make seeing the first man I ever loved with someone else any easier. Hopefully, we'll be able to put all of this behind us and laugh about it in the future. Or he and Everleigh will rag me for eternity over it.

"Gemma." Tyler's voice lowers and sounds huskier as soon as the shower comes on. "That night at your cottage—"

I wasn't prepared to talk about this right now and wasn't sure I wanted to, either. "I don't think Robert knows what happened between us."

He flashes me a pearly side smile. "I don't give a fuck if he does. However, I need to clear the air about some things I said afterward that weren't true, like how it meant nothing to me."

I swallow hard as my heart races, and the blood drains from my face. Admittedly, that hurt when he said those words to me. "Why'd you lie?"

"I needed to keep you away. Though I didn't want to, I told myself I had to come to terms with you getting married to someone else, so my only option was to ignore you and keep my distance. It's why I got a job at the gym and filled my nights with other things to do besides dwell on what it felt like to kiss you again. It's another reason I was okay with you believing Ruby and I were dating. It was to protect my heart, Gemma. And to protect yours too."

My words are lodged in my throat, and I open my mouth to speak but nothing comes out. The air between us sizzles, and I'm ready to combust at his admissions. I suck in a deep breath, needing to say something as he stares at me.

"I guess that makes sense. The only reason I said it was a mistake is because I'm not the type of woman who cheats. I'm faithful. Until you came back, I thought I was in love with Robert. Seeing you again peeled back the layers of the fake relationship I had built up in my head, and it exposed too many ugly truths. I was literally having an existential crisis. But the chili was *great*," I say, trying to lighten the mood.

He laughs. "I was gonna ask you about that actually."

"I would've brought some leftovers for you the next day, but I thought it'd be awkward, so I happily ate the entire pot by myself." *While pathetically crying and rereading his letters.*

He's full-on laughing. "At least that night wasn't an entire waste."

I smile and squeeze my legs together, trying to push away the thoughts of straddling him again. It's almost as if he can read my mind because he adjusts himself. The water turns off, and our private time is about to be over. I still haven't told Everleigh about that night, and I'm sure Tyler hasn't said a word about it, either. It's something I'd like to keep between us for now.

"So when are you gonna drop the bomb on your dad?" he asks.

"I'm not sure. His disappointment might kill me, though. I need to do it soon before he hears about it from someone else. If I'm gonna spread the news that we broke up, then he needs to hear it from me," I explain.

Tyler glances down at my ring finger. "You can start by not wearing that anymore."

I groan at the sight of it, forgetting I even had it on. "You're right. I need to give it back to him. And I should text Winnie before it gets too late." I pull my phone from my pocket and notice my hand is shaking as I type the message.

"I'm sorry you're having to deal with this," Tyler says, offering a smile.

"Me too!" Everleigh shouts from the hallway before she comes into view with Sassy on her heels.

"Thank you. Not sure what I'd do without you two."

"Probably marry that asshole," Everleigh blurts, which makes me snort. She grabs Sassy's leash and takes her outside.

I reread the message I typed to Winnie before hitting send.

Gemma: Hi, Winnie. I want to be respectful and let you know that Robert and I are no longer getting married, so I'd appreciate it if you'd canceled all the plans. I'm grateful for the work you've done planning this wedding, but your services are no longer needed.

Considering how quickly she responded to me this weekend, I expect an instant reply but wonder if I'll get one. Everleigh returns with Sassy who trots over to Tyler and jumps in his lap.

"Hey, girl." He pets her head, and she starts licking his face. "Too much, too much."

"Sassy!" Everleigh snaps. "Come get a treat." Once the magic word is said, Sassy jumps down and rushes to the kitchen.

I start yawning and feel as though I could fall asleep sitting up. When I check my phone to see if Winnie's replied yet, I realize it's almost nine. After sleeping like shit for the past few days, I think it's finally caught up to me.

"I should probably get going," I say, getting up from the couch. Tyler stands, and Everleigh gives me a hug before telling me good night. She looks just as exhausted as me right now, but she's been working extra hours at the boutique.

"Let me walk you out," Tyler suggests, and butterflies flutter in the pit of my stomach.

"Okay," I mutter as Everleigh goes to her room, and I swear I hear her chuckling under her breath.

I grab my keys from the counter, and Tyler follows. I wish I could take him home with me because when he's around, I feel like nothing bad could happen. Tyler would protect me no matter what, and he's been doing so since he showed up a few months ago. I was just too stubborn to realize I was in danger. While I never could've predicted that Robert was a wolf in sheep's clothing, I should have recognized the signs.

We go outside, and the mid-autumn breeze paints across my skin. This season has always reminded me of when Tyler left. The heartbreak that brought on was almost too much for me to handle. But now he's here, and we have the opportunity to start over and rekindle our friendship that I cherished so damn much.

When we get to my car, I turn and meet his gaze, and my breath hitches. It's almost as if I'm eighteen again, noticing the fire in his eyes for the first time. Tyler looks up and down the street, then his gaze meets mine again.

"I'm sorry for ever hurting you, Gemma. It's one of the biggest regrets in my life," he admits. I watch his tongue dart out and lick his lips, and the urge to taste him again nearly takes over.

"You don't have to keep apologizing to me. You couldn't stay, and I couldn't leave. We shared an amazing summer together, which I've never forgotten. You mean a lot to me, Tyler. You're one of the only people who really understands me on a deeper level. There are a lot of things I regret too, but I've realized that all we have is the present and the future. So I'm trying to cherish the good and not harp so much on the past. It's time for us to forget about the heartache and start over. I'm willing if you're willing."

He brushes my loose strands of hair behind my ear, and I have to force myself not to lean in to his touch. "I'm willing to try," he tells me. "Not to be selfish, but I'm glad the wedding is off. As I've always said, you deserve the world, Gemma. And a man who'd fight to give that to you. I'm not giving up hope that someday you'll get your happily ever after like in all those rom-coms you love so much."

When the silence drags on, I realize I'm stalling. Doesn't he know he was that person for me? That he was always the only man I ever wanted for *years*?

I don't want the night to end yet, but it has to. It's too dangerous for us to be together, to be close, and I think he understands that too.

"I want that too. Thanks again for everything," I say, shifting off the car so I can get inside.

Tyler reaches around and opens the door for me. "Be careful

driving home. Watch your back. Be safe. We'll figure this out together, Gemma. I promise," he reassures, and I have no doubt he means it.

"I will, and thank you again. Good night," I offer with a smile as I climb in.

"Night, see you tomorrow." Standing in the driveway with his arms crossed over his chest, he watches me leave. I wave, and he returns the gesture.

As I drive down the street, my mind races, replaying tonight.

After just ending a long-term relationship, I shouldn't be thinking about Tyler. Though falling *in* love with Tyler isn't possible because I never fell *out* of love with him.

I stay alert and aware of every set of headlights behind me and the cars parked on the street in my neighborhood. When I enter the cottage, my phone vibrates. I expect it to be Tyler or Everleigh, but it's from Winnie. I open the message, and my adrenaline rushes as I read it.

Winnie: The wedding plans are moving forward per Robert. I don't work for or take orders from you, Gemma. If you have an issue with that, contact your fiancé.

I should've known that'd be the response I'd get. They can continue all they want, but neither of them can force me to walk down that aisle. I guess only time will tell who'll get the last laugh in the end, and I just hope to God it's me.

CHAPTER TWENTY-SIX

TYLER

After walking Gemma to her car and watching her drive away, I go back into the house. It's been a long ass day, and I'm tired, though I probably won't get much sleep now. As soon as I walk into the living room, Everleigh charges toward me and hugs me tightly.

"Whoa. You okay?" I wrap my arms around her, squeezing her back.

"Thank you," she whispers before pulling back. "Thank you for caring so much about Gemma and being there for her. She probably won't ever admit it, but she feels safe around you."

"I've always cared about her," I confess. "I won't let anything bad happen to Gemma."

"I know. That's why you're the best." She grins. "Well, and because you're an amazing cook."

Everleigh walks toward the kitchen, and I follow. She grabs a bottled water from the fridge, then offers it to me.

"Sure, thanks," I say, taking it.

She pulls another one out for herself and immediately takes a sip. "I didn't wanna say anything when she was here, but you should've seen the look in Robert's eyes. He was deranged."

"I swear, that asshole has some serious issues."

"You're telling me. There's possessive in like a sexy, alpha way, and then there's psycho in a needs-a-straitjacket kinda way. I could hardly sleep that night, worrying about what he would've done to her if I hadn't gone to pick her up."

My jaw clenches at the thought. I don't understand how someone as amazing and beautiful as Gemma ended up with such a tool bag. I get the feeling that if her mom were alive, she would've warned Gemma about Robert from the beginning. Her letters talked about her mom and how she wished she were around to ask about girl stuff. Gemma's dad only gets glimpses of what Robert wants to share and has no idea who he really is.

"I'm gonna go to bed so I can get up early and beat the punching bag before work since I have to train tomorrow evening."

"You're working too much," she says. "I feel like I never see you these days. We spoke more when you were in prison than we do now."

I roll my eyes when she laughs, then chug half the bottle. "Not true. I have this thing called a cell phone now, and you can call and text at any time."

"Oh, shoot. I totally forgot about that."

"And you wonder why you're single with that smartass mouth."

"Maybe it's because all the guys in town are taken?"

"They can't *all* be."

"Oh, you're right. Some live in their parents' basements and play video games from sunup to sundown."

"Come to the gym with me tomorrow. Plenty of men there."

"Hard pass. I'm not getting up a minute earlier than I have to. Not to mention, gym rats care more about their muscles than women."

"Whatcha trying to say?" I lift my sleeve and flex.

She snorts and playfully pushes my chest when she walks around me. "Good night, Arnold Schwarzenegger."

I take a sleeping pill so I can fall asleep. By the time my alarm goes off, I'm ready to blow off some steam. Once I'm finished working out, I shower and feel a lot better. It's exactly what I needed before heading to the shop. When I walk in, I see Gemma's pretty face behind the counter.

With bright eyes, she smiles at me with dark-colored lips. She's acting as though she has no worries in the world, almost as if she hasn't been crying for the past few days.

"Morning," I say, lowering my eyes to her orange shirt and smirking. "Getting ready for Halloween early?"

She frowns. "No. It's my favorite—"

"Color. Yeah, I remember."

Gemma sighs with a grin. "Of course, you do."

I step closer to her. "It looks good on you."

"Thanks." Gemma stares into my eyes as I study how green hers are, neither of us speaking.

"Did you sleep okay last night?" I ask, breaking the silence.

"As good as expected, I guess. You?"

"I took some meds so I could, then got up early this morning to hit the gym."

"You like working out there?"

I smile. "I do. My offer still stands to teach you some self-defense moves if you wanna learn a few techniques."

Gemma raises her brows. "You think I should?"

Shrugging, I grin. "Wouldn't hurt." It'd also mean I'd get to spend more time with her.

"Maybe. I'll think about it."

I nod, then pour a cup of coffee and nod. "Alright. Well, if you decide you wanna, come in around seven."

Once I enter the garage, I glance over my shoulder and catch Gemma watching me. I flash her a smirk, and I swear she blushes before turning away. Something's happening between us, but I'm not complaining. Even though her life is a little messy right now, I want to be there for her. After our conversation last night, I won't be letting her go ever again.

Dear Tyler,

The seniors are putting together a Pumpkin Ball to raise money for our class trip in the spring. It's Friday, and as much as I wanna go and be with my friends, I'm the only one without a date. Well, technically I have one, Ben Bernard, whose boyfriend lives in Texas. Since we can't take the people we want, we're going together.

He's a great dancer, so it'll be fun at least, but I still wish you were here. I feel like it's taking forever for June to get here. The countdown on my phone isn't moving fast enough. It's labeled "graduation," but really, it's for the day you'll be home. Everyone always says not to rush growing up, but this is the worst kind of torture. We've been writing letters for almost four years, and at this point, it's like the day will never come.

To keep my mind busy, I've started cleaning out my mom's cottage behind my house to make it a space of my own. It's filled with her paintings. I love them all, but my favorite is the morning glories watercolor. The pinks and purples are super vibrant, and it has so much detail that it almost seems real. When I'm able to move in, I'm gonna frame a few and hang them on the walls. I can't wait to show you when you're here.

Everleigh told me you called her the other day and that you sounded really good. Though I wish I could've heard your voice, I imagine it every time I read one of your letters. I hope you're safe and staying healthy wherever you are right now. Watching the news makes me so damn worried about you, but I don't mention it to Everleigh because she's concerned enough. I'll just be so relieved when you're back in the States.

Oh, I've included a picture of me in my dress too. It's orange, my favorite color, but I think it makes me look like a pumpkin. I was surprised my dad approved because it's strapless, and I can't wear a bra with the low back. Hopefully, I can wear it for you in person.

Until next time,
Gemma
P.S. 226 days!

A few weeks into our relationship, Gemma modeled that dress for me. I also stripped her out of it and kissed every inch of her body afterward. I've thought about that orange gown for years and wonder if she still has it hanging in the back of her closet. The way it hugged her breasts and showed off her smooth skin had me hard as fuck.

We chat between customers and tasks, then eat lunch together. Once I'm done for the day, I head to the gym and train Luke. I shower in the locker room and change into shorts and a T-shirt to get ready for my session.

"Hey," I greet as soon as I see him standing by Ruby.

"You ready?" I ask, tossing him some gloves. "I'm about to whip your ass into shape."

"Uh-oh. Blackwood's in a mood." Ruby cackles.

"Aw, shit." Luke's eyes widen, and I laugh.

"Nah, don't worry. I'll go easy on you, kid." I pat his shoulder. "At first, anyway."

Luke and I practice for an hour straight, and by the time we're done, he nearly collapses on the floor.

"What'd you do to him?" Ruby stands over him, offering some water.

Sweat drips down my chest, and I wipe it away with a towel. "Made him into a man."

Ruby snorts and holds out her hand to Luke. She pulls him up, and he chugs the entire bottle before coming up for air.

"You gonna make it?" I shoot him a grin.

He nods, his face red and splotchy. "I need a shower. Same time next week?"

"You got it. Stay hydrated."

I grab our gloves, then stuff them into my bag so I can wash and sanitize them at home. Checking my phone, I notice it's almost seven, but there are no missed calls or messages.

"So what's new?" Ruby moves to the front counter, and I follow her. "How's your sister?"

"Ha-ha." I roll my eyes. "She was just complaining that there are no eligible men in town, so hey, you might have a chance after all."

"Don't mess with me, Blackwood."

Laughing, I shake my head, then look around. I was hoping Gemma would actually take me up on my offer and stop in tonight. I'd love to teach her how to take that asshole down in five seconds.

"Are you waiting for someone?" She peers around the empty gym.

"Huh?"

"You keep glancing at the door."

"Well, I offered Gemma a lesson, but I guess she's gonna chicken out."

"Gemma, huh? You sure that fiancé of hers would let her off his leash?"

I smirk and shrug. "Sure do, considering she called it off."

"Ahh. Now it makes sense." Ruby's full-on laughing as she moves around the desk. "Swooping in as soon as the ring's off her finger."

Frowning, I explain, "It's not like that. We're just friends."

"Yeah, and I like big cocks. Please, Tyler. I'm not blind, and I notice the way you two lust after each other."

"Maybe, but she's going through some shit right now, so I'm only trying to be her friend."

"Well, if that's the case, then give her my number. I'll show her a good time. Get her mind off the breakup and show her what she's missing."

I shake my head, brushing a hand through my hair. "You really need to get laid."

"I did last night, thank you *very* much."

My eyes widen as she bursts out laughing. "What? I have a no-strings relationship."

"Oh, really? Do I know her? Is she local?"

"As a matter of fact, you don't because she lives in the next town. Wanna watch our sex tape?" She pulls her phone from her pocket.

"Alright, I'm out." I grab my duffel and toss it over my shoulder.

"What? I bet you could learn a thing or two." She licks her lower lip, and I can't stop chuckling. "Give Everleigh my number too while you're at it!"

"Not a chance," I grumble. "I need new friends. You're too much."

"Suck it up, Blackwood. I'm your *only* friend."

"Bye," I call out as I push through the door and leave.

Ten minutes later, I'm home, and Everleigh's lounging on the couch with a wine glass.

"Hey, bro. You got some mail today." She gestures toward the coffee table. "A letter from the prison came, and I've been anxiously waiting for you to open it."

Dropping my bag, I furrow my brows, then kick off my shoes. "Why?"

"Well, I don't know. It just seemed weird. Do they want you to go back?"

I bark out a laugh. She's probably on her third glass. "Relax. It's probably from my old cellmate."

"The hot one with the sleeve tattoos?" She perks up.

"Down, girl. I've heard enough sexual shit for one night."

"Huh?" she asks as I rip open the envelope.

"Ruby," I say. "Saw her at the gym and now I know *way* too much about her sex life."

Everleigh snorts. "At least she has one."

"Stop," I say before she continues. "Don't wanna hear about yours either."

"Don't worry." She chugs her wine until it's empty. "The only action I get is from Victor the Vibrator in the shower."

"For fuck's sake." Shaking my head, I walk to the kitchen and pray we have a case of beer left. "I need my own place," I mutter when she's out of earshot.

After I grab a bottle of Bud Light, I go back to the living room and sit down next to Everleigh. She's watching some dating reality show, but I'm too tired to complain.

"So what's the letter say?"

I unfold it and begin reading. Meeting and getting to know Archer was the only silver lining while being locked up. I thought of him as the younger brother I never had. He's five years younger than me, only a year older than Everleigh, and has a lot of life left to live once he's out.

"He's asking how I'm adjusting after being locked up for five years. Says he's proud that I started over and that he wants a fresh slate too but refuses to go home. Then he mentioned some ideas of what he could do when he's released in a few years. I've already told him he could come here if he wanted."

"That long? Geez. That sucks. He totally should move here. Noah will be out by then too. You guys could start an ex-con's club or something." She giggles as though it's the best idea she's ever had.

"Har har. Time to cut you off." I reach for her glass, but she quickly pulls it away.

"Don't you dare!" She presses it to her chest, then gets up to refill it. "I'm not driving anyway, and I've had a rough day."

"Oh, yeah? Hard day of gossip and folding shirts?"

She glares at me, which causes me to laugh. "What'd Archer do anyway?"

I brush a hand over my scruffy jaw and debate whether I should say. It's not my story to tell, but he's not a bad guy either. She sits back on the couch and leans forward, waiting for me to continue.

"He took the fall for his sister so she wouldn't go to jail for murdering her abusive boyfriend."

"What? Seriously?"

"They grew up poor and knew it'd be believable if the kid from the wrong side of the tracks was the one who did it. There was a fabricated story about how he tried to get him off her but couldn't because the boyfriend was high on something and uncontrollable. Archer explained that he walked in on the guy beating his sister and knew where the gun was kept and took the blame. When he realized what his sister had done, he wiped off her fingerprints and planted all the evidence needed, then called the cops."

"And you believe him?"

"A hundred percent. Archer loves his sister more than his own life. She'd gone through so much already, and he wanted to protect her. It worked out because a few weeks later, she found out she was pregnant."

"Oh my God."

"Yeah, it was messy. I met her during visitation hours while I was waiting for Maddie and Liam."

"So how long was his sentence?"

"Six years. His lawyer did a good job at claiming defense and unintentional homicide. It helped that the guy's tox report showed he was loaded with drugs and alcohol."

"Wow. That's awful. I can't believe he did that."

"Once you meet Archer, you'll understand. He's loyal to a fault and basically raised his sister while working and going to school."

"Hmm…kinda sounds like you." She smiles.

"He's a good person. I hope he really does take me up on my offer because Lawton Ridge isn't so bad. But don't get any ideas in that horny head of yours."

"*Me*? Why not?"

I chuckle at the last line he wrote but keep it to myself.

P.S. Make sure your sister is single in three years. Hahaha.
Goddamn bastard.

"Because the last thing he should do once he's released is get into a relationship. He needs to find work, save money, and get settled again first."

"And he can't do that while relieving six years' worth of sexual frustration?"

I groan. "Nope. I'll be forcing you as far away from him as possible."

"That's rude and hurtful!"

"You really think you'll be single in three years anyway? You'll probably be married and knocked up by then."

Everleigh snorts. "Do you see what I'm doing on a Thursday night?" She gestures around the room and wiggles her toes in her fuzzy socks.

"Well, Ruby's been begging me to give you her number, so…"

Everleigh bursts out laughing. "Reminds me of that one summer after graduation with Layla Monroe."

"Wait, what?" I look at her with wide eyes. "Never mind. I do *not* wanna know. I'm gonna take a shower, then pass out."

"Oh, come on! We can have a friendly brother-sister chat! In fact, you've been without sex for five years. How are you not jumping every single woman in town? Is that why you shower so much now?"

I stand and finish my beer. "Good night, pain in the ass."

"Fine, fine. I already know the answer anyway."

"Sure, you do," I say, grabbing my bag off the floor, then walking away.

"It's because you're waiting for Gemma. Duh! I wasn't born yesterday! You two are a canceled-wedding day away from banging. Oh wait…" She laughs at her own ridiculous joke.

"Go to bed!" I shout as I step into the hallway, trying to escape her.

It's impossible not to think about Gemma while I'm under the hot stream of water. My cock hardens at the thought of her and the sweet way she looks at me. When we lost control with each other, I was ready to tear off every inch of clothing and make her mine forever. I don't give a fuck that she was still engaged to that asshat because she was *never* his in the first place. I want her as badly as I did before, but this time, I want to do it right.

I fist my dick and stroke it hard and fast. Squeezing my eyes tight as images of her flood my mind, I desperately need the relief. Thinking about how tight her cunt squeezed my fingers and how sweet she tasted brings me over the edge in minutes. Whispering her name with a grunt, I feel my orgasm take hold. I imagine Gemma on her knees licking me clean.

Once I'm in bed and under the covers, I grab my phone to text her. I won't be able to sleep without checking on her first.

Tyler: Missed you at the gym tonight.

She replies moments later.

Gemma: Sorry, I fell asleep right after work and just woke up. Rain check?

Tyler: Absolutely. Whenever you're ready. Even if you just want to hit the punching bag, it's a nice stress reliever.

Gemma: I'd like that. Maybe this weekend when I'm not so exhausted.

Tyler: Sounds like a plan.

Gemma: How was your night?

Tyler: It was good. Nothing special since I didn't get to hang out with you.

Gemma: Smooth. Haha.

Tyler: Just telling the truth ;)

Gemma: I'm gonna make some dinner, then take a hot bath so I can hopefully fall back asleep.

Tyler: Okay, if you need someone to talk to later, I'll leave my phone on. Otherwise, sweet dreams.

Gemma: Thank you. See you tomorrow.

Gemma's going through an emotional time right now. Even though I wish I could hold her, I'm giving her the space she needs to process the breakup with Robert in her own way. But if there's one thing I *can* do, it's letting her know I'm here if she needs me.

This time, I'm not going anywhere and will wait as long as it takes for Gemma to be ready.

CHAPTER TWENTY-SEVEN

GEMMA

I'M glad it's finally Friday. This week has been a roller coaster of emotions, and I'm ready to have a relaxing weekend. I want to open the windows, enjoy the cold front that's moving through, and clean my house. Adulting at its finest.

I'm extra excited this morning since Mrs. Wright delivered maple bacon donuts. She only makes them a few months out of the year, and I nearly die when the aroma fills the room.

"I know you love them, so I threw in a few extra." She winks.

"Dad's gonna be really happy," I tell her. "Thank you so much."

"Welcome, hon. Have a good day." Mrs. Wright leaves with a smile and a bounce to her step.

When I take one out of the box, I'm surprised it's still warm. I pour a cup of coffee, then enter the garage.

"Daddy!" I shout.

"Yeah?" he answers, standing by his toolbox. As I walk over to him, his eyes widen in excitement.

"It's that season again already?" He grins and takes them from my hands. "Thanks, sweetie. You deserve a raise."

"You should tell that to my boss," I tease just as Tyler comes through the door with wet hair.

"Good morning," he says, then quickly gets to work.

"Mornin'," Dad says around a mouthful.

"Morning," I mumble softly, studying him. He must've worked

out this morning because he's freshly showered. Our eyes meet, and I smile before heading back to the lobby.

It's insane how much he affects me with just one look.

I try to push the thoughts away and concentrate on my to-do list. As is usual on Fridays, the schedule is jam-packed today.

The morning passes so fast that I'm shocked when lunchtime rolls around. Tyler comes in and hands me a set of keys for a customer's vehicle. His fingers brush against mine, and I try to hold back a smile.

"I parked it on the side," he tells me, lingering for just a moment. He glances down at my hand and lifts an eyebrow when he notices I'm still wearing my engagement ring. While he doesn't say anything, he also doesn't have to. The expression on his face and the way he tilts his head show me exactly what he's thinking.

"I'm telling my dad this weekend. Tomorrow, actually. That way he can have some space to process the news. It's not something you drop during a workweek," I explain.

Tyler shrugs. "It's not my business, Gemma. You have to do what's best for you when the time is right."

"Any plans for lunch?" I ask.

"Who's asking?" Tyler leans against the counter, throwing me a smirk.

Damn. Has he always been this sexy?

"I'm thinking about going to the pub for a burger. If you wanna join…"

"Let me text Ruby and ask." He barely gets the words out before chuckling.

I'm tempted to reach over and smack him. "You're never gonna let me live that down, are you?"

"Nope. It's filed away next to you stripping down naked in your cottage after the bar that night."

I tuck my bottom lip into my mouth and blush. "You suck."

He leans in a little farther. "I lick too."

My breasts rise and fall rapidly, and the only thing that pulls me away is my father coming inside. He looks over at us, and Tyler immediately straightens his position.

"Daddy, I'm running down to the pub for lunch. Want anything?"

He shakes his head. "Nah, thought I'd go down to the deli and get a turkey sandwich. Thanks, though."

"Alright, sounds good," I say as Tyler goes back into the garage.

My dad stares at me as he pours a cup of coffee. "Gemma," he says, and I can hear the warning in his voice.

"Don't." I stop him before he can continue. "It's not what you think."

He studies me, but I stand my ground, not wanting to have this conversation right now. Thankfully, an older gentleman walks in and steals my attention away. I'm happy for the interruption as Dad leaves the lobby.

I don't like him thinking poorly of Tyler, who should be the least of our worries in my current situation. Robert has been too quiet, which is more frightening than his vicious threats.

Soon, it's time for lunch, and I wait for Tyler, but when he comes into the lobby, he's frowning.

"Gem, I think it's best if I don't join you for lunch. I'm sor—"

"Don't apologize. I completely understand. How about I bring you a burger instead? I mean, it's not shrimp and grits, but it's a hot meal." I smirk, hoping to lighten the mood.

He instantly perks up. "Sounds great."

Tyler goes to the break room, and I take a stroll down the pub. Instead of eating at the bar as I intended, I place our order to go. As I'm waiting for our food, my phone vibrates.

When I see who the text is from, all the color drains from my face. I knew it was only a matter of time.

Robert: You're joining me for dinner tonight. I'll pick you up at 7.

My mouth falls open at the audacity of his demand.

Gemma: No, but hell no.

I'm not going anywhere with him ever again.

Robert: My client specifically requested you come. You will be there.

Gemma: I won't. Your client is not my problem. I'm not marrying you. It's over, Robert. Stop texting me!

My blood pressure rises and so does my anger level. I'm half-tempted to block his number so I'll never have to hear from him again.

Robert: It's not over. We will work this out because we belong together.

His last message nearly sets me off.

Gemma: You're INSANE. Leave me alone.

I lock my phone and shove it into my crossbody purse. Thankfully, the food comes soon after because I'm so damn annoyed I can barely stand to be in public.

When I walk inside the shop, Tyler instantly notices my mood change.

"Did you step in dog shit or something?"

Shaking my head, I set the food on the small table. "It's nothing."

Tyler doesn't push the conversation. Instead, he changes the subject, which I'm grateful for. It's obvious he's keeping his distance from me at the table, but I get it. My dad is already suspicious, which motivates me to tell him tomorrow even more.

I take my phone out of my purse and snap a picture of my lunch and send it to Everleigh. Immediately, she responds with a drooling face emoji.

Everleigh: Should've gotten you to deliver me lunch. Drinking a shitty protein shake.

I feel bad for not asking her since the boutique is so close.

Gemma: I'm a horrible best friend.

I frown, and Tyler glances up at me. "I'm chatting with Everleigh.

She didn't bring her lunch again. You're slacking on your brotherly chef duties."

He lets out a roar of laughter. "I bet you a hundred bucks she ate last night's leftovers for breakfast because I cooked. Don't let her play you for a fool. She's good at that sometimes."

I gasp. "Seriously? I'm so calling her out! I felt sorry for her for two seconds."

I type out a message, spilling what Tyler said.

Everleigh: That little shit! Tell him to keep my secrets to himself.

I snort at her antics. My phone buzzes again, and when I lower my eyes, I notice it's Robert again. Knowing it will put me in a bad mood, I ignore it. When Tyler and I are halfway finished eating, Dad returns with a milkshake in his hand.

"You didn't bring me one?" I pretend to be offended. He's in a better mood than earlier at least.

"Shoulda asked! Belinda makes them extra chocolatey for me." He takes a sip of it and beams.

"Tease," I say, cleaning up our mess.

"Belinda's shakes are the best," Tyler admits. "She made me a strawberry banana one, and it was pure heaven."

"I'm gonna have to try that one. I had no idea she was the queen at making shakes," I retort, actually wishing he would've gotten me one now.

"I think I've gained ten pounds because of her." Dad laughs, patting his belly.

"You're the one who keeps going down there, Daddy," I remind him. "She's just making sure you're a happy customer."

"Or she knows the way to a man's heart is his stomach," Tyler taunts, waggling his brows. I chuckle at his insinuation that Belinda is flirting with my dad by making him shakes, though it'd be super cute if that was the case.

The two of them get back to work, and I busy myself with the financial statements, ignoring my phone and all the messages Robert keeps sending me. When I think about him, my anxiety spikes, and I feel as if I can't breathe.

For the rest of the afternoon, I deal with spreadsheets, receipts, and customers. I'm nonstop busy, which keeps my mind occupied. Once the shop closes for the day, I'm ready to go home and take a bath, then enjoy a movie on the couch. Just as I'm about to lock the front door, Robert rushes past the large windows wearing a scowl. Seconds later, he's pushing himself past me and staring with a menacing grin.

"Gemma, sweetheart." He leans forward, trying to kiss me, but I take a step back, nearly tripping over myself.

"What're you doing here?" I hiss, confused. I thought I was *extremely* clear in my text messages that he needed to fuck off.

His lips turn up farther. "I'm here to pick you up for dinner. I told you I'd be here earlier. Didn't you get my messages?"

"I'm *not* going. You need to leave," I grit out, placing my hand on my hip, ready to scream and hope my dad or Tyler hears me.

Robert moves toward me, but I step back, keeping my distance until I'm pressed against the counter.

"Are you trying to make me look bad?" he snaps, his face flushing with the same anger I saw at his house.

I cross my arms over my chest, not cowering to his stance although his large frame looms over me. "What don't you understand, Robert? We are *done*. Over! You need to leave before my dad sees you here," I warn.

He sneers and rolls his eyes as if he's not concerned because he's not. "Victoria specifically requested we *both* be there. You know I'm trying to sign this fucking deal. Do you want me to lose one of the biggest contracts of my life over your selfishness?"

I shrug. "Your business dinners and your clients are no longer my concern."

Reaching out, he grabs my arm firmly, not caring if he's hurting me or not, and he yanks me closer. "You're being such a self-centered bitch!" he shouts.

Before I can open my mouth to scream, Tyler rushes through the door and moves toward Robert with his chest puffed out.

"Don't you fucking talk to her that way," Tyler barks, and instead of Robert letting me go, he only holds me tighter. Seconds later, Tyler's in his face and pulling me away from Robert's grasp. My arm throbs where he grasped me, and I'm sure it'll bruise.

"You touch her again, and I'll fucking make you *wish* you were dead," Tyler warns. "You need to go."

Robert scoffs. "Is this how convicts threaten people? Pathetic. Come on, Gemma. We're leaving." He snaps his fingers at me as if I'll just follow his command. "Now!"

Tyler crosses his arms over his broad chest and stares him down. I notice how uncomfortable Robert becomes, and he even takes a few steps away from us.

"*We* are leaving," he seethes.

"You really are a dumb fuck, aren't you? She's not going anywhere with you," Tyler tells him. "And if you lay a hand on her again…"

As if things couldn't get any worse, my dad enters and looks back and forth between us. Dread coats me like ice cold water in winter.

"What's goin' on here?" he asks.

Robert instantly snaps on a smile, and I follow his lead. He clears his throat, changing his persona, and speaks. "I was just picking Gemma up for an important dinner, sir. We were just leaving."

Robert holds his hand out and waits for me to take it.

I'm livid and need to figure a way out of this. Then a thought comes to me.

"Yep, and Robert just asked Tyler if he'd like to join us," I add with a wide smile.

Robert's grin slightly falters, but he slaps it right back on. My dad doesn't notice at all, but Tyler's face contorts as if I've lost my damn mind. Maybe I have.

"Son, I think that's a great idea for you to go with them. Might be fun," Dad suggests, patting Tyler on the shoulder. Tyler's actually at a loss for words, and for the most part, so is Robert.

"That's really nice of you, Robert. I always knew you were a good guy," Dad continues, and I want to groan, but I hold it back. "So are you going?" he asks Tyler.

"Tyler said he didn't want to go," Robert declares.

"But we're trying to convince him to come because the food is amazing. Plus, we're meeting one of Robert's clients, so it should be a fun time," I squeal, acting excited. I won't let Robert get out of this that easy.

Robert's nostrils flare. If he wasn't so concerned with impressing every Tom, Dick, and Harry, this wouldn't be an issue, but I know his weaknesses and will use them against him. I just hate that he has my dad believing he's a goddamn saint when he's the devil in disguise.

"You know, I think I will go," Tyler agrees, and I want to scream out in victory.

"Fantastic," Robert mutters, showing his pearly whites. "So, are you ready, darling?"

I love how my dad proudly watches this unfold, having no idea how much of a cluster fuck the reality is.

"I still have some things to finish up first. Tyler and I will meet you at the restaurant, if that's okay, sweetheart? What time should we be there?"

"That's fine. Six. Sharp," he says between gritted teeth, and it's obvious he's furious about Tyler tagging along. Watching Robert squirm is the highlight of my whole day.

"Perfect," I sing-song. "We'll be there."

Dad's so damn happy that he looks like he's ready to explode.

"Welp, you kids have fun. I'm gonna head home," Dad says, then leaves through the back door.

Robert glares at me. "What the hell is wrong with you?"

I take a step forward, more confident than before because Tyler's beside me. "I'll join you on *my* terms, so if you want me to go, you'll agree to it. And afterward, I'm giving you this damn ring back because we. Are. *Over*."

He narrows his eyes as his entire body tenses. He's losing control, and if Tyler wasn't here, there's no telling what he'd do to me.

"Fine. Have it your way, but this isn't over, Gemma. Far from it," he warns, then glances over at Tyler. "Make sure to clean up. I usually like to take the trash out, not bring it inside with me. Don't be late, *sweetheart*." The term of endearment comes out venomous. Robert turns on his heels and walks out, allowing the door to slam behind him.

"What the fuck?" Tyler groans as soon as Robert is out of sight. I feel as if I'm having a panic attack and brace myself on the counter, trying to breathe and gain control as the world collapses around me.

Tyler rushes over, his hand bracing my elbow. "Gemma, are you okay?"

I nod. "Too much adrenaline rushing through me at once."

"You're absolutely sure this is what we should do?" he asks me as I straighten my stance, then turn off all the lights. "We don't have to go anywhere."

"I wanna get this over with so I can give him this ring back and be done with it all. At least now, Dad won't think the worst of you. Silver lining, I guess. Plus, now I won't have to be alone with him and his client. Robert won't be a dick in front of her or you. But right after dinner, I'm handing it over. It's a final fuck you, leave me alone gesture," I explain.

He sucks in a deep breath as we walk to my car. "I'm letting you make the decisions here, but if you want me to punch his face in, just say the word." He cracks his knuckles, making me laugh.

"Thank you. It means a lot," I say honestly as we get inside and drive to Everleigh's.

Tyler showers and changes clothes but not because Robert demanded it. It's his daily routine since he's covered in grease and sweat. Tyler is always handsome, even filthy from work, but he also dresses up really nice. He's wearing sleek black slacks and a dark blue button-up.

As we head across town to Fancies, I notice how tight Tyler's jaw clenches and know he's not happy about this situation. I'm not either, and I'm half-tempted to turn around, but I know that'd only stir shit up more. Also, I have a point to prove. I'm not afraid of Robert as long as Tyler is with me. Robert will get his perfect business dinner with the rich client, and I'll return his ring. Then it'll all finally be over.

"We should all be thankful Jerry walked in when he did. Otherwise, Robert would've been eating my fist," Tyler finally says.

"You can't. He wants you to hit him so he can make you out as the bad guy, and considering your past, Robert wouldn't have to try very hard. I don't want you to get into any trouble because of me. He's just not worth it. Trust me," I say.

"Maybe not but breaking his big ass nose would give me so much satisfaction." He turns and flashes me a smirk.

I roll my eyes, grinning. "You say that now."

We pull into the parking lot of the restaurant, and I turn off the engine. Sucking in a deep breath, I lean back on the headrest and close my eyes. Being at this restaurant brings back bad memories.

"You're sure about this?" he asks again.

"It could be a huge mistake, but I'm glad I won't have to pretend everything is fine because he wants me to. You have no idea how much it means to me that you came with," I admit, already feeling overwhelmed. I just want to get this over with and make it known to *everyone* that the relationship is over.

He takes my hand in his, brings my knuckles to his lips, and presses a soft kiss on them. "I promise I'll do whatever I can to help and to make sure you're safe. Even if it means going to a bougie ass restaurant and wishing I were somewhere else. But I'll go anywhere with you, Gemma."

His words have my heart melting. "It seems upscale, but the food actually sucks, especially compared to yours." I smirk, then check the time. "I guess we should put our game faces on and go inside."

"Yeah. Don't worry, we'll get through this together," he reminds me, then we get out of the car and walk toward the entrance.

Tyler glances over at me and tilts his lips up. "Just in case no one has told you today, you look beautiful."

Heat rises from my core, and I tuck my bottom lip into my mouth as Tyler opens the door for me. When our eyes meet, the intensity is enough to steal my breath away, and it only reinforces that I made the right decision by deciding not to marry Robert.

CHAPTER TWENTY-EIGHT

TYLER

I'M NOT sure what I should expect when we walk inside. The waiters wear dress shirts with ties, and each table drinks wine from crystal glasses. It's the type of place you take a date with the expectation of getting fucked afterward. I can't even imagine how expensive the meals are, but it's not any of my worry because Robert's paying. Perhaps I'll order the most expensive dinner I can.

When Gemma moves toward the host stand, I can tell she's uncomfortable.

It's reserved seating only, so she gives them Robert's name. Moments later, they're escorting us through the dining area to a semi-private room in the back. As we pass the tables, I feel as if there's a spotlight on me, and everyone knows I don't belong. At times like this, I'm convinced I have the word *convict* tattooed on my forehead. We continue and are finally brought to a secluded area where Robert's sitting at a table with a blonde. The way he creepily studies the woman, who I can only see from behind, is disgusting. It's as if he's undressing her with his perverted eyes.

Gemma glances over at me, and I flash her a wink of comfort. It's enough to make her lips turn up as we move closer. Robert stands to greet and kiss Gemma's cheek, but she takes a step back. When I step forward, the woman turns her head. The room briefly fades and goes black as the shock of who's in Lawton Ridge settles.

"What the hell?" My voice booms as I zero in on her—*Victoria O'Leary*.

Her plump lips turn up into a sneer as she finds joy in my expression, and I can barely control my temper.

"Oh, fantastic." Victoria crosses her legs, showing off her bare thighs. "How lovely to see you again, Tyler. It's been a while, hasn't it? About...*five years*?" She forces out a malicious chuckle as I narrow my eyes and ball my hands into fists.

Gemma looks back and forth between us. "You know *her*?"

I glare at Robert and Victoria. "That's the bitch who framed me and got me locked up."

Victoria's hand flies to her chest, and she cackles so loud it pierces my ears. "You got exactly what you deserved."

"Did you know about this, Robert?" Gemma asks in an accusing tone, crossing her arms over her chest. "This is low, even for you."

The room is tense as hell, and I gently grab Gemma's arm and pull her back so she's not too close to Victoria.

"I had no idea," he claims, huffing as if he's insulted she'd even ask.

I move closer, putting space between him and Gemma. "Cut the shit, Robert. You knew exactly who she was. Fuck you."

"And fuck you too," I say, turning to Victoria.

"We're not staying here." I grab Gemma's hand to lead her out of here, knowing exactly how dangerous it is for us to be around Victoria. Seconds later, Gemma is being jerked away. Our hands break, and Robert has her pulled close to his body.

"Let me go!" she shouts.

"I didn't know, Gemma." Robert pleads with his eyes.

"Bullshit," I say.

"I didn't!" He raises his voice, and I catch sight of Victoria watching us with amusement. We argue back and forth before Victoria walks over to us with her wine glass in hand.

"He really didn't know," she admits, drinking her alcohol as if she's having the best time.

"And why should I trust a goddamn word that comes out of your mouth? I learned my lesson already." I scowl.

She flashes her million-dollar smile. "Believe what you want, Tyler. I wanted to find you after I saw your name on that witness list.

Which was far too easy, by the way. I knew we'd meet again, though honestly I didn't think it would be this early in the game. It's a nice surprise, even more so that it involves some weird love triangle." Victoria's obviously proud of herself as she arches a brow with a cunning smirk.

"Mission fucking accomplished," I throw her way, blocking Gemma from both of them. Victoria's dangerous and so is Robert.

"My previous sentiment still stands," I say. "Fuck off."

Gemma and I move toward the door as Robert follows us, begging her to stay like a little bitch. He continues to mutter Gemma's name under his breath as the exit of the restaurant comes into view. Once we're outside, he cries for her to stop. Gemma sucks in a deep breath and breaks away from my hold.

"I have to talk to him," she whispers.

I plead with my eyes not to give in to him, but she does, though she keeps her distance.

"Honestly, I didn't know," he says again. "You have to believe me."

Watching with my arms crossed, I'm ready to pounce if he lays a hand on her.

"Maybe you didn't, but as you mentioned before, there's zero trust between us. I don't think I can believe anything you say anymore, Robert. Not that it matters since we're no longer together."

He acts as if she slapped him in the face, but Gemma continues. "She's dangerous. And if you're as smart as you claim to be, you'll walk away from her and that deal now before she turns on you, too."

Robert opens his mouth, then shuts it. "I'm not scared of her..." His eyes snap to me. "Or you."

Gemma shrugs. "Fine, but don't say I didn't warn you. I'm leaving."

"You're not going anywhere. You agreed to have dinner with me tonight. We have other things to discuss." Robert growls.

He must have a death wish if he's talking to her that way.

"No." She doesn't explain herself and takes the ring off her finger. She steps closer, then hands it to him.

"If you go, you'll be sorry," he threatens, studying the diamond he thought would be enough to make her happy.

Gemma shakes her head, and when she's next to me, she smiles.

"Ready?"

"This isn't fucking over, Gemma!" Robert yells from behind us.

She looks over her shoulder. "Go to hell, Robert. And take Victoria with you."

I can't wipe off my smug grin as we walk to her car. I grab her keys and offer to drive. Once I unlock the doors and we're inside, I notice her breaths are ragged. When our eyes meet, sadness is in her expression.

"I'm so sorry you had to see her, Tyler."

"It's not your fault. Victoria is a sneaky bitch and lives for drama," I explain.

"Is she why you went to Vegas?" Gemma asks as I turn onto the main road. Swallowing hard, I don't want to lie, but I don't want to get her involved any more than she is, either. The less she and Everleigh know, the better.

"Yes," I admit.

"I never put the pieces together. It didn't cross my mind that she was the same Victoria that you knew, and I didn't care to ask questions." Gemma shakes her head. "I've met her before."

"When?" I ask, trying to figure out the timeline.

"Monday night. We met her for dinner. She was the one who dropped the bomb about the wedding."

I'm lost in my thoughts for a moment. No wonder she was quiet when I was in Vegas. Victoria was here planting the seeds for her evil plan, whatever it is.

"No telling what Robert's told her," I say honestly.

She groans. "I hope he kept his mouth shut, but considering she knew about the wedding, I highly doubt it. Robert has a habit of running his mouth if it means building a relationship with someone. His main priority is getting them to sign the contract, and he'll do whatever it takes, including selling them the dream."

"The more I hear about Robert, the more I can't stand him," I admit.

We sit in silence until the light turns green. She glances at me. "Wanna come over for a little while and keep me company?"

"Sure," I say, my heart hurting for her.

It doesn't take long before we're pulling into her driveway. The lights in her father's house are on, and I feel like we're sneaking around like we used to when she didn't want her dad to know I was sleeping over. Though, we should be careful because Jerry's already suspicious as hell. Until he knows the truth, it'd be best if we're not seen together outside of work.

When we walk inside her house, she sets her purse on the counter and sighs. "Today has been weird as hell. I need a *strong* drink of something."

"It definitely has."

When I look around the cottage, I glance at all of her mother's paintings on the walls. There's a large canvas of an open field surrounded by a forest with an absolutely stunning use of colors. "She was so talented," I say as Gemma stands next to me.

"Sometimes when I look at this painting, I imagine myself going through the plush grass and running straight into the forest." Her voice trails off, and I try to picture what would be beyond the landscape.

I search around the room for a specific painting, but I don't find it. "Where's that morning glories watercolor painting?"

Moving into the kitchen, I notice an abstract canvas with bright colors splashed across it—another beautiful one her mother created.

She tilts her head with amusement in her eyes. "You remember that too?"

"Of course. I thought it was in the dining room. Where'd it go?"

A blush hits her cheeks. "I put it in my bedroom. Wanna see it?"

"Sure." I force down the lump in my throat as she moves toward the hallway, and I follow her. There were many summer days and nights spent tangled together in the sheets of that room.

Leaning against the doorframe, I notice not much has changed in here. She still has the same headboard and dresser with framed photos of her, Everleigh, and Katie. I wait until she waves me forward. A pair of panties and bra are crumpled on the floor, and she kicks them to the side. "Sorry. I forgot about those."

"Not like I haven't seen them before," I say with a chuckle, moving closer to the painting. The morning glories are so detailed they almost look real. Bright purple and pink stand out among the green grass. "Wow," I mutter. "Just as beautiful as I remember."

"I wish I could paint like her—or rather, I wish my mother was here to teach me," she confesses.

"You can still learn," I encourage. "It's not too late."

She cocks a brow. "I've tried *many* times, and they look like something a four-year-old made. It's embarrassing, considering I should have her creative genes, but I obviously don't. Just imagine if Bob Ross's son was a terrible painter!"

I laugh. "Is he?"

"No! He's brilliant, just like his dad was. The mountainscapes he creates…it's ridiculous. Then you have me, who can barely paint a sun—the simplest thing ever, and I still managed to screw it up."

"I'm sure it's not that bad."

"Ha! I'll show you," she says and opens her closet. That's when I notice the orange dress hanging on the rod, bringing back memories of her letter. She still has it, after all. Up on top is an old Converse box, and I'm curious what's inside. Gemma pulls a canvas from the back and hands it to me, stealing my focus.

It takes everything I have not to lose my shit at the blob of paint. I tuck my lips into my mouth, but it's impossible to hold back a smile.

"See!" she exclaims and points at me.

"What is it?" I ask, tilting it.

"It's supposed to be a nest on a tree branch. Inside are baby birds and different colored eggs."

"Ooh, sure, I see that." I nod, but she sees through my lie and playfully smacks me.

"Hey! Picasso's art was strange and is still extremely popular." I throw her a wink.

She rolls her eyes, and I hand her the painting, which she shoves to the back of her closet.

"What's in that box?" I ask, curious.

"Um. All your letters."

"Really? You saved them even after all these years?"

She nods. "Every single one."

We're frozen in a heated gaze, and while I'm happy my words meant as much to her as hers meant to me, it somewhat saddens me too because when I moved away, those were all she had left of me. No telling where we'd be right now if I hadn't. I wouldn't have met Victoria or gone to prison, but then Maddie and Liam wouldn't be in my life either. She notices the somber mood and swiftly changes the subject.

"Are you hungry?" she asks, walking toward the doorway.

"I'm starving. I'll be happy to make something," I offer as I follow her to the kitchen.

"No, no, no, you're *my* guest of honor and have cooked for me several times already. It's my turn."

I take a seat at the marble island. "Okay, fine."

It's hard not to think about the last time I was here when we both lost control. Just imagining her soft moans in my ear as she rode her release has my dick getting hard, but I try to think about something else. We cannot cross the line right now, regardless if she's single and she's all I think about.

She opens the fridge and glances inside. "Hmm."

I chuckle at her uncertainty. "Are you sure you don't want me to help?"

She pulls out cheese slices and butter, then sets them on the counter. "How about a grilled cheese sandwich?" she asks. "It's been a while, but I think I can make one."

"I just hope you're a better cook than Everleigh," I tease. "Because the look on your face has me worried."

She chuckles. "My cooking isn't as bad as my painting skills."

"Thank God for that," I mock, and she rolls her eyes.

"Joke's on you, though," she says, grabbing a skillet. "Because you'll eat it even if it sucks. I know how nice you are." She turns on the burner, and I watch as Gemma scoops a gigantic spoonful of butter and slaps in down on the skillet.

I cringe because she's already screwing this up. "Let me help."

She turns and points the spatula at me. "Not happening. Want a drink while you wait?"

The butter sizzles, and I'm convinced it's burning. "Sure." I might need one to swallow down her food.

She quickly reaches inside the fridge, then hands me a Whiteclaw.

"What in the hell is this?" I look at the can, and my face scrunches.

"That's all I have!"

I laugh and crack it open. "Well, it's no beer, but I guess it'll do." I take a sip and nearly spit it out.

"Don't you dare waste a drop of that. It's basic bitch gold." She opens a loaf of bread and puts it in the skillet, then turns to me. "Will you tell me what you did in Vegas when you went?"

I bite the corner of my lip, thrown off by her question. "Are you sure you want all the details?"

She nods. "Yes. Now that Victoria is here, I wanna know everything."

I swallow, then blow out a shaky breath before telling her about Eric and what Victoria did to his girlfriend, Amara. It's impossible for me to leave out the details because Gemma needs to understand how dangerous Victoria really is. Her mouth falls open, and she gasps, pressing her hand to her chest.

"No way..." Her eyes widen in shock.

"So, I went to Vegas to testify in a deposition as a character witness for the case against Amara to discuss what I saw and heard when I worked for Victoria. The lawyer who represented me before went too," I explain. "Afterwards, I flew with Serena to Sacramento and visited Liam and Maddie until the next day."

"Do you think it actually did any good?" she questions, but before I can respond, I smell something burning. As if she reads my mind, she turns around, and the skillet is smoking. The fire alarms start beeping, so I quickly open the front door and try to fan some of it out. Gemma opens a window, then throws the burnt bread in the trash. "Whoopsies. That was only a warmup round," she claims. As if she's well practiced, she grabs the broom, and the beeping finally stops.

I walk around the island, not allowing her to embarrass herself anymore as she grabs the loaf for more bread.

"I'll help," I say, and this time, she willingly hands me the spatula. "We'll do it together."

"Perfect," she whispers, noticing how close we are. It's not lost on me either.

I go back to the previous conversation. "Long story short, I don't know if it'll help Eric. But I suspected Victoria would retaliate at some point. I just didn't think it would be this fast, but I should've known better. That woman is always three steps ahead of her enemy. She lives for this shit, and probably gets off to it when she's alone," I groan. Talking about her puts me in a sour mood.

"Gross," Gemma adds, which causes me to laugh.

I wipe out the skillet, and we get started on round two.

"The secret to making an amazing grilled cheese is buttering the bread, then putting it down. Otherwise, you can't control how much butter it soaks up." Our eyes meet for a brief second as I flip the bread. "Now, you put the cheese on while this side is still hot, then put the second piece of bread on top."

Gemma unwraps American and cheddar, then adds them both. A minute later, I flip the sandwich and wait until it's golden brown. When it's good and toasty, I slide it on a plate.

"No fair. I was supposed to make dinner for you," she playfully pouts.

"Cooking is my thing. I don't mind," I tell her as we continue our process. "Plus, it's more like teamwork. I butter, and you add the cheese." I smirk.

After I cook three more sandwiches, she grabs a bag of chips from the pantry. We fill our plates, then go to the couch.

"What do you wanna watch?" Gemma asks, turning on the TV before handing me the remote.

I flip through the channels and settle on a Bruce Willis movie. It's nothing but action and explosions, but Gemma enjoys it. After we're done eating, she cleans up the kitchen, and I join to help her.

"I've got this," she says around a yawn. It's then I realize how exhausted she is. Too much shit has happened this week for her not to be, and we've had a long day.

"You should get some rest," I tell her, grabbing the dishes she rinses to put in the dishwasher.

"Yeah, but I'll just lie in bed. I won't be able to sleep because my mind runs too much."

"I totally get that," I admit. Drying off my hands, I think back to the countless nights I've stayed awake because *she* was on my mind.

"Let me take you home," she offers. "It's getting late."

"I can walk."

"Absolutely not. There's a murderer in Lawton Ridge who has it out for you. It's not an option, Tyler." Gemma grabs her keys before I can argue.

"Valid point," I admit, chuckling lightly, though it's really not funny. Victoria's unpredictable. "But *I'm* driving, just in case."

She hands over the keys, then grabs a light jacket before we walk out. On the way home, I think about all that's changed between us since I first showed up a few months ago. As Gemma sits next to me and hums along to the radio, I know now more than ever that coming home was the right decision.

We chat about nothing, and the conversation flows so easily that I'm pulling into my sister's driveway in no time at all. After I turn off the engine, we sit together for a second, not wanting the night to end even though we're both exhausted as hell.

"Tyler," she whispers. "Thank you again for everything. You've surprisingly been my rock through all of this."

A small smile meets my lips as I study her face and take in how genuine her words are. "I'm just returning the favor for all those letters you wrote me when I needed someone."

Right now, I want to pull her into my arms and kiss her like there's no tomorrow—in a way I've dreamed about since I saw her again for the first time. By the way she licks her lips, I know she's thinking it too, but we can't.

"Good night, Gemma," I say.

"Night," she tells me as I reach for the handle, then we both get out so she can hop in the driver's side. Being with her is so damn electrifying, and it's so hard to walk away, but somehow I do. I'll kiss her when the timing is right, when she's ready, but that's not now.

As she backs out of the driveway, I send her a text.

Tyler: Drive safe. Let me know when you get home.

Before she pulls away, she messages me back.

Gemma: I will.

When she's out of sight, I go inside and force myself to take a cold shower. By the time I get out, she sends me another text to say she made it safely back, and I tell her sweet dreams. I have a feeling tonight I'll be staring at the ceiling for hours thinking about her before I finally drift off.

Gemma's always had that effect on me.

CHAPTER TWENTY-NINE

GEMMA

After last night's shitstorm, I'm a ball of emotions. I have to give Dad the news that Robert and I won't be getting married. Even though he'll be disappointed, I hope he understands why. We've always been close, and there's nothing I wouldn't do for him, but I hate letting him down. I don't plan on going into detail about Robert's pushiness or how he tried to mold me into a Stepford wife. It will be short and to the point—we just weren't meant to be together.

"Hey, Daddy," I greet as soon as I walk into the kitchen. He's drinking a cup of coffee and reading the paper at the table.

"There's my girl." He kisses my cheek when I lean down to hug him. "How ya doing, sweetheart?"

"I've been better, but I'm okay." I move around him and go straight to the coffee maker.

"Gonna explain what's goin' on?" he asks with concern etched on his face. "Everything okay?"

"I'll explain. Do you want me to make breakfast first?"

"Sure, just somethin' light is fine, though," he insists.

I drink my coffee while I cook western omelets, and he talks about the local news. Though I'm more occupied with how to start this conversation, so I'm barely listening.

"Gemma?"

"Hmm?"

"What's burnin'?"

My mouth falls open as I smell smoke coming from the toaster. "Shit!" I quickly unplug it and remove the dark, crisp bread. "Whoops. I'll make more, hold on."

"You sure you don't want any help?"

I turn off the stove and slide the pan from the burner before I burn that too. "No, I've got it. Just sit tight."

Ten minutes later, I have our food plated and set on the table with coffee refills.

"Smells delicious, sweetie." Dad beams as he dives into his omelet.

"Thanks. Sorry, I'm distracted."

"I can see that. What's goin' on?"

Swallowing hard, I stare at my food and blow out a ragged breath. It's now or never.

I look up at him, trying to stay strong. "I called off the wedding," I say, ripping off the Band-Aid.

Dad immediately lowers his fork and frowns. "Oh."

I close my eyes to keep the tears from falling. I'm not crying over the loss of my relationship with Robert. It's the disappointment on my dad's face that makes me emotional. I tried to prepare myself for his reaction, but it didn't do any good.

"Did you two break up last night?"

Nodding, I wipe my wet cheeks with my napkin. "I ended it earlier this week. Marrying a man I wasn't in love with anymore didn't feel right." It's the truth, just not the *whole* truth.

"I only want you to be happy, Gemma. I hope you know that."

"I do, but I feel awful because you've been so excited to walk me down the aisle and have talked about it for months. I was scared you'd be upset with me."

Dad reaches across the table and squeezes my hand. "Of course, I like the idea of you getting married and starting a family, but it has to be with the right man. That's all that matters to me. Maybe I got excited by the way Robert could take care of you, but I only want what's best for you."

"I can take care of myself, Daddy," I assure him with a small smile.

"You sure can. C'mere."

Pushing my chair back, I walk over to my dad and wrap my arms around him. When he hugs me tightly and kisses my forehead, relief floods through me.

"The whole town is gonna know in a matter of hours," I whine. "I hate how they all gossip."

"Don't worry about them. They'll talk about it for a couple of days, then move on to the next big thing."

God, I hope so. I just want to put this all behind me and start over.

"I have to ask," he mutters when I take my seat across from him. "Does your change of heart have anything to do with Tyler?"

"Dad!" I gasp, shocked he'd ask that. "I've already told you that we're *only* friends."

"I've noticed the way he looks at you, Gem. I may be old, but I'm *not* blind."

That causes me to snort, and I shake my head. "My feelings for Tyler are…complicated, but regardless, marrying Robert hasn't felt right for a long while. Way before Tyler returned."

"If it helps, I like Tyler a lot. He's a hard worker, and it's obvious he wants to get his life back on track. But I didn't appreciate the way he left you all those years ago. I could tell you were heartbroken."

The memory of my dad trying to help me through that sad time of my life brings back bad memories. "I was, but we were only kids. He's grown up since then. We both have. We're friends who work together and talk. That's it."

I'm not sure if he buys my casual way of ending this conversation, but he doesn't push it any further. We continue talking while we eat and finish our coffee. After we clean the kitchen and wash the dishes, Dad suggests we walk to the farmers' market, and I agree.

We stop by the boutique that's packed with teenagers and their moms. I notice her new inventory and fall decorations and feel so damn proud of what she's accomplished.

"Hey!" Everleigh wraps me in her arms. "Sorry, we're swamped."

"I see that! No worries. It's a good thing."

"Hey, Jerry." Everleigh gives him a side hug, and he kisses her cheek.

"Hey, sweetie. How're things goin'?"

"Great!" Her eyes light up when she focuses her attention past me.

Over my shoulder, I catch a glimpse of Tyler walking in with Sassy. My heart races as butterflies swarm my stomach. After the protective way he got me out of the restaurant last night, my mind has been running wild. He's wearing dark jeans and a blue T-shirt that shows off his arms. The facial hair on his jawline is longer, and though he typically keeps it trimmed, I kinda like it this way too.

"Hi," Tyler says to all of us when he gets closer. I sheepishly grin, embarrassed that my dad is with me and watching our interaction. "Thought I'd take the dog for a walk and stop in to visit."

"Yay! My girl." Everleigh immediately drops to her knees and loves on Sassy. "Are you being good for your daddy?"

Tyler chokes and backs away, causing me to chuckle. "What? Don't say that. It's creepy."

"No way! Whether you like it or not, you're the only male figure in her life right now."

I snort, shaking my head.

"This isn't funny."

Wrinkling my nose, I laugh harder. "It's a little funny."

He scowls, which is super adorable, considering Tyler's all man and muscle.

"I'm your brother, so if anything, that'd make me her uncle," he corrects Everleigh.

"Stop being dramatic. Don't forget to give her treats when you get home," she reminds him.

"Yeah, yeah. I know the drill."

"Don't fight it, son," my dad says, patting Tyler's shoulder. "Women bring home pets, and they become yours."

"So I'm learning." Tyler scoffs.

"Be thankful I never got a cat. Then again, it's not too late," Everleigh taunts.

"Please don't. I need to save up more money before I can move out, so at least wait until then."

Everleigh's hands move to her hips, and she pouts. "Ha-ha. You're staying with me forever."

"I'm sure your future husband would approve of that, no problem." Tyler rolls his eyes.

"Oh, he would. You'll just be included in all the baggage I bring to the relationship. He already has to accept that my first loves are my job and Sassy. Next, is you—my brother who lives with me and cooks for me."

"And there it is. The only reason you want me there."

"I thought I was clear on that?" Everleigh teases.

As they bicker, Katie and Owen enter and make it a reunion. My dad greets them, then tells me he'll meet me outside when I'm done.

"What's going on?" Katie asks.

"Just siblings fighting like cats and dogs while literally arguing about cats and dogs."

Katie bursts out laughing. "Damn, I missed all the fun."

"Swear word!" Owen shouts, then opens his palm.

Katie groans as she digs into her purse. "He was a lot cuter before he could talk."

Everleigh and I giggle as she hands Owen a dollar bill.

"My parents are watching him tonight. Wanna get Mexican food and drink margaritas?"

"I'd love to," Tyler interrupts with a shit-eating smirk.

"Girls' night, sorry," Katie sing-songs sarcastically. "If you're there, we won't be able to talk about you."

Blood rushes to my face, and my cheeks heat.

"And trust me, I hear there's a lot to talk about," Katie says pointedly.

I turn to Tyler, who's shooting daggers at Everleigh, who must've shared what she knew. She's so busted.

"What? Katie and I chatted this morning, and it kinda slipped out." Everleigh gives me an apologetic look, then shrugs it off. It grows awkward, so she busies herself by reorganizing a rack of clothes. "Oh, Cara needs help at the register. Gotta go! But count me in for tonight! Bye!" She shoots me a wink.

I glare at her, knowing she's full of shit because her new employee is handling it just fine.

"Alright, well I better go too. Don't want all the fresh fruit to sell out." Katie smirks, then glances back and forth between Tyler and me. She and Owen walk out, leaving us alone.

"Sorry, I told Everleigh."

"It's totally fine. They would've found out eventually. Guess I need to accept that it's only a matter of time before everyone else does too."

"I'd ask if you're okay, but that feels like a dumb question."

The roughness in his tone makes me smile. He's nervous.

"Nah, it's alright. I talked to my dad this morning and told him about the wedding."

"Really?" His eyes light up. "How'd he take it?"

"Surprisingly well. I feel a huge weight lifted off my shoulders now."

"Good. I'm happy to hear that. I know how worried you were about having that conversation." Seeing Tyler's genuine concern makes my heart burst.

"He asked about you too," I add.

With an arched brow, he gives me a cocky grin. "Yeah?"

"I explained we were just friends and you had nothing to do with the breakup. Though I'm not sure he believed me."

"What's the real reason then?"

I lower my gaze, noticing Sassy's getting restless. "It's...complicated?"

Tyler chuckles with a nod. "Guess that works."

Sassy whines and pulls on her leash. "You better go before she makes a mess in here," I tell him. "Have a good weekend."

"Yeah, you too." Tyler turns toward the door, and I quickly stop him, then step closer.

"Thank you again for last night. I owe you one."

"Owe me one, huh?" One side of his lips tilts up. "Guess I better think of something then."

His insinuation causes me to blush. "Get out of here."

Tyler flashes me a wink that causes my insides to melt, and I watch as he leaves with the dog. I recompose myself then meet my dad outside so we can head to the farmers' market like planned.

As I soak in the tub, I can't stop smiling while thinking about Tyler. After Dad and I came home, I did some laundry, then decided to take a bath before meeting Katie and Gemma for our girls' night.

Dear Gemma,

You're a real fresh breath of air, you know that? I love reading your letters even when you go in-depth about the movies you've watched. Helps me picture the scenes in my head and imagine I was there with you.

A few of my friends and I have leave this weekend. We're gonna hit the bars and will most likely drink till we're good and stupid. We're meeting a bunch of locals and will probably regret everything on Monday morning, but letting loose has been a long time coming. We could use some time to forget about the long, shitty days, especially in this grueling heat. Let's just say, I'll never complain about Alabama summers again. If I do, you have my permission to kick my ass.

Every picture you've sent was hanging on the wall near my bed. Everleigh sent me a few too, and the bastards I share a room with were constantly staring at your photos. I even had to punch a guy for stealing one. Sick fuck. So they're now tucked safely inside my notebook. I still look at yours every night before I go to sleep because they remind me of home. Although there isn't much for me there, I can't wait for the moment I'll see you again.

I recently heard a new song, and it made me think of you. Look up "Power Over Me" and listen to the lyrics.

Talk soon.
Love, Tyler

I had just turned eighteen when he wrote that letter, and I immediately rushed to find that song. Then I searched for the lyrics, and they had my heart lodged in my throat. I even found an interview where the singer explained what it meant to be completely enamored with somebody. And I instantly understood.

For weeks, I was in shock and giddy. Though I wasn't positive, I felt like my unrequited feelings weren't one-sided after all. No matter what Tyler wrote, my teenage brain was insecure and thought he was just trying to be nice since I was his sister's best friend.

It turns out, he'd been falling for me for a long time. Even knowing now what happened between us, I still wouldn't have done anything different. I'd do it all over again.

As I sip a glass of wine, surrounded by bubbles, I think back to when I first met Robert. It hadn't been instant attraction, and I'd rejected him the first couple of months he asked me out. Eventually, I convinced myself it was time to move on and that I was pathetic for not pursuing a relationship at my age. I pressured myself to open my heart again so I could prove I wasn't broken.

Robert was charming from the start. He always sent gifts and gave me countless compliments. In a way, he was too good to be true, but everyone kept telling me I was lucky and deserved him. So we kept going on dates, and I wanted to desperately believe what people said about his character. It'd been a long time since a man's hands had touched me, and I'd finally had the desire to feel that again.

Within six months, Robert was calling and texting me all day long, reminding me how much he loved and wanted a future with me. It happened so fast that I told myself I wanted that too, but now I realize I was only covering my pain.

I knew if I couldn't give myself to someone as great as Robert, then there was no hope for me.

I wanted the loving husband and kids. I wasn't getting any younger, so when he proposed in front of a crowd, I couldn't say no. All the red flags were there, yet I ignored them. If I wouldn't have put so much pressure on myself to get married, I might've seen who he truly was—a manipulative asshole.

As I drown in regret, my thoughts wander to the idea of having a future with Tyler. My heart wants to believe he's staying, but my head wonders if Lawton Ridge will really be enough for him—or if *I* could be.

Whatever happens between us can't be rushed. Though my body remembers his every touch, we need a fresh start.

After an hour of soaking, I dry off and get ready to hang out with the girls. We're meeting at Everleigh's, which means Tyler will be there at some point. While I should be wallowing in the loss of a two-year relationship and broken engagement, the idea of seeing Tyler gives me butterflies.

"Heeeey!" Everleigh pulls me inside after she opens the door.

"Good lord. Did you start drinking already?" I giggle when I catch a glimpse of Katie behind the counter with the blender.

"I couldn't wait any longer."

"I'm thirty seconds late," I deadpan, glancing around for Tyler.

"Well, I *was* pre-gaming."

With a snort, I walk to the kitchen. "Then I better catch up."

When the three of us have full glasses and a large bowl of popcorn, we get cozy on the couch. Everleigh grabs the remote and turns on a movie.

"*Pretty Woman*," I say. "Haven't seen that one in years."

"It's a classic and totally girls' night movie worthy," Katie smacks and pops some kernels in her mouth, then continues. "Who doesn't wish they'd get swept off their feet by a handsome, rich man after he's paid you thousands of dollars to be his escort?"

"Sounds like my kind of happily ever after." Everleigh nods.

"You two are twisted. Minus the hooker and falling madly in love part, that was almost my future, remember? It's not as great as it sounds."

"Oh shit." Everleigh covers her mouth. "I'm sorry, Gemma. I wasn't thinking." She holds up her drink. "Clearly. We can turn off the movie and talk about it."

"There's nothing to discuss," I insist. "Y'all knew I was second-guessing everything, and now that the wedding is officially called off, I feel confident about my decision. I wouldn't have been happy as his wife."

"I'm glad you came to that conclusion on your own," Everleigh says in a serious tone. "Now we can work on making you my future sister-in-law," she adds with enthusiasm.

Rolling my eyes, I take a long chug of my margarita to avoid responding.

The door whips open, and we turn and look.

Speak of the devil.

Tyler walks in with Ruby, and they greet us with wide smiles.

"Hey," he says in a sexy baritone.

"Ruby, join us!" Everleigh squeals, then stands and grabs her hand, dragging her to the couch. "Sorry, Tyler. No *boys* allowed."

"Alright, I was salty before for not getting invited, but now you stole my guest, and I *still* can't join?" The sarcasm in his voice has Katie and me bursting out in laughter.

Tyler and Ruby are sweaty and in workout clothes. Though Tyler looks nice dressed up, I enjoy seeing him in gym shorts and a sleeveless tee too.

"This is why I don't date straight chicks. They always wanna watch romantic comedies," Ruby says, nodding at the screen.

"Wait. That's an option?" Katie snickers.

Ruby chuckles. "Sometimes. They like the *idea* of being with a woman because they assume we're less complicated, but a couple of months later, I always get the 'I'm leaving you for a man' talk."

"Maybe they're just bi-sexual?" Everleigh suggests with a grin.

"But the D always wins," Tyler adds with a wink. The four of us stare at him. "What?" He shrugs, then walks down the hallway.

"He's not wrong." Everleigh smirks.

Moments later, I hear the sounds of water running and imagine Tyler naked in the shower. The girls chat as they watch Julia Roberts wear the smallest miniskirt ever, but my mind wanders elsewhere.

Halfway through the movie, my phone vibrates in my pocket. I suck in my lower lip to hide the goofy smile on my face when I see Tyler's name on the screen, but it's helpless.

Tyler: You look really pretty tonight.

I blush at his words and wish I could talk to him in person, but I promised Everleigh and Katie I'd hang out with them tonight. Plus, I never wanted to be that girl who ditched her friends for a guy. Though I have a feeling they'd understand.

Gemma: You're too sweet. Sorry we stole your friend. Do you want some company?

Tyler: I mean it. Nah, that's okay. I don't want to steal you from them, even if my sister is being obnoxious and loud.

Gemma: She was drinking before I even got here. Katie too.

Tyler: I overheard Everleigh and Katie talking the other day about Noah. I think Katie's getting anxious about it.

Noah has over a year left in prison, but I think Tyler being back has made her think about him more. I imagine she's wondering how she'll face him when he comes home.

Gemma: Maybe after a few more drinks, I can get her to spill the tea.

I laugh at the GIF of a woman sipping tea and hit send.

Tyler: Haha. Isn't that what girls' nights are for? Just make sure to talk slow and loud so I can eavesdrop.

Gemma: Ha!

Not wanting to be rude, I put my phone away. I'm half-listening to them chat as my mind circles back to Tyler. Could we actually work as a couple and be happy again? My heart says yes, but my head is skeptical. The chemistry between us is as strong as ever, but I'm still scared he'll leave again.

And if that happens, I won't be able to survive it twice.

CHAPTER THIRTY

TYLER

IT'S BEEN a week since Victoria showed her ugly face. Though Robert acted like he had no idea who she was, I don't buy it. The guy's a sleazy motherfucker, and even if he's being truthful, Victoria's vindictive. I called Eric to tell him, and he was just as shocked as I was when I saw her. He believes she's up to something and might be planning to retaliate for partaking in the deposition. If she knows what's good for her, she'll take her shady ass back to Vegas where she belongs.

The garage has been busy, but I have no complaints. Now that Gemma doesn't avoid me anymore, I look forward to arriving early and staying late. She and Everleigh hung out a few nights ago, but this time, they let me crash their girls' night. I didn't even care that they made me watch *Hocus Pocus* because I got to be near Gemma.

I don't have to work at the gym today and just want to spend my Saturday with Gemma. After I drink a cup of coffee, I work up the courage to text her.

Tyler: Do you have plans tonight?

Gemma: Besides eating ice cream with Tom Hanks, nothing.

Tyler: You have a weird obsession with him.

Gemma: Not any weirder than your Jack Nicholson infatuation.

I laugh because she has a point.

Tyler: Well, speaking of which, I'd like to make you dinner tonight. Then maybe we could watch The Shining since you've never seen it. What do you think?

Gemma: Just the two of us?

My throat tightens because I can't decipher if she's asking with excitement or panic.

Tyler: Yes, just the two of us. Well, and Jack Nicholson ;)

Gemma: I guess I can squeeze it into my very busy schedule for you and Jack.

I can hear her sarcasm in my head, and her smart mouth causes me to chuckle. I don't want to freak her out and call it a "date," but I like the idea of us moving in that direction. I'm okay with going slow so we can see where things go, as long as she wants the same.

I'm sure she won't mind hanging out in private because there's no prying eyes. Now that the rumor mill has started about her and Robert breaking up, everyone suspects she's heartbroken.

Tyler: Well, thank you for making time for us. We appreciate it.

Gemma: Of course. What time?

Tyler: Six? We can eat, then watch the movie after.

Gemma: Sounds good. I'll see you then.

She ends her text with two red hearts, and I've officially lost my man card because it makes me giddy as hell.

Now I need to figure out what I'm going to make, grocery shop, and perhaps find a new shirt.

I'm glad Everleigh's at work this morning so she can't give me shit for overpreparing, though I wish I had her insight on what to cook. It's been so long since Gemma and I have spent an evening together, and I want it to be special.

After researching some recipe ideas and making a decision, I text my sister.

Tyler: I'm hitting the grocery store soon. You need anything?

Everleigh: As a matter of fact, I do. Hold on, I'll send you my list.

This can't be good.
Moments later, I get a screenshot with a list of items.

Bread, buns, eyeliner, orange juice, eggs, tampons.

Everleigh: Make sure the eyeliner is black and the tampons are regular. Thanks!

She can't be serious.

Groaning, I grab my wallet and keys, then head to the store. Everleigh walked to work this morning and left me her car in case I needed it. I can't wait till I can buy a vehicle so I won't have to rely on her so much. Though I appreciate it, I hate having to ask.

I decided to go with steak tips with mushrooms and gravy. I haven't had it in years, and I think she'll love it. Then for dessert, we'll have cheesecake, and if I remember correctly, she liked hers topped with fresh strawberries.

After I grab everything along with Everleigh's grocery items, I head to the other side of the store. I have no idea what I'm searching for or what the hell eyeliner looks like. I snatch the first one I find and toss it into the cart. Then I make my way over to the next aisle and find no less than a dozen varieties of tampons. *How did me offering to buy food turn into looking through the makeup and feminine product aisles?* I find a box that has the word *regular* on it and hope it's right. Otherwise, Everleigh is shit outta luck and can do her own damn shopping next time.

Once I check out and pay, I drive to a shop on Main Street to find a new shirt. Most of my wardrobe consists of workout tees or sweatshirts. But tonight, I'd like to wear a button-up and something more formal. An older gentleman helps me find what I'm looking for, then talks me into a new pair of jeans and a belt. He's a great salesman, and I have to cut him off before I blow my budget.

"She's a lucky lady," he says as he rings me up.

"Excuse me?" I pull my wallet from my back pocket.

"I assume you have a date."

"No. Well, yes, kinda."

He grins. "Kinda? I think she'll get the memo as soon as she sees you. In fact, walk around to the barber shop and find Vin. I'm sure he can fit you in for a cut."

Brushing my hand through my hair, I realize it has been a while. "You think I need one?"

He casually shrugs. "Your beard could use a trim, too."

Well then. People in this town are sometimes too honest for their own good.

"Thanks for the tip."

"No problem." He smiles and gives me my total.

I put my bags in the car, then walk to the place he mentioned. Couldn't hurt to get cleaned up I guess, though Gemma's definitely gonna notice. I'm not sure if that'll be a good thing or not yet.

"Hello," an older man with a beer belly greets me.

"Hi, I'm Tyler. Do you have time for a haircut and a beard trim?" I ask, explaining the guy at the store recommended him. His mouth turns up, and he ushers me over to his chair.

"Let me take a look at you, son."

We discuss what type of cut, and I give him free rein. Forty-five minutes later, the hair on my head and face is trimmed, and I feel like a new man.

"Wow. You did a good job." I smirk.

"Thank you. Come back in four weeks."

I chuckle at his demand. "Okay."

After I'm finally home, I unpack the groceries and my clothes, then take a shower. Everleigh comes home and nearly squeals when she sees me.

"Holy shit. Where're you headed?"

"You're home earlier than usual," I deflect.

"Cara's closing tonight. And don't change the subject. You have a date."

"It's *not* a date," I counter. "I put your lady things in the bathroom."

"My lady things?" She giggles. "I can't believe you bought them."

I snap my eyes to her. "You told me to!"

"I added them as a joke, but it's nice to know that when a woman's in crisis, you'll rise to the occasion."

"You're such a brat."

"You love me."

I shake my head and make a mental note to get her back later.

"Now, tell me where you're going."

"Gemma's," I mutter as I grab all the ingredients and place them in a bag.

"Oh em gee!" she squeals.

I look at her and glare. "Stop that."

"I knew it. You two are destined together."

"I don't believe in destiny."

"What? Why not?"

I shrug. "I just don't. Things happen due to actions, not because of some special universe game."

"You're just jaded. I bet you'll think differently in a few months."

"Doubtful." I move around the kitchen counter and into the other room to find my shoes.

"You're all dressed up for a date and now you're packing food. Are you cooking?" she asks with way too much enthusiasm.

"Yes," I say, then explain what I'm making.

"Then eating *her* for dessert?" She waggles her brows.

I groan and grab my shit. "I'm leaving now."

"Alright, have fun! I won't wait up for you," she calls out, snorting. "Don't be loud when you come home tomorrow morning."

"You need to get a life so you can stay out of mine," I tease.

"Don't count on it since you'll be marrying and making babies with my best friend." She smirks when I shake my head and open the door. "Which means no using protection! You can't make a baby that way."

"You should stop drinking before five. It's a bad habit." She's gotta be wasted if she's talking about marriage and kids.

"It's almost six," she gloats.

"Then by all means, get smashed."

"Not that I need your permission, but Ruby and I are hanging out at the pub later tonight."

"What about Katie?"

"She couldn't find a sitter."

I would've offered to hang out with Owen if I didn't already have plans.

"Okay, well I gotta go. Behave yourself," I mock, then walk to the car and load everything.

By the time I park in Gemma's driveway, I'm a ball of nerves. I shouldn't be this damn anxious, but I am.

Grabbing my stuff, I go to her door and knock. As I inhale a deep breath, she opens it and beams at me.

"Wow," I exhale and scan my eyes down her blue dress that coincidentally matches my shirt. "You look beautiful."

Breathtaking, actually.

"Thank you." She licks her lips and blushes. I love when her cheeks tint that shade of pink. "And you look quite handsome yourself." Gemma steps back, allowing me to enter. "Did you get a haircut?"

I chuckle as I head to the kitchen. "I did."

Then I tell her about the guy who recommended the place and fill her in on Everleigh's shopping scheme as I unload the items.

"I can't believe you fell for that." She laughs as she opens the bottle of wine I brought. Gemma pours it into two glasses, then hands one over.

"She's feistier than I remember," I defend. "When I left, she was a sweet angel. You and Katie must be to blame."

"Trust me, she was anything but *sweet*. She was handing out condoms at a school fundraiser."

I take a sip of my drink and nearly choke. "Wait, what?"

"Yep. She made a sign too. *Our body, our choice, our right.* Then threw condoms like confetti."

"For fuck's sake." I let out a breath. "How did I not hear about that?"

"She almost got expelled, but your grandma marched down there and had 'words.'" She uses air quotes, and I snort.

"That couldn't have been good." I chuckle, digging around and grabbing a pot and pan. "Wow. So, she's always been this way."

"Ohhh yeah. Between the three of us, she's the instigator. Katie's the logical one, always trying to reason with her bad ideas."

"And what are you?"

She lowers her eyes. "The gullible one, I suppose."

I frown. "That's not true. You're the *sweet* one."

"Sweet and gullible," she counters.

"Sweet and gorgeous," I correct, flashing her a wink.

She tilts her head with a smile. "I guess I'll take it."

"Good. Now, I'm gonna make you the *best* meal of your life." I drizzle the oil, then add the pieces of steak.

"And what masterpiece are you creating tonight, *Chef Tyler*?"

Fuck. She just made that sound so goddamn sexy.

I tell her while adding seasoning, and I swear her mouth waters.

"And for dessert…" I hold up the cheesecake I bought.

"I think I just had a food-gasm. It already smells delicious." She hums.

My cock jerks at the sexy noise, and I quickly shift so she doesn't notice. As much as I'd love to feel her come on my fingers again, tonight is about us starting over.

It takes an hour to cook, and we chat the entire time. There's no awkward silence or weird tension and being with her feels as easy as it did before I left. Gemma relaxes, and I grin every time I hear her sweet laughter. She teases me, and I love every moment. As she watches me move around the kitchen, she offers to help, and I replay the memory of her disastrous attempt to make grilled cheese sandwiches last weekend.

"I got it," I insist, plating everything before we sit.

"Wow, Tyler." She closes her eyes as she moans around a forkful of food. "This is seriously so good. I think it's my new favorite meal."

"Yeah? That makes me happy to hear. I'm not quite up to the level I was at before prison, but I'll get there eventually. Especially if you keep letting me cook for you."

She smiles sweetly, and my gaze lingers on her lips that I'm desperate to kiss again.

"There's no way you were better because this is a ten outta ten. Maybe even an eleven with dessert."

"It's nice having someone else to cook for. I mean, if you don't count my mooching sister who literally takes food off my plate."

"What about before? Did you cook only for yourself then?"

"In Vegas, yes. When I was with Maddie and Liam, I was in the kitchen a lot. It helped the slow days go by as we played the waiting game. Maddie was a dancer in college and always sucking down protein smoothies, so I tried to help her break that habit."

"I bet she loved it."

"Oh, she did. Then when I stayed with them for a few weeks after I got out, I spoiled them with breakfast and dinner a handful of times. At first, it felt strange, but it's like riding a bike. Plus, it helps that I can follow directions."

"Well, if this meal is any indication, I think so too."

Gemma and I talk and laugh through the rest of dinner, then decide to save dessert until after the movie since we're both stuffed.

"You sure you're ready to watch this? It's a scary one."

"Do I have a choice?" she mocks, curling up on the couch with a blanket.

"It's not scary scary…more a psychological thriller."

"If I have nightmares tonight, I'm blaming you."

"Oh, don't be a baby. Jack Nicholson is amazing in this film."

"Hmm…we'll see." She smirks as I press play and then plop down next to her.

"Just by his expressions, I can tell he's crazy as hell," she says after a while.

I wrap my arm around her and pull her against my chest. "Here, I'll protect you."

Gemma beams, then snorts. "Smooth."

"Hey, gimme a break. Like my cooking skills, my game is a little off."

Gemma bursts out laughing until tears form in her eyes. "How do you always make me smile? After the past couple of weeks, I should be in a sour ass mood. But I don't think I've been this happy in months."

"You should always be laughing and smiling, Gemma. It's a beautiful sight to see and sound to hear." I turn and brush my thumb over her jaw, then pluck her bottom lip from between her teeth.

"Thanks for being here."

"Thank you for agreeing to hang out."

"No, I don't mean just tonight. I mean, for coming back. I know you didn't do it for *me*, but I'm glad you're home."

"I wasn't sure it would be the right choice, but it turned out to be one of the best decisions I've made in years."

She stares at my lips, and I battle with my head and heart on what to do next. Before I decide, a loud scream comes from the TV, and we both jump.

"Jesus." She rests a hand on her chest. "That scared the shit out of me."

I chuckle and take it as a sign. Tonight's not the night to cross that line.

We finish watching the movie, and when the credits roll, Gemma curses me out for the ending.

"You really thought it'd have a happily ever after like one of your cheesy romance films?" I tease as I cut the cheesecake.

"Well, I was holding out hope." She crosses her arms.

"Alright so, besides that, what'd you think?"

"It was…*interesting*. Not something I'd ever watch again, though."

"That's fine because you have fifty more to choose from." I smirk.

"I need a break before suffering through another, okay? Like maybe something with Patrick Swayze."

"Let me guess, *Dirty Dancing*?"

"Yep. One of my favorites."

"I remember," I say softly. "You and Everleigh went through a whole phase when you were like thirteen and played the soundtrack on repeat."

"Oh my God, that's right." Her eyes light up with excitement. "We tried to learn all the steps, just like Baby and Johnny."

"I wanted to bash my head into a wall. That was probably why I started going to the gym and taking out my frustrations on a punching bag."

"Very funny."

"Oh, I'm serious. Y'all were always so loud, singing the lyrics at the top of your lungs."

"We were teenagers," she defends.

"Exactly and, at the time, extremely annoying." I chuckle. "But don't worry, I only think you're a little annoying now. So that's progress."

She scoffs with a small smile.

"Alright, let me add the toppings, then we can dive in." I slice the strawberries, then add whipped cream.

"You ever thought about working as a chef, like for real?" she asks.

"Maybe, but I'd rather get my hands dirty and sweaty in a ring. Perhaps, getting hired at a restaurant will be my plan C."

"Must be exhausting to have so many talents," she teases, stealing a piece of fruit.

"It is," I say dramatically. "Good thing I've been celibate for the past five years. Wouldn't wanna be a complete show-off."

Gemma chokes and gasps for air. For a split second, I worry she won't be able to catch her breath, but then she swallows and chuckles.

"Jesus, are you okay?"

She wipes the tears from her eyes as she continues grinning. "Yes, but I think you're trying to kill me."

"I didn't realize you were so sensitive."

"I wasn't expecting that!"

With a smirk, I shrug. "Sorry. Next time, I'll make sure you don't have any food or beverages near your mouth."

"How generous," she muses.

Once our desserts are ready, we take them and sit on the couch. That sexy moan that escapes her tests my willpower to be a gentleman.

"So, can I ask about Robert?" I ask carefully, and she nods.

"I haven't heard from him since last Friday," she admits. "I hope that's a good sign, and that he'll leave me the hell alone."

"You think he will?" I glance at her.

She sighs. "I hope so. I have nothing to say to him. Most of the town knows anyway, so it'd be pointless to try to 'fix' what's broken between us. Not to mention, I have no desire to give him another chance."

"Maybe we'll both get lucky, and he'll become Victoria's focus, then they'll both be out of our lives for good."

"One can dream, right?" She licks some of the whipped cream from the strawberries, and I quickly look away before she catches me.

"So I have a question, and you can totally say no."

"I probably won't." I smirk. "What is it?"

She sets her empty plate down on the coffee table and faces me. "I'm driving over to Clayton tomorrow to see Noah. I'd really love it if you'd come with me, unless you feel uncomfortable."

I wasn't expecting that. Though I have no desire to set foot in a prison again, I'd be on the other side this time.

"Never mind, I shouldn't have asked. Of course, you don't wanna go," she quickly says, then waves it off.

"Gemma, I'll join you," I quickly tell her. "Might be good for Noah to see what his life can potentially be like after, and perhaps it'll give him some hope."

"Really?"

"Yeah, really. If you don't think he'd mind." Based on what Katie said, Noah hasn't wanted many visitors, so it may be crossing a line.

"He won't. I told him about your situation years ago after it happened, and we spoke not too long after you came home. I think you're right. It'll give him some peace knowing life isn't over after prison."

"Then count me in."

CHAPTER THIRTY-ONE

GEMMA

Spending time with Tyler yesterday was amazing, and it felt like old times. We laughed so much, and it took my mind away from reality, which is exactly what I needed. At the end of the night, I walked him outside, and he kissed my cheek. I blushed when he caught me off guard, and nearly stuttered over my words as I told him what time I'd be at his place the next day.

I was dying for him to kiss me, but I fought the urge to make a move. Though we haven't really talked about what we're doing or where this is going, it's obvious we love being around each other. There's no use denying what we both want.

Rumors and gossip be damned.

I've spent the past two years of my life worried about what others thought of me, and I was miserable. I won't let those concerns run my life anymore. People's opinions won't stop me from doing what makes me happy.

After giving myself a pep talk, I drive over to pick up Tyler. When I spoke to my brother last week, he didn't seem against the idea of Tyler coming with me when I mentioned it. Hopefully, he's okay with it because I called the prison this morning and added his name to the visitors' list.

"Good morning," he says with a smirk as he gets into the car.

"Hey." He's dressed in another nice button-up, and I stop trying to imagine how I'd strip that shirt right off him. "Wanna grab coffee first? It's about an hour away."

"Sure. Want me to drive?"

"I can since you don't know how to get there, and then you can drive us back."

Tyler buckles, then surprises me when he takes my hand. "Deal." He brings it to his lips and presses a gentle kiss on my knuckles. "I'll buy the coffee since we're taking your car."

I'm so focused on his mouth that I nearly forget where we are. Sighing, I put the car in reverse, then drive us to the Coffee Palace, a newer hip cafe that opened last summer. They serve fun theme drinks, and I can't wait for Tyler to try it.

"Happy Sunday!" Marjorie exclaims the moment we enter. She has her hair parted and put up into two messy buns that look adorable.

"Hey!" I reply, and when my hand brushes Tyler's, he grabs it and interlocks our fingers. I try to hold back how giddy I am, but when I glance at him, I can't stop the stupid smile that fills my face.

We step up to the counter and browse the menu. "Y'all gotta try one of my new seasonal lattes for fall!"

"Ooh, which ones?" I ask, excited. I love all the tasty drinks she creates.

"Pumpkin cream, apple butter spice, and harvest caramel."

"I literally can't imagine what those would taste like," Tyler blurts out, and I giggle.

"Oh, darling, you can't go wrong with any of them. *Trust me*," Marjorie gloats.

I snort at Tyler's wide-eyed expression. "Can I just get a regular coffee with cream?"

"What flavor?" she asks, typing on her cashier's screen.

"Just black."

"There are different types," I explain, then point at the options.

"Uhh…a dark roast?"

"I have Southern blaze and sunshine rain."

Tyler looks at me, and I hold back a laugh. Marjorie roasts her own beans and makes her own unique blends.

"Surprise me," Tyler finally says.

"I'll take a pumpkin cream with almond milk," I confirm.

"Comin' right up." Marjorie tells us the total. Tyler lets go of my hand and grabs his wallet, and I immediately miss his touch.

After he's paid, she pours a plain coffee and directs Tyler to the cream and sugar on the other side.

"That's Tyler Blackwood, right?" she asks when he's out of earshot.

"Yep," I respond, waiting for her inevitable question of whether we're dating.

"Wow." She smirks. "Talk about a glow-up, amiright?" Marjorie waggles her brows, and it causes me to snort.

"Definitely." I nod. Though Tyler was always handsome, he's definitely bulked up and matured over the years.

"One pumpkin cream latte with almond milk," she calls and hands it over.

Tyler and I thank her, then head to the car.

"Well, that was interesting." He reaches my door and opens it for me.

"Thank you." After I take my seat, he closes it, then jogs to his side and slides in. "You'll get used to it. I'm guessing they didn't have premium lattes in prison?" I tease.

"If you consider stale coffee premium, then yes. Otherwise, hell no." Tyler winks. "How's your Halloween in a cup?"

I take another sip and hum. "Delicious. Wanna try?"

"Sure, but if it makes me gag, I'm blaming you."

"Now you're just being dramatic like Everleigh."

He glances at me before trying it, almost as if he's questioning his decision. "That's pure sugar. Damn." He makes a face, then hands it back.

"That's the point. Sugar rush and caffeine. It'll wake my ass right up."

Tyler's eyebrow lifts. "If you say so."

We chat the entire time, both of us cracking jokes and talking about random topics. He mentions I should try another Jack Nicholson movie, and I agree but only if he watches a romantic comedy with me. After we shook on it, he captured my hand and placed it on his lap.

By the time we arrive at the prison, giddy butterflies swarm my stomach. I can't wait to see Noah again and am grateful I can spend time with Tyler too.

"You ready?" I ask. "We'll sign in, they'll do a quick body search, then we'll wait for them to release him."

"Ready as I'll ever be." He shrugs and gives me a wink. I imagine this is hard, and I appreciate him being here with me.

Thirty minutes later, we're finally in the visitation room, and I notice Tyler's leg shaking.

"You okay?" I whisper, reaching for his hand, and he takes it.

"Just some overwhelming flashbacks, but I'm alright."

Moments later, a guard ushers Noah forward, and I light up with excitement. I wish I could wrap my arms around him, but there's a no touching policy.

"Hey!"

"Hi, sis. You look good."

"Thank you. Remember Tyler Blackwood?" I nod toward him.

"Of course. How's it goin', man?"

"Can't complain. Hope you don't mind me being here."

"It's fine. As long as you go back and tell everyone in town I'm ripped as fuck now." Noah chuckles.

I shake my head, grinning. "And still cocky as ever," I add.

"Yeah, well, that'll probably never change." Noah shrugs. "So fill me in on what's happening. Anything new with Robert?"

We spoke the day after Robert's and my huge blowout, and I told him I'd ended it.

"He hasn't reached out to me since the dinner last Friday, and I'm hoping it stays that way."

"You know I love you, Gem, but I'm happy you called it off."

"Have you met him?" Tyler speaks up.

"Once, and that was enough to confirm I didn't like him, but even so, Gemma was gonna do what she wanted anyway."

"I asked him to come here with me, but he'd always say he was too busy with work," I explain. Looking back, Robert always acted too good to be seen visiting a convict in prison. He judged and mocked people who had criminal records, my brother included.

"Fine by me. Less times I had to fake being nice." Noah flashes a smirk.

"Just wait till you come home. Everyone's polite to your face but talks shit behind your back," Tyler warns. "Hope you got some thick skin."

"Tyler…" I mutter and give him a look. The last thing I want is to scare Noah about going home.

"Gem, it's fine. You don't need to sugarcoat anything for me. Without a doubt, it's gonna be rough, but since Tyler is there, I won't be so alone." Noah shrugs, and it breaks my heart that he'll have to deal with this when he's out.

"I'm not trying to. I just wanna make sure you don't change your mind and move to Alaska or something."

"That's way too damn cold for me." Noah grunts. "Plus, I don't have any money, remember? I'll be a thirty-three-year-old man living the dream at home."

"I'm thirty-four, and I'm staying with my baby sister," Tyler mocks. "She said we can start a convicts club when you're back."

Noah laughs, and I love hearing that sound come from him because it doesn't happen often.

"I've been working out at the gym, training a few people."

"So what you're saying is I have less than eighteen months to bulk up so I can kick your ass?"

"Yep, something else to look forward to," Tyler says, and I'm glad he's being so positive.

Glancing back and forth between the two of them, I beam because they're getting along so well.

"So you're dating my sister now?" Noah asks bluntly.

"Noah!" I whisper-hiss. "I just ended my engagement."

"Exactly. You're a free woman. He better hurry before another old guy swoops in and steals you away."

Tyler tries to hold back his laughter, but fails, as I hang my head. "You're both jerks."

"Hey, I just said what Tyler is probably thinking."

"What the whole town is thinking," Tyler adds.

"How'd we get on the subject of me anyway? We're here to talk about *you*," I deflect. There's no way Tyler and I are having this conversation in front of my brother in a prison.

"There hasn't been anything *new* with me in over eight years." Noah leans back, crossing his arms. "Well, unless you consider us getting two new flavors of Jell-O this month."

"Ooh, which ones?" Tyler acts interested.

"Watermelon and strawberry banana," Noah confirms.

I burst out laughing at his excitement. "If that makes you happy, just wait till Tyler makes you one of his amazing dinners. He's practically a chef."

"No," Tyler argues. At the same time, Noah says, "Can't wait!"

"Stop being so modest. Considering you could've lived on ramen and PB&J sandwiches but decided to teach yourself how to cook so you and Everleigh could eat a home-cooked meal is something to be proud of," I tell him genuinely. He probably doesn't think he did anything special, but he did. Tyler was all Everleigh talked about in middle and high school, and those stories are what had me falling for him in the first place.

Tyler and Noah mostly chat about Noah's plans when he's free. Though I know better than to mention Katie's name, Tyler has no shame in doing so.

"Since our time is almost up, I gotta ask. Why didn't you ever write Katie back or let her visit?"

The moment his question comes out, Noah's face pales.

Shit.

Bowing his head before shaking it, Noah blinks at us with glossy eyes. "It's *complicated*."

When I spoke about it with Tyler and explained Noah's version of "it's complicated," he said he understood Noah's reaction. However, Tyler looks like he's ready to bust Noah's balls for pushing Katie away.

"You gotta man up," Tyler insists. "Life's too short."

"Trust me, I'm aware of that. I live with the guilt of what happened every single day. I wanna be able to see Katie in person, not with a table between us and no privacy."

Everyone was shocked when Gabe died and more so when Noah was convicted of his murder. The whole situation is a tragedy, and though Noah didn't mean to harm our cousin, he acted on emotions instead of logic. Katie stayed with Gabe for the baby and because she always wanted a family. Eventually, I think she would've left him after his cheating scandals, but in the heat of the moment, Noah didn't think about that.

And it will cost him a decade of his life.

"You know I love you, but I'm not sure your relationship with Katie is repairable after all the times you denied her visitation and ignored her letters," I blurt out even though I hope it's not true. Katie deserves closure after all this time, but Noah better be ready to grovel.

Staying quiet, Noah just nods.

"But hey, look at me. If I can win my girl back in two months after twelve years, there's definitely hope for you." Tyler flashes me a wink.

His girl.

I could definitely get used to hearing that.

"So you two *are* dating. I knew it," Noah says, chuckling.

I shake my head, denying it. This isn't the time or place to decide that.

"We're seeing where things go." Tyler gives me a smirk, and my insides melt. Though we haven't discussed it, we have an unspoken mutual understanding between us.

"And if I managed to get a job—*two* jobs—after moving away, you won't have any problems. People might be wary at first, but a lot of them have big hearts." Tyler squeezes my hand. "At least that's what I'm seeing. They just need some time to warm up to ya."

I nod, agreeing. Lawton Ridge is a close-knit community, and everyone deserves a second chance, even Noah.

For the remaining ten minutes, we chat about Dad and the garage, then the guard announces visiting time is over. I always get a little sad when I watch the cuffs go on his wrists before he's ushered out of the room.

"I love you!" I call out before he's out of sight.

"Love you too, Gem. See you soon." He smiles, a genuine one this time, and it warms my whole body.

Tyler and I walk out to my car, hand in hand, and I can't stop the giddiness in my voice. "You guys really hit it off."

"Noah's easy to get along with. Now, we just have a little more in common than before." He grins, then opens my door.

"It means a lot to me. He's gonna need someone besides family on his side when he comes home."

Tyler brings his fingers to my cheek, then tucks loose strands of my hair behind my ear. I stare at his lips, hoping he'll finally kiss me.

"I'll be happy to help or do whatever I can for him."

Tyler's rough exterior is crumbling to his feet as he shows me his softer, sweeter side that I never forgot. He was a hardass around other people and kept to himself a lot, never revealing more than he needed, but I always saw the real Tyler. After spending that time in the military, he had a sexy broodiness to him, but this loyally fierce side of Tyler is the best I've ever seen.

And I'm falling for him all over again, except harder and stronger this time.

As promised, Tyler drives us home. He lets me pick the music even though I offered him the choice. Time flies as we talk and hold hands. Before I know it, he's pulling into Everleigh's driveway.

We both step out of the car, but Tyler's quick and is in front of me before I can go to the driver's side. He cages me in, and I meet his gaze.

I wait, hoping he'll make the first move, *begging* him with my eyes to lean in, but he doesn't. Tyler's letting me set the pace because I'm the one with everything to lose if we don't work out.

But I've never been more sure of anything in my life. I want him. No, I *need* him.

Without giving it another thought, I wrap my fingers around the back of his neck and pull his face to mine, allowing our lips to crash together. Tyler slides his hands down my body and grips my hips, grinding himself against me. My back presses against the car as our tongues battle in a heated kiss. When I moan against his mouth, he tilts my head up and slides in deeper.

Arching my back, I feel his hardness against my stomach, causing an ache between my legs. I thread my fingers through his hair and grip him tighter, not wanting this to end.

By the time we come up for air, I'm flushed, and my whole body tingles.

Tyler smiles. "Wow. What was that for?"

Blushing, I bite my lip. "To say thank you for coming with me today. It really meant a lot." I pause before adding, "And also for cooking me dinner last night."

"I'll cook for you anytime. And thank you for asking me to come. I didn't realize how much I needed to do it until I got there. Though I felt anxious at first, it wasn't as bad as I thought it'd be."

"I think you helped Noah more than you realize. He'll have more hope now than what I could've given him. You have firsthand experience, and I can tell he trusts you."

"I'm happy to tag along anytime you want," he reassures me. Tyler looks down and notices his bulge that's impossible to miss. He lowers his arm and crosses his hands over it. "I better get inside before I embarrass myself out here."

Arching a brow, I smile. "Alright. See you tomorrow morning."

"I'll text you later, okay? I'm gonna work off some…" He clears his throat. "Frustrations." Then he lowers his eyes, and I hold back my laughter.

He walks me to the other side of the car, opens my door, then gives me a sweet kiss before I get in and buckle. As I back out, Tyler waves. My heart pounds hard as I drive home, and I can't wipe the stupid grin off my face.

I've been dying for his kiss since the last time our lips touched, and I already want to drive back to his place and do it again.

CHAPTER THIRTY-TWO

TYLER

If I could bottle up my time with Gemma this week and relive those moments a million times over, I would. As crazy as it sounds, it feels like the last twelve years apart never happened, and we picked up right where we left off. Talking to her is as easy as it was when I wrote her letters and we spilled all our secrets. She's the last person I think of before bed and the first when I wake up.

I want to give Gemma my heart and let her keep it forever. Hell, she's had it for over a decade.

Ever since she kissed me on Sunday, we've been inseparable. Seeing her at work is equal parts amazing and torturous because all I want to do is pull her into my arms and never let go. Though it's mid-week, we're meeting up tonight after my training session. The plan is wine, pizza, and *One Flew Over the Cuckoo's Nest*. I chuckle to myself, knowing she'll groan the whole time, or we'll be too busy exploring each other's mouths to pay attention to the screen. I'm hoping for the latter.

We've only been at work for a couple of hours, but I already miss her. I tell Jerry I need a coffee refill so I can sneak a quick moment with her. Luckily, the lobby's empty so I'll get her to myself for a few minutes.

Gemma smiles, and I swoop her into my arms, pulling her close to my chest as I press a soft kiss to her lips.

"What're you doing?" she whispers, glancing around to see if her dad's near.

Grabbing her hand, I lead her into the break room and move forward until her back pushes against the wall. "Trying to get to second base."

She giggles, and I steal a kiss. "Okay, make it quick. A customer could come in at any minute."

Smirking, I dip my head and suck her neck, tasting her soft skin. I slide my hand up her body, then cup her breast and squeeze.

Pulling back, I meet her eyes. "Thanks, that should hopefully last me through lunch."

Gemma's jaw drops with a gasp, then she smacks me playfully on the chest. "You're bad. Get back to work, Mr. Blackwood." Her voice lowers in a commanding tone, which makes me hard as hell.

"Fuck. It's hot when you call me that."

Gemma lowers her gaze and gives me a cheeky grin. "Good luck with that. Just remember, you're working with my father."

I adjust my dick and grunt. "Thanks, that killed it."

The door chimes ring, and she quickly paints her lips across mine. "Now go! Before you get us both in trouble."

As I nonchalantly make my way to the shop, I think about Maddie and how she'd be losing her shit right now if she knew that Gemma and I were...*something*. I should probably give her an update so she'll stop sending me links to dating apps.

"Tyler, why don't you start your lunch break? I'll finish up here, then take mine."

"Alright." I wash my hands and scrub as much of the grease off as I can. Today, I plan to get Gemma one of her froufrou lattes she loves so much. Gemma watches me as I make my way to the door, and I turn and give her a wink before leaving.

The moment I walk into the Coffee Palace, I'm greeted by the smell of roasted beans and the sound of espresso machines. Marjorie lights up when she sees me. I tell her to pick something for Gemma and a black coffee for me.

"Are you absolutely sure I can't talk you into trying our new harvest caramel latte? It's very sweet *and* salty. Best of both worlds."

"No, no. But thanks. Just a dark roast."

After I pay, she hands me my cup with a flirty wink and gives me Gemma's pumpkin cream.

Lord, the people in this town are a little too friendly sometimes.

Just as I'm about to leave, my phone rings, and when I see it's Serena, I set the drinks down.

"Hey," I answer, surprised to hear from her. We typically text unless it's something important.

"Tyler, hi. Sorry to bother you during work, but I just got some news and wanted to pass along the details."

Her words and tone have my heart racing. "Involving what?"

Serena hesitates and inhales a deep breath, which means it's not good. "The case against Victoria was dismissed. Her attorneys got it thrown out on a technicality."

"What?" I roar. "You're fucking joking."

"I wish, Tyler." She sighs, and it's obvious she's just as upset about this as I am. "I'm sorry."

"It's not your fault, but man, I feel awful for Eric. Does he know yet?"

"Yes, the prosecutor called me right after the announcement was made. I don't think he's gonna take it lying down, though, and honestly, I'm a little worried about him."

Considering Victoria is already scheming her revenge, I'm worried for him too.

"Thanks for letting me know. I'll speak to him."

"Stay safe, Tyler."

We hang up, and I blow out a frustrated breath. I can't believe this.

Then again, I definitely can.

Victoria has more money than God, and she'll use it to her advantage to get out of every-damn-thing she can.

I quickly text Eric since I wanna get back to the shop before Gemma's latte gets cold.

Tyler: Hey, man. I just heard the news. I'm so sorry.

Eric: Don't worry, I'll get my justice for Amara another way.

I cringe when I read his message because he's not going to let this go. Though I don't blame him for wanting to fight, we both know Victoria's dangerous.

Tyler: What do you mean? Don't do anything that'll get you killed or locked up. It's not a life you want, trust me.

By the time I walk into the lobby, I'm tense as hell, but I try to shake it off so I can enjoy the rest of my break with the woman who drives me wild.

"Hey, beautiful. I got you something." I hand her the cup, and when she smells it, she smiles wide.

"You're so sweet," she hums before taking a sip. "Oh God, it's so delicious."

"Save those moans for later, please. I can't keep trying to hide my chubby around your dad."

Gemma nearly spews out her drink but quickly covers her mouth and swallows it down. "Tyler!" she laugh-hisses.

We go to the break room and talk while we eat. I check my phone for Eric's response, but one never comes.

The rest of the afternoon goes smoothly, and by five, I'm on my way out to do my training session with Luke.

"I'll be over at seven thirty," I remind her. "That okay?" It'll give me time to shower and hopefully grab something to eat beforehand.

"Sounds good. I'll be waiting…" She bites her lower lip, and I groan.

"Stop that."

I give her a quick kiss before Jerry can catch us. Though I'd be okay with him knowing we're casually dating and hope he'd approve, I'm letting Gemma decide when she wants to share the news. After her breakup with Robert, I think she's waiting to tell him.

Luke and I train hard for an hour straight. He's getting pretty good, and I'm proud of how far he's come in such a short amount of time. Afterward, I chat with Ruby for a few minutes, then head home.

"Who's there?" Everleigh dramatically shouts when I walk in. "It can't be my brother! He doesn't live here anymore."

"What's up your ass?" I tease. "Missing me?"

She rolls her eyes before moving to the kitchen and grabbing a corkscrew. "Your cooking? Yes. Your bad jokes? Not so much."

"Oh, come on. You're the one who was all Team Tyler and Gemma get married and have babies. How's that gonna happen if we never spend any time together?" I set my bag down and flash her a mischievous smirk.

Everleigh groans as she grabs a bottle of wine. "I didn't think it all the way through. Now that you two are…" She waves her hand around. "Whatever you two are, I don't get to see either of you. Can't you squeeze me in and still fall in love?"

"You need a boyfriend," I mock. "Then you wouldn't be in my business."

She pours herself a glass and makes a face. "Not true. Unlike the both of you, I can balance work and still make time for my friends and family."

"Alright, fair enough. We'll hang out tomorrow, okay? I'll even make Cajun chicken pasta."

"Ooh, carbs. Now you're talkin'."

I chuckle as I wrap an arm around her shoulders and give her a hug. "I'll tell Gemma to make some brownies too."

She glares. "So by 'we'll hang out,' you meant *all* of us."

"Well, yeah." I shrug. "Why not?"

"So I'll be the awkward third wheel."

"Invite Ruby or Katie. Or I dunno, a *date*."

"You've been out of the game for several years and don't understand how unpredictable and flaky people are in today's climate. Every guy on every dating app, 'Hey, beautiful. Wanna see a dick pic?' Then proceeds to send it before I respond. After that happens a good thirty to forty times, you kinda just give up hope and realize there aren't any decent single men left."

"Okay, point taken. That's gross, by the way."

"Especially when they're so proud of their balls." She makes a face. "Then they ask for a boob shot, and I send them a picture of Sassy's nipples." She laughs at her own joke.

Shit, that makes me especially glad I didn't take Maddie's advice and join those apps.

"Well, you have fun with that. I need to shower and grab a pizza and wine before I head to Gemma's."

"The perfect couple's date night." She gags, then snickers. "I really am happy for you guys. Robert wasn't right for her, and I'm just glad she realized that before it was too late."

Me too.

"So are you two official yet? Or just friends with benefits?"

I snort. "Are we gossiping like high schoolers now? I'm not one of your girlfriends, Ev."

"Maybe not, but you're dating one of mine, so…"

She does have a point.

"We haven't talked about it, but we're going slow, and I'm letting her set the pace."

"I love you, brother, but if you break her heart again, I won't forgive you twice."

Nodding, I frown because I know Everleigh was there for Gemma and helped pick up the broken pieces I left behind.

"Trust me, I'm not planning on it. I don't want to lose her this time, and I'd marry her now if that was an option."

And it's the truth.

Gemma is the *only* girl for me.

"That's more like it." Everleigh grins. "Now, go have fun with my best friend and reiterate that she's yours and always will be."

Thirty minutes later, I arrive at Gemma's with goodies in hand and excitement in my step. As much as Everleigh's a pain in my ass, she makes valid points. Gemma is mine now, and I want her to know I'm in this for the long haul.

"Hello, gorgeous," I say when she lets me inside her house.

"Mmm, smells delicious," she purrs. "The pizza, I mean."

I laugh. "What every man who's trying to win over the girl of his dreams loves to hear."

She looks at me and tilts her head. "I don't think you need to worry about that, considering I just ended a relationship. All I wanna do is spend time with you."

After I set everything down on the kitchen island, I close the gap between us and wrap her in my arms. Tilting up her chin, I bring her mouth to mine and slowly brush my lips against hers. I slip my tongue inside, tasting her sweetness, wanting to devour her.

"I hope one day we're doing a lot more than just *spending time* with each other." I flash her a wink.

"Same." She smiles.

"According to my sister, we should already be married with a baby on the way, so caution to the wind the next time you speak to her."

"Oh, trust me, I'm aware. She's already sent me a list of baby names."

I snort. "We seriously need to get her a boyfriend so she'll stop obsessing over us."

"Oh, I've been trying to hook her up for years. She'll go on a couple of dates, then find something wrong with them all. It's stupid things too, like the way the guy chews or the type of socks he wears. Never fails. Every. Single. Time." Gemma shakes her head. "She'll sleep with them, though."

"Ahh, okay, that's enough about my sister's sex life. Moving on to our dinner and movie."

Gemma chuckles, and we fill our plates and glasses.

"So what torturous movie are you making me watch tonight?" she asks as we sit on the couch.

When I tell her the title, she rolls her eyes. "Tomorrow night, we're watching *27 Dresses* or *Knocked Up*."

"Actually, tomorrow…" I linger after taking a bite of pizza. "I promised Everleigh we'd hang out with her because she's getting cranky we're always together. She said she'd be the third wheel, but I told her to invite someone." I shrug, certain she won't.

"Perfect! Definitely a Katherine Heigl movie then."

"I'll make sure we're stocked up on whiskey."

"You mean margaritas?" she counters.

"No, I'm gonna need the hard stuff to get through one of your movies."

Gemma lifts her glass of wine with a smirk. "Exactly why I'm planning to drink the whole bottle tonight."

I laugh, but it doesn't matter because at this moment, we're more focused on each other.

There's no doubt about it—I'm falling even harder and faster for Gemma Reid, and I don't ever want this feeling to stop.

CHAPTER THIRTY-THREE

GEMMA

Though it's Sunday and I typically sleep in, I get up early. Once I'm dressed and drink a cup of coffee, I head over to Katie's house. We're going to some open houses, and I've been looking forward to it all week. Considering she wants a fixer-upper, it'll be fun to walk through rooms with character that have actually been lived in. It'll be a stark difference from the brand-new cookie-cutter mansions Robert stages with pricey furniture. When I park in her driveway, she opens the front door wearing a smile and waves me inside. Though when I walk in, she seems anxious and fidgety.

"Everything okay?" I ask.

"Yeah, just nervous about today. Plus, Owen threw a fit when my mother came to get him. He thinks he's old enough to stay home alone. Boys," she groans, rolling her eyes. "It's times like this when I wish I would've had a girl."

"Yeah, but she probably would've been worse, especially if she'd been anything like you. Young Katie was a high-maintenance, bratty know-it-all," I tease.

Katie chuckles, grabbing her purse. "You're probably right. I should be careful what I wish for and more thankful for what I have. I'd rather deal with a boy because our biggest arguments revolve around showering and video games."

"Exactly." I nod as we go to her car.

After we buckle in, Katie hands me a piece of paper with several addresses written down. I notice one's a block down from my house. "Oh, I recognize this one. I think an older couple used to live there, and after their kids grew up, they moved to Alaska or something."

"Really? So it's not haunted. Noted." She snickers as she drives us across town.

"So how's the single life?" Last week, I told her all the details of Robert's and my breakup and how I have zero plans to work it out with him.

I hold back a grin but fail miserably.

"Oh, excuse me," she says all dramatically. "What I should've asked was how are you and Tyler?"

"Good. Actually great, if I'm being honest. We've been inseparable, and while we haven't put a label on it, it feels official. I can't stop kissing and touching him anytime he's near. It's never felt like this with anyone but him."

Katie glances at me. "Happiness fits you, Gemma. Have y'all… you know?"

"No," I rush out. "Not *yet*. We're taking things one day at a time. I appreciate how patient he is, though I'm ready to jump his bones," I admit, and Katie chuckles.

"Don't blame you a bit." She drives to the end of the cul-de-sac and turns off the car.

The street is packed with vehicles, and other people are taking the sidewalk that leads to the perfectly landscaped yard. The suburban neighborhood is cute, and I could picture Katie living here.

"If you're already like this and you haven't banged it out, I can only imagine how you'll be when you finally do." She waggles her brows, and I snort.

"*If*…we do," I correct, but I know it's just a matter of time.

"You might be able to pull that on someone else, but it's more than obvious how you both feel. Always has been." We go to the front door and are escorted in by a real estate agent. While the outside of the house is brick with picture-perfect shutters, the inside is a living time capsule. Brown shag carpet and flowered wallpaper are in the main rooms. Katie and I give ourselves a tour, and when we enter the bathroom, the Pepto pink fixtures and tile nearly blind us.

She turns to me with her mouth in a firm line. "Okay, this is where I draw the line."

"But you can remodel and make it however you want," I remind her with a snicker, but she's not convinced. The rooms are large, but the ceilings are low, and it all needs work. While I think she could handle it, this place would be a huge undertaking. Before we go, the real estate agent hands her a card.

"Thank you," Katie says. "How's the neighborhood? Are there a lot of children?"

The woman contemplates as though searching for the correct answer. "Not really. Lots of older people." She pauses with a smile. "But it's very quiet, and the crime rate is low," she adds.

"Great. Thanks so much," Katie politely says before we leave. "No, but hell no," she mumbles when we're out the door.

"We still have four others to see. That's just the first," I remind her.

She nods and laughs. "Hopefully, it gets better. Too bad I don't have Chip and Joanna with me. They'd be able to help me find a good buy."

"Who?" I ask as she cranks the car, then takes off.

"The Gaines. *Fixer Upper*! They had a show on HGTV." She glares at me as though I've committed a crime.

"I don't watch much cable," I explain. "Just movies and Hallmark."

"There are tons of reruns you can watch. They're amazing and gave me a lot of inspiration for what I want. I highly recommend it if you have any spare time." We make our way into an older neighborhood with trees so large they shade the streets. Once she parks, Katie turns to me. "Is this the right address?"

"Yep, this is it," I look at the paper and confirm.

"This house looks creepy, doesn't it?" She stares at the two-story mansion that hasn't been touched in decades, the paint chipping and flaking on all the boards. It seems like the kind of house where a villain in *Scooby Doo* would hide, and I'm kinda scared to go inside.

"Welp, let's go find the skeletons in the closet," I suggest, trying to lighten the mood. I love Halloween, but I'm actually a wuss when it comes to things like this.

"I'm good." She nervously laughs. "Totally not *that* desperate. I've watched way too many horror films."

I shrug and snort. "Just know, I would've walked in and gotten possessed for you."

"You're a true friend." She snorts. "But I'm too chicken." Katie sighs, and we continue down the list. The next is on the outskirts of town, so it takes us fifteen minutes to get there. It's cute and needs a lot of love, but it has potential. An older lady's selling it, and she walks around with us, nearly explaining her life story and why she's moving. Apparently, her husband passed away and she wants to move closer to her sister in Texas.

"Not in the house, right?" Katie asks, and my eyeballs nearly bug out of my head.

"No, but that would've been something." The woman smiles, keeping the conversation lighthearted. "Gonna be real honest with you, honey. This house is adorable, but it's a damn money pit."

"I appreciate the honesty. I'm trying to find a forever home for my son and me. I'm a single mom and want to give him the best life I can," Katie admits.

The older woman's demeanor softens, and I wonder if she's aware of Katie's story. Lawton Ridge is small, and news travels fast, but it happened so long ago that many people have forgotten.

"You're gonna need to install new plumbing and have gas lines run again. There's an electrical issue in one of the bedrooms that I've never been able to have sorted out. I'm sure it will eventually cause a house fire, or at least that's what my late husband always said, bless his soul. If you're willing to spend a lot of money, you could really fix it up nice, but I wouldn't feel right not telling you everything that's wrong. My conscience would kill me, and I still have a few good years left in me," she says, placing her hand on Katie's shoulder.

"Thank you," Katie tells her. "But you're never gonna sell this house if you keep explaining to people why they shouldn't buy it."

"Oh, I know. Eventually, someone will offer me a price I can't refuse, then doze it down and rebuild on the lot." The old woman frowns. "But that's not here nor there."

I give her a sad smile.

"If you want the house, I'm sure it will still be here," the woman assures her.

Katie and I thank her again on our way out.

"She was really nice." Katie gives me a half-smile.

"She was," I admit. "And honest."

"No kidding. Cross that one off. I'm okay with spending money to fix whatever I can, but big issues like that scare me. Electrical. Plumbing. Gas. Those are all huge things. Plus, it needs to be leveled too. She's right, it's a money pit, and I appreciate her telling me because I thought it was cute. So you've seen Tyler every night this week?" She quickly changes the subject.

Just hearing his name gives me heart palpitations. "Yep, since last week. He's been so helpful and actually listens when I talk. Prepares the most delicious dinners ever. I swear I'll finally be able to gain that twenty pounds I've always wanted if he keeps this up. We talk about everything and don't hold back on anything. Last weekend, we went to visit Noah, and it was like a dream."

Katie snaps her eyes to mine, and I swallow hard. "Wait, he saw Noah?"

I hate that I slipped and mentioned him. "Yeah, we did. I only asked Tyler to join me because Robert always refused. I wanted Tyler to talk to him about life after prison, so Noah could have some idea what to expect," I explain, and the mood turns sour. "I'm sorry, Katie."

"It's okay. I'd go with you, but your brother is such an asshole, he refuses to let me visit. It's ridiculous. *Fuck him*." She grabs the steering wheel tighter and exhales. "But I'm glad Tyler went with you. That's really nice of him. We talked about Noah at the bar that night after the double date. I explained everything, how Noah refused to see me, and the way it all made me feel. Tyler actually made me understand the situation from Noah's perspective a little more, but I'm still pissed. If your brother knows what's good for him, he better never ever, *ever* reach out to me. Not after how he cut me off when I needed him the most."

"I'm not sure if I should warn him or just allow him to get his ass kicked by you if he gets brave. And I completely understand."

Katie clenches her jaw. "He deserves it after what he did to me and the way he made me feel. While he might be behind bars, the loneliness I've experienced is more like being in prison than anything he's experienced."

I go quiet, not really sure what to say, so I quickly change the subject. "So...only two more on the list."

"Yep! I kinda get why everyone has warned me away from a fixer-upper. But I'm determined," she says with a smile, and we turn down a gravel road. The houses are spread far apart, and the lots are acres large. We continue driving until we come up on a large brick house.

"Better get a tractor for this one," I say, noticing the vastness.

"Geez, you're right. I didn't realize this was a whole farm." She glances around, and I see a wooden barn in the back. I start laughing and can't seem to stop, and when Katie joins in, we're like silly teenagers again tickled to death over nothing. A guy in overalls shows us around, and I can tell Katie doesn't care for the layout. Considering she's already got enough on her plate with working full-time and raising Owen, I don't see her adding farmer to her list of things to do in life anytime soon.

"Okay, last one." She lets out a long sigh once we thank the guy and head out. "I hope this one doesn't suck, or I'll be renting forever."

"Well, considering it's down the street from me, it's already promising," I try to encourage her. "And as I said, there are a ton of kids Owen's age in the neighborhood. I see them riding their bikes and fishing in the creek. They seem friendly and always wave when I pass them. Plus, Dad has them decorating a scarecrow for the Harvest Festival or something. And they'll mow your grass for twenty bucks."

"That's awesome!" Her tone is hopeful.

"They're good kids," I assure.

It doesn't take long before we're slowing in front of the two-story farmhouse. The outside needs some updating but has potential, and it doesn't look haunted either.

"Ready?" I ask, reaching for the handle, and she nods.

We take the wooden steps that lead to the wraparound porch. The door is open, so we let ourselves inside.

"Hello?" Katie studies the tall ceilings. There's a formal dining area and a gigantic living room with huge windows that oversee the fenced-in backyard. Some of the floorboards are soft, so those will need to be replaced.

"Just up here," a woman shouts. Katie and I take the stairs and find the seller. She's in her mid-fifties with strands of gray mixed in with her jet black hair.

"Hi," she offers, holding out her hand. "I'm Aurora. Welcome. Feel free to wander around. Also, I'm entertaining any offers."

Katie thanks her, and we take our time walking through every room on the top floor. "The closets are huge!" Katie's voice is an octave higher, and I can tell she likes the place. None of the others had her so jazzed.

"There are enough rooms in this house to give Owen a few brothers and sisters," I say, waggling my eyebrows.

"Artificial insemination *is* becoming more popular. Otherwise, it might be an immaculate conception." She shrugs.

We go downstairs and check out the kitchen, which is bigger than my entire cottage. The counter space alone is enough to prepare a feast for twenty on. The walls need painted and flooring redone, along with the appliances and bathroom fixtures being replaced too. But other than that, it seems like a solid house. With some TLC and elbow grease, it would be stunning.

"I really like this place." Katie looks at me and smiles wide. "It does need a lot of work, though."

"That's true, but this might be your forever home, remember? You just have to decide if you love it enough to live here forever. After it's fixed up, it will be gorgeous," I admit, seeing why Katie would adore it. "Like something out of a magazine."

"Yeah, totally!" I can sense the excitement in her tone.

"Sleep on it for a few days. Make sure not to jump into anything you might regret. Meanwhile, do some research on the property," I suggest, loving how happy she is.

"Yes!" She grabs her phone from her back pocket and snaps a few shots of the downstairs area. Aurora meets us at the edge of the staircase and gives Katie her personal number to call if she has any questions.

"Have you had any offers yet?" Katie asks bravely.

"Not yet! But I don't think it will last too long. There have been a few people who seemed interested, but we'll see." She tucks her hair behind her ears. "Thanks for checking it out."

"Yeah, it's a great house," Katie admits, taking one last look before we go outside. She's nearly giddy when we drive away. "This one gives me a good vibe."

"I felt it too!" I say. "Plus, you'd be close to the cottage. It would be fun!"

She agrees. "Wanna do lunch?"

"Sure! I could go for a turkey wrap from the cafe."

A few minutes later, we're parking on the street in town. Belinda greets us with a big laugh when we enter. "Come in, sit, sit," she says, then she looks at me. "The usual?"

"Yes, ma'am." I nod.

"And I'll have what she's having," Katie adds.

Moments later, Belinda returns with two sweet teas.

Katie's giddy about the last house. It's going to be a lot of work, but if anyone can handle it, she can.

It takes less than five minutes before our wraps are delivered, which is good because I'm starving.

"Did any of the other places really speak to you?" I ask, taking a bite.

"Not really. I need to keep my eyes open for more in the area, just to make sure."

"Absolutely, there's no need to rush. And honestly, that house has been there for a while, so I don't think it's going anywhere fast. You've got time."

This seems to please her. "Gotta lot of thinking to do."

"That's for sure. But you'll make the right decision for you and Owen. Though I selfishly want you close, I know something better might pop up."

"Thanks, Gemma. I appreciate you joining me today," she says as we finish eating. "I would've been a nervous wreck going alone."

"If you would've invited anyone else, I'd have been mad at you. I love this kind of stuff," I admit. We pay, leaving Belinda a fat tip, then head back to Katie's house. We exchange hugs and say our goodbyes.

On the way to the cottage, I can't help but think of how much of an asshole Robert is. He's known Katie was searching for a while and refused to help because he was too busy. Though I know Katie's extremely independent and would probably rather handle this herself without the help of a man. That's just how she is or rather, how she's learned to be over the years.

I can't believe it's already the middle of the week. It seems like I blink and the time just passes me by. Though I can't complain because the view of Tyler is a nice one to have. All it takes is a single glance and a smirk and I'm putty in his hands. It's more than infatuation, and never in my life did I think this is where we'd be. I honestly thought it was over between us.

Sometimes, it takes the long road for people to get together, and destiny doesn't allow love like we have to be wasted. Even though it was a beautiful mess to get here, it's a journey I don't regret.

After lunch, the florist delivers a pot mixed with purple and pink morning glories. My eyes go wide and my hand shakes when I open the note attached.

Because they're your favorite and you're *my* favorite.
-Tyler

My heart melts as I read the letter, and I want to burst through the garage doors and wrap my arms around his neck and kiss the hell out of him, but I refrain. I'm sure my dad doesn't want a show. My emotions tend to get the best of me, though, and I push it to the side.

An hour passes and Tyler comes in and hands me a pair of keys. His fingers brush against mine, and butterflies flutter in my stomach. As he leans against the counter, he smirks.

"Flowers?" He laughs, pretending they're not from him.

"Thank you," I whisper. "I love them so much. And I love how thoughtful you were to get me my favorite. Plus, they won't die. I'll plant them in my mother's flower garden." I recall the moment Tyler walked into my bedroom to see the painting he remembered from my letters. These look identical to the art my mother created.

He swallows hard when tears brim on the edge of my eyes. Tyler reaches out and grabs my hand and squeezes it, being so damn gentle with me. Something I'm not used to after being with Robert. Instead of being pushed to the side, Tyler puts me first, which is a huge change that I'm adjusting to.

"What are your plans tonight?" Tyler asks.

"Spending time with you," I whisper.

"That's the correct answer," he quips with a wink, then goes outside. He's trying not to spend too much time with me during our shifts so my dad doesn't get suspicious. I haven't told him about me and Tyler yet, and I'd like to keep it to myself for a little while longer.

After my day is over and Dad tells me goodbye, Tyler comes to me, pressing his body and lips against mine. I'm desperate and needy for him, though we still haven't crossed that line yet. When we finally break apart, I'm breathless, and my head is swimming, drunk from him. I'm convinced Tyler feels it too.

"I need to go home and take a shower first," he mumbles.

I tuck my bottom lip into my mouth. "You can shower at my house," I suggest.

His eyebrow pops up. "Perfect. Maybe you'll join me then?"

"Maybe," I purr, grabbing my flowers. "I am a dirty girl."

"Hot damn, baby. Keep talking like that and …" He pushes back. "Just mmm." Tyler kisses me one last time before we lock the shop and leave. On the way to the cottage, I'm all smiles as we chat about the weather and how oddly happy my dad's been acting.

"You think Jerry's dating someone?" Tyler asks, and it makes me giggle.

"He doesn't date." I shrug. "Maybe it's just all the fall vibes putting a pep in his step or something. It's his favorite season too."

"Could be." Tyler chuckles. We park and make our way to the cottage, and we can't seem to keep our mouths and hands off each other.

"I need that shower now," he whispers against my lips as I unbutton his shirt. "You coming with me?" His eyebrow arches.

"Yes," I murmur desperately. Tyler grabs my hand and leads me down the hallway. When we're in the bathroom, he devours my lips.

When we come up for air, I light some candles I keep on the counter for when I take bubble baths, then flip the switch. "Just creating a little ambience," I whisper as Tyler undresses me.

He peels off my blouse and skirt as his lips trace my collarbone. I'm nearly breathless, my breasts rising and falling as he nibbles on my neck and ears. With my eyes closed, I unbutton his pants and slip down his boxer shorts, then grab his hard length. He lets out a deep groan when I stroke him.

"Gemma," he growls, his head rolling back on his shoulders. "Fuck."

We finish undressing each other. It's the first time we've been without clothes together in over a decade. Tyler studies every inch of me and grins.

"You're so goddamn beautiful," he mutters as my lips crash against his.

"How about that shower now?" I ask, knowing if we don't get in now, we might not.

"Good idea." He chuckles, reaching over and turning on the water. Tyler steps in and holds his hand out for me. The water is warm and falls over my skin as Tyler grabs the soap and washes me. His hands feel so fucking good as they caress every inch of me. I'm nearly panting by the time I'm clean. I wrap my arms around his neck and kiss him.

"When are you going to make me yours?" I finally ask.

"When you're ready," he replies genuinely. "I don't want you to rush into a relationship, considering what you've been through."

I wrap my arms around his neck. "I've been waiting for you since the day you left, Tyler. I'm ready."

He plucks my lip into his mouth, then kisses down my body. Flicking my nipple with his tongue, Tyler moves lower until he's on his knees. Carefully, he loops my leg over his shoulder, then devours me whole.

"Oh." I let out a ragged cry as his tongue flicks my clit. "Tyler, *yes*."

One finger slides inside me, then a second. It won't take long before I lose myself with him, not with how much I've wanted him for the past few weeks. I was his for the taking from the moment we entered the cottage. Tyler takes his time, making sure to properly please me by adding just enough pressure with his mouth. The orgasm builds quicker than I ever expected, and I try to steady myself by grabbing him so I don't bust my ass.

"Mmm," he moans against my pussy, keeping his pace as the release rushes through me. The groan that comes from his throat is guttural as I ride the wave. He steadies me by gripping my ass, allowing me to fully lose myself in the moment, which I do.

Tyler pulls away and stands, then adds shampoo to his palm and washes my hair. I'm so damn relaxed as he massages my scalp while my body recovers. Once he adds the conditioner and I rinse, Tyler smiles.

"Hungry?" he asks, and I guess he doesn't realize we're not done here yet.

I fall to my knees, wanting to show him the same pleasure he's given me. "Gemma," he warns. "You don't…" His words trail off as soon as I place him in my mouth.

I look up at him, noticing his eyes rolling to the back of his head as I try to give him the best blow job of his life. Not wanting to rush, I trail my tongue down his shaft and around his tip before I stroke him a few times. He's long and hard, and his girth nearly fills my mouth as I take most of him in.

"Fuck. That feels amazing." He places his hand against the wall as I pick up my pace. I want him to understand how much I love pleasuring him. As his body tenses, I slow to a snail's pace, teasing the fuck out of him. His pants tell me everything I need to know, and he warns me before he comes. Grabbing his ass, I shove his cock to the back of my throat, wanting to swallow him down.

Moments later, his body convulses as he loses himself. I continue pumping him and don't stop until his orgasm does. Tasting him again is something I've dreamed about for so damn long, and something I've only ever shared with him.

"You're delicious," I say, and I can see his pulse still racing in his neck when I stand and meet his eyes.

Tyler leans his forehead against mine. "You're mine, Gemma. You understand that, right? I was stupid to ever let you go."

"I won't argue with any of that." I beam, our mouths crashing together in a white-hot kiss. Though our bodies are clean, our actions were dirty and hot. I'm living for every moment I get to spend with him like this.

We step out of the shower, and Tyler takes his time drying me. It's sensual and sweet, and my heart is full of adoration for this man. It seems like it's too good to be true, and I keep waiting to wake up and find out it was a dream.

"Let's order a pizza and snuggle on the couch," I suggest, just wanting to be as close to him as I possibly can. "Or we could have sex until the sun rises."

Tyler pulls me closer, tracing his lips with mine. "I don't wanna rush things with you, Gemma. I've waited all this time to be with you, and I want it to last forever."

My cheeks heat at his admission. "Same," I whisper.

He paints my lips with his, and I don't want the night to end. "I'm not letting you go this time, Gem. Now, let's order that pizza."

CHAPTER THIRTY-FOUR

TYLER

I'VE HAD a permanent smile on my face since Wednesday when I told Gemma my true feelings, and I meant every word. Everleigh has called out my change in demeanor a dozen times, and Jerry's even made a comment about my giddiness. Though we're not announcing our relationship status to the world, it's not being kept a secret either. It's fun to give the whole damn town something to talk about.

I woke up fairly early this morning because I had a training session from six to nine. While I was tempted to wake Gemma before I left, I've kept her up late all week, so I didn't. Instead, I told her to text me after she's had a cup of coffee. Once I'm home and showered, she sends me a photo of her lying in her bed, hair disheveled, looking like a goddess.

Tyler: Damn. I'm so lucky.

Gemma: And why's that?

Tyler: Because you're my girl. What're your plans today?

Gemma: Thought I'd lay around naked and wait for you to come over.

Tyler: You're making this really hard.

Gemma: Well, if you're hard, get over here! ;)

I totally set myself up for that response.

Tyler: Get up. Eat breakfast. Put on some clothes because I'm taking you somewhere this afternoon.

Gemma: OOH! Where?

She always ruins her surprises.

Tyler: I'm not telling you, but dress to be outside until after dark.

Gemma: Okay! How much time do I have?

Tyler: I'm picking you up in 2 hours :)

Considering it's the third week of October and the temperature has dropped significantly, I dress in a long-sleeve T-shirt and jeans. I even grab a light jacket because it's been brisker at night. Before I leave, I take Sassy for a walk and think about hanging out with Gemma and creating new memories together. Once we're back, I feed Sassy some dog treats, then head to the boutique to get Everleigh's car.

Everleigh has the place decorated from head to toe in black and orange. Each corner has witches and wizards, the mannequins are skeletons, and spiderwebs dangle from the ceiling. She wanted to create a haunted house vibe with the music and sound effects. Every customer who enters is greeted by Cara, who's dressed like a ghost and hands them bags of candy. Everleigh has outdone herself with the decorations, and it makes me chuckle. When she pops out from behind a mannequin wearing black lipstick, I pretend to be scared. "Got me!"

"Shut up, you didn't even jump," she says.

"Prison will do that to a person," I remind her, and she shakes her head. "Keys, please?"

"I'll give them to you under *one* condition only," she teases.

I groan. "Walking Sassy was the only thing you asked. Anything else isn't a part of the deal we made."

"Oh well." She shrugs. "I want you to bring Gemma by the shop so I can finally see you two together in public." She dangles the keyring on her pointer finger. I try to swipe them from her, but she's too fast. "Say you will…"

"Oh my God. You're so annoying."

"Uh-uh, *promise* me," she continues, and I finally give in.

"Okay, fine. But we're not staying long."

She drops them in my palm. "Works for me."

"You little shit," I throw back before I turn on my heels.

"You love me!" she shouts across the way just as an animated ghost wiggles and flies on a string across the ceiling. Cara tries to hand me a bag of candy, but I refuse.

Once I'm in the car, I let out a laugh. Everleigh's something else, but she's right, I do love her along with all her ridiculous antics. She's Gemma's and my number one fan, and I appreciate how much she supports the idea of us being together. It's something she's wanted for longer than I can remember. She deserves a matchmaker award because she's so damn sly.

It doesn't take long before I'm turning into Gemma's driveway. I'm almost twenty minutes early, but if I know her, she's dressed and pacing, trying to figure out where I'm taking her. She won't guess, and I threatened to feed Everleigh TV dinners for the next month if she slipped.

I knock on Gemma's door, and she immediately wraps her arms around my neck and plants her lips on mine. "I've missed you."

"I *always* miss you," I admit, taking in the sweetness of her skin. "You taste delicious."

She grabs my hand and drags me inside. I cross my arms over my chest and smirk when I see what she's wearing.

"Am I dressed properly? Should I change?" Concern covers her face.

I grab her hand and pull her closer. "It's the season when all the basic ladies dress like Han Solo, so I'd say you nailed it. And you've even have a scarf with candy corn on too."

She snickers and playfully smacks me. "Blame Everleigh! All of this came from *her* shop. She's a bad influence and makes me want to buy everything in there."

"She's really good at that, but truthfully, you're dressed perfectly for the occasion. You're beautiful." I slide my lips against hers. "Ready?"

She sighs. "If you only knew how bad I wanted you right now."

"It's worth the wait, I promise," I whisper, kissing her again. "Let's get going."

"Okay, fine! You're so determined to drive me crazy." She whines and pouts, but a smile meets her lips and ruins her act. We drive across town, and her brows furrow when she realizes where I'm taking her.

I park outside the shop, and Gemma narrows her eyes at me. "We're visiting Everleigh?"

"She made me promise I'd bring you to see her," I admit.

Gemma chuckles and shakes her head but doesn't say anything because she's aware of how my sister is. Hell, she knows her better than I do. We get out of the car and walk inside, and Gemma immediately lights up when Everleigh rushes and nearly tackles her to the ground. "I've missed you so much!"

"The shop is amazing! You added way more stuff and have completely transformed it into Halloween central." Gemma studies the outlandish decorations with wide eyes. Everleigh might've gone overboard, but neither of us admits it.

"Every customer has loved it." My sister snickers and goes to a giant cauldron with smoke billowing from inside. A moment later, she dramatically grabs a bag of candy from it as if she magically made it appear, then hands it to Gemma.

"You two have fun," Everleigh squeals and whispers something in Gemma's ear. When she pushes away, a blush hits Gemma's cheeks, and I can only imagine what was said.

"We're leaving now," I sing-song, grabbing Gemma's hand and interlocking my fingers with hers.

"Aww," Everleigh says loudly, and I keep moving forward. When we're outside, the crisp fall breeze hits my cheeks, and when I glance over at Gemma, she's smiling wide as she opens the bag. "I love candy corn."

"The whole town is going to have a sugar rush, compliments of Everleigh," I throw out.

Gemma walks toward the car, and I shake my head.

"Don't we have somewhere to be?" she asks, confused.

"Yep, we do," I say, squeezing her hand. When we round the corner, she finally realizes what I planned.

"The Harvest Festival? I haven't been since I was a teenager," she beams with a hop to her step and a grin so wide it's contagious.

After four blocks, we're in the middle of the town square. Everywhere I look has some sort of activity going on or kids running around in costume. I wrap my arm around Gemma as we stroll along the street full of vendors and booths.

"Ma'am, wanna get your face painted?" a young girl asks. There's a poster board full of different designs. Gemma grins and looks back at me, almost as if she's waiting for my approval. It almost breaks my heart because I'm sure Robert didn't like things like this.

"If you want," I encourage. "It'll be fun."

A moment later, Gemma sits on the stool as the girl moves her long brown hair away from her face.

"What kind of design?" she asks, pointing at the choices.

Gemma taps her index finger on her mouth, then smiles. "What about a cat?"

The girl's face lights up. "Sure!"

Grabbing her supplies, she dips her brush in the black paint. Carefully, she paints whiskers on Gemma's cheeks, then a pink upside-down triangle on her nose. When the girl is done, she grabs a mirror and shows Gemma.

"You're the prettiest cat here!" she compliments, and Gemma laughs.

"How much do I owe you?" Gemma unzips her crossbody purse, but I've already got my wallet open and cash ready.

"Six dollars," the girl says.

I hand her a twenty and tell her to keep the change. She holds it, and her eyes go wide. "Really?"

"Yeah! Consider it a tip for being an amazing painter." I grin.

"Thank you so much." She's so excited that she nearly squeals.

When we leave, Gemma loops her arm in mine. "That was really sweet of you."

Glancing over at her, I admire how adorable she looks with whiskers. "She did a good job, and I think she's right. You *are* the prettiest cat here."

"Maybe I can have her teach me how to paint." Gemma snickers, then leans into me.

We continue viewing the different fall-themed items—plastic pumpkins, wreaths, candles, pretty much everything a person could imagine. At the end of the block, a photo booth is set up, and it seems to be a popular area because the line is long.

"We should check this out," I suggest, and she nods.

"Yes! We totally should, so we have photos to remember our first date." She winks. Right now, in the middle of the street, all I want to do is kiss her, not caring who sees, but I don't.

"First of many," I admit. She tucks her bottom lip into her mouth, and I'm tempted to pluck it free. After we wait in line for ten minutes, it's our turn to walk inside. After I pay, she gestures to the props if we want to use them. Gemma places a wizard's hat on my head and hands me a wand as she grabs a sign that reads "All Tricks" and a crown. The photographer moves us in front of a backdrop of a haunted mansion.

"You get five poses," the photographer explains.

"Perfect." I give him a thumbs-up, and he counts down. We make silly faces and laugh our asses off for another. Next, I wrap my arm around her and pose like high schoolers at prom. For the last two, I place my hands on her cheeks and kiss her, something I've wanted to do since we arrived.

"Those turned out great," the guy admits, directing us to where we can get our photos.

"Can we pick them up later?" Gemma asks, seeing how many people are already waiting.

"Yep, we close at nine! They'll be in an envelope waiting for y'all."

After we leave, my body buzzes from being so close to her.

We pass Disney princesses, Marvel characters, and the occasional devil and vampire.

"I've always loved Halloween," she admits.

"I remember," I say, interlocking our fingers as we enjoy being together.

In the middle of the square is a big stack of wood where the ceremonial bonfire will be lit at dark. I glance over and see a stage where a band will perform at seven. Purple and orange lights are strung from poles, creating an area for a dance floor. I make a mental note for us to come back later, but we still have a few hours before sunset.

Gemma and I play a few games, and she randomly takes out her phone and snaps selfies of us. As we pass people on the street, I wonder if news has fully spread about Gemma and Robert's breakup. We have no reason to hide anymore, though it's a little awkward with so many wandering eyes. Honestly, though, I don't give a fuck what anyone thinks. For the first time in a long ass time, I'm happy. I won't let town rumors and whispers ruin a good thing.

"We should do the hayride." Gemma points across the way where a tractor is pulling a trailer of hay. When it comes to a stop, the kids hop off, smiling like they had the time of their life.

"Deal." We make our way over and climb aboard. I sit on some hay with Gemma on my lap. The trailer quickly fills with children and chatter. Gemma and I are nothing but smiles as the tractor takes off and drives us up and down the streets. I wrap my arms around her waist and hold her as she grins wide. We pass all the decorated businesses, the haunted maze filled with zombies, and the pumpkin patch. Most people look like they're having a good time, and the weather couldn't have been any better. I've never really cared about any of the town activities and always skipped them, but doing things like this with Gemma might be one of our new traditions.

The cool breeze brushes against our skin, and she snuggles even closer to me. Resting against me, she lets out a contented sigh. Eventually, the tractor returns us to the unloading area, and I'm sad it's over. We stand and jump off, and we're each handed a candy apple wrapped in cellophane.

"Thank you!" Gemma tells the lady and immediately digs in. Though I'm not into sugar like that, I join her. We eat our sticky food and notice scarecrows are strategically placed throughout town. Each one is hosted by a business. "Did Everleigh decorate one of these things?" I ask.

Gemma shrugs. "I dunno. She didn't mention it, but considering she goes all out, I wouldn't be surprised. Dad donated one but let the neighborhood kids decorate it. I'll have to find it and take a picture for him. It was a fundraiser for the local food bank or something."

Spooky music plays throughout the square, and after we've finished our apples, we stop for some hot cider to take the chill away. I glance over at Gemma as she grips her cup, and her gaze meets mine. A wave of heat rushes through me, and I swallow hard.

Our afternoon has been full of unspoken words and stolen glances, and I don't want it to end. As I study her, there's not a doubt in my body about returning to Lawton Ridge. I'm just so damn grateful she's giving me another chance.

"Let's paint a pumpkin," I suggest as we pass a makeshift pumpkin patch. Brushes and paint are set out for those who want to decorate it here. Gemma nearly squeals, then gives me a look. "My painting skills suck, but we'll make a Picasso pumpkin if you want."

The rows are long with at least three hundred pumpkins of all different shapes, sizes, and colors. Children rush past us, and Gemma smiles sweetly at them.

"What?" I ask her as we knock on a few.

"I can't wait to bring my kids here," she admits with a blush to her cheeks. "Not that I'm ready to have kids right now, but I'm not getting any younger."

"Yeah," I agree. "I think you'll make a great mom, Gemma. You have a big heart and care."

"Do you want children?" she asks. It's not something we've discussed. When we were younger, we were too busy living between the sheets and in the moment to talk about our future.

"If I found the right woman," I say. "I've thought about it a few times, but considering my childhood wasn't the greatest, I'm wary about bringing kids into this world."

She swallows, watching me. "Would you have kids with me?"

I wrap my arms around her waist until I can feel the warmth of her skin against mine. "Without a doubt."

Her gaze seems to pierce through me, and her expression softens. "How about this one?" she eventually says, quickly changing the subject.

"It's great." I lift the pumpkin, not realizing how damn heavy it is, but I should've, considering he's the daddy of the whole patch. I set it down by the decorating supplies with an oof. "I swear he weighs seventy-five pounds."

She snickers. "He? Are we naming him?"

I let out a chuckle. "Yeah, let's call him Big Daddy."

"I honestly just wanted to see if you could lift it. And you did." Her smile touches her eyes.

"You are *so* wrong for that," I tell her, grabbing a brush and squirting different colors of paint on a paper plate. We both sit cross-legged and look at the giant orange pumpkin.

"What if you decorate one side, and I do the other?" I suggest.

Gemma laughs. "Deal!"

We get to work on our masterpieces. There's enough space for me to put what I want, and I can't wait for Gemma to see. When I glance up at her, she's deep in thought, and I chuckle, trying to imagine what she's creating over there. If it's anything like her canvas, I'm taking this pumpkin home and displaying it right next to the front door. Once I'm finished, I sit patiently and wait for her to finish. She claps her hands together and brings her knees close to her chest.

"Are you ready for me to see?" I ask, and she covers her face with her hands.

"I guess!" she says excitedly, and I crawl close to her. When I look at what she's drawn, I'm at a loss to what it is.

"Do you see it?" She's smiling wide, and I nod.

"It's a..." I try to figure it out quickly but fail miserably.

"It's a spider!" Gemma reaches over and tries to tickle me, and the next thing I know, I'm leaned over, pushing her back against the grass and kissing her. Her palm rests on my cheek, and her warm, ragged breaths brush against my lips as I devour her. We're lost in a moment of time as the sounds of children fill the background along with music in the distance. Our tongues twist and dance, and the only thing that stops us is a clearing of a throat.

"Gemma?" a woman asks, standing over us. I push away, and Gemma sits up, trying to fix her hair. The woman zeros in on us.

"Where's Robert?" she questions, wearing an accusing expression.

Gemma clears her throat, tucking loose strands of her hair behind her ears. "I'm not sure. We're not together anymore. *Clearly.*" Just by the tone in Gemma's voice, it's obvious she's annoyed.

"Oh." She looks at me again, then back at Gemma. "Sorry to hear that."

"I'm not," Gemma snaps, and the woman makes small talk about the weather before scurrying off.

"Bitch," Gemma whispers under her breath.

"Who was she?" I ask curiously, considering she felt the need to confront Gemma as if she was an adulteress or something.

"One of Robert's secretaries. I swear she's always had a thing for him. Honestly, though, she can have him. He's available now, so go get him!" Gemma waves her hand, then laughs before leaning over and capturing my lips. "I haven't seen your side yet," she says when we break apart.

Moving around to what I painted, Gemma smiles wide when her gaze lands on it. "Tyler…"

"What?" I smirk.

"You drew a heart with our initials inside. That's so damn thoughtful." Leaning forward, Gemma places her palms on my cheeks and kisses me. "I love it. Way better than my blob."

I run my fingers through her hair. "Well, we all know cats can't paint."

She snorts. "You're right."

Standing, I hold my hand out for her, and she takes it. When she's eye level with me, she grins. "So what're we gonna do with Big Daddy?"

"Several painted ones are placed at the entrance of the pumpkin patch. Maybe we should put it there until we leave? Then we can pick it up on the way out," I say, and she nods.

"You're so smart," she says as I bend over to lift him, careful not to touch the paint. Carrying him to the front, I place it with the spider side showing.

"Oh no, turn it around." She twirls her finger. "I want everyone in this damn town to see what you did."

With a wink, I do what she says, making sure our initials are on full display.

"Best damn pumpkin ever." She claps her hands together, and I stand beside her, smiling.

"I agree."

We look over the other decorated ones, then we head back to the square. Members of the city council give the announcement that the bonfire will be lit in ten minutes. In the meanwhile, they pass out metal skewers and set up a table with ingredients for s'mores. I can't remember the last time I had one.

Once the crowd disperses, Gemma and I head over and stuff fluffy marshmallows on the ends of our sticks. After the fire is roaring and the kids have gotten their fill, we step up and roast our mallows.

"The trick is not to let it catch on fire," she explains, twirling hers carefully as I hold a plate with graham crackers and chocolate stacked. When it's to her specification, she puts the gooey whiteness between and squishes it together. "You eat this one."

"No, you go first," I insist.

"How about we share? They always seem like a great idea until you eat half and realize it's too much." She chuckles, and I agree, taking the other side.

We sit on a bench and eat our messy dessert. "You might not be able to cook grilled cheese, but you're the queen of s'mores," I say around a mouthful.

When Gemma looks at me, there's a bit of marshmallow on the corner of her mouth. I smirk.

"It's on my face, isn't it?"

Nodding, I lean over and scoop it off with my thumb, then lick it from my finger. She watches me intensely as the underlying current streaming between us nearly takes me under. "I'll get some napkins."

Gemma keeps her eyes on me as I get up and stalk across the way to grab a few, then bring them back. Once finished, we sit enjoying the evening breeze until the band begins and the twinkle lights come on. Couples move to the dance floor, and I stand and hold out my hand.

"Will you dance with me?"

She nods, and I lead her to the middle, then wrap my arms around her waist, pulling her close. Our bodies move together as we rock back and forth. I'm ready to swoop her into my arms and carry her home. Gemma hums the melody of the song, and listening to her tugs at my heartstrings. This woman is everything I've ever wanted, and I can't believe she's actually mine.

The beat picks up, and I twirl her around, then dip her down. When she's face-to-face with me, she moves forward, allowing her lips to crash against mine. We lose ourselves in the music, and she's so ravenous for me that my control slips when she tugs on the hem of my shirt. The song fades off and "Cotton Eye Joe" starts playing, which is a crowd pleaser. Children rush to the center as we laugh and get out of the way.

"Let's get out of here," I suggest, and her cheeks flush. I grab her hand and lead her away from the crowd. The music echoes off the buildings as we walk toward the patch to get our pumpkin. I hoist it up on my shoulder, and Gemma chuckles at the size of it. Before we leave, we stop at the booth and pick up the envelope with our pictures waiting for us.

Gemma opens it, and I see her emotions bubble when she pulls them out.

"Look at us," she says, showing me the prints.

"T&G," I whisper. "Forever."

"Forever," she repeats. "I'd like that."

CHAPTER THIRTY-FIVE

GEMMA

THE LAST WEEK with Tyler has been unreal, and I question if I'm living in one of my favorite romance movies. It's different to be in a relationship where my partner actually cares. Tyler is different and wants to spend every free moment with me.

Every day after work, we've had dinner together and hung out. Most of the time, he cooks, and I watch, but I'm happy to learn a few things in the kitchen. Our night typically ends with us watching a movie, and even though I want more, we still haven't had sex. Although I just ended a long-term relationship, when I'm with Tyler, it doesn't feel like we're moving too quick. He's not a rebound and has always meant much more to me than that.

When I think about Tyler and our past, and liken it to what I had with Robert, there's no comparison. The feelings I have when I'm with Tyler run deeper than the surface level and nearly cut to the bone. While I haven't voiced that to him because the thought is scary, I can't deny I'm falling head over heels in love.

On the way to work, I can't stop thinking about seeing him. I never thought I'd enjoy working with the man I'm dating, but I do. Seeing him gives me something to look forward to. When I walk in, the donuts are already there, and Tyler's standing with a cup of coffee in his hand. He studies me and smirks.

"I love it when you wear skirts like that."

I move across the room. Meeting his eyes, I grin. "I love it when you take them off."

Tyler groans and shakes his head. "Thanks. That's what I'll be thinking about for the rest of the shift."

A smile plays on my lips when he adjusts himself. "Maybe you can come over tonight and show me how it's done."

He frowns. "I have two training sessions tonight, and I volunteered to close for Ruby so she could leave a little early. But afterward..." He takes a step closer until his face is inches from mine. I smell the hint of his body wash and cologne, and my panties nearly melt. "I'll be happy to."

My heart nearly beats from my chest, and I'm tempted to kiss him, but my dad enters, so I create space between us. Though Dad is well aware Robert and I are no longer together, it's still awkward for him to see me close to Tyler, and I want to respect our workspace. Plus, I don't want the whole world in our business, not while we're still trying to navigate being together after all the Robert drama.

When his secretary confronted me at the Harvest Festival, I nearly lost my shit. Too many people don't know how to mind their own damn business, and considering Robert flaunted me around everywhere, it's a shock to most. I wish I could post fliers on every light post saying we broke up. Telling people doesn't seem to be getting around as fast as I thought, so I'm not sure what else to do. But considering I've stopped wearing my ring, many have noticed, though they haven't said much.

Lunch comes quick, and Tyler and I eat together in the break room. It's quiet, and we talk about Halloween since it's this weekend.

"I've never been to an adult Halloween party, but I'd like to go to one," I admit.

"We should plan one next year. It'll be fun. We'll get Everleigh in on it too. She's seriously obsessed with everything black, orange, and purple."

I giggle. "She's always like that. Every. Single. Year."

"I thought she would've grown out of it, but guess not," he says and shrugs as he finishes his burger.

"What time do you think you'll be done tonight?" I ask, wishing I could fast-forward time so we can be together.

"Probably around ten. I've been keeping you up late each night, and I feel bad. Maybe you should get some rest, and we can have breakfast in the morning?"

I pout, but he's absolutely right. I am tired. "Will you have *me* for breakfast instead?"

His eyebrow pops up. "Absolutely, sweetheart. I'd love to spend time with you all weekend. We should do something."

"I've wanted to hike some trails since the weather has been so amazing and the leaves are changing colors. It's been a while since I've been up there, but I remember how well maintained the paths were."

"I'd love that, baby. I haven't been since I was a teen. It's a date then." He winks and looks up at the time. "Lunchtime's over."

"It goes by too quick." I pout. We've been trying to be punctual with our breaks so my dad won't have anything to say. When Tyler stands, I can't help but to notice how damn sexy he is. What's even better is he's all mine. We pick up our mess and go our separate ways, but before he walks out to the garage, he takes a quick glance at me. I lift my skirt, just enough for him to see my upper thigh, then move it down. "Miss you already."

"Devil woman," he says, then enters the garage.

The afternoon is busy, and customers come in for last-minute repairs, something that never fails to happen every Friday since we're typically closed on the weekends. By the time I look up at the clock, it's past closing time, and I can't stop yawning. After Tyler and Dad finish cleaning their messes, and I'm done picking up the lobby, we lock up and leave.

Tyler and I hang around outside for a moment, but I know he has to get to the gym because he's particular about being on time with his clients. "Drink some wine and go to bed at a decent time," he demands, leaning forward and giving me a kiss on the cheek.

"I will. See you in the morning," I murmur, stealing another kiss.

"Bright and early," he tells me. We linger for a moment, then break apart. I go to my car with a smile and drive home elated. Feeling this happy should be illegal, but I'm so damn glad it's not.

I turn into my driveway, grab my purse, and head toward the cottage. I'm on cloud nine as I unlock the door and go inside.

"About fucking time," a booming voice barks, and my adrenaline spikes when I see Robert standing in front of me. He's wearing a grimace from the pits of hell. I take a step back, ready to bolt through the door and run to my dad's house, but he grabs me before I can escape.

"How did you get in here?" I grit my teeth.

"I've got my ways," he warns, his beady eyes trailing over my outfit. Robert narrows his gaze. "You disgust me."

With every passing second, I grow more scared.

"You need to leave," I say, trying to find my courage. "Get out of my house."

He flashes an evil smirk. "No. Do you know how long I've been waiting for you? There are things that need to be settled *tonight*, and I'm not going anywhere until they are."

He tightens his grasp on my upper arm. "Let me go!"

"Everyone saw the little performance you and Tyler put on at the Harvest Festival. Do you have any idea how fucking embarrassing that was for me?" he seethes, and I force myself away from him, backing up until I'm against the door.

"I don't care. We're not together, and everyone knows it now. I don't know what you want from me." My eyes widen in fear as I live in a continual nightmare loop where I can constantly repeat myself, but Robert doesn't hear me.

"I want you to marry me, Gemma. Do what you said you'd do."

The rage comes quickly as I glare at him. "How many times do I have to explain to you that it's over? I'm not marrying you. I won't!" My voice is loud and guttural, the emotion pouring out of me like a summer storm.

"Because of you, my deal with Victoria is no longer on the table. It's all your damn fault I didn't get that contract signed. You owe me, Gemma. You owe me your fucking life for messing with my future." He begins pacing in front of me.

My feet won't move as if they're stuck in quicksand as I suck in air. "There *never* was a deal. Don't you see that? She was manipulating you to get to Tyler."

"The only person who's manipulated me is you. I wouldn't be surprised if you had planned to string me along all this time so you could gain popularity around town."

I scoff because that's the last thing I ever wanted. "Are you delusional? I won't play into this false narrative, Robert. If anyone has manipulated anyone, it's you with your games and need to keep your perfect public image. I'm done. I've had enough. Now, get the hell out of my house." I grab my phone from my purse and type in 911. This time, I want him arrested for harassing me. I turn the screen and show him. "I'm not playing anymore. Leave."

"Call them. They won't come. I've made sure of it. Don't believe me? Try it out. I dare you."

But I don't because he's paid many people off over the years, and they're still in his pocket.

"Why are you doing this?" I ask, defeated but trying to stay strong.

"Because I've invested too much goddamn time in you and our relationship. I'm not sure if you've noticed, but I'm not letting you go. I've told you this, and it's like you can't comprehend what I'm saying. I refuse to let you make a fool of me in front of the people of Lawton Ridge." He rakes his fingers through his hair. When I meet his demented expression, I shudder.

"I've worked to make a name for myself, and I don't appreciate you parading yourself around like a whore and letting everyone see how unfaithful you are to me. You're moving in with me, and you're going to be my wife and the mother to my children. You will be quitting your job as soon as we get married."

Laughter escapes me. "Not happening." I cross my arms over my chest.

Robert shrugs. "Fine then. How much do you love this cottage?"

I narrow my eyes at him, not sure what's going to come from his mouth next. "What are you talking about?"

"Just wondering, because I hold all the cards in my hands right now, Gemma. So you need to choose your words wisely."

My heartbeat pounds in my ears as adrenaline rushes through me. He strolls through my cottage and looks at the canvases on the walls. After he makes a face, he moves over to the next, acting as if my mother's work disgusts him.

"I own the deed to your father's land. To his house and this cottage." He continues wandering around. "And I'll bulldoze it to the ground. All of it."

"You're a liar!" I shout, not wanting to believe a word he says.

He looks at me with his arms crossed, wearing a sneer. "See, your irresponsible father was late on paying the hospital bills after your mother died, so he took out a second mortgage on the house."

I wish he'd stop talking. I wish he'd disappear.

"And he was nearly eight months late on payments. The whole property went into foreclosure, and the bank was ready to sell it off. Considering I'm privy to things that will soon go to auction, I paid his debt. And now you'll pay his."

"Shut up," I snap. "Why should I believe a word you say?"

"You think I'd lie about something like this? Trust me when I say this house will be gone by the end of next week. I'll flatten it all to the ground with all your precious memories inside. It is mine, after all. Just like you."

I glare at him, shaking my head in disbelief. He's so full of shit.

"What? You want proof?" he muses.

Robert pulls out his cell phone and brings up the tax documents for the property. He shows it to me, and I press refresh in the corner. It's real, and the realization nearly smothers me to death.

"No," I whisper. "No, no, no." I bend over, tears rushing out of me as I try to come to terms with this. Why didn't my father tell me? Why didn't I know? I suck in air, hoping not to hyperventilate.

"So you'll do exactly what I say, or you'll both lose everything."

I focus on the ground, feeling lightheaded and weak in the knees. I refuse to pass out in front of him, refuse to let him see how much this really affects me. He's the type of psycho who gets off on having control. I straighten my stance, pushing my emotions to the side, and realize I don't have a choice in the matter. He'll take everything from my father and me. He won't stop until I do what he says.

"I'm sorry, I didn't hear you. You're going to have to speak up," he says sarcastically, cupping his hand over his ears.

"I hate you," I say between gritted teeth, and it's obvious he's finally found a way to break me.

"Good. So we're going to tell everyone that after a short breakup, we realized how in love we were and decided to get back together. And since we can't live without one another, we will be getting married as planned."

"Robert, you can find someone else. Plenty of women would marry you in a heartbeat and do everything you want and say.

People will understand you've moved on. It's not as big of a deal as you're making this out to be." It's the truth, but also my last resort to help him change his mind.

"The date is set. November. And it's final. You love your dad so much, and I'm aware of how you'd never want anything to happen to this land or his business. So start wearing your ring again." He pulls it from his pocket and forces it on my finger. "Prove your loyalty to me publicly. You'll do what I say, or everyone you love will pay the *ultimate* consequence. I know you, Gemma. You care too damn much to let that happen." He smirks, proud of himself.

I speak up. "What's that threat supposed to mean?"

"Threat?" He moves until he's inches from me and grabs my cheeks, forcing my mouth closed. "It's not a threat, dear. Keep our arrangement or I'll make sure Victoria gets her revenge on Tyler without any consequences. I'm sure you don't want anything to happen to your criminal lover." He lets me go and laughs. "I'm sure I can start adding your friends to the list too. Everleigh. Katie. Owen. Your brother, who may conveniently find himself doing more time. I'll hurt every person who means anything to you."

"You're a monster." I replay his words.

Robert has the financial stability to pay anyone hush money. He and Victoria would both win at that point. Robert would get rid of the man I'm in love with, and Victoria would finally be able to bury the hatchet. Tears well on the rims of my eyes, and I don't think I'm strong enough to hold them back, not as everything crashes around me.

"Break up with the boy toy. Tomorrow. Then we can go back to hosting the wedding of the century. We'll plan a public appearance, and you'll wear that black dress I love so much," he demands.

Bile crawls up my throat, and I might empty my stomach, though there's nothing in it. "Tyler will never agree to this."

"He will as long as you convince him. You've apparently been acting while you're with me, so turn on the charm. Be demanding and make it believable. You'll marry me, Gemma. Because there's too much at stake for your fuck buddy's life and your own. Not to mention, your father's livelihood and this piece of shit cottage. The choice is yours, but don't make the wrong one." He chuckles.

"Cheer up, buttercup." Robert comes closer and forces his mouth against mine. I try to push him off, but he's too strong. He tastes like stale coffee and sweat, and it's enough to make me gag.

"Fuck you," I mutter as he moves past me. He opens the door, and before he leaves, he silently threatens me with a glare.

"We'll have plenty of time for that during our honeymoon." Once he's gone, my knees give out, and I fall to the ground. No matter how much air I try to suck in, I can't breathe. Hunched over, I'm hyperventilating, and my head feels like it might explode.

Tears stream down my face because Robert's words aren't threats. He's a man of action and will do every single thing he said. I'm not stupid and fully understand that from being with him for so long.

Somehow, I stand and walk to the couch. I cover my face with my hands and let my wails release. The pain is too much to comprehend. The loss I already feel nearly destroys me.

How will I ever be able to let Tyler go and marry a maniac who's determined to ruin my life? I'm damned if I do and damned if I don't, but Robert uses my weaknesses against me. He knows I'll do whatever I can to protect the people I love, even if that means being miserable for eternity.

He'll never allow Tyler and me to be together.

I wipe the tears away, trying to figure out how to convince the man I love that we're over. It'll destroy me—and him—but I have to be strong because our lives are on the line.

CHAPTER THIRTY-SIX

TYLER

I'VE BEEN STROLLING around the gym with a cheesy grin on my face that I can't wipe off. This past week has been amazing, and nothing could piss me off right now. Gemma's mine again, and everything between us has worked out perfectly. Our mutual attraction and the feelings we have for each other are beyond my wildest dreams.

After I close the gym, I walk home and immediately jump in the shower. Gemma and I have breakfast plans in the morning, and if the weather cooperates, we'll go on a hike too. Honestly, I don't care what we do as long as I'm with her.

Thoughts of her take over as the water streams down my chest, and my dick comes alive at the memories of her mouth on me. I loved the way her hands slid down my chest before she gripped my shaft and stroked it hard and fast. Or how she moaned when I growled out in satisfaction.

It's all too much.

I pump my cock, squeezing tightly as flashes of Gemma flood through my mind. The way she simultaneously looked at me with so much hunger and tenderness has me increasing my pace. Resting one hand on the shower wall, I pump with visions of Gemma kneeling in front of me and am soon grunting out my release, exhaling roughly as my head tilts back in relief.

Fuck.

I miss her so goddamn much.

Though we see each other every day and most evenings, I can't seem to spend enough time with her. Everything's still new and exciting, but it's always felt that way when we were together.

Once I'm out of the shower and have dried off, I slip on a pair of shorts and look for food. I see a note on the counter from Everleigh.

Hanging out with Ruby at the pub and will probably crash at her place. See you tomorrow!
P.S. Can you take Sassy out for me PLEASE?

That little shit.

She probably didn't text me because she knew I'd give her hell for leaving me to dog-sit.

Quickly, I slip on some gym shorts and a T-shirt.

"C'mon, Sassy. Let's go for a walk." She immediately bounces when she hears her favorite word. I grab her leash, and we go around the block. She stops at every tree and sniffs every yard. By the time we get home, it's been thirty minutes, and my stomach is raging with hunger.

After warming some leftovers, I sit down on the couch and click on the TV. As I flip through the channels, I scarf down the food and stop on an old episode of *Seinfeld*. Once I've finished eating, I take my plate into the kitchen and grab a beer. Just as I settle back in my spot, a knock sounds on the door.

It's late, which means Everleigh's probably drunk as fuck and can't find her keys again. I'm gonna give her so much hell for this.

As soon as I open it, I'm pleasantly surprised to find Gemma standing there.

"Hey." I smile. "Wasn't expecting you."

"I know." She steps in when I shift to the side. "But this couldn't wait."

After I close the door, I notice something's wrong. She looks like someone stole her prized possessions—bloodshot eyes, tousled hair, fidgety hands. Gemma frowns, and when I scan down her body, I notice red marks on her wrist.

What the fuck?

"Gemma, what's going on?"

We walk into the living room, and I cross my arms over my chest as I wait for her to answer.

"Did something happen?"

She swallows hard as if she's trying to find the courage to tell me the worst fucking news on the planet.

"I don't wanna hurt you, Tyler, but I have to be honest with you."

My jaw immediately tightens. "Alright."

"I've realized we can't rewrite the past and just pick up where we left off twelve years ago. I can't pretend you didn't crush my heart when you left. I still carry resentment from how badly you hurt me, and because of that, we can't be together. Robert has always been there for me, and I was having mixed feelings, but they're clear now. I love him."

Blinking hard, I wait for her to admit she's kidding, and this is some cruel joke.

"Excuse me?" I nearly stutter.

"I love Robert, and the wedding is happening. I'm so sorry, Tyler." She stares at me emotionless, and it's obvious something isn't right.

"Bullshit," I blurt out, lowering my arms. "I can see right through you, Gemma. You're lying."

"I'm not. It's the truth. Robert and I are getting married in a couple of weeks, and I'm quitting my job after I find a replacement."

Now I know she's playing me for a fool. She'd never quit working at her dad's shop.

"What happened between today at work and now?" I challenge, not taking her words at face value.

"I already told you. I had a realization…"

"Goddammit, Gemma," I hiss, stepping closer and causing her breath to hitch. "What'd he say to you? Why're you doing this?"

"It's not gonna work out between us, so stop trying to—" I close the gap between us, cup her face, and crash our mouths together. Her words are full of fucking shit, and the way her body responds gives her away.

At first, she tenses, but then she quickly relaxes in my hold and wraps her arms around my waist. Sliding my hands down, I grab her ass and lift her off the ground. Her legs wrap around me, and I push my erection against her. She releases a moan, and I've undoubtedly got her. Walking to the couch, I sit with her straddling my lap. She grinds against my cock as I hold her in place.

"You wanna tell me again how we're over?" I growl, moving my lips to her neck and sucking on her soft skin. "Tell me you don't love me. Convince me you love him. C'mon, repeat it," I demand.

Gemma shakes her head and looks down. I cup her face and watch as tears form in her eyes. "What'd he do to you, baby? Please, tell me."

The tears fall, and she becomes visibly more emotional. "He showed up at my house and told me he owned my dad's land. If I don't marry him, he'll bulldoze it to the ground, and everything my dad and I love will be forever gone. Robert's fucking crazy, so I have no doubt he'll actually do it."

"What?" I look at her in shock. "How's that possible? Are you sure he's not just BS'ing you?"

She nods. "He showed me the paperwork. It's confirmed. I guess my dad took out a second mortgage to take care of my mom's medical bills years ago and wasn't able to keep up with the payments. Right before it went into foreclosure, Robert bought it and waited for the opportunity to use it against me so I'd bend to his will. He's a monster." She wipes her cheeks, and I hate that bastard for putting her through this.

I grip her face and rest my forehead against hers. "Why didn't you just say that?"

"He threatened your life, too."

Rolling my eyes, I scoff. "How?"

"He said he'd make sure Victoria got her revenge without any consequences. Though they aren't working together—another thing he blamed me for—I believe he'd find a way to cover up her crimes."

Fuck, fuck, fuck. Victoria already has an endless amount of money and can pay anyone off. She doesn't need him to get away with murder. She's done it several times already.

"Sweetheart, listen to me," I mutter softly, and she meets my gaze. "I'm in this for the long haul, you got me? Be honest with the shit he says or does to you, and we'll get through it together. Promise me."

She nods again. "You're right, I should've, but I was so scared. He's worse than usual and admitted that even though we don't love each other, he wants me as his wife for his public image. I'm not sure what I'm going to do. I can't lose my cottage or the house my mom and dad built together. He'd be devastated."

"I don't have the answers right now, baby, but we'll figure it out. Okay? If we have to be together in secret until we find a solution, then so be it. It'll suck, but there's gotta be a way out of this."

"There isn't much time," she insists. "The wedding invites went out today."

"Well, he's not the only person who knows people. I'll do whatever it takes to keep you safe and for us to be together."

She wraps her arms around my neck and presses into me. I hold her to my chest and inhale her scent. "We've got this, baby," I whisper in her ear. "I'm not letting you go this time. *Never*."

"I'll have to keep up the act until we have a plan," she explains. "In public, I'll have to pretend we're a perfect couple, but hopefully, we can find a way to end the charade before the wedding day."

"We will," I promise.

She leans in and presses her mouth to mine. "Before you kissed me, how'd you know I was lying?" she asks, searching my face.

"Because I can read you, Gemma. Your mouth said one thing, but your body said another. I learned a lot of weird shit in prison, one of them being body language—a defense mechanism—but the two weren't lining up."

"Well, you were definitely right about one thing." Her lips shyly tilt upward.

Brushing hair behind her ear, I grin. "What was that?"

"That I love you. I'm completely crazy, out of my mind in love with you," she states confidently.

Her confession has my heart nearly beating out of my chest, and I can't hold back the wide smile on my face.

"You have no idea how happy that makes me, baby. I'm madly, deeply, *insanely* in love with you. I love you so damn much that it physically hurts when I think about how I almost lost it all."

Gemma laughs and smiles at the same time, wiping away happy tears. "I can't believe we're finally together again and have to pretend we aren't."

"It won't be for long, sweetheart. We can sneak around, and

when it's all over, we'll be able to appreciate every single minute we get together." I press my lips to hers.

"I hope so. As long as he doesn't throw anything else at me, I think I'll be able to pretend for a couple of weeks."

"You're stronger than you realize, Gemma. You always have been."

She leans into me and presses her mouth to mine. Our kiss quickly grows hungry and desperate, and her hands grasp me as I squeeze her ass cheeks. Gemma rocks her hips, and that sexual urge returns, greedy and eager.

"I don't wanna wait anymore, Tyler. Please. Make love to me," she begs with little whimpers that have my cock aching.

"You're sure?" I ask, hoping she doesn't change her mind after how she's touching me.

"*Yes.* I want you."

Without muttering another word, I stand and take her with me. She squeals and tightens her arms around me, holding on. Gemma feathers kisses on my face and neck, driving me more insane. I take us to my room, then move to the bed.

Setting her down, she lies back with her legs hanging over the edge. I stand between them and lean over her with a smirk. "How do you want it?"

"What are my choices?" she muses, and I growl.

Grabbing her thighs, I wrap them around my waist, then rest my elbows on either side of her. "Well, I can make love to you, sweet and slow…" I arch my hips and press my cock between her legs. Her head falls back as she releases a moan. "Or I can fuck you, deep and hard."

She gulps, then slides her hand between us until she feels my bulge. "Both."

I chuckle at her indecisiveness. "You keep doing that—" I nod down to where her hand is. "And you may not get a choice."

"I'm okay with that. Just take off your clothes," she demands.

Ignoring her request, I drop to my knees and keep her legs parted as I slide my palms up her thighs and press the pad of my thumb against the outside of her panties. She's still wearing the pencil skirt she had on at work, which works fucking perfect for me.

Before I do anything, I plan to taste and feast on her pussy.

"You're soaking wet for me, aren't you, baby?" I taunt, playing with her clit.

Her eyes slam shut as she bites down on her lower lip. "Mm-hmm," she hums.

"Move your skirt over your waist. I wanna see you," I instruct. It's been over five years since I've been with a woman, and I'm not rushing this—especially not with the woman I love.

Gemma does what I say, giving me a front row seat to her sexy black thong. "These for me?"

"I won't deny I think of you every time I put them on." She smirks.

I move them to one side and brush my finger over her, immediately feeling her wetness and sliding up and down her slit. Her breath hitches, and she gasps, though I've barely touched her. It's obvious she's as eager as I am, but I'm taking my time tonight. I want to cherish every second and remind her why we're amazing together.

Slipping my finger inside, she grips the blankets and arches her back as I explore her sexy body with my mouth. I flick my tongue against her clit, and she writhes underneath me. I add a second finger and drive deeper as I suck hard. Her hands fly to my hair as her legs curl around my shoulders, and it won't be long before she completely unravels.

"God, that feels amazing." She moans. "Don't stop."

Not a fucking chance.

Gemma rocks against me as I bring her closer to the edge. She pushes my head into her harder as I thrust my fingers faster.

"Yes, yes, oh my God…" She nearly flies off the bed as she comes on my tongue. I widen her thighs and devour her as she screams out my name.

Leaning back, I wipe my mouth and grin. "That was fucking hot."

"That was…*so* good."

"Glad to hear being rusty hasn't affected my ability." I flash her a smirk.

"Don't get cocky." She chuckles. "Now, clothes off."

I waggle my brows. "Yes, ma'am."

Standing, I pull my shorts down and take off my shirt. My cock springs free, and Gemma doesn't hesitate before reaching for it. She places my length between her lips, then lowers her body as she strokes me into her hot mouth.

"Fuck, that's incredible," I murmur, resting my palm on the back of her head to guide her. "I came in the shower to the very thought of this."

Gemma stares up at me with pure amusement.

"Couldn't help it. You consume me." I flash her a wink, and she sucks faster.

"You better slow down…" I warn, but she doesn't listen.

I want to be inside her when I come. Pulling back, she releases me, and I reposition her. She raises her arms, and I remove her shirt and unclasp her bra. Cupping one of her perky breasts, I lean down and drag my tongue over her nipple until it's hard.

"You have amazing tits, baby." I caress the other before switching my mouth to it.

I help her out of her skirt and panties, and when we're both naked, I direct her to lie on the bed. Lifting one of her legs, I rest her ankle on my shoulder as I stand and position myself between her.

"I might not be able to last long," I warn. "I've been waiting for you."

"Our night isn't ending anytime soon," she says sweetly. "And I don't plan to sleep tonight."

"Goddamn," I hiss, stroking my cock as I press the tip against her pussy. The anticipation is almost too much as I slide inside her.

"Mmm…" Her eyes flutter closed as she grins.

"Jesus fuck," I grunt, nearly biting off my tongue as I try to hold back. The moment I speed up, I'll embarrass myself and come in five seconds. It's been so goddamn long, and I don't want this to end anytime soon. "You're so tight, baby. It's too good."

I position her other leg on my other shoulder, then lean down until her knees touch her chest.

"You're so deep," she purrs. "Go faster, it's okay."

Gripping the back of her thighs, I move back slightly until I easily thrust in and out of her. Her pussy squeezes my dick with every movement, and it's pure heaven.

Gemma slides her hand down between her legs and rubs her clit as I pound into her delicious cunt. She cups her breast with the other and makes sexy little breathy noises. As she gets closer to the edge, her hips rock faster, and the moment she unravels, her body tightens. Her loud moans are music to my goddamn ears.

"Yes, sweetheart...*fuck.*"

She shakes, riding out her release, and before I lose control, I pull out completely. Gemma furrows her brows, but before she can ask, I flip her over on her belly.

"Lie in the middle of the bed," I order. She does, and I crawl to her, grabbing her hips and tugging her upward. "Stick your ass out, baby."

She looks over her shoulder and smiles, then spreads her thighs. I dip a finger inside her again, and she's wet and ready for more.

"Hang on," I warn when I enter and squeeze her cheeks apart. She gasps as her chest falls to the bed, and I dive deeper.

At this angle, I can increase my pace while filling her full with my length.

"Shit," I mutter as her pussy clenches, and I give her ass a hard smack. Gemma rocks against me as I pound in and out of her, and in seconds, she's screaming out again. Her moans echo against the walls, and I've never been happier that my sister isn't home. I'm thankful we don't have to worry about being quiet, though our neighbors might have a different opinion.

I reach around and rub her clit, but she squirms. "It's too much, but don't stop," she pants. "Oh my God, it's so good."

Smirking, I move back slowly before slamming hard again. She loses her balance, and her arms slide above her head as her body goes flat against the mattress. The new position makes her pussy tighten around me even more, and I'm seconds away from coming inside her.

"Goddamn, Gemma...I'm so close, but I don't wanna stop. You feel too amazing."

"Come inside me," she pleads. "*Please.*"

"You're sure?"

"Yes." She pants harder. "Fuck me," she demands. "*Faster.*"

Leaning over until my chest covers her back, I bring my mouth to her ear. "You have any idea what you just said? I'm already losing my fucking mind."

"Don't stop until you do," she says, and I can tell she's grinning.

When she's steady on her hands and knees, I kneel securely between her legs. The headboard is about to dent the motherfucking wall from hitting it so much. Fisting her hair, I tug her head back as I push inside, and she gasps. Grabbing her hips as she rocks into me, I pound fiercely into her, over and over. I release her hair and bend my knees. Squeezing her waist, I ram into her wet cunt deeper and faster until the build is too much, and I explode.

Grunting and groaning, I curse as the orgasm takes over. Gemma collapses on the bed, and I nearly fall on top of her but hold myself up with my elbows.

"Jesus Christ," I choke out. "I can barely breathe after that."

Gemma giggles as I situate myself next to her and hold her in my arms.

"You gettin' old?" she taunts.

"Not sure I can keep up with you youngster," I tease, brushing the hair off her cute, sweaty face. "That was…"

"Incredible," she finishes for me.

"So incredible. And sexy. And hot. Fuck, I'm getting hard again."

"Guess you aren't too old then." She smirks.

Leaning down, I cup her jaw until our mouths touch. "I love you, Gemma. We're meant to be together. I have zero doubts about that."

"I love you too." She wraps an arm around me and brings us closer. "I wish I had waited longer for you. We wouldn't be in this weird mess if I hadn't started dating him in the first place."

"Don't you dare blame yourself for his behavior. Robert's on a power trip, and we aren't gonna let him get away with it," I reassure her.

"I hope not." She rests her head on my chest and snuggles into me. "So how's having sex again after five years?" she asks with a cute chuckle.

Threading my fingers through her hair, I laugh. "Better than I could've ever imagined. But it's only because it's always felt unbelievable with you—that still hasn't changed."

Gemma tilts her head up and flashes a small smile. "I'd be on board with the housewife duties and stay-at-home mom gig as long as it was with the right man."

"I'd never ask you to do that. I respect you and know how much you love working with your dad."

"But when I picture you coming home to me, I like the idea of us spending as much time together as we can. You'd cook dinner because *obviously*..." She chuckles. "I'd give the kids a bath, and after we tucked them in, we'd snuggle on the couch with a glass of wine and talk about our day. Afterward, we'd climb into bed, make love, and then I'd fall asleep in your arms. I wouldn't even need to dream because nothing would be better than the reality I'd be living with you."

"You have no idea how much I wanna give that to you, baby," I tell her sincerely, brushing the pad of my thumb over her cheek. "I never felt worthy enough for you, and it's partly why I had to go. I needed to make something of myself so I could have that title. Didn't quite go as planned, though." I frown, then press a soft kiss to her forehead.

"I don't understand why you'd ever think that. To me, you hung the damn moon, and I couldn't care less about anything else."

"Young and filled with insecurities, I guess. I think that happens when you grow up with no role models and wonder why your mother couldn't stay sober long enough to be in your life."

"Have you seen her since you've been home?"

I shake my head. "Nope. Don't even care enough to find out where she lives."

Gemma nods. "She's the one who missed out."

"Especially since I'm so damn loveable..." I waggle my brows, and Gemma releases the sweetest giggle.

"I think we should take a shower," Gemma suggests.

My eyebrows pop up. "Already?" I know what her insinuation implies.

"You need a break, or do I need to remind you of what you'd be missing?" She slides her hand between our bodies and wraps her fingers around my cock. "I think he's on board."

"You're insatiable," I growl, pushing my hips into her hand as she continues to stroke me. "*Fuck.*"

"That's what I thought." She climbs on top of me and pushes me back as her pussy rubs against me. "I'm not wasting a minute I have with you, so you better meet me in the bathroom in thirty seconds. Otherwise, I'll start without you."

CHAPTER THIRTY-SEVEN

GEMMA

THE MOMENT I leap off the bed, Tyler's chasing me, and I squeal all the way down the hallway. He quickly catches me in his arms and spins me until I'm facing him.

"Nice try." He flashes a devilish smirk as his arms slide down my back. "You have an amazing ass, by the way. I can't stop touching it."

Tyler has no idea how many years I've spent hating my body—too flat, too skinny, too ugly.

He notices my expression change and tilts up my chin. "Whatever negative thoughts are filling your mind right now, stop. You're *beautiful*. Your sweet tits and fine ass are just a bonus."

I burst out laughing and pull his lips down to mine, sinking my tongue into his mouth. "Thank you," I mutter. "I appreciate you saying that."

"I fucking mean it, Gemma. Nothing will ever affect how I feel about you. I'm in love with you because of who you are. Not anything else."

"And that's why I love the hell out of you. Now, get me in that shower now," I demand. "I have some wild fantasies to fulfill."

Tyler chuckles and shakes his head, then turns on the shower. Once the water's warm, we step in. Immediately, I'm swarmed by the hot stream and Tyler's hands and mouth. I can't get enough of him. I never could, and I most definitely won't be able to now.

The anticipation of Tyler claiming my body again is almost too much for me to handle. As the memories of our summer together flood in, I remember why I never stopped loving him.

I spin around in his arms until his chest is to my back. His thick cock presses against my body as I arch my back, allowing him to slide it up and down my pussy. Leaning down and flattening my palms on the shower wall, I widen my legs to give him access. Squeezing my hips, he pushes in deep, making me gasp out in relief. He ravages me from behind with desperate thrusts, and I can't control the moans that escape from my lips. Tyler grunts and slides his hands up and down my body. He circles my clit, massages my breasts, and pounds into me as if his life depends on it.

Once the buildup is too much, my pussy clenches, and I unravel around his dick. This feeling is almost too much yet at the same time, not enough.

I want more.

I *always* want more of him.

Tyler's close, and when I look over my shoulder, his eyes are closed tight. I whisper sweet words and tell him to fuck me harder. Moments later, he's growling out his release as he spills inside me again.

The connection between us is so intense that I get emotional thinking about it. He holds me in his arms after we clean up. When he kisses me slowly, he nearly steals my breath away.

Once we're satiated, it doesn't take long before we're ready to pass out. I immediately fall asleep in his arms without a worry in the world.

The next morning, Tyler wakes me with his tongue between my legs. After he devours me as if I'm his queen, he crawls up my body and kisses me, allowing me to taste myself, which is a real turn-on.

"I could get used to that," I say. "Who needs coffee first thing when you can have an orgasm instead?"

"Exactly." He smirks. "But just to be extra nice, I'll make you breakfast in bed *with* coffee."

"You keep treating me to sex and food like this, and I'm never gonna leave your bed."

Tyler smiles, then kisses my forehead. "That's my plan."

I lie down while he goes to the kitchen to cook. I honestly don't know how things could get any better.

Thirty minutes later, Tyler brings a tray with two steaming hot mugs and two plates of eggs and toast. I sit up, and he grabs his, then settles next to me.

"So what's the plan today?" I ask after gulping down half my coffee. Though I'm definitely not complaining, I don't think either of us got enough sleep.

"Well, my only plan was to ravish you, but maybe after you shower and change, we can go on that hike?" he suggests.

"I'd love that! We just have to be careful in public. I have to amuse Robert's ridiculous idea for a bit. I should probably speak to my dad and triple-check that Robert's telling the truth. And if he is, then maybe my dad will have a solution. But unless he drags me by my hair down that aisle, I'm not saying *I do*."

"We'll think of something, baby. I promise," he reassures me. "Don't forget I have some connections in Vegas who could easily take care of him," he teases with a wink, but I don't think he's joking.

After we finish eating, I help him clean the kitchen and take every opportunity to kiss him. It's almost eleven when I get dressed, and Tyler walks me to my car. We look around to make sure we're not being watched or followed before he kisses me goodbye.

"I'll call you after I speak with my dad," I tell him. "Then we can pack some snacks and hit the trails."

"Sounds good. I love you."

My heart nearly leaps out of my chest when I hear him say that. "I love you more," I say.

"Pfft. Not fucking possible." He gives me one final kiss and then opens the car door for me. "Drive safe."

I can't wipe the foolish grin off my face as I drive home. Every part of me is lit up with happiness, and nothing could bring me down when everything feels so perfect and right.

The moment I pull into my driveway, I realize I spoke too soon, and my world comes crashing down.

A moving truck is backed in, and a crew is loading up my belongings. I glare at them, confused, wondering what they think they're doing. When I pick up my pace and turn the corner, I see Robert. "What the hell are you doing?" I shout as I storm toward him.

"Good morning, darling." His eyes scan down my body in

disgust. "Hope you enjoyed your final night of being a whore because *today*, you're moving in with me."

"What?" I put my hands on my hips. "Have you lost your ever-loving mind?"

He steps toward me, closing the gap between us. "Watch your goddamn tone," he hisses. "That was the deal. We get married, you move in, and you quit your job. Don't like it? Then say goodbye to all of this because I'll get a team out here this afternoon to bulldoze it down."

Tears threaten to surface as I take in his angry tone and the bulging vein in his forehead. He's not messing around, and I have no doubt he'd do exactly that.

"I *hate* you," I seethe.

"Get over it, princess. They've already started packing and moving your shit."

"You can't do that! You can't touch my personal property!" I argue. "I'll call the sheriff!"

He leans back, pure amusement on his ugly face as he crosses his arms over his chest. "Go ahead. Remind him to bring a case of beer to our barbecue tonight while you're at it." Robert laughs as he walks away and goes toward the cottage. I'm going to lose my shit if they've touched my mother's paintings.

At that thought, I march past him and barge through the door to check what they're doing. "Stop! Get out. Don't move anything else," I demand.

Three men stare at me, expressionless, then glance over at Robert. When I turn and look at him, he shakes his head, and the guys continue working.

Goddammit!

Everyone's on his fucking payroll, so no one will listen to me.

"You'll never get away with this," I say between gritted teeth.

"I already am."

I storm out and go back to my car, feeling hopeless. Knowing Everleigh's at work, I call Katie, and when she answers, I lose it. Tears fall and there's no stopping them.

"Gemma? What happened, sweetie?"

"Robert!" I say between harsh breaths. "He has a company

moving everything out of my place. He's forcing me to live with him and get married to help his image."

"What? That's insane, Gemma!" she shrieks. "Tell him to kick rocks!"

"I tried!" I grow more hysterical with every passing second. "He owns my dad's property. If I don't do what he says, he'll tear it all down."

"What the hell? How's that even possible?" she asks, and I explain all the details. I feel awful for not knowing or helping, but my father's a prideful man and keeps his problems to himself.

"So it's either marry him, have his children, and quit my job, or my dad loses everything."

She lets out a long breath. "What about the shop?"

"I think that'd be safe, but he'd have no place to live, and it's more than just a house to him. It's the home where he and my mom made memories, and where Noah and I were raised. And to dig the knife even deeper, Robert knows how much the cottage means to me. Even if I can't live in it, I'd be devastated if he destroyed it." I cry harder at the thought. "I don't know what to do, Katie. I love Tyler. We finally made love last night, and now everything around me is falling apart."

"Does Tyler know about Robert's ultimatum?"

"Yes, I told him, and he said we'd figure something out together."

"Tyler should kick his fucking ass! Charge him caveman style and use his boxing skills to rearrange his ugly old face!"

I'd laugh at her dramatics if I wasn't in the middle of a crisis.

"Trust me, he's ready to do just that." I sigh. "I need to ask my dad about this. It's going to kill him, but I have to make sure Robert's not lying to me. I don't know how I'm going to get out of this without hurting Tyler or my father."

"Robert seriously thinks you're going to marry him after this whole stunt?"

"He's got me by the damn throat and has made sure I have no other options. The minute I defy him again, he'll make his threats a reality."

"Which means he could literally hold this over your head for years. If you don't do what he asks during your marriage, he'll throw it at you again. You'll be miserable, Gemma. You can't marry him," she pleads. "There has to be a way out of this without jeopardizing your dad."

"I'm listening," I say between tears. "Because I can't think of any solutions."

"Make him sign the deed over to you. Negotiate a deal with him. A trade, of sorts. He gets the wife and kids, and you get what you want too. After a year, file for a divorce."

"A divorce? He'd never go for that. That'd be against his *values*."

"Well, then leave that part out for now and just say the only way you'll agree to marrying him is if after the wedding, you get the deed in your name. I mean, that's pretty damn reasonable because if you're miserable, you'll make his life miserable too. Tell him that."

I swallow hard, contemplating it. "But I still lose. I'll be married to him, forced to have his children, and won't get to be with Tyler." I let out a sob. "The only man I've ever loved."

"Well, yeah…there's that part." Her voice softens. "I'm so sorry, Gemma. Want me to kill him for you?"

I snort, wiping my cheeks. "No. It would only make things worse. There has to be something I can do to get out of marrying him and get the paperwork signed over to me, like you said."

"You'll think of something."

Katie and I speak for a few more minutes until I let her go.

Next, I call my father.

"Daddy," I say, trying to keep it together.

"Hey, sweetie. You didn't come over for breakfast this morning, so I went to the deli and chatted with Belinda."

"Shoot, sorry, I forgot to tell you I wouldn't make it today."

"That's okay. What's wrong?"

I chuckle at how he just knows.

"I need to ask you something, but promise you'll be honest with me, even if it's not something I wanna hear."

"Alright," he says cautiously. "What is it?"

I ask about the second mortgage, the almost foreclosure, and if Robert owns the property. Then I tell him about Robert's threats.

"It's true," he responds in a somber tone.

"Daddy, *no*…" I hold back from more tears falling. "Why didn't you ever tell me? I could've helped." I would've taken out a loan or picked up a second job to help pay the mortgage.

"I was ashamed and embarrassed. I'm supposed to be taking care of you and had no idea he'd use it as motivation to blackmail you. I thought he was helping so the house would stay in the family. Gemma, I'm so sorry." He chokes up.

"Don't apologize, this isn't your fault. I'm going to find a way. I won't let him do this."

"Don't marry him because of me, sweetie. You told me it was over, and I can see how much you love Tyler. He can threaten it all he wants, but it doesn't mean he will."

"You don't know him like I do, Daddy. He's a monster. Movers are emptying the cottage as we speak because he's forcing me to live with him. If I don't, he'll take everything."

"Gemma, you listen to me," he says sternly. "If he takes the land and the house, so be it. I won't trade any of this for your happiness."

My mother's cottage is everything to me, and it's all I have left of her. I'll be damned if I let him take that away from me too.

"I'll think of something," I confirm, hoping I actually will. "For now, I'll play his game and somehow get him to do what I want for once." Katie had a good idea, but I'm not sure what it will take for him to agree with that either.

We talk for a few more minutes, and when Robert strolls toward my car, I end the call. I gotta put on my game face and not let him think he can push me around.

Opening my door, I step out and wait for him to speak.

"Everything's packed and loaded on the truck. Follow me back to our house." He doesn't give me a chance to respond before he turns and goes to his SUV. My mind goes wild as I try to think of what the hell I'm gonna do.

Once I arrive, I watch as they unload my things and stand numbly as they stack boxes on top of boxes. I want to ask where my mother's paintings are, but I'm so emotionally drained that I don't know if I can even speak. Robert looks at me with a shit-eating grin and walks toward me, closing the gap between us. Flinching, I take a step back so he can't touch me.

The thought that I once allowed him to touch and kiss me makes me sick to my stomach. The way I'd cook him breakfast, clean his house, and bend to his every demand disgusts me. It's like I've woken up and don't recognize the person he molded me into.

"Well, that's it. Home sweet home, darling," he says once the movers leave.

"You had no right to do that without my consent," I scold.

"Oh, don't frown. It's not a good look on you." He grins like the devil he is. "Don't worry, you can even have your own room until our wedding night. The invites went out today. We're getting married in two weeks."

"And you'll leave my dad's house and the cottage alone?"

"Yes. That's the arrangement. And I am a man of my word, Gemma darling."

I suck in a harsh breath and glare at him. "Fine," I agree between clenched teeth. "But I have one condition if you want me to walk down that aisle."

He tilts his head at me with amusement. "You really think you have a right to negotiate?"

"Unless you want me to go public and *ruin* your image, then yes, I do. Might be a little awkward if your bride is kicking and screaming down the aisle."

He scoffs with an eye roll as if I wouldn't. "Fine, I'll humor you. What do you want?"

I cross my arms over my chest and stand firm. "After we're married, you get your lawyer to draft up a deed transfer and sign my father's property over to me. It legally becomes mine, and this marriage stays purely transactional. I don't love you, and you *clearly* don't love me."

Robert ponders it as he looks intently at me. "Alright, but I have my own addendums to our agreement then. If I sign it over to you, then you can't turn around and file for divorce. If you do, I'll make your life a living hell, and you have no idea what I'm fully capable of. Also, I want a prenup as an extra layer of protection for myself. Also since you so kindly mentioned my image and reputation, you'll attend all business dinners, events, and you'll play the part of being my perfect, *happy* wife."

I stare at him when it hits me like a ton of bricks.

"Fine," I concede. "Not a problem."

Robert takes another step with his infamous victory grin. "See? Wasn't that easy? We should pop a bottle of champagne to celebrate. Oh, and don't forget, we're having a barbecue tonight to formally announce to everyone that we're back together. Better get ready soon. Don't want you looking like a cheap two-dollar whore."

Grinding my teeth, I glare at the disgusting man in front of me. God, I hate him so much.

"I'll be in my room until they arrive," I announce, turning and walking down the hall. At least the spare room is on the second floor and away from him.

"See you soon, my bride-to-be," he calls with an annoying chuckle, and it causes angry tears to spring to my eyes.

I need to call Tyler. This will break his heart but not nearly as much as it's already breaking mine. We were so fucking close to finally being together again after loving him for so damn long.

Locking my bedroom door behind me, I sit on the edge of the bed and try to mentally prepare myself for this conversation. If I break down, he'll want to come and rescue me, and I have no doubt Robert would call Sheriff Todd and have him arrested for trespassing. It wouldn't be good for Tyler, considering his record. I can't risk Robert making Tyler's life a living hell too.

I grab my phone before I can chicken out and click on his name.

"Baby, I've been waiting for you. Didn't you get my texts?"

"Sorry, I haven't had the chance to check them. But we need to talk."

"Okay. What's going on?"

I release the tight breath that's lodged in my throat and squeeze my eyes shut. "I'm so sorry, Tyler, but I'm marrying Robert."

CHAPTER THIRTY-EIGHT

TYLER

THE PAST THREE days at work have been absolute torture. Every time I look at Gemma, I want to pull her into my arms and kiss the hell out of her. But I can't, and I know she wouldn't let me anyway. The woman I love is six feet away, and I can't do a damn thing.

As I refill my coffee for the third time today, I think back to Saturday and the phone call that changed everything. At least I'll be able to get it off my mind for a bit with Eric coming to visit. Everleigh and I are picking him up from the airport after work, and it'll be a nice distraction. Plus, with him close, I'll be able to keep my eye on him to make sure he doesn't do anything stupid.

No one seems to know where Victoria is, which can only mean bad news. I'm waiting for her to pop up unexpectedly, and knowing how she is, it's not out of the realm of possibilities. I'm not naïve enough to think she's given up because the O'Learys don't work that way.

After my shift is over, I grab my shit and leave. Gemma doesn't look my way, and I keep my eyes off her. The invisible wall between us is too high to scale, and I'm not convinced that Robert doesn't have someone watching the garage.

The walk to the boutique gives me time to think about everything I want to say to Gemma and can't, so I tuck it inside. It disgusts me to know she's going back to his house every night when she should be sleeping in my bed. When I walk inside the boutique, the animated ghosts swoop down and nearly smack me in the face.

"This is a hazard," I say, trying to hold back a smile. If anyone can make me laugh with the mood I'm in, it's Everleigh.

"Lock the door behind you," she says, but I don't see her. Moments later, she comes into view with a pile of red and green Christmas sweaters in her arms.

"Already?" I ask, looking around, noticing half the store has already been transformed.

"Halloween will be over in a few days, and then it'll be time for hot cocoa, chestnuts, and Santa!"

I groan and shake my head. "I forgot how much you love the holidays."

"Well, get ready for it because I'll be this crazy about decorating until Easter, then it starts all over with summer!" she squeals. I glance at the clock, and before I can say anything, she speaks up. "I'm almost done here. Get the broom and help a sister out."

With a huff, I do it because we need to be at the airport within the next hour. It doesn't take very long for Everleigh to start turning off the lights. She keeps the purple and orange twinkle strands on, and then we leave. On the way to her car, she's all smiles.

"I love this season," she says, nearly twirling before she unlocks the door. I offer to drive, and she happily lets me. Once we're buckled, I turn on the radio, not wanting to talk, but she's not having it.

Reaching over, Everleigh turns the music down and looks at me.

"So, you gonna explain what's going on between you and Gemma?"

I glance over at her. "I don't wanna talk about it."

"She doesn't want to either. I'm just confused. I'd already planned your wedding, the kids' names, and started buying baby clothes. Then out of the blue, it's over, and she's marrying that asshole because of his stupid threats. You were supposed to live happily ever after. This is messed up!" Her face contorts.

"It is," I offer, not wanting to say too much more about this. Gemma has been very quiet and has given everyone the same answer—she's marrying Robert. I grab the steering wheel tighter, hoping she's taking care of herself while with him.

"I tried to talk her out of it. Katie did too. So did her dad. But she's moving forward regardless of the fact she'll be miserable for the rest of her life. I can't watch my friend do this, Tyler. I can't."

"You're gonna have to, sis. It's her choice. She doesn't love him, but she does love her dad and everyone else in her life who Robert threatened to destroy. It will all work out in the end. I promise."

"I don't see how it can with the wedding happening," she mumbles, and I tense. Everleigh notices the mood change and thankfully talks about something else. "Next week, you wanna help me decorate the trees at the shop?"

A small smile touches my lips. "Trees?"

She nods. "Yes, trees. You can't have just one. Come on."

This makes me chuckle. "Maybe, but isn't it tradition for it to be put up *after* Thanksgiving?"

"Not when you're in the business of slinging candy cane leggings like they're drugs." She laughs at her own joke.

"Okay, okay. I'll help." I agree just to appease her.

Everleigh's satisfied with my answer and turns up the volume on the radio. Taylor Swift blares through the car, and soon, it's followed by Lady Gaga and Nicki Minaj. But instead of complaining, I deal with it because it's much better than talking about Gemma.

We eventually make it to the airport, and soon, we see Eric exiting with a duffel bag swung over his shoulder. I honk, and he waves, then gets inside.

"Thanks, man, appreciate you letting me stay with you for a little while."

I look over my shoulder at him, and he doesn't look any better than the last time I saw him. "No problem. This is my sister, Everleigh."

Everleigh shifts her body and turns and gives him a grin. "Nice to meet you," she offers. On the way home, we stop and eat at a diner because we're starving. He doesn't bring up Victoria, which I'm grateful for because Everleigh would ask too many questions.

Once we walk inside the condo, Everleigh showers and packs a bag.

"Leavin' already?" I grab a beer from the fridge and hand one over to Eric.

"Yeah, Ruby and I have a date with *The Challenge* on MTV, and it starts at eight, so I don't wanna be late. Be back on Saturday, or maybe I'll see you when I come see Sassy after work each day," she explains, giving me a quick squeeze, then leaves.

Eric and I sit on the couch, and I flick on the TV for background noise.

"Glad you're here," I offer with a smile.

"Yeah, me too. Sorry to bring this up, but I'm just gonna come out and ask. Have you run into Victoria lately?"

I turn to him. "No, is she still here?"

"Yes. I hired a few trackers in Nevada, and no one has seen her since Sunday. She returned here a few days ago. My source told me her private jet is currently sitting in a hangar in Birmingham, which means she's close. I don't know what she's planning, Tyler, but I can guarantee nothing good will come out of it. So, I'm doubly glad I'm here."

He gives me a serious look, and I take a swig of my beer, processing the information he shared. She might be in town, but she better keep her ass far away from Gemma and me.

"It's not surprising. She's already meddled with people who are in my life. I figured she was still scheming, working out her next move to take me down. I wonder where she's staying." I trail off, allowing my thoughts to get the best of me. "Do you know why the case was thrown out?"

Eric huffs, and he looks like he's chewing on rocks. "They told me it was because of a technicality, but my lawyer got with me off the record and said her alibi was sealed airtight, and no weapon was found. It's essentially my word against hers. Victoria claimed I blamed her as revenge for firing me. I couldn't believe how she was able to twist the fucking truth and how people took her word as the Holy Grail. She's a goddamn murderer who's freely walking the streets because she's rich."

"Money makes people turn a blind eye on unethical things, even those who are supposed to protect and honor the law. All of it is bullshit, and I'm sorry you have to go through this," I say, putting myself in his shoes and thinking about what he's lost. Though I spent time in prison, the woman I love is still alive, even if she's not with me right now.

"It does. And that's exactly why I need to end this. Because if I don't, she'll continue this destructive path of ruining other people's lives. I can't allow her to get away with what she did, Tyler. I won't." He's tense as hell as he tightly holds his beer bottle.

I suck in a deep breath and nod. "I know there's nothing I can say that will stop you from going down this road. I'll help you however I can, Eric, but I can't get locked up again because of her. I've lost too much already."

"This is my fight. You already did what you could, and allowing me to stay with you is enough. I appreciate you, man. Glad to have someone who's sane in my corner for once and happy to help you and return the favor."

A chuckle escapes me. "So what's your plan?"

He shakes his head. "The less you know, the better. I just need to find her first, and then I'll figure out the rest."

His words cause a chill to run up my spine. I hate that he's going to these lengths, but there's no changing his mind. If Victoria would've done to Gemma what she did to Amara, I'd hunt her like the animal she is, consequences be damned.

Eric finishes his drink and stands. "I think I'm gonna get some sleep. Gotta get the rental car early in the morning."

"Sure thing," I tell him, showing him around the house just in case he needs anything. Everleigh offered to stay at Ruby's for a few days so I could have her room and Eric could have mine. "Sheets are clean."

"Thanks again," he tells me. I grab some clothes from my drawers before I walk away and give him his space. Sassy jumps off Everleigh's bed when I pass to go into the living room, and I decide to take her for a walk. It gives me a little time to blow off some steam, but now that I have confirmation that Victoria is in town, I watch out for anything out of the ordinary. Sassy stops every ten seconds, but I don't rush her, especially with how nice it feels out.

Once we're back inside, I feed her some treats, then she runs back to my room and hops on the bed. "You're so lazy," I say with a grin as she puts her head down.

Considering I didn't take a shower after work, I go to the bathroom. I step under the hot stream and can't stop thinking about the last time Gemma was in here with me. The pain of her going through with the wedding nearly destroys me. She'll stand in front of a room full of people, and they'll witness her exchanging vows with that asshole. The whole thing makes me so goddamn sick to my stomach, and I feel like I'm suffocating. I turn off the water and get out of the shower and dry off. My thoughts over this whole situation are fucking with me, but above all, I just want her to be safe. My stress levels are through the roof, so I promise myself I'll get up in the morning and hit the gym regardless of how shitty I've been sleeping lately.

After I get dressed, I go to Everleigh's room and climb into her bed. As I close my eyes, I think about a letter Gemma wrote to me. It squeezes at my heartstrings, and as I recall each word she said, it nearly guts me.

Dear Tyler,

Your last letter nearly broke my heart. When you get home, I'm going to kick your ass for that. I don't know why you think you're not good enough to have a real relationship. You're caring. Honest. You've got all the qualities that a woman looks for in a man…or at least from what I've watched on TV and read online. Everleigh has shared with me all the things you used to do for her when she was younger. I'm aware that you didn't have a good example, but she turned out just fine, though a little crazy, but I don't think that's your fault. :) Your grandparents love you, and they love each other, and I'm also happy they were in your life. Honestly, without your grandma pulling the reins back on Everleigh, I think she may have gone wild. Also, one last thing. Just because your mom wasn't a good role model doesn't mean you're destined to follow in her footsteps when you decide to get married and start a family. And you will have all of that—a wife, kids, and an amazing job. I don't doubt that. Your heart is huge, and whoever you end up with, I know you'll do whatever you can to make her really happy. She'll be the luckiest woman alive…and I'm kinda jealous thinking about it.

I'm not giving up on you yet, so don't give up on yourself either.
With Love,
Gemma
P.S. I'm still kicking your ass.

. . .

Though time passed and I ended up hurting her, I'm relieved that Gemma never changed her stance. Right now, going through with this wedding is the best decision. The bottom line is, I'm not giving up on her either, and in the end, we'll be stronger for it.

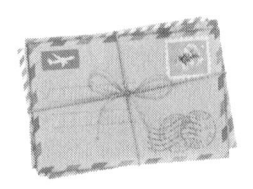

I can't believe it's already Friday, but then again, every day since Gemma told me she was marrying Robert has been exactly the same. Gym, work, gym, home, sleep—rinse and repeat. Today, Gemma wore that miniskirt I love so much with an orange fuzzy sweater. Roses were delivered promptly at lunchtime, and Robert made sure to order so many that the smell nearly knocked me down when I entered the lobby.

Gemma pretended they weren't a big deal, but I wonder if she despises them and if she wants to trash them the same way she did the others he sent. While drinking my coffee, a customer enters, complimenting her on the roses, and Gemma gushes. It takes everything I have to keep my expression neutral.

"So the wedding is happening soon. Are you excited to get married?"

"Oh, yes ma'am," Gemma says with a saccharine sweet smile. "Can't wait to start my life with my husband. I love him so much."

I glance at her, grab my cup, and walk into the garage, busying myself with tasks. Jerry gives me sad eyes but doesn't say anything. He's aware of how Gemma felt about Robert and was just as frustrated as everyone else to hear the wedding was happening. Though neither of us have brought it up, we feel the same. Robert's threats are total shit, but Gemma has to do this to protect her dad's property. It's the only way.

After work, I go to the gym. Luke and I throw punches for an hour, and I don't go easy on him. Over the past few months of training him, he's grown much stronger and has started using his head more. I'm like a proud big brother when he swings and punches me right in the chin. Fighting on the mats helps me work out my aggression just as much as it helps him.

Once the session is over, Ruby asks me if I want to get a drink with her. Everleigh is still staying at her house, but she's been walking Sassy each day after work and spending time with her. Though I'm sweaty, it's not like I'm trying to impress anyone, so I agree. We walk down to the pub, and she gives me shit about my demeanor.

"You gotta quit moping around like this, Tyler. Move on. Date again. Find you a side piece." She elbows me as we sit at the bar and our beers are placed in front of us. She doesn't know all the details about Robert and Gemma's arrangement. I didn't feel as if it was my place to even mention it.

I give her a look. "I'm good. Honestly. The wedding will be over soon, and I'll eventually get back to the life I had before it."

"The one where you did nothing but work and had no social life?"

I shrug. "Maybe."

She sips her beer and watches parts of the football game playing on the TV. "I just worry about you. I know how much Gemma meant to you, and I hate to see you like this. That's all."

"Hey, I'm gonna be just fine. I just need a month or so to process it all. Things will go back to normal, I promise."

She lifts her glass and grins. "Good. I'm gonna hold you to it. Everleigh is worried shitless about you too."

I scoff. "She needs to make up her mind. She was lonely when I was spending time with Gemma every night, and now, she's annoyed that I'm home. The girl needs to date."

Ruby smirks. "If only she'd give me a real chance."

I narrow my eyes at her. "She denied you?"

"Well, not exactly. There was a night when I thought—"

Shaking my head, I tell the bartender to bring me a shot. "I don't wanna hear about you making moves on my sister."

"She's a great kisser." Ruby winks.

"Ruby," I warn, not knowing if she's joking or not. All she does is laugh her ass off.

We decide to order food, and after we finish eating, we say our goodbyes.

"If you're bored, my schedule is free until the end of time," she tells me, then adds, "unless your sister changes her mind."

Considering Everleigh is staying with Ruby until tomorrow, I don't know what to think about any of this. Instead, I huff and turn on my heels. I'm two seconds from pulling my phone from my pocket and asking Everleigh if Ruby was fucking with me, but then I decide I don't want to open that can of worms. The thought has me chuckling. My phone vibrates, and I answer when I see it's Eric calling.

"Where are you?" he says breathlessly.

"Outside of the pub. Everything okay?"

"I'm close. I'll be right there," he rushes out before hanging up.

I notice headlights in the distance. The vehicle looks like it's going at a high rate of speed when it turns the corner, coming toward me. My adrenaline spikes, and I look at my surroundings, hoping to hell it's Eric. When the car comes closer, I recognize his rental and breathe a little easier. I'm thankful it's not Victoria because his voice sounded strained. He rolls down the window and demands I get in the car. By the expression on his face, there's no time to argue.

"What the fuck is going on?" I ask as I buckle, and he picks up his speed. He's driving erratically, but I know he's been trained for this.

"I found Victoria, and she's looking for you. You're not safe," he warns, making a turn.

"Where are we going?" I ask.

"To beat this bitch at her own game. I got some news from one of her bodyguards who used to be an old friend. Victoria crossed him, and he just happened to reach out to me," he explains. I haven't ever seen him this happy.

"Are you serious?"

He nods. "I also learned she's been watching you, Tyler. And Gemma. Neither of you are safe."

I open my mouth, but he interrupts me before I can continue.

"And I found out even more information." He's so damn giddy I want to slap the smile off his face because these are serious allegations.

"Go on," I demand.

"She's been cheating on Mickey. With the same bodyguard who snitched her out to me yesterday."

My mouth falls open in shock. Mickey DeFranco is the father to Victoria's children and is also the man who Liam was forced to fight. He's the reason Victoria murdered her brother in cold blood too. The family feud between them ran deep, but Victoria doesn't follow anyone's rules but her own. So she hooked up with Mickey and used Liam as a decoy husband. One thing is certain, Mickey is crazier than she is. I knew that the moment I laid eyes on him in the ring. "I don't know what to say."

"I made a few phone calls." Eric looks at the clock.

I glare at him as he pulls into a neighborhood with million-dollar mansions. Somehow, he was able to get a gun and put the clip in the bottom, then loads a bullet in the chamber. I notice the silencer on the end and that he's wearing gloves and tactical gear.

"Eric," I warn.

"Don't worry. I'm not gonna do anything stupid. This is for our protection. Come on." He opens the car door, and I hesitate.

"What about the not getting me involved thing that you said on Wednesday?" I ask, following him as we nonchalantly walk down the sidewalk. We look suspicious as hell.

"Considering you're her current target, I think it's best we make sure the situation is properly handled." He checks the time on his phone. "Any minute now."

He studies a large house with gigantic windows and a circle driveway. The lights flicker in the distance, and he pulls me behind some tall bushes, and we walk the property line. Eventually, he squats, and I follow his lead.

"What are we waiting for?" Curiosity is getting the best of me as my heart races.

"You'll see," he whispers.

A few minutes later, Victoria leaves the house with the boy toy following her.

"Fuck!" Eric hisses and begins texting someone. She climbs into the passenger side as her bodyguard drives. Eric and I jog back to his car and try to find her. Victoria may look like a princess, but she's actually the fucking devil, and I can only imagine what she's doing.

Eventually, we catch up to her, and my heart hammers in my chest when she drives into my neighborhood and sits outside of Everleigh's. By the flicker inside, I know the television inside is on, and my sister is inside playing dog mom before going to Ruby's. If Victoria gets out of that damn car, I swear I'll take her down myself.

"What's your exact address?" Eric asks, typing it into a text as I tell him.

Ten minutes pass, and I can smell the sweat on my skin from the gym. Eric pulls out a pair of binoculars. "Are you fucking kidding me?" he hisses.

"What?" I ask.

"She's going down on him right now. This is gonna be messy."

I keep my focus on the street and notice a black van driving at a snail's pace. Eric ducks down slightly and so do I. The seconds feel like minutes when I see Mickey DeFranco, looking hopped up on drugs, exiting the vehicle. He's holding something in his hand. I can't make out what it is as he stalks toward the Mercedes with fogged windows.

There's commotion in the car, then Mickey slams the metal into the passenger side, shattering glass on the street. He reaches inside and pulls Victoria out by her hair.

"Holy fuck," I whisper as Eric watches with a satisfied grin on his face.

I hear screaming and notice Everleigh's porch light flicker on. "No, Ev. Stay inside."

"Shit." Eric panics, as Victoria's guttural cries echo through the neighborhood. "They're being too loud, and they'll wake everyone up at this rate."

The bodyguard gets out of the car and tries to run away, but Mickey pulls a gun from his waistband and caps him. The guy falls to the ground, but I can't see him any longer. Everleigh opens the front door, and I want to scream for her to go inside and pretend she didn't see anything. But I can't because she can't know Eric and I are here. The less she knows, the better.

"Help me! Help!" Victoria screams as Mickey drags her toward the van. She trips in her high heels as she tries to fight him.

Shock washes over Everleigh's face as she pulls her cell phone out and slams the door shut.

Mickey's booming voice calls Victoria every curse word under the sun. "You thought you could fucking cheat on me? After everything we've been through?"

"Let me go," she demands with a shriek.

"You stupid whore. You're going to pay for this." She slips again, but he continues to jerk her around like a caveman who's come to claim his woman. Victoria gains her footing and reaches for Mickey's gun. Somehow, she gets a hold of it, and when he tries to take it back, it's too late. Shots ring out, and Mickey tumbles to the ground. As if she's making sure he's dead, she puts another bullet in his temple. My heart nearly stops at what I just witnessed, but there's no time to react because Eric exits the car with his gun drawn and moves toward her.

I'm still as I watch him move closer, pointing the barrel at her. "This is for Amara," he roars. She doesn't notice him until he speaks, but she's not fast enough to recognize what's happening. A shot pierces her arm that's holding the weapon. Metal crashes to the ground as Eric takes another shot, then another. She falls and doesn't move. I see blood pooling next to Mickey's body and am frozen in shock.

Eric looks over her for a few seconds, puts her fingerprints on the gun before dropping it next to her, then hurries back to the car. Not wasting any time, we zoom down the road and end up outside the pub.

"Wanna get a drink?" he asks nonchalantly.

"Are you serious?" I don't even know what the fuck just happened, and my brain is trying to catch up. I've seen some crazy shit, but that takes the cake.

Eric gets out, then heads inside. Not knowing what else to do, I follow him. Once I'm next to him, I flash him a glare as my body buzzes from adrenaline. He's not fazed by my shell-shock expression and orders a shot of tequila.

"What the fuck just happened?" I whisper when he downs it and orders another.

He peels off his gloves and tucks them inside his jacket pockets. "It's over," he says in the calmest voice ever. "It's finally over, Ty."

After twenty minutes, my phone buzzes with frantic text messages from Everleigh.

Everleigh: Where are you?

Everleigh: I need you to come home. I'm so fucking scared. There was a shooting on the street outside of the house. It's all blocked off, and I had to give a statement to the police of what I witnessed.

Tyler: I'm at the pub. I'm heading home now.

"We've gotta go," I tell Eric, and he nods after he signs the credit card receipt. Since the road is closed, we decide to walk home, and my heart is hammering in my chest the entire way.

"Want to explain some things to me?" I finally turn to him as I see the ambulance lights in the distance.

"The gun was one of Victoria's and had her fingerprints all over it. Chris, her bodyguard gave it to me. From what I can tell, what happened out there was nothing more than a lovers' spat."

"You called Mickey DeFranco?" I'm putting the pieces together.

"I just called a few people who could get the word back to him. He's a jealous man, so I knew he'd lose his shit." Eric shrugs. "She got what she deserved."

When we walk up the sidewalk, Everleigh runs over and wraps her arms around me. She's shaking like a leaf, she's so frightened.

"Are you okay?" I ask.

She nods. "There was a fight, and this couple ended up shooting each other. I thought this was a good neighborhood," she says, and tears spill down her cheek.

I let out a cool breath, realizing she never mentioned another person. She never saw Eric. "Wow."

"I already gave my statement," she tells me. "No one else heard anything. It was crazy and is no doubt gonna be the talk of the town tomorrow." She buries her head in my chest.

"You should go inside and have a glass of wine."

Everleigh nods and does what I say. I look at the street and see three covered bodies. What a traumatic fucking experience for my sweet little sister to have to witness. Before we go inside, I turn to Eric. "Why did we go to the pub?"

"For an airtight alibi. I did some research on the sheriff and learned he was lazy as hell. There won't be a proper investigation, forensics, or any of the shit we do in the city. Lovers' quarrel that ended poorly. The ultimate Romeo and Juliet story." He smiles, and we go inside.

I sit on the couch, my body almost feeling numb because I can't believe this is really over, and Victoria is dead. For the first time in five years, I feel free.

CHAPTER THIRTY-NINE

GEMMA

My life as I know it is changing, and all my freedoms are gone. Every day, a black cloud seems to hang over me, and I can't get away from it. At work, Tyler and I have kept our distance, but sometimes, I find myself staring at him, longing to be close again.

The last time I spoke with him, he quickly explained that Victoria died, and Everleigh witnessed it. She had told me what happened, something about a lovers' spat and a shooting outside her house, but I hadn't pieced the two together. Victoria did terrible things to Tyler and Eric that changed the entire outcomes of their lives. I was just shocked that her boyfriend came here to take care of the problem. I'm so relieved for Tyler, knowing he now has the freedom he's been seeking since he met that woman. It might not have been the kind of justice he was after, but justice was definitely served for what that woman has done to people.

After having lunch alone, I get a group text from Katie and Everleigh, and that's when the dread really settles in.

> **Everleigh: I know the circumstances aren't really ideal, but since you're getting married in two days, I think we should have some fun. Let us throw you a bachelorette party tomorrow night. We can drive over to Nashville and do it up real big! Cowboy strippers and lots of alcohol!**

Katie: I would totally save a horse and ride a cowboy. Count me in!

Everleigh: Gemma?

I swallow down the lump in my throat, not in the mood to celebrate my defeat. It's not a happy moment, and I feel as though I'm planning my funeral. I find some courage and text them back.

Gemma: I'd rather not go all out, if possible. Can we have drinks here instead?

Katie: I'm fine with whatever you wanna do! It's your choice.

The knife drives in deeper, and I don't know what to say. They're just trying to be nice when I'd rather just hide away from it all. We're all trying to make the best of a shitty situation.

Everleigh: Gemma...you really don't have to go through with this. We're here to support you.

I've had to reiterate my decision to them both so much over the past week like a broken record. They're aware of how I feel about Robert and the ultimatum he gave me. And though I've tried to convince them this is the right thing to do to save my dad's home, they're not convinced no matter how many times I say it.

Gemma: I know. Appreciate and love you both so much. I don't know what I'd do without you.

I think about Tyler. I think about everything we've shared. I think about that night that I went over to his house and explained everything. What I'm being forced to do makes me feel sick. If I could blink and take away every moment that Robert and I spent together, I would. They say people learn something from every relationship, but the only thing I learned is I trusted him too much.

After work, I leave and go to his house where I've been forced to stay since he moved my shit there. Robert shows up late as I'm warming up a frozen entree. While I'd rather pretend he's not home, he forces my attention to him.

"You look like utter shit," he hisses as soon as he sees me. He doesn't sit but rather crosses his arms. "When you quit your job, I expect you to look put together and at least try. I won't have you staying home, lounging in filth like this."

I have no energy to argue with him. "What do you want?"

The quicker he says what he needs to say, the sooner he'll leave me alone, and right now, I want my distance from him more than anything.

"There's one more thing we need to add to our agreement," he says with a pushy edge to his tone as if I'm one of his clients and still need to sign on the dotted line. Though he may have gotten the upper end of the deal—considering he wants me to have his children, quit my job, and play the role of the perfect housewife and mother for the rest of my life—I plan to get the last laugh. Happy wife, happy life, right? I can guarantee I'll be miserable, and so will he.

"What is it?" When the microwave dings, I grab my shitty enchiladas and a fork, then plop on the couch. He looks so damn offended that I'm not eating at the kitchen table and will probably explode at any second now. Crossing his arms, he moves where he's in my view and blocks the TV.

"The night of our wedding, I want us to have sex. I think it's important we consummate our marriage properly."

This has me nearly choking on my food, and I glare at him. Has he lost his damn mind?

I've never been so damn thankful to be on birth control. There's no way in hell I'm going off it, either. But he's so ate up in his own damn self that he doesn't even realize I'm still on the pill. Hell, I might take double doses to ensure I don't get pregnant. While I do want kids someday, I don't want *his*.

"That wasn't a part of the original agreement. You can't just change things two days beforehand because you didn't think about it."

"Gemma. I want to have children as soon as possible to please my family and continue my legacy. That's always been a part of our plan. And the sooner we try, the quicker it'll happen. You know it's tradition for a husband and wife to sleep together on their wedding night."

"Will the deed be signed on Monday then?" I ask.

"I will sign when we return from our honeymoon," he states matter-of-factly. "It should be obvious how much trust I have for you, and I need to make sure you'll keep your end of the deal before I give you anything. You're too conniving."

I bite my tongue at his audacity. "This is purely transactional, Robert. All of it. The wedding. Having children. All you're doing is checking boxes on your life list, and I'm disgusted that I'm being forced to be a part of it. So you give me what I want, and I'll bow down and do what you say."

He chuckles. "Force you? You agreed to it, Gemma. Don't you fucking forget that. Every night on our honeymoon, we will be having sex. I want you pregnant as soon as possible."

"I'm compromising a lot for you. I have to know you're gonna follow through and give me what I want because I *don't* trust you. I can't *unhave* sex with you if you decide not to fulfill your end of the bargain. If you can't agree, I'll walk away right now and deal with the consequences. It'll be much worse to call everyone and let them know the wedding is off forty-eight hours beforehand," I threaten, and he seems to finally understand how serious I am.

"You're not gonna play me for a goddamn fool, Gemma. You're nothing but a selfish bitch, something that you've proven to me time and again over the past year. You're only worried about yourself. I honestly don't understand why my parents love you so goddamn much."

I scoff. "You're a hypocrite. If anyone has been selfish, it's you. You pushed me away. You made me feel like I was second class next to your work and your clients. The only time you *ever* fucking wanted me around was to show off. Maybe if you weren't a damn sociopath and had an ounce of empathy in your body, you'd be able to see why we didn't work out. Just so you know, it wasn't because of me. I'm convinced you're incapable of loving anyone or anything other than money," I throw back at him.

My words don't faze him, but it seems he's considering what I've said. Canceling the wedding this soon would be too devastating for him to handle and would take a lot of cleanup. He huffs, and for once, I think I have him by the balls. "Fine. I'll sign the deed on Monday, but only if you agree to my additional terms."

I suck in a deep breath. "Okay. If that's what it'll take."

"Saturday after the wedding, we'll make love and have a proper night as husband and wife. Monday morning, I'll sign over the deed. Friday, we leave for our honeymoon, and you know what is to take place there."

That gives me another idea. "One more thing. If you screw me over and don't sign, I won't be going on the honeymoon. The whole town will hear about it because you know how fast gossip spreads here."

He glares as if he's annoyed by my audacity to assume he'd find a loophole out of giving me what I want after I give him what he wants. But I wasn't born yesterday. I've heard a lot of his negotiations, and the key is to think of every opportunity that can screw you over.

"Then I expect you to quit your job immediately. If you agree to all that, it's a deal." He holds out his hand. I contemplate not taking it, but I know I have no choice. I reach out and shake it, and he grins. I want to throw up in my mouth as he walks away with a bounce to his step. Instead of eating my gross food, all I can do is cry. All of this is almost too emotionally taxing for me to handle.

I put on my wedding dress and hate the way it looks on me. I would've never chosen this for myself, but I'm sure he'll love it. Before I go out and exchange I do's with the man I hate, I drink myself stupid. There's no way I can do it sober. Everleigh and Katie try to convince me to leave, but I continue to take shots of Fireball and act as happy as I can around Robert's family. I have no plans to be a runaway bride today because too much is at stake. Anyone who doesn't know me probably thinks I'm ecstatic. The persona he's created makes him seem like the whole package. People think I'm the luckiest girl on earth for finding such a catch, and I want to scream that this is hell. Money doesn't buy happiness or orgasms.

When it comes time to walk down the aisle, I reek of cinnamon and booze. Dad gives me a once-over, and I see a flash of concern on his face when I nearly trip over my heels, but he doesn't say anything. He didn't want me to go through with this, but I put my foot down. Losing the house and cottage wasn't an option, and I explained that several times. As soon as the wedding song plays, I wish I would've brought the Fireball with me because I could use another shot. I wear a fake smile and continue forward, one foot at a time, knowing what I have to lose and gain.

The ceremony passes by in a flash, which I'm thankful for. I don't remember anything that happens during. I don't recall his mouth pressing against mine or the photographer snapping a hundred photos. Afterward, I go straight to the bar and order more shots. Though Everleigh and Katie are concerned for me, they encourage and join in. Robert's friends and family stare, but I don't give two shits what they think. Instead, I'm determined to be the life of the party, even if it's in my head, and I'm happy to give his boring, stuck-up rich friends something to talk about. Robert scolds me like a child when we dance, but I don't care.

You only get married once, right? The thought has me laughing because all of this is a damn disaster.

If he wants to have sex with me, I'll be so drunk I won't remember his hands on me. When the world tilts, and I feel as though I'm going to throw up, I realize I've accomplished my goal. A mischievous grin spreads across my face as he's forced to keep me from falling on my ass. He cusses at me for ruining our wedding night, but for me, it's mission accomplished. Tonight, I win—not Robert—regardless of what he thinks.

Monday morning comes quickly, and I'm determined to make Robert keep his word despite not being able to consummate our marriage. He suggested we could Sunday night, but I told him I still felt hungover and nauseous. That was enough to make him walk away.

I get up and dress for work, but he's already gone by the time I roll over. He told me he'd meet me at the notary office, so I'm going to make sure I'm not late. If he tried to get out of signing the paperwork today, there'd be no honeymoon. Rumors would spread like wildfire, and he'd have to create more lies to cover that lie. Considering he invited nearly five hundred people to the ceremony and bragged about where we were going, everyone would be suspicious if it was suddenly canceled. I acted surprised and excited when he announced it on stage, and they all stupidly bought it. He continued on about the first-class tickets to Hawaii and the private villa he rented, and I was the envy of all the single women. Knowing how many people witnessed what took place still gives me hives, but he's always wanted to be the center of attention. He finally got what he wanted, and me being sloppy drunk is what he deserved.

Just as he promised, he meets me at eight with the drafted deed agreement his lawyer finalized. I told Dad I had some errands to run this morning and would be late to work.

When we enter, the woman and all her jingly bracelets and big blond hair greets us. She pulls out her official stamps and looks through the paperwork, then asks for our driver's licenses.

"I haven't changed my information yet," I explain.

Robert glares at me. "Why haven't you?"

"Sweetheart..." My tone is venomous. "It's only Monday. We've been married for two days. Don't worry, I plan on taking care of it before we leave for the honeymoon."

"All documents have to be signed in your full legal name and need to match what's on your license," the clerk informs me.

"That's fine," I confirm.

"Maybe we should wait until you get an updated social security card and can go down to the DMV and change your license."

I narrow my eyes. "That won't be necessary." Leaning over, I whisper, "A deal is a deal. Don't make me cause a scene."

He acts as if I just slapped him across the face, even if my voice was only loud enough for him to hear. The smile on the woman's face doesn't falter, but she begins to tap her nail. Though Robert hesitates, he eventually does exactly what I need. Even if he's an asshole most of the time, I can respect that he keeps his word, *sometimes*.

When the paperwork is stamped, the woman hands it over to me, and I feel like I won the damn lottery. We thank her, and I hold it tightly in my hand as if it will disintegrate. Though I never wanted to stand in front of a crowd of people, wearing the same dress his mother wore while saying I Do, having this deed makes that torturous ceremony all worth it. Before we leave, Robert makes sure to pull me into his arms and kiss me for anyone who's looking our way to witness.

After I'm in my car, I wipe the taste of him from my lips and pop a piece of gum in my mouth. I can still smell the faint hint of his cologne on my shirt from where he got too close and rubbed against me. Just the thought of him touching me makes me want to soak in bleach. At the beginning of our relationship, I wondered why he was single because he's good looking, has a ton of money, and seemed to want to make me happy. Now, I realize he's crazy as hell and probably pushed every single woman away. What a disaster.

The first place I go is to the courthouse to file the paperwork. There's no way I'm going to allow anything to get in my way. Considering it's Monday morning, the line is long, but I don't mind waiting. Hell, I'd wait the rest of the week right here as long as it meant this was finalized and recorded in the deed book. When I get to the window, I'm relieved to see a woman I don't know because I really don't want anyone in my business right now. I happily pay the filing fee to get everything transferred over to my name. For the first time in a couple of weeks, I feel as if I can breathe again.

Afterward, I go to the bank and pay for a lockbox so I can keep all of my important documents in one place. I don't trust Robert, and I have no place safe to keep things. I sign the paperwork, and eventually see Katie who's with a customer. She waves and gives me a curious look. The papers in my hand are worth their weight in gold, and I need them to stay safe. The ladies here won't break the rules for Robert, especially with Katie watching everything like a hawk.

Before leaving, I go over to her area and say hello.

"Whatcha up to?" She smiles.

"Not much. Just had to take care of some business," I explain.

"Awesome. You doing okay?" she asks, just as her phone rings.

"Doing good. And it's fine, answer it. I gotta go anyway," I tell her, waving goodbye and leaving. The weight on my shoulders isn't as heavy as it was before, but the fact that I'll have to appease Robert and make sure I keep my word makes me feel ill. I head to work and try to hold back the sliver of happiness I have. It's been a while since I've smiled, but as I replay what's happened over the past few weeks and all the threats Robert spewed, I know I made the right choice. There isn't a single doubt in my body.

As soon as I walk in, Dad comes and greets me. "Hey sweetie, take care of everything?"

He grabs a cup of coffee and pours a mountain of sugar in it. Just so Dad doesn't worry, I put on the act.

"Yep, got it all sorted out. Thanks for letting me come in late," I say just as Tyler walks in.

He glances at me, then turns his head. It's awkward as hell, but I keep up the act for Dad's sake.

"Don't forget about dinner Thursday night before you leave," Dad reminds me, not paying any attention to how uncomfortable Tyler is.

"I haven't. I'll be there come hell or high water," I promise. This seems to make Dad happy, but Tyler leaves halfway through the conversation.

Somehow, I keep the smile on my face, and Dad gives me a sad expression. "I wish you wouldn't have done this, Gemma. It's destroying me."

"I know, Daddy." I offer him a smile. "But it's all gonna work out in the end, I promise. I got the deed to the property today. The house and cottage are safe now." I lean forward and give him a tight squeeze, wishing he'd understand that I did it all for him, and he's worth it.

CHAPTER FORTY

GEMma

Each day I wake up to an empty house, I'm relieved. The last person I want to see first thing in the morning is Robert, but lately, I haven't been so lucky. While Robert lives in a beautiful house, the stark white walls makes it feel like a prison. I can't believe I never noticed how much of a robot he is. There's nothing personal inside this four-thousand-square-foot home. It's a cookie-cutter version of all the others he's built down to the interior design. While it's a nice place, it looks like it came from a magazine, and I hate it more than anything.

I want color on the walls, and my mother's paintings splashed around my house. There needs to be character and for it to look lived in. Right now, I feel out of place as if I might break something, and that's no way to live. It's obvious I'm just another item in Robert's collection placed inside his pristine house.

After I get dressed, I walk into the kitchen where I find Robert drinking coffee at the table. The morning after the wedding he was up early to have breakfast with a client and was gone most of the day. Not surprising, considering he doesn't know how to stop working. When I glance in his direction, he's wearing a grin as though he's happy to see me, and I want to tell him to go straight to hell. But I'm trying to control my anger. The last thing I need is an argument before my coffee.

"Good morning, dear," he sing-songs, indicating he wants to chat about something. This is typical of him, and I swear at this point, I can predict his next moves.

I grunt, grab a mug from the cabinet, and pour some cream before filling it to the top with liquid caffeine. I sit down with my eyes barely open because I've slept like shit since I've been here.

"I wanted to explain my plans for the rest of the week so we're on the same schedule."

I take a big sip, thankful the creamer cooled it down enough to drink immediately. Impatiently, Robert waits for my reply, and I just glare at him. I never agreed to pretend to *want* to be with him, just that I would, so this is as good as it's going to get. When I don't speak up, he continues.

"I have a new client that I'm meeting in Cedar Pines today. Considering it's five hours away and we have a lot of properties to view, I'll be there for a couple of days. I'll be leaving this afternoon and won't return until Thursday evening. I'll have no time to prepare for the honeymoon since our flight is early Friday, so you need to pack both of our bags."

He's not asking, but rather he's demanding it.

"Make sure to clean the house and do the laundry too. Just because your mother died when you were young and you weren't taught the proper way to keep a household, that's no excuse. I need to know you're at least trying here, Gemma."

"I'm sorry?" I finally ask, not ready to write down all the tasks he has for me. It's absolutely bullshit that he keeps bringing up my mother, and it infuriates me to the point of no return each time he does. If my mother were here, I'm sure she would've warned me away from him. Instead of answering, Robert goes back to his newspaper.

I've stayed here for less than a week, and he's already treating me like a damn child. He gives me zero credit and doesn't respect the fact I'm still working full-time at the garage. Maybe he should hire a maid since he has so much money. Being his housewife who cooks and cleans up after him is time-consuming and disgusting. Somehow, I'm supposed to magically make it all happen with a smile on my face. I'm no Disney princess.

"It's a part of your duties." He finishes reading an article, then looks at me. "Speaking of, when do you plan on quitting your job? I need specifics, no more being vague. We've already discussed this several times, and if you weren't up there all day, you'd have more time to be here."

"You're such a sexist pig," I mutter, tired of listening to this rhetoric.

"I didn't hear your answer," he snaps. "You know how I feel about you working there with Tyler. He's a *criminal*. And he basically forced you to be with him publicly," he says, repeating the story he told people because Tyler and I were seen together at the Harvest Festival. Robert still hasn't gotten over it and hates that I'd rather be with an ex-convict than him.

"That's a lie *you* made up, remember? Please tell me you don't actually believe that because it's not true." I want to tell him to go fuck himself too, but I don't.

"Doesn't matter because he's still a loser." He scowls.

Somehow, I'm able to play it cool, though it's too damn early for his games. Maybe I've learned a thing or two from him manipulating me so much over the years. Knowing I need to change my tone, I decide to answer him. Or rather, give him the answer he needs to hear. Not because I want to please him, but because I want to stop talking about this and enjoy my morning in silence.

"I'm planning to hire someone so I can train them after the honeymoon. Then I can leave without putting my father in a bind. I know you don't care about any of that, but it's important to me. So there's the timeline you want so badly."

"Fantastic," he quips. "Oh, and my mother wants to have lunch with you tomorrow to discuss the thank-you notes that need to be written and mailed out. She's very concerned about things being done in a timely manner, and considering we got so many gifts, it's gonna take a while. They should be sent before we leave on Friday."

I haven't even opened any of the cards or presents, and they're all still in the living room. When he treats me this way, it puts me in a bad mood for the rest of the day, which isn't fair to any of the customers who come into the shop.

"What time tomorrow?"

"I believe she said eleven sharp at the cafe downtown," he tells me.

I wouldn't be surprised if Robert planned this because his parents adore me so much. The deli is always busy during the week, so I'm sure he wants people to physically see me and his mother together. I half wonder if they know how much of a monster their son is or he got those qualities from them. Now that I think about it, it's probably the latter.

"Okay," I say. "Oh, also, don't forget we're supposed to have dinner at my dad's house on Thursday at seven. He wants to wish us well before we leave for the honeymoon because I'll be gone for ten days."

Robert huffs. "Shit. I forgot about that."

Of course he did. He's only concerned about *his* plans, never the ones I had.

"It's important to my father and me, so it'd be in your best interest to be there," I say.

"Absolutely. I agree." He grins, not realizing my dad knows the full story. "I'll make sure to leave by two on Thursday so I can make it on time. If I'm gonna be a little late, I'll text you. Never know how traffic will be." Robert looks at the clock on the wall. "I've gotta go."

He stalks to me and places a wet kiss on my forehead. I don't react until he's out of sight, but then I wipe it away as if it's poison.

I'm actually grateful the next two days crawl by because it gives me time to make plans. It's been nice not having Robert around, but I miss being home, in my bed, and seeing my mother's paintings on the wall.

Thursday at work is uneventful and we're slow, which gives me too much time to think about dinner tonight. I won't be happy until the food is cooked and Robert is sitting at the table. When it comes to socializing with my friends or family, Robert tends to find a last-minute excuse to bail. If I were to do that, he'd lose his shit, but if he does it, I'm supposed to accept it and move on.

The only reason I don't think he'll ditch tonight is because he wants to please my father and prove how perfect he is for me. Too bad Dad already knows the truth. Regardless, my adrenaline spikes thinking about us all being in the same room in a matter of hours.

After work, I think about how much I miss Tyler. We haven't talked about even the most trivial things like the weather, donuts, or coffee. It's been radio silence at the garage.

Before I go to my dad's house, I stop by the grocery store and pick up a few steaks and ingredients for loaded baked potatoes. It's one of Dad's favorite meals, so I thought I'd surprise him with it. I even spent some time watching a few YouTube videos so I can prepare his ribeye just the way he loves it. I'm not sure the last time Dad has had a proper sit-down dinner at home. We eat breakfast together a few Saturdays a month, but nothing fancy.

As soon as I knock on the front door, Dad opens it wearing a big cheesy grin. I noticed he had enough time to shower after work and even changed clothes for the occasion.

"You're wearing a polo?" I ask, not used to seeing him in a shirt with a collar. It's bright blue and looks good on him, but it's different, considering I see him in his uniform ninety percent of the time.

"You know how judgey Robert is." He releases a sigh. My heart begins to race when he mentions his name. He's on both of our shit lists right now. I bite my tongue and continue inside, trying to gather my courage. As soon as Robert arrives, I'll be forced to put on a show of a lifetime.

Dad helps me unload everything, then I pull out a skillet, the butter, and the seasoning. I even grabbed a loaf of garlic bread too. As I turn on the flame, I take a deep breath and follow the directions I found online. Once the potatoes are wrapped in foil and roasting in the oven, I place the steaks in the skillet. The kitchen quickly fills with the delicious smells of spices, and my stomach grumbles even though I have no appetite. My nerves have replaced my need to eat.

Before the food is ready, the doorbell rings, and Dad quickly answers it. Hearing Robert's voice makes me anxious, and I try to push down all of my thoughts, not giving them the opportunity to swallow me whole. I refuse to wear that stupid look I used to have when I'd see him. I'm sure Robert had hoped I'd stay under his spell much longer.

Robert comes in and kisses me on my cheek. He makes sure to tell me how lovely I look and how great the food looks and smells before he sits next to my father at the table. Dad gives me a look, but Robert doesn't notice. They shoot the shit, talking about the garage, and Robert mentions his new client. I make our drinks and set them down on the table. He vocalizes how much he appreciates and loves me. Actor Robert is great. The real-life one is a nightmare.

I place the steaks, potatoes with all the fixings, and garlic bread on the table, then serve everyone. The conversation is light and pleasant, even if it's fake and awkward as hell.

"So how did the meeting go?" I ask, wanting to fill the time with something other than silence.

"I have a verbal agreement on a contract for an *eight-figure deal*," he nearly screams with excitement. I haven't seen him this giddy...*ever*.

"Really?" I ask, trying to hold back my laughter.

"Yes." He looks at me, then my father as he cuts his steak, then pops a huge bite in his mouth. "It's even bigger than the job I was gonna do for Victoria, so I'm thrilled." He glares at me, then turns his smile right back on.

The asshole is still throwing jabs at me, but I keep grinning, listening to how worked up he is over this.

"Once we return from the honeymoon, he's going to come to the office and sign all of the paperwork. He wants to build a damn outlet mall on the outskirts! Can you believe this, Gemma?" Robert's smile is so wide, I think I see his teeth sparkle.

"Wow," I reply, faking amusement.

He grabs my fingers and kisses them, and I see how uncomfortable my dad is, so I pull my hand away.

"It seems everything is finally working out just perfectly. We're officially married, and now we'll go on the honeymoon of a lifetime. Make a baby, expand our family, and we'll have everything we both ever wanted in life. Everything, sweetie."

I try not to throw up in my mouth.

"Wow, that's impressive," my dad says, glancing at me.

"It's very impressive." I temporarily stroke his ego, and I swear I see his chest puff larger. My heart beats rapidly, but I'm ready for this. Clearing my throat, I add, "Too bad it isn't real." Tilting my head, I shrug, then fill my mouth with potato.

"What're you talking about?" Robert asks.

Dad looks between us, confused.

"It's fake, all of it, all of...*this*." I wave my fork around before setting it down.

"Please explain, Gemma," Dad interrupts.

I giggle, really enjoying this. Grabbing my glass, I take a sip. "What was your client's name, Robert?"

"Excuse me?" he snaps, his brows furrowing.

"His name. The *multi-billionaire* you met." I speak slowly as if he doesn't comprehend my words.

"Eric," Robert barks. "Why?"

I'm full-on laughing now, and tears stream down my face at how Eric performed the role perfectly. He was more than willing to act like a wealthy businessman and fool Robert. I'm bent over, gasping for air at this point. Dad narrows his eyes at me as though I've officially lost my mind. The doorbell rings, and I grab my napkin and wipe my cheeks, then stand.

When I open the door, I see Tyler. I flash him a wink to let him know it's all going as planned. We both smile as we walk into the dining room holding hands. Dad turns and sees him just as Robert slams down his silverware, completely infuriated.

"What's he doing here?" he hisses.

Tyler wraps his arm around my waist and pulls me close before kissing and stealing my breath away. I melt into him, finally tasting him again, and I'm happy to have an audience to witness it all.

Dad's lost, and Robert looks as if he's going to blow a damn gasket. Before either of them can speak up, Tyler pulls a piece of paper from his back pocket. He takes his time unfolding it and holds it for Robert and my dad to see.

"What the fuck is this?" Robert says between gritted teeth after he studies it. "Is this a damn joke?"

I smile like I'm Vanna White presenting the key phrase. "It's our marriage certificate."

"Whose?" Robert furrows his brows.

"I'm so glad you asked. It's Tyler's and my marriage certificate," I proudly say.

Dad's eyes are as wide as saucers, and Robert lets out a growl.

Tyler clears his throat. "Right. And it's dated seventeen days ago, which means when you filed your certificate, we were already married." He turns and looks at me, placing another soft kiss on my lips. Nothing else in this damn room matters right now, but him.

With a grin, Tyler continues. "Which means, your marriage isn't legal because you can't be married to two people at the same time."

"But the deed in my name certainly is," I confidently add. "Oh, and just in case you haven't figured it out by now, I won't be going anywhere with you tomorrow. I guess what I'm saying is you can fuck off."

As the realization sets in, Robert grows more furious. Dad is smiling, so damn proud of what I've done. It's impossible not to notice how humiliated and angry Robert is, and I burst into hysterical laughter as Tyler pulls me closer.

"You stupid bitch! Do you have any idea what you've done?" Robert barks, forcefully shoving his plate out of his way and standing.

"Beat you at your own fucking game. When I ended things, I told you I wasn't marrying you, Robert. I meant every single word."

CHAPTER FORTY-ONE

TYLER

NINETEEN DAYS EARLIER

My phone rings, and I see it's Gemma. Just seeing her name has my body buzzing. We had the most amazing night last night. I can't wipe off the stupid grin on my face as I think about how it felt to be inside her and claim her as mine.

Quickly, I answer it. "Baby, I've been waiting for you. Didn't you get my texts?" She dropped me off hours ago, and I'd been waiting to go hiking with her.

"Sorry. No, I haven't had the chance to check them. But we need to talk about."

"Okay. What's going on?"

She lets out a breath that has me concerned. "I'm so sorry, Tyler, but I'm marrying Robert." Her voice trails off.

"*What*? What happened?" I ask, slipping on my shoes, ready to go to her and have this conversation face-to-face.

"Please listen," she says in a strained tone. "Robert came to my cottage and—"

"I'm on my way," I tell her, not waiting any longer.

"You can't. I'm not home. I'm at Robert's."

I stop moving as my heart pounds hard in my chest. "Why?"

Gemma lets out a whimper, and I swallow hard. "He moved everything out of the cottage and into his house. I was given an ultimatum to marry him or…" She chokes up, and I wait patiently for her to finish. "He'll destroy my dad's house and the cottage."

"Baby, he can't do that." My anger level increases, and I become volatile, ready to beat the fuck out of him. The consequences be damned.

"He can, Tyler. He's backed me into a corner." She continues explaining the deed and how Robert weaseled his way into owning her dad's property. With each sentence, she becomes more emotional, and I can't handle it. She's never been this upset before, and it's breaking us both in the process. Robert needs to pay for hurting her.

"You don't have to do this," I press.

"I don't have a choice. I'm so sorry." She sniffles, and her voice gets quieter. "I never wanted to marry him, but it's the only way he'll sign it over to me. Once we're married, I'll get the deed, and Dad's property will be safe."

I pace my bedroom and realize I'm chewing my bottom lip as I try to think of something to get her out of this. Never would I have imagined he'd stoop so low, but I should've. I didn't trust the guy the first time I laid eyes on him.

"Did you ask your dad about any of this? Double-check that Robert wasn't making shit up?" I run my fingers through my hair and sit on the edge of my bed, then suck in a deep breath.

"I did," she nearly whispers, the defeat in her tone evident. "It's true."

Staring at the wall, I think about our future, and I refuse to let it slip through my fingers. Not this. Not ever.

Over the years, I've dated, but it was never anything serious. Nothing compared to what I have with Gemma. When I imagine getting married and having children, the only woman I dreamed of having that with is Gemma, and I refuse to allow Robert to take that away from me.

She's supposed to marry *me*, not him. The idea hits me, and my heart races at the prospect.

"Gemma…" A smile fills my face, and I'm so damn anxious that I can barely contain myself. "I have an idea. It's a crazy one, though."

She's still crying, and I hear her sniffles. I wish she was sitting in front of me so I could place my palms on either side of her cheeks and press my lips against hers.

"Considering I have no options, I'm all ears."

I lick my lips, my nerves getting the best of me. "When I think about marriage in general, it makes my palms sweaty. But when I think about marrying *you*, it's different. It feels so damn right."

Gemma continues getting emotional. "But I have to marry Robert, and he'd kill me before giving me a divorce. So that could never happen for us."

"Unless you marry me *first*."

The line goes quiet, and I almost question if she's still there. "Tyler…"

"If you were in front of me right now, Gemma, I'd get down on one knee and tell you how much I fucking love you and always have. You're the only woman I've ever imagined myself growing old with, and if you'd allow me, I'd spend the rest of my life trying to make you happy." My heart races, and I wish I didn't have to do this over the phone.

"Tyler Blackwood," she whispers. "Are you asking me to *marry* marry you?"

"Yes, yes, I am." I smirk. "Because if you're married to me, you can't legally be married to him. He'll think it's legit and sign the paperwork. By the time he realizes what's going on, it'll be too late for him to do anything about it."

"He'll never see it coming," Gemma says with a sweetness in her tone.

"Hell no, he won't. I can't imagine a future without you, baby. You're my everything. And I wish you were here so I could propose properly, then make love to you all damn night. I know it's a wild idea but—"

She interrupts me. "Yes," she blurts out, and I can tell she's smiling. "I love you so damn much that I can barely put it into words. I just don't want you only doing this because—"

"Trust me, it's not because of Robert. It's because I love you, need you, and want you forever, sweetheart," I admit.

She lets out a hum. "You've made me the happiest woman."

I chuckle. "I'll get all the details together. We can go down to the courthouse and file the paperwork together. We'll slip out of work separately and take care of it. It's gonna be the best kind of satisfaction, knowing you're my wife and not his."

She lets out a relieved breath. "This really could work."

"It will. I'll always protect you, Gemma," I reassure her. "Now we just have to figure out how to get him away for a bit so we can move your things back to your place and change the locks. Should do a security system, too. Once everything's done, you can tell him to fuck off."

She chuckles, and the sound is so goddamn sweet. "I feel like I can finally breathe again. I can't believe we're really doing this—getting hitched," she gushes.

"I told you we'd get through this together, and I meant it. Though I still want you to have the wedding of your dreams, sweetheart. The one you always talked about having when you were a teenager. I don't want you to be robbed from that," I say genuinely.

"I'd get married to you anywhere, Tyler. Courthouse. Church. Hell, even inside the deli if we had to. You're enough for me and always have been," she confirms. "As long as it's *us*, I'll be the happiest person alive."

I chuckle, almost shocked by where this conversation has gone because it wasn't promising ten minutes ago. "I promise to give you the wedding you deserve one day, but right now, we need to just make it legal. Let's go to the courthouse on Monday. Maybe ask your dad if we can go in to work late. I'll borrow Everleigh's car and meet you in Birmingham so no one can tip Robert off. Since there's no waiting period in Alabama, it'll be official as soon as we sign and they file it," I explain.

"That's perfect. I'll get with my dad and make sure we can get off. Then the only issue left is getting Robert out of town for a couple of days."

I plop down on my bed and think this through. Knowing what I know about Robert, he's easily deceived. When it comes to money, he'll do anything. "I think I have another idea. What if he has a rich client out of town that he needs to meet? Think he'd fall for that?"

"Absolutely, as long as he thinks it's worth his time. So it'd have to be a huge investment, someone with a lot of money. And I've been to so many of those boring dinners that I could literally write a guidebook on what to say." I can tell she's beaming by the tone of her voice. "He's made this too easy for me."

"Don't get cocky." I chuckle. "But who are we gonna have to do it? Someone who could pull it off. A man who could act and look the part." After a moment of silence, it hits me. "Eric's coming to town next Wednesday and owes me a favor from doing the deposition. He'd do it without a doubt."

"Eric? Really? He's already been through so much already."

"He has, but he told me if I ever needed anything, he'd be happy to help. We can rent him a fancy car and buy him an expensive suit. You could coach him on what to say and how to act, and trust me, he's got that douchebag vibe down. I hated him when we first met, so I'm sure Robert would adore him."

Gemma laughs. "I'm sure he will. I'll even use the money in Robert's and my joint checking account to fund it."

I chuckle as the adrenaline rush has me smiling nonstop. "Great, so I'll talk to Eric, and you take care of your dad. Change my name in your phone to someone else, a girl's name or something, just to cover your tracks. If it gets too dangerous, call me. I'll be there to beat his ass within ten minutes," I say seriously.

"I'm sleeping in one of the spare rooms until the wedding, so I'll be able to avoid him for a couple of weeks, but good idea. I'll get things together on my end, and we'll meet Monday. God, I'm so happy right now," she adds at the end. "I don't know how I'll ever be able to repay you for rescuing me."

I smirk. "I can think of a few ways."

"Blow jobs every morning for a year?" she suggests.

"For eternity," I add with a chuckle. "We've got this, babe. It's all gonna work out, and in the end, it's gonna taste like sweet, sweet victory."

"It will," she whispers. "I should let you go, though."

"Okay, baby, please be safe. I love you," I say.

"Love you more."

The call ends, and I blow out a relaxed breath, trying to put all the pieces together. If this doesn't work out, it could piss Robert off even more and then who knows what he'd do to get back at Gemma. But if we play our cards right, Robert would get a dose of his own manipulative medicine, something I would pay my life savings to see. He needs to be knocked down a few pegs, and I think we've found a way to beat the bastard at his own game. Now, I just need to call Eric and get him on board.

SEVEN DAYS EARLIER

It's been twelve days since Gemma and I came up with our plan. In only two days, she'll walk down the aisle and marry that stupid fucker. While I know it's not real, it bothers me to no end that it's not us getting the beautiful ceremony. Though after we filed the paperwork at the courthouse last Monday, I painted my lips across hers as if it might be the last time. Even though it wasn't, it would be until this was all over.

We've kept up the act that we're not together since the whole town is invited to the "wedding of the century." Even when we aren't in public, we've kept our distance. Neither of us trust that Robert wouldn't have us followed again. It was better to play it safe, but it still doesn't make it easy—especially seeing her every day at work.

Jerry has been in a bad mood over it all because Gemma told him she was marrying Robert despite him telling her not to. Everyone except him and her two best friends think they're truly in love. They know about his ultimatum but not about our plan to pull the rug out from under him. We're keeping it a secret just between us so there's no chance of him finding out. Assuming everything goes smooth, we'll share the news with them after it's all done.

Each day that I see her at work and can't kiss her pisses me off. Finally, just when we managed to find our way back together and be happy, this bastard barges in and takes it away from us. What he doesn't realize is it will just make our reunion that much sweeter.

It's surreal not to feel threatened by Victoria for the first time in years. All the pieces are finally starting to snap together, and I can't wait to spend time with the love of my life once this is over. After that night, Eric flew back to Vegas to take care of some work stuff, but will be back tomorrow to start preparing for his meeting with Robert next week. He's been texting with Gemma on how to fool Robert into thinking he's a multi-billionaire interested in dozens of acres of land for development. It's quite comical when I think about all those meeting Robert dragged Gemma to, and now she's going to use it against him in the biggest fucking way. I can't wait to see the look on his smug ass face.

No one will suspect a thing either because hardly anyone knew Eric came to town or what he'd done. Fortunately, the case was filed as a triple homicide just as he thought it'd be. Everleigh's witness testimony also helped since she never saw Eric or me. The O'Leary family was completely outraged by the sheriff's lack of investigation, but Todd's a lazy asshole. He'll close anything up to avoid more paperwork. Regardless, it's no longer my problem, and it's finally over. Right now, all I can focus on is getting through this next week and ensuring Gemma gets that deed. After my training session at the gym, I get a text from her.

Gemma: Robert just added a stipulation to our agreement. Two days before the wedding! I'm so furious, I can't even think straight.

Tyler: I hate him more every day. What is it now?

Her text bubble pops up and disappears, and it takes her almost two minutes to send it.

Gemma: You're not gonna like it. Hell, I fucking hate it.

Tyler: Just tell me, baby.

Gemma: He says he won't sign the deed unless we consummate our marriage on the wedding night. If I do, he'll sign it Monday morning, but if I don't, he won't sign until after our honeymoon.

The rage I feel nearly makes me burst a blood vessel. Gemma is mine, and the thought of him touching her makes me want to beat his fucking face in, but I understand what's at stake here.

Tyler: I want to fucking kill him.

Gemma: I do too. I hate him so much. But I have two options—don't do it and if he refuses to sign on Monday, I'll threaten him with not going on the honeymoon and the aftermath of that would have rumors flying. He bragged all about how he's taking me to Hawaii at the reception, so everyone is expecting us to go. However, the risk of that option is not knowing if that'd be enough to persuade him to sign before the plan with Eric is supposed to happen. Which means getting him out of town those two days would go to shit.

She's right. If he doesn't sign on Monday, the big reveal on Thursday will mean nothing. He'd still own the property, and this will all have been for nothing. The only benefit is that Gemma and I are married, but she'd lose her cottage. Robert's a horrible excuse of a man, and I can't wait to see the look on his stupid face when he realizes Gemma's and his marriage isn't legal. It's the only thought that's keeping me sane right now.

Tyler: What's option two?

I hold my breath because I have a feeling I'm not gonna like it.

Gemma: Cry.

The urge to pull her into my arms weighs heavy on me, and I want to find Robert and bash his head in. What kind of sicko blackmails a woman into having sex with him? I try to calm down and am so happy Everleigh isn't home to ask why I'm rage-pacing the living room.

Needing to get some fresh air, I grab Sassy and we go on a walk, but Gemma and I continue our conversation.

Tyler: What if there was a legitimate reason you couldn't have sex that night where you could still persuade him into signing on Monday?

Gemma: What do you have in mind?

Tyler: Fireball?

Gemma: Fireball? So, get fucking smashed to the point of not being able to walk...which means the following day, I'd have too much of a hangover to have sex that night too. Hmm...I think that just might work.

Tyler: You could even tell him you think someone slipped something in your drink if he asks you why you got so drunk and use that as an excuse so he doesn't try to get out of going on Monday.

Gemma: You know...that's actually not a bad idea. Robert's a dickhead, but he's not a creep like that. He'd want me to be an active participant, but if I were too sick or passed out drunk, he'd be forced to wait until the honeymoon. It's worth a shot! (Haha, get it? Shot!) WHY ARE YOU SO SMART?

I chuckle at her corny joke.

Tyler: We make a great team, baby.

Gemma: I miss you so much, hubby. Love you.

Tyler: I miss you too, wifey. Love you more. This will all be over soon. You've got this.

Gemma: I gotta go, but can you put a bottle of Fireball on my desk tomorrow? I'll sneak it into my bag with my wedding shoes.

Tyler: I'll make sure it happens, sweetheart.

Sassy is ecstatic when I take the corner and walk to the liquor store that's close to the boutique. The owner loves dogs, and she nearly dies when she sees Sassy. I grab the biggest bottle of Fireball they sell and cross my fingers this works.

FIVE DAYS EARLIER

Today is the goddamn wedding.

Everleigh knocks on my door as I'm lying in bed staring at the ceiling when she walks in.

"Hey, bro." She offers me a smile. "I'm gonna head out." She and Katie are in the bridal party, and she's leaving to go meet them at the venue.

I sit up and look at how pretty she is. "You look great, Ev."

Her eyes are sad. "I wish this wasn't happening. I'm really sorry, Tyler. My heart is breaking for you and Gemma."

"It's gonna be okay, I promise," I tell her, but she's not convinced. "Just be there for your bestie. She's gonna need you today."

"I am. I won't take my eyes off her. But anyway, I'll be home later tonight. If you need anything, let me know."

"Thanks," I say, running my fingers through my hair, knowing they're all going to watch a fake wedding with a bride who'll be too drunk to stand. I almost smirk but make sure I don't. "Have fun."

"Fun?" She groans. "Yeah, right. It's like going to a funeral." She gives me a half-smile. "See ya."

When I hear the front door close, I go to the kitchen and make a sandwich. Though I hate the thought of Gemma pretending to marry him, I have the satisfaction of knowing she's *my* wife, and soon, everyone will know the truth.

FOUR DAYS EARLIER

It's barely past eight, and I've already worked out, made breakfast, and done a load of laundry. The tension of not knowing what happened last night is bothering the fuck out of me. I can't get my mind off it. After I take a shower, my phone rings, and I immediately light up when I see it's Gemma.

"Hey, hubby," she purrs, and I can hear the sheets rustling. I know she's alone, and I wish I could barge over there and kiss her all over.

"Good morning, wife. Well, how'd it go? I've been going crazy waiting to hear."

She laughs. "The Fireball did the trick. And if you're wondering, yes, it's absolutely still my kryptonite. By the time I got home last night, I was puking, and he was so disgusted. Never seen a grown man get so squeamish over vomit. After he cussed me out for drinking too much, I told him I'd make it up to him over the honeymoon and made him believe I actually wanted him to knock me up. That seemed to butter him right up. He said he'll keep his end of the deal then and will meet me Monday morning after his lawyer drafts up the deed agreement. He then asked if that earned him a BJ on the plane." She makes a gagging noise. "Too bad I won't be going."

I chuckle at the way she sing-songs that last part. "Thank God." I blow out a relieved breath. "So how's the hangover?"

"Oh, it sucks, but having to screw him would've been much worse."

"Absolutely." I know Robert isn't there because she wouldn't risk calling me. "So where'd he go?"

"Client breakfast and will be schmoozing them all day at the golf course. I could really use one of your amazing breakfasts right now to soak up all this cinnamon in my stomach. Each time I burp, it's horrible," she tells me. "I may never drink that crap again."

"Everleigh said the same thing." I smirk, remembering her stories about her twenty-first birthday. "I'm glad you're okay and so damn relieved he didn't touch you. Less than a week and we'll get to be together, baby."

"I can't wait. Anyway, just wanted to hear your voice before I called Eric next."

"Alrighty, have fun! Teach him all the tricks of the trade," I say.

"Will do," she tells me, and we exchange "I love you's," then the call ends. I plop down on the couch and force myself to wipe away my grin because I don't need Everleigh busting my balls.

THREE DAYS EARLIER

Monday morning comes bright and early. I won't be able to concentrate until Gemma texts me and confirms the deed has been signed and filed. Since Gemma's coming into work late, Jerry and I have been taking turns helping customers. All morning, I've been busting my ass, moving around like I drank ten cups of coffee, and Jerry notices.

"You good?" he asks.

"Yeah, fine," I tell him and grin, though he's not convinced.

"You know, I'm really sorry about all of this, Tyler. I know you love my da—"

"Mr. Reid. With all due respect, there's no need to apologize. Gemma's a smart woman, and I know she's made the right decision. It's water under the bridge." I pat him on the back and get back to my tasks.

He offers me a sad smile, and I wish I could tell him the truth because it's obvious how much this has affected him. He'll know soon enough, and it's what keeps me going.

When my phone vibrates in my pocket, I tell Jerry I'm taking a quick coffee and donut break because cell phones are his pet peeve. Once I'm in the lobby, I pull out my cell and see a text from Gemma.

Gemma: It's signed and notarized. Just filed it at the courthouse. It's a done deal, baby. We'll be together soon.

I quickly text her back with a shit-eating grin on my face.

Tyler: Fuck yeah, sweetheart. I'm counting down the days.

I'm so damn happy I can barely contain myself as I walk into the garage. When she finally arrives at work, we keep up our avoidance act, but I can't help but notice how beautiful my wife is. Jerry and I both go into the lobby for refills, and he reminds her about dinner on Thursday night. I just want to kiss her luscious lips and make love to her all night long. The urge to be with the woman I'm crazy about nearly takes over.

I grow tense and anxious knowing our big reveal is right around the corner. Wanting to give Jerry and Gemma some privacy, I walk back to the garage, giddy as a fool. I can't fucking wait to see the look on his face when he realizes what we've done. And better yet, how he's *lost*.

TWO DAYS EARLIER

By the weekend, I'll be holding Gemma in my arms where she belongs. At lunch, I decide to walk down to the cafe and have some chicken and dumplings. While I'm there, I get a text from Gemma.

Gemma: All of my stuff is back at the cottage! OMG, I can't tell you how happy I am right now.

Tyler: Good, baby! I told you it would all work out.

Gemma: This will be over so soon!

Tyler: 2 days!

When Belinda walks up, I set my phone down, not wanting to be rude. I compliment her dumplings, and she gives me a cheesy grin. After I'm done eating and pay, I walk down to the Coffee Palace and grab a black coffee and a Candy Cane Mocha for Gemma since the temperature has dropped. Before I leave, I get a text from Eric.

Eric: About to meet this stupid fuck for lunch. Pray I don't punch him in the face before this is all done.

I smile, wishing I could give him the green light to do just that.

Tyler: Good luck with that.

Eric: I'm looking forward to making this asshole pay for what he tried to pull. I'm gonna make you proud.

Tyler: I appreciate you, man. Thank you again.

I tuck my phone back in my pocket, then head to the garage.

When I walk in, Gemma isn't around, but I set her coffee by her keyboard. It's a small gesture, but one I know she'll love.

ONE DAY EARLIER

While I'm busying myself with an oil change, I get a text. Quickly, I pull my phone from my pocket and look at it, hoping Jerry doesn't catch me.

Gemma: Security system is installed! Yay!

Tyler: Awesome! So close now, baby!

Our conversation is short because we're still at work. Afterward, I leave and go to the gym so I can train Luke and one of his friends for a few hours. As they're grabbing some water, Eric calls me. I tell them to give me ten minutes, then step out.

When I answer, he's laughing his ass off.

"Do I even wanna know?" I ask.

"He's such a fucking tool bag and fell for a *twenty-million-dollar* deal. Hook, line, and sinker, sucka!" He's full of so much energy, it has me laughing right along with him.

"Damn, twenty million? I'm impressed, man."

"That's because I'm impressive!" he gloats. "I'll keep you updated if anything changes. We're meeting for drinks and dinner tonight. I plan to make him spend a few thousand." He barks out a loud chuckle.

"Good! He deserves it. Keep me posted," I say.

"Will do. Talk soon."

We end the call, and I immediately text Gemma.

Tyler: Eric just set up an eight-figure deal with Robert.

Gemma: I TOLD HIM SEVEN! Robert fell for that?

Tyler: Totally. Tomorrow night, I'm devouring you from head to toe.

I adjust myself, just thinking about it.

Gemma: Gah! Tease.

Tyler: Not a tease, sweetheart. That's a promise.

Luke and Samuel are finished with their break, so I tuck my phone in my pocket. Tomorrow can't come soon enough.

PRESENT DAY

It's the day I've been waiting for. It's been nineteen days since Gemma and I made our plan, and tonight, it'll all finally be over. Over the past few weeks at work, there were many stolen glances. The underlying current that streamed between us nearly had me taking her into the break room and kissing the hell out of her. Somehow, I refrained, though.

After work, I go home and take a shower, then get dressed. I'd be lying if I said I wasn't nervous—not because of Robert but because of Gemma's dad. I don't want him to be disappointed in me, and I just hope he's supportive of what we've done. There's no going back on it now.

I tell Everleigh I need to borrow her car this evening, and while she questions me, she's happy I'm getting out. She's convinced I'm depressed over Gemma marrying Robert, so she is more than willing to let me do whatever I want. While I appreciate her going easy on me, I made sure not to take advantage of it because she'll know the truth about Gemma and me soon enough. And she's gonna flip her shit when she does.

My heart thumps erratically on the way over to Jerry's house. I arrive at the exact time Gemma told me. I can't imagine the conversations they've had, but I'm ready to do this. Sucking in a deep breath, I knock.

Gemma answers the door with a cheesy ass grin. I meet her eyes, and she gives me a wink, silently telling me everything's good to go. We stroll into the dining room together, hand in hand. Jerry turns and looks at me, confused as hell. As soon as Robert sees me, he throws a mini tantrum.

"What's he doing here?" he hisses, his nostrils flaring in anger.

Seeing him like this before our secrets are spilled gives me all the courage I need. I wrap Gemma in my arms and pull her close before sliding my lips across hers. She's already breathless, her body instantly responding to me. Instead of pulling away, she deepens the kiss, and I can't wait to get the hell out of here and be alone with her.

When we pull away, Jerry has confusion written all over his face, and Robert's face is beet red. Before they can respond, I pull the wedding certificate from my back pocket. Making a spectacle out of it, I slowly unfold it, then hold it up like I found the golden ticket to Willy Wonka's Chocolate Factory.

"What the fuck is this?" Robert grits, reading it. "Is this a damn joke?"

Gemma holds out her hand and grins. "It's our marriage certificate."

Robert looks as if he's solving the hardest Sudoku puzzle. "Whose?"

"I'm so glad you asked. It's Tyler's and my marriage certificate," Gemma tells him.

Robert growls as though he's ready to attack, and Jerry still looks lost.

I clear my throat. "Right. And it's dated seventeen days ago, which means when you filed Gemma's and your certificate, we were already legally married." I study her, so damn happy that she's my wife. Not caring, I lean forward and kiss her sweetly. "Which also means, your marriage isn't actually legal, because you can't legally be married to two people at the same time."

"But the deed in my name certainly is," Gemma quips. "Oh, and just in case you haven't figured it out by now, I won't be going anywhere with you tomorrow. I guess what I'm saying is you can fuck off."

Robert looks about to explode as Jerry smiles wide. The only thing that takes my mind off this is Gemma hysterical laughter. The sound is so contagious that I pull her close to me and chuckle too.

"You stupid bitch! Do you have any idea what you've done?" Robert screams, moving his plate, then stands.

"Beat you at your own fucking game. When I ended things, I told you I wasn't marrying you, Robert. I meant every single word," Gemma gloats.

"I need an explanation right this goddamn minute!" Robert demands. If he knows what's good for him, he'll keep his feet planted where they are.

"Sure thing." Gemma shoots him a wink as I trail my fingers across her arm. "Eric, your *eight-figure* client was completely fake. I needed you out of town so I could move all of my shit out of your house. Locks are changed, and a new security system has been installed in my cottage. Also, Eric was on your dime. His car, suit, hotel, all of it. Thought you could use some more business expenses."

"Bullshit," Robert seethes. "You're not smart enough to pull something like that off."

She rolls her eyes, and the urge to knock him on his ass gets stronger with every dumbass word he says. "I told him what to say to make it believable. All those times you thought I wasn't paying attention at your business dinner? I was, and I learned a thing or two about you as well. Forcing someone's hand in marriage isn't right, Robert, but you gave me no fucking choice. You made this bed, and now you'll sleep in it...*alone*."

"You fucking cunt!" Within seconds, Robert charges toward Gemma. Jerry stands, and I move her behind me as Robert sloppily swings his fist. I throw one punch right into his big ass nose, something I've wanted to do since the moment I met him. Robert stumbles backward, but his rage is too much. He growls and makes me his new target as blood runs down his face and splashes on his white button-up shirt.

As he throws punches and misses, Jerry shouts, "That's enough!"

Robert turns, and that's when I see Jerry holding a long-barreled shotgun in his hand. He racks it, putting a shell into the chamber. All I can do is cross my arms over my chest and smirk. He'd be a dumb motherfucker to try to cross Jerry Reid.

"Get the fuck outta my house." Jerry points the shotgun at Robert. "I'm a crack shot, so I wouldn't press your luck, boy."

Robert straightens his stance, then glares at Gemma. "This isn't over," he threatens, pointing a finger at her.

Gemma walks to the living room and grabs a stack of papers. When she returns, she slaps them down on the table. Robert snatches them up and flips through them. His eyes bug out of his head as he continues to read the bank statements that could destroy him and his business.

"If you don't want that getting reported to the district attorney, the papers, and the local news, I'd suggest you drop it. Considering the amount of money laundering and fraudulent activity that's in that stack, I believe it is over, Robert. Don't make me ruin you because I will. Oh, and don't worry, I have plenty of copies, so feel free to keep those as a reminder." Gemma stands firm, showing no mercy toward the man who made her life miserable.

Robert snarls before walking out, slamming the door behind him. When we hear his car start and speed off, Jerry lets out a sigh. "Oh thank God, you didn't marry that asshole."

Jerry wraps Gemma in a big hug, then pulls me in too. The three of us laugh and break apart.

"Are you two really married and stayin' that way?"

I look at Gemma, who's beaming with happiness. Pulling her close, I interlock my fingers with hers, then look back at Jerry. "Yes, sir. She's the love of my life."

He places a firm hand on my shoulder and squeezes. "Good. You two deserve all the happiness in the world with each other."

"Thank you, Daddy." Gemma hugs her dad again, and I notice tears in her eyes when she pulls away. "I told you it would all work out, didn't I?"

"You did," he exclaims. "Never saw any of *this* comin', though."

"You're the first to know," I explain. "Well, you and Robert."

He chuckles. "I'm honored and thrilled to have you as my son-in-law, but that doesn't mean I'm gonna go any easier on you at the garage."

"Wouldn't expect anything less."

Gemma squeezes my hand, and I meet her eyes.

"Thank you, Gem. I know you did this for me," Jerry says sincerely, and I see the flicker of emotion in his eyes that's starting to boil over.

"I did, Daddy. And it worked out for the best. Now, we all get our happily ever after."

"Yes. And oh, you two go be together. You've been married for seventeen days and fooled the world. Go, go! I'll clean up 'round here." He shoos us away, and we don't argue.

I've been waiting nearly three weeks for this night, and I don't want to waste another second of not being alone with my wife.

CHAPTER FORTY-TWO

GEMMA

I CAN'T WIPE the smile off my face as Tyler and I leave my father's house and go to the cottage. I'm so damn happy all my things were moved back, along with new locks and a security system so Robert can't weasel his way in again. The look on his face when the realization set in that he'd been duped was priceless, and it's something I'll never forget.

Best. Moment. Ever.

Tyler opens the door, then pulls me to him before I go inside.

"Wait." He lifts me in his arms, and I tighten my hands around his neck. "It's tradition for the husband to carry his new wife across the threshold."

I laugh. "Then by all means, hubby."

He dramatically steps through the doorway, and I press his lips to mine. "I can't believe we're really married."

"I can't either," he whispers, setting me down. Cupping my face, he brings our mouths together. "I love you."

"I love you, too." I rub my nose against his, and he grins as I continue. "Now, let's consummate our marriage. Like, *all* over this place."

"Is that so, Mrs. Blackwood?" He arches a teasing brow.

"That's the hottest thing I've ever heard."

I jump back into his arms, and he easily catches me as my legs go around his body. He holds me tightly as our tongues swirl together, and I feel his hard cock pressing into me.

"Tyler, I need you. Right now," I demand.

"I'm here, baby." He moves down my jaw and slides his tongue up to my neck. "Tell me what you want."

"Take off your clothes."

He chuckles. "And then what?"

"Fuck me against the wall. Then bend me over the island. Then on top of the counter."

"Jesus Christ," he growls in my ear. "Been thinking about this for a while, haven't you?"

"I have lots of fantasies that involve you, and in all of them, we're naked and moaning."

Tyler carries me into the kitchen, then sets me down. I watch as he removes his shoes, his shirt, and finally his jeans. I lick my lips at how hard and ready he is for me standing in only his boxer shorts.

"As sexy as you look in that dress, it needs to come off," he demands.

I spin around so he can do just that. Tyler brushes my hair to one side and slowly lowers the zipper. The dress falls to my feet, leaving me in only a thong and strapless bra. Before I can tell him to remove them, he kneels behind me, threading his fingers inside the thin panties and pushing them down my legs.

"Fucking hell, baby. I wanna devour you so badly. Taste your come and sink my tongue deep inside you." He stands behind me, pushing his throbbing length against my bare ass.

I unclasp my bra and toss it to the side. Looking over my shoulder, I flash him a devious smirk and arch a brow. "Then what are you waiting for?"

Flattening my palms on top of the island, I part my legs and give him the view he's so desperate for. Dropping to his knees again, he grips my thighs, and spreads my ass cheeks. I lower my stomach to the counter and when he swipes his tongue along my clit, the sensation has me nearly combusting.

Tyler licks, sucks, and flicks my clit, and he doesn't let up until I've given him two orgasms. By the time he stands, my knees are shaking.

"Oh my God." I blow out a ragged breath.

Tyler kicks off his boxers, then grabs my hand and leads me to a bare spot on the wall. "Put your hands above your head and spread your legs."

His deep voice sends a thrill down my spine. I love when Tyler's tone is demanding. When I hear it, I become so eager to please him.

Once I'm positioned to his liking, he moves behind me.

"You have me so fucking hard, baby." I hear him stroking himself and grin. Tyler grabs my waist as he slides against my pussy, coating the tip with my juices. "Hang on."

He pushes inside, slow and easy at first, then pulls out before sliding back in. The intense feeling has my head falling back on my shoulders. Tyler drops his mouth to my neck, fists my hair, and continues thrusting. His other hand slides up my arm, and he threads our fingers together.

"Fuckin' perfect, sweetheart. You and me."

"Always," I say around a moan.

Tyler switches from hard and fast to soft and slow. It's enough to drive me wild, and by the time my orgasm builds, I'm crying out his name. Slipping his hand between my legs, Tyler rubs my clit until I fall over the edge again. He squeezes my breast, kissing up my throat before capturing my lips. As he whispers sweet nothings, I fight to catch my breath and unravel for the third time.

It's too much. But so goddamn good.

"I love how responsive you are, baby. Your body craves my touch," he growls.

"I can't get enough," I admit. "We could hibernate in here all winter long, and it still wouldn't be enough."

"That sounds like fucking heaven," he says against my mouth.

Before I can respond, he spins me around and leads me to the kitchen. Tyler turns me again until my stomach is flat on the counter. I stick out my ass as he slides back inside me, and I gasp at how deep he goes.

"Shit," he hisses, ramming faster. I release a breathy moan as he holds my hips tightly. My pussy clenches, and he pants harder. "Sit."

He nearly gives me whiplash as he pulls out and flips me over until the cold marble hits my ass.

"Jesus," I say with a laugh, gripping his shoulders.

"We have one more position to check off your list." He flashes me a wink, stroking his length before sliding between my legs. "You're so tight, Gemma. I'm using all the willpower I have not to come yet."

Clinging to him, I wrap my arms and neck around him as he roughly pounds me. He's a saint for keeping up the pace this long, and I want him to unravel with me this time. The buildup is intense, and I'm close again. With my lips to his neck, I press a soft kiss against his skin, then whisper in his ear, "I love the way you fuck me, *husband*. Come with me."

Moments later, Tyler releases a roar of a moan and sinks as deep as he can, spilling inside me. I lean back, my palms flat on the counter as he grabs my hips and pumps into me one more time.

"Fuck, baby." His voice is hoarse and sounds even more sexy. "You nearly killed me."

I grab his face and bring our mouths together. "And we get a lifetime of that."

Hours later, we're in my bed, naked and tangled in the sheets. We haven't stopped ravishing each other, sucking and licking, fucking and making love. I've never experienced anything like this before, and the fact it's with Tyler makes it a million times better. The love I feel for him is so strong, and I can barely contain the bursting happiness with every kiss we share.

"Thank you for marrying me," I say as I rest my head on his chest. "And keeping me close even when I tried to push you away."

He tightens his hold around my back and tilts up my chin. "Thank you for loving and trusting me enough to say yes."

"So if we're doing this—staying married and all—don't you think a husband and wife should live together?" I ask nervously. Though I don't know why I'm anxious about mentioning this, I know it's still a big step.

"You sure you're ready for that?" he asks. "I mean, besides us being married and all, that's making it official-official." He smiles.

"According to the State of Alabama, we're already official," I quip. "But yes, I've been ready since I was eighteen. Every night, I wanna come home to you in this cottage—where it all began."

"You gonna let me do the cooking?" He pops a brow.

"Just so you know, I can make a mean omelet. Ask my dad."

"No offense, sweetheart, but your father is too nice to tell you it's not good."

My jaw drops as I release a gasp. "Just for that…" I lower my hand and cup his balls.

"Better be nice down there if you ever want me to be able to give you children…" he warns, and dammit, he has a point.

"Fine," I pout, releasing him, then wrapping my palm around his length. "You can man the kitchen as long as I control the TV."

As I stroke his thick cock, his eyes close, and he's no longer listening. "Okay, deal," he stutters out. "Whatever you want."

I giggle, increasing my pace. "And you do the laundry and dishes."

"Okay, now you're pushing it." He chuckles, towering over me until I'm on my back. "No using sexual favors to get what you want."

"I thought that was the whole basis of marriage." I snicker. His lips drop to the shell of my ear, and in seconds, I'm putty in his hold.

"If that's the case, then it goes both ways." His erection presses against my thigh, teasing my clit. "But you'll probably win because I can't fucking get enough of you."

"Now who's insatiable?" I recall from the first time we had sex at his place.

"When it comes to the love of my life, definitely me."

"Let me ride you," I demand. "And cuff you to my bed so I can take full advantage."

"Never thought I'd want to be handcuffed again…" He lingers, and I mentally slap myself for being insensitive. "But in this case, I'm all for it."

"Shit, I'm sorry. I'm a horrible wife."

Tyler wraps his arm around me until he flips us over, and I'm straddling his waist. "Not possible. Get those cuffs and have your way with me."

Laughter spills out of me as I watch the man I love more than anything put his wrists together. I find the handcuffs I got as a gag gift, then lock them around him.

"Guess I can do whatever I want to you now…" I taunt, walking my fingers down his chest toward his throbbing cock.

"As long as you remember I'll be using these on you later," he counters.

"I don't recall that being a part of the deal."

"In fact, I might get some rope and a whip for when I really need to punish your ass," he threatens in a husky voice, but that actually sounds hot as hell.

Grinning, I lower myself down his body until my mouth is at his cock. "That's the kind of honeymoon I can get on board with. But you have to feed me in between."

For the next forty-eight hours, we stay hidden inside the cottage, enjoying each other and Tyler's delicious cooking. By Saturday evening, my phone is loaded with missed calls and text messages. Everyone thinks I left for Hawaii yesterday, and as soon as the news spreads that I didn't, the gossip mills will be running wild.

"I suppose we should tell Everleigh and Katie we got hitched," I say as we curl up on the couch after eating his famous chili.

"Who do you think will freak out the most?" He laughs. "I think Katie will flip her shit that you didn't invite her."

I shake my head in disagreement. "Oh, your sister, by a landslide. She's gonna ask a million questions, including when we're giving her a niece or nephew, and if we're having a real ceremony."

"Yes."

I blink. "Yes, what?"

"Yes to both. A niece *and* a nephew. And if you want a big country wedding, then I'll give that to you too."

I blink again. "You've already thought about this?"

"I've thought about *you* for years."

"You're perfect," I tell him, bringing my lips to his. "I don't need any of that as long as I have you, but if *you* want one, then I say let's do it."

"We have time to figure it out."

"True. Okay, let me get Everleigh and Katie on a group call so we can hear their squeals." I chuckle.

Once I have them both on the line, I say, "You both there?"

"Yes," they respond in unison.

"Aren't you in Hawaii?" Everleigh asks.

"Did you murder Robert already?" Katie snickers, and I hold back laughter.

"I'm not in Hawaii," I blurt out. They both start freaking out, and I haven't even gotten to the exciting stuff yet. "Okay, listen. I have a bet going with someone, and I need your help with it."

"Where are you?" Everleigh asks again, ignoring me.

"I'm at my cottage," I tell her so she'll calm the hell down. "Just wait, and I'll tell you everything."

She groans, growing impatient with every ticking second.

"So the bet is which one of you will freak out the most when I tell you this particular news. Okay, ready?"

"This is weird, Gem." Katie blows out a frustrated breath. "But okay, I'll play."

I cover my mouth with my hand so they can't hear my fit of laughter. Once I've calmed myself, I clear my throat.

"Robert's and my marriage wasn't real, which is why I'm not on the honeymoon, because I got married beforehand."

The line goes silent, and I check the screen to make sure I didn't lose them.

Finally, Everleigh speaks up. "You were legally married to someone else before the wedding?"

"Yes, that way I could get Robert to sign the deed over to me, and I didn't have to actually marry him.

"That's fucking brilliant!" Katie squeals. "You played him! I should've thought of that."

"Wait!" Everleigh shouts between Katie and me laughing. "Who'd you marry?"

"Well, it's someone I know you'll both like..." I tease.

"Ruby?" Katie shouts.

I snort and make a mental note to have Tyler call her later. "No!" Tyler's dying next to me, trying his hardest to keep quiet.

"Oh my God..." Everleigh drawls out. "Did you marry my brother?"

"Hey, sis," Tyler says.

"Holy shit!" Katie shrieks. "You and Tyler got married? No

fucking way…"

"Are you serious?" Everleigh's voice shakes, and I can tell she's nearly in tears.

"Yep. He helped me come up with the whole plan. Got Robert out of town for a couple of days to get my shit back, put up security cameras, and scammed him into giving me the property."

"That's some genius shit right there," Katie says.

"Are you guys staying married? Or…what's going on?" Everleigh asks.

Tyler and I look at each other with stupid grins on our face. "We sure are," Tyler responds. "I'm moving in with Gemma, and we're starting our life together."

"I have goose bumps!" Katie squeals.

"I'm so happy for you guys!" Everleigh's full-on crying. "And how dare you not tell me this beforehand! For two miserable fucking weeks, I had to watch my best friend make the worst decision of her life, and there was nothing I could do. I'd hate you both right now if I wasn't so damn happy you're finally together."

"Sorry, we had to keep it a secret so there was no way Robert would catch wind of it before he signed on Monday."

"Then I kept her hostage for two days to…" He pauses, waggling his brows at me, but I shake my head at him to keep his mouth shut.

"Yeah, yeah. To bang each other's brains out." Everleigh groans.

We talk and laugh for the next ten minutes before we end the call. I'm so happy, my heart feels like it'll burst out of my chest.

"Who should we call next?" he asks.

"What about your friends Liam and Maddie?"

"Hmm." He ponders it for a moment. "How would you feel about telling them in person? Maybe over Christmas?"

I instantly perk up. "I'd absolutely love that, Mr. Blackwood."

"It's no Hawaiian honeymoon, but I promise to give you everything you deserve. Including a real wedding ring." He rubs over my bare ring finger.

"Being your wife is all I ever wanted," I say truthfully. "The rest is just a perk."

Our lips collide, and I taste the wine we had with dinner tonight. "I love you, Mrs. Blackwood."

"I love you more."

CHAPTER FORTY-THREE

TYLER

SIX WEEKS LATER

"Good morning, beautiful," I whisper into Gemma's ear as she curls into my chest. The sunrise is barely over the horizon, but today, we're flying to Sacramento to visit Liam and Maddie for a week. They have no idea Gemma's joining me or that we're married.

Maddie's gonna lose her shit.

I'm excited to see both them and the kids.

"It's too early," she mutters. "And cold. You're nice and hot. Keep me warm." She slides her palm down my stomach and inside my boxer shorts. I chuckle, knowing exactly where it's going to lead.

"We don't have time, baby," I warn when she brushes her fingers along my half-erect shaft. "You didn't finish packing last night."

"Mmm...I can throw some sweaters and jeans in a suitcase within two minutes."

My chest rumbles with laughter because there's no way she'll do that. It's taken her a week to pick the three outfits she managed to pack.

"You know we won't be able to fool around when we're there, so we need to before we go."

"Gemma, I literally heard them banging every single night when I was there. Trust me, us going at it in their spare room would be payback. Actually, now that I'm thinking about it, we should do it just so I can finally get even."

She laughs before sliding her leg over mine and straddling my waist. "So let's have a practice quickie. Lord knows you haven't mastered that yet."

"Wouldn't most wives appreciate that?" I arch a brow, grabbing her hips as she rocks on top of me.

"Of course, but sometimes, there're only ten minutes to spare, and you're more of a…*teaser and pleaser*."

I snort, then groan as she moves her panties to the side and rubs her pussy along my cock.

"Alright, if you want *fast and dirty*, I can do that."

She lifts slightly, giving me enough room to grip my dick and slip it inside her entrance. Bending my knees, I thrust up hard and deep, squeezing her breast with one hand and rubbing her clit with the other. I keep up my pace until she's gasping and hanging on by a thread.

"Like this, baby?" I breathe out, panting.

"God, yes. Don't stop. I'm so close…" Her head tilts back as I pinch her little bud, and she falls off the ledge, exploding on my cock. Moments later, I follow and release inside her tight cunt.

Gemma collapses on top of my chest, breathing hard and nearly gasping for air. "Holy shit."

"You wanna take your words back now?" I brush my fingers through her sweat-filled bedhead.

"Don't get cocky, but yes. *Best. Quickie. Ever.*"

I bring my hand to her ass and give it a hard slap. "Now, go pack," I demand.

"Shower first," she pleads.

Grabbing my phone off the nightstand, I check the time and blow out a breath. "Alright, but it's gotta be lightning fast."

"Yeah, yeah." She sticks out her tongue before climbing off me and running toward the hallway. I leap off the bed and follow, racing her into the bathroom.

Once we're under the warm water, I pull her to my chest and press a kiss to her nose. "I can't wait for you to finally meet them. Maddie's gonna be all over you, so just a warning."

"I figured, but that's okay. She'll spill all your secrets and tell me all about your days living together."

"Okay, never mind. We're not going."

She grabs my face and lowers my mouth to hers. "Stop worrying. I'm already in love with you, and I'm already your wife, so there isn't anything she can say that'll make me change my mind. But I'm betting it's all good stuff anyway."

Wrapping my arms around her waist, I smile against her lips. "As long as you ask Liam about all the times I kicked his ass in the ring."

Gemma giggles and looks up at me. "And I plan to tell them how amazing you are and that when I needed you the most, you were there for me. Loyal, honest, hardworking. The sexiest traits in a man that I could ever want."

"My cock doesn't even make the top three?"

She rolls her eyes, then grabs my shaft and starts pumping it. "You have four minutes to prove to me why it should be."

I spin her around, and when she places her palms on the shower wall, I thrust inside her tight pussy and do just that—though I make it happen in three minutes, which earns me her number one spot.

"Oh my God!" Gemma squeals as our plane lands in Sacramento. "I'm so nervous now."

I squeeze her hand and smile at her. "Don't be. You'll be ready to move here before the end of the week I bet."

"Everleigh and Katie would kill me. And I think Ruby would be devastated if you left."

"Hmm...I don't know. I think she's pretty occupied with her new girlfriend right now." I chuckle because Ruby doesn't commit, but the woman she's seeing has become serious over the past month. She freaked out when I told her we'd gotten hitched, and Gemma claims that inspired Ruby to want something more serious. Of course I laughed, knowing Ruby, she doesn't do commitment longer than a few weeks. But never say never.

Though it'd be nice to get her out of Alabama and farther away from her psycho ex-fiancé, it's not really a concern anymore. Robert's completely out of the picture. After their fake marriage became one of the biggest scandals of Lawton Ridge, he moved three towns over and brought the secretary who stopped us at the Harvest Festival with him. Apparently, they're engaged now. I roll my eyes at the thought, wondering what he did to make that happen. Probably blackmailed her too.

Once we deplane and grab our luggage, we get our rental car. Liam offered to pick me up, but I didn't want to inconvenience them. Plus, this way we can surprise them when Gemma walks in with me.

"It's chillier here than I was expecting." She turns the heat on in the SUV, and I laugh.

"That's because you're a Southern heat baby."

We talk for the hour drive and so many memories come to the forefront. It feels like a lifetime has passed since I lived here.

"We're here," I call out.

"Wow. This house is beautiful."

"You should see the inside. Maddie went crazy with the décor, and Liam loves her too much to stop her."

Gemma looks at me and smiles. "I have a feeling Liam's a lot like you."

I shrug, then turn off the engine. "Maybe a little."

Once we're out, I grab her hand and give it a little squeeze, trying to calm her nerves.

We step onto the porch and ring the bell. Moments later, Liam swings open the door, and his eyes widen in excitement.

"Tyler! You made it, man!" He immediately pulls me into a hug and slaps my back.

Laughing, I bring Gemma to my side. "I brought a guest. Hope that's okay."

"Absolutely!" He puts his hand out, and she hesitantly shakes it. "I'm Liam."

"It's great to finally meet you, Liam. I'm Gemma."

"*The* Gemma, huh? Wow." He brushes his fingers through his

hair and chuckles. "You're gonna give Maddie a stroke. I hope you prepared her." He looks at me, then at Gemma.

"The best I could," I admit.

"Well, come on in. I was just cleaning the kitchen. Tyler made a huge mess at lunch, and Maddie's getting the boys down for their naps. She's gonna blow a gasket." He chuckles again, ushering us to the living room. "Hold on. I'm gonna have fun with this. Sit on the couch, and I'll blindfold her."

"Didn't you tell her I'd be here?" I ask, taking a seat with Gemma on one of the sofas.

"Of course not. She would've driven herself—and me—crazy with cleaning nonstop, and this way, I get to take credit for you being here," Liam boasts.

"It wasn't your idea," I retort, grinning.

"But she doesn't have to know that," he says pointedly.

"Okay, hang tight. I think I hear her coming down the stairs."

Gemma gives me a wary look, and I bring her knuckles to my lips and press a kiss to them. "I told you they were a crazy couple."

"Liam! What are you doing?" I hear Maddie screech. "Why do I need my eyes covered? This is dumb. I'm gonna trip over a toy."

"Baby, I have a huge surprise. Trust me, you'll *love* it," Liam reassures her.

Maddie releases a deep sigh. "Is this like the time you *surprised* me with caramel sauce on your cock and a whipped-creamed bra?"

I quickly cover my mouth to hide my laughter as Liam and Maddie come into view, and Liam's face falls. "No," he says sharply. "Possibly better, though."

Liam motions for us to stand, so we do, and I brace myself for her to flip her shit.

"Alright, sweetheart..." Liam uncovers her eyes, and when Maddie's gaze lands on me, she screams.

"Oh my God! Tyler!" Within two seconds, she charges for me and wraps her arms around my waist. "What are you doing here?"

I hug her back and laugh. "To see you, of course."

When she draws back, she's wiping tears from her cheeks. "I can't believe it. You came back to visit!" She slaps my chest. "How could you not tell me? My house is a fucking mess." She moves her hands to the top of her head. "Not to mention, I haven't brushed my hair yet."

"We didn't come here to judge your house, Mads. I wanna introduce you to someone, though." I wrap an arm around Gemma and close the gap between us.

"Am I finally getting to meet your sister?" Her voice goes up an octave.

Gemma chuckles and holds out her hand. "I'm Gemma."

Maddie beams. "Gemma *Gemma*? The one you're 'just friends' with?" she asks, using air quotes.

"Well, not anymore, but yes, that Gemma," I say.

Liam comes closer and gives Maddie a hug from behind. "I think they're finally together," Liam mutters to her.

"It's about goddamn time!" Maddie blurts out. "Do you know how long I've been waiting for him to finally admit he was in love with you? Even when I told him to go after you, he was all *she's engaged…blah blah blah*. What the hell changed? And why didn't you say anything?" she scolds, flashing me a scowl with her hands on her hips.

"It's a long story," I explain. "But Gemma isn't my girlfriend."

Maddie's face drops.

Turning to Gemma, I ask, "You wanna tell her?"

"We're married." She clings to my arm and smiles up at me. "Got hitched six weeks ago."

"Shut. The. Fuck. Up." Maddie's booming voice is so loud, I'm shocked she doesn't wake the kids. "You got *married*?"

"Dude, congrats!" Liam pats my shoulder. "I'm guessing this story is gonna call for some whiskey."

"I want all the details!" Maddie exclaims as she starts picking toys and random items off the floor. "After I shower and clean up this mess."

Gemma and I help tidy up so Maddie can get clean and change.

An hour later, we're sitting on the deck, sharing the story of how Gemma and I got married. We talk about Robert, Jerry and the garage, and all the drama that unfolded with Victoria.

Maddie's shaking her head at me in disbelief. I know she's thinking about her sister Sophie and her crazy ex-boyfriend who kidnapped and tried to kill her. Liam, Mason, and Hunter found her just in time.

"That's batshit insane!" Maddie's jaw drops. "Why didn't you punch in his face?"

Gemma chuckles. "He wanted to and offered plenty of times, but he knew with his record, he had to be extra cautious."

"Especially in small towns. Everyone knows you and your business," I explain.

"And the gossip flies around faster than mosquitos at a summer barbecue."

"Aw...sounds like a Hallmark movie. Who doesn't love a small-town romance with drama and gossip?"

"God," I groan. "I forgot you're horny for Hallmark, too."

"I love it," Gemma tells Maddie.

"I already have ten Hallmark Christmas movies recorded! We'll make the boys cook while we start one."

"Putting me to work already, Mads?" I flash her a wink. "I'm on vacation, you know?"

Maddie smirks with an eye roll. "Oh, *puh-lease*. You're here to cook for me. Don't even deny it."

She's not wrong. I anticipated being in the kitchen, and I don't mind. It gives Liam and me some alone time to shoot the shit and catch up. The girls can drink their wine as they watch their corny holiday movies—as long as I get my wife back by the end of the night.

By Saturday, the entire house looks like it vomited Christmas decorations. I helped Liam put up a real tree, and Maddie's sister and even Serena and her son came to help decorate. They all brought their kids and packed all the rooms. It was great to reunite with Mason and Sophie too.

That night was their annual sisters' Christmas dinner and gift exchange. I helped cook a ham and turkey, and Gemma offered her not-so-great baking skills. Though she tried, which was cute. I didn't think I could be any happier, but being here surrounded by my closest friends and new wife, I'm nearly bursting at the seams with joy.

Perhaps it's because it's a special time of year, but also, it's the first Christmas I've celebrated in over five years.

And so far, it's been one to remember.

"I brought one of your gifts," I whisper in Gemma's ear when I come up behind her.

"You did?" She spins and faces me. "I didn't pack one! Why didn't you tell me you wanted to exchange presents here?"

"Don't worry. It's an early one. We can still do ours Christmas morning, but I want you to have this particular one now."

"Okay." She smiles as I grab her hand and lead her to the tree.

Everyone quiets as they watch me kneel in front of her and reach in my pocket for the velvet box.

"What're you doing?" she whispers.

"Giving you what you deserve." I take her hand and smile up at her. "A real proposal and a real ring."

She tilts her head and tries to smile through her tears. Though she's already said she doesn't need anything fancy, I want to show her how much she means to me and how much I love her.

"Gemma, sweetheart. After everything we've been through, I can't imagine my life without you in it, and I hope I never will again. You're the woman I always want to fall asleep next to and wake up to. We might've gotten hitched unconventionally, but I'd marry you again in a heartbeat." I open the box and show her the ring. "Will you marry me again?"

She wipes her cheeks and immediately nods. "Of course." She bends down until our lips collide. "I can't believe you bought me a ring."

"Well, technically, I didn't…" I take it out and slide it on her finger. "Your dad gave me your mom's engagement ring, and I had it set on another band."

Gemma gasps as she stares at it, holding out her hand and watching it sparkle under the light. "Oh my God." She barely gets the words out before she falls to her knees. Wrapping her arms around me, she cries into my neck, and I hold her tightly against my chest.

Even though over a dozen eyes are on us, it feels as though we're the only two people in the room. I know how much this means to her and how special this ring will always be to us.

"This is unreal," she mutters. "I can't believe you did this."

I tilt her chin until our gazes lock. "I love you, more than anything."

When I mentioned to Jerry that I was saving to buy Gemma a wedding ring set, he said he had something even better than an expensive diamond. He told me the story of how he proposed and how special his wedding day was. After five years, she lost the ring, so he bought her a new one. It wasn't until after she passed that he found it and kept it in an old jewelry box. Jerry planned on giving it to Gemma but was waiting for the right time, and he told me the time was now.

"I can't take all the credit, though. Your dad offered it, and I ran with it."

"I thought she lost her solitaire ring." She stares at it in awe.

"Not this one," I tell her and plan to tell her the whole story later when we don't have an audience.

"You better invite me to *that* wedding this time, Tyler!" Maddie blurts out, and everyone laughs.

"You got it, Mads."

"We should do it on our one-year anniversary. Give us time to plan something amazing," Gemma suggests, and I nod in agreement.

"I love that idea. A fall November wedding," Maddie gushes.

"With lots of pumpkin spice," Gemma adds.

"Of course." I smirk, then kiss the top of her nose. "Anything for you."

We end the night tangled in the sheets, proving my quickie skills have been moved up to the *expert* level—three orgasms in five minutes.

The next morning, I wake up before Gemma and sneak into the kitchen to start the coffee. I'm surprised when I see Liam sitting there with a cup already.

"Hey, morning," I say quietly. "Up early?"

"Yeah, thought I'd hit the gym before the kids get up."

"Wow. Good for you, man." I open the cabinet, grab a mug, then fill it full.

"You still thinking you'd like to buy the gym in your town?"

"We've talked about it, but not right now. Gemma wants to wait until Jerry retires so we can focus on it together. It'd need a complete remodel and new equipment. She wants to add tanning beds." I snort. "So perhaps in a year or two."

"That's great, Tyler. I couldn't be happier for you." He grins. "But I do miss you."

"I miss you guys too."

"I still can't believe Mickey found Victoria in Lawton Ridge, and they're all dead. Blows my goddamn mind, but then again, it doesn't. He was crazy as fuck and overly jealous. He nearly killed me, and I wasn't even into her like that." Liam sips his coffee and shudders. "Glad it's all in the past."

"Me too," I admit. It still feels surreal. "So glad."

After an incredible week at Liam and Maddie's, Gemma and I have to return to Lawton Ridge. Maddie cries as we hug goodbye, and she exchanges phone numbers with Gemma. I love that they became friends and grew close this week, but I have a feeling Maddie will be in my business even more now. I'll get texts full of wedding ideas for the next eleven months.

"I love your friends," Gemma says as we're on the plane. "I wish we were closer."

"You say that now," I tease. "No, they're great. I'm glad you and Mads hit it off."

"So I have to ask something, but you can't get mad."

I arch a brow. This can't be good. "Okay?"

"Did you and Maddie ever…" She lets the word linger, and I wait. "Hook up?"

I nearly choke on air as I look at her in shock. "You think I'd still be alive if I touched Liam's woman?"

That causes her to smile, and she shrugs. "Well, didn't you say you two were in a cabin in the woods or something? That sounds kinda romantic."

"Trust me, it wasn't. Victoria was watching our every move. I had to cut the power just to get us out of there, and since she had backup generators, it gave us only a few minutes before they came on. We barely escaped. Maddie and I have only always been friends," I reassure her.

"Okay. Just had to ask."

"She's really friendly, that's all. Maddie's easy to love and knows how to get you to spill your guts even when you don't want to," I recall, remembering all the times she got me to admit shit.

"I believe you, babe. Liam seems very protective of her, so I'm sure if you two had done anything, he would've broken your neck."

"Well, he would've tried at least." I chuckle, then grab her hand and press a kiss to her knuckles. "I'd do the same if another man tried to touch you, just so you know."

"You have nothing to worry about. You're all I want."

I lean down until our lips crash. "And you're all I'll ever need."

EPILOGUE
GEMMA

FOURTEEN MONTHS LATER

Dear Gemma,
You're too young to be worrying about your wedding day, but I will say the way you described it sounds perfectly you. Something simple, but elegant. To answer your question, I've never thought about getting married. Considering my mom and dad divorced and didn't even want to be parents, I never had that desire, but never say never. Maybe if I meet the right woman, I'll get down on one knee and propose, confessing my love...

Tyler wrote me that letter after I told him about how Everleigh, Katie, and I binge-watched *Say Yes to the Dress* all weekend long. The girls and I started talking about what dresses we'd wear and what theme we wanted. The next day, I wrote Tyler a detailed letter explaining my dream wedding.

As I look at our vow renewal photos from three months ago, I notice all the similarities that I told him when I was only sixteen years old. A part of me wonders if he remembers what I told him. Next to the one of Tyler and me kissing at the altar is a framed picture of our eight-week ultrasound from two weeks ago.

Sharing the news with Tyler over Christmas that I was pregnant was one of the most exciting and emotional days of my life. We'd only had our one-year wedding anniversary a month before that. We talked about starting a family soon, and it happened quicker than either of us anticipated, but we're both over the moon about it. I have no doubt he's going to be the best father because he's already the most amazing husband.

Since we're adding a bundle of joy to our family, we'll be looking for a bigger house in the next year or two. I'll be sad to leave the cottage and all the memories we've made, but we'll need more room once the baby is able to walk. Until then, I'm soaking up every day being here.

The best part of still being in my first trimester is my brother will be here for some of our pregnancy journey. For the first time in ten years, he'll be living back in Lawton Ridge, and though I'm nervous for him, I can't wait to hug him again. Noah and I were very close growing up, and a part of my heart went with him when he was charged with unintentional manslaughter. He's done his time, and now he'll have to figure out how to be a part of society again. People in this town haven't forgotten what happened, and they'll judge Noah, as well as anyone who's associated with him. I can only hope some of them will be forgiving, and I pray one of those people will be Katie.

Though I have a feeling she's not gonna make it easy.

Tyler comes up behind me, wrapping his arms around my stomach, and nuzzles his nose in my neck. "Morning, baby." He slides one hand up and cups my breast. "Morning, *sexy*."

I snort with laughter at the cute way he always tells me and our baby good morning or night. He's ecstatic and already running wild with ideas and making a list of things we'll need. Telling my dad was another highlight of my life. I'd only seen him cry a handful of times, one including the moment we gave him a custom mug with the words "Best Grandpa Ever" written on it.

"What're you doing?" he asks.

"Just looking. I can't wait to add more photos on this wall. Hopefully some with Noah."

"I'm glad he'll be able to meet the baby," he admits. "It'll be nice having another man around, too."

"Me too. And I'm happy you two get along so well. That definitely helps."

After the first time Tyler visited Noah with me, he joined me every month after. It became our thing, and when we told Noah we got hitched, he had to stop himself from reaching over and hugging us. He was so ecstatic for us and also because he was getting a brother he liked. I hate that he wasn't able to celebrate the wedding with us, but after missing a decade's worth of important events, I'll take whatever I can.

"We should eat and get moving if we wanna meet the contractors on time. I'm gonna need extra coffee today," he warns, slapping my ass. "Especially since my hot wife kept me up half the night."

I turn around in his arms and scowl. "Hey, you started it! I was almost asleep when I felt your cock pressed against me."

"And that's an automatic invitation to jump me?" he taunts, flashing a smoldering grin. "I mean, I'm not complaining, but it definitely wasn't one-sided."

Rolling my eyes, I push past him and walk toward the kitchen. "Yeah, yeah. You blame my hormones, but you're all over me all the time."

"Is that a bad thing?" He arches a brow when I glance over my shoulder. "You definitely weren't mad about it last night, or the night before that, or the night before that, or the night…"

"Stop!" I burst out laughing, and he comes around the island, wrapping me up in his arms. "I get it. Over a year later and we're still hot for each other."

"Insatiable," he adds.

"Do you think that'll change once the baby's born?"

"Only for the first six weeks. Then I'll go back to trying to knock you up again."

"Oh my God, no you're not! I'm not taking care of two babies under the age of two."

"Why not? I bet we make adorable kids. Hell, let's have ten."

I groan, pushing back so I can start the coffee maker. "You're insane. Let's get through one pregnancy before you start renting my uterus out for nine more." I grab a mug, then the creamer from the fridge. "Plus, with us remodeling the gym and planning the re-opening, I don't know that we should be biting off more than we can chew. I'll already be juggling a newborn by the time it's open plus all the paperwork and office stuff. I'll be lucky if I don't go crazy."

"Gemma, I already know you're gonna be an amazing mom. Stop worrying." Tyler cups my cheeks and brings our mouths together. His tongue swipes along my bottom lip, and I hum at the sweet gesture.

This past year, he really reminded me *why* I love him so much. After moving in together, we got to know each other on a deeper level. Even after all this time, he still cooks me breakfast every morning. We spend our lunch breaks together, and soon, we'll see each other throughout the day even more. He's worked so hard to save money and between the two of us, we were able to get a business loan to buy the old gym downtown. The owner, Sam, was finally ready to sell it, and after Dad started dating Belinda six months ago, he's ready to retire early. He claims it's because he wants more time to spend with Noah once he's out, but we all know the truth. It's his first girlfriend in over twenty years. I'm happy for him, even if it's still a little weird for me.

The plan is to gut it from top to bottom and replace all the old equipment and put in a boxing ring. Tyler's already told Noah he'd hire him to help rebuild the place and work on whatever we need him to. Noah's excited for the project since it'll keep him busy and give him the opportunity to make money. My brother's always been good with fixing things, like our dad, and with the shop closed, he'll need the work.

Katie got that promotion at the bank she was hoping for and finally bought a fixer-upper. Though Noah could help her remodel, she's too damn stubborn to ask for help. She thinks she's going to be able to tear out walls and fix the plumbing by watching YouTube tutorials.

I have faith in my best friend but not *that* much. I'm hoping to convince her to at least give him a chance, but ever since we got Noah's official release date, she's been in a weird mood.

"You really think we'll get the whole place gutted and ready to open by midsummer?" I ask as Tyler drives us downtown. "That only gives us four to five months."

He reaches over and squeezes my hand. "It's my full-time job now, baby. I'll be there every day doing shit and working with the contractors to make sure it's finished on time."

"You have no idea how happy I am that you're gonna let Noah help. It will ease him back so much smoother."

"I have no doubt he'll be a hard worker. After seeing how he's bulked up, he'll probably run circles around the other guys." He chuckles, but it's true. Noah will be the most eager out of them to prove himself and do a good job.

Tyler parks in front of the gym, and when he looks at me, I can't stop the smile from forming on my face. "I can't believe, by this time tomorrow, we'll be picking him up from prison."

"Been a long time comin'," he confirms, and I nod.

"Then let's get this meeting over with so you can triple-check your dad's house is ready for his arrival like I know you're dying to."

"Hey!" I squeal. "I just want it to be perfect."

"Babe, he's been sharing a tiny ass cell for the past decade. He'll appreciate a nice warm bed and privacy more than you know."

I frown because he's right. I can't even imagine the conditions Tyler and Noah have experienced.

"We should at least grab a few pies for dinner tomorrow night. He's probably dying for homemade desserts."

"I'm sure he'd love that." Tyler places a kiss on my knuckles. "Now, Club Blackwood is waiting for us."

I snort at the name, shaking my head, but this is his pride and joy, so I let him name it whatever he wanted. He plans to add a juice bar, a boxing arena, and a couple of private studio rooms for training and classes. He has so many great ideas, and I can't wait to watch him fulfill his dream.

TYLER

I watch as Gemma changes out of another dress and rummages through her closet yet again. She's a nervous wreck, and nothing I say has been able to calm her. Walking up behind her, I squeeze her shoulders, trying to release the tension.

"Sweetheart," I say calmly. "If we don't go soon, we're gonna be late picking him up."

"Babe, I know," she snaps. "Nothing fits me!"

I hold back from saying anything that might upset her. Her hormones are out of control—some days are better than others—but with the added nerves, she's been a tad moodier.

"You could wear sweatpants and a ratted T-shirt for all Noah cares," I remind her.

"I don't wanna look like a fat, tired pregnant woman in our pictures. He promised we'd take some as soon as we got home, so I need to look nice."

"Okay, how about this...you put that dress back on, and we'll buy some maternity clothes tomorrow. Everleigh's boutique has some cute new ones."

As soon as my sister found out we were expecting, she expanded her inventory to include maternity as a surprise for Gemma. She messaged me this morning that it's all arrived, and she's ecstatic and impatient for Gemma to see.

"Wait, what?" She turns around, blinking.

I tell her the news, and her whole face lights up.

"Seriously?"

"Yep. She wanted to surprise you tomorrow, so can you pretend you didn't know?" I smirk. "I tried to wait, but seeing you freak out like this, I didn't know what else to do."

Gemma wraps her arms around me, and I hold her to my chest. "Sorry, I'm a mess."

"You're perfectly fine, baby. But we really do need to leave."

"Okay, gimme five minutes." I lean down and collide my lips with hers. "Thanks for telling me the secret."

Twenty-five minutes later, we're finally on the road, and Gemma's knee is shaking next to me. Jerry's in the back seat of the SUV with Belinda. I don't even know if there's gonna be room for Noah at this point, but we'll make it work.

"Oh my God, I'm so nervous!" Gemma squeals as I pull into the parking lot. There's a process for when an inmate is released, and we'll have to wait out here until he comes out the door.

"I'm so relieved we'll never have to be here again," Jerry says. "Can't wait to hug my baby boy."

Gemma snorts. "He's hardly a baby, Dad."

"He'll always be mine and you too. I don't care how old you two are; you'll always be my babies."

I smile and flash a wink to Gemma. She's lucky to have such a loving and caring father.

"There he is! Noah!" Gemma opens the car door, and the three of us follow suit.

He's carrying one small bag and wearing the biggest smile I've ever seen. Jerry stands next to Gemma as Belinda and I stay behind. The moment he's close enough, he wraps his arms around the both of them, and soon, I hear sniffling.

Moments later, he releases them, and I hug him next. "Good to see you, man."

Noah wipes his cheeks. "You too. I was just about to say you have no idea, but..." He chuckles, and so do I.

Walking out of the gates six years ago is still fresh in my memory. Seeing Maddie and Liam for the first time outside was something I couldn't actually prepare for, no matter how much I envisioned it. I imagine it's the same for Noah.

"Well, let's get out of here and get ya settled at the house." Jerry beams.

"And eat," Gemma adds. "Belinda made her famous fried chicken, and we bought pie."

"I can't wait." Noah grins. "But before we go home, I need to make a stop."

"Sure, wherever you wanna go," I tell him as we pile back into the SUV. "Just tell me where."

"I don't actually know the address, but I'm sure you do."

I look at him through the rearview mirror and see the guilt written on his face. Gemma isn't gonna like this.

"Wait, where?" Gemma asks, looking over her shoulder.

Starting the engine, I put my foot on the gas and exit the parking lot. I know exactly where he wants to go.

"Katie's," Noah finally answers. "I need to see her before we go home."

"Noah!" Gemma scolds. "No. She specifically said she didn't want to see you, and I'm not gonna be the one who forces her."

"You aren't," he argues. "Tyler's drivin'."

I snort at the way he just threw me under the bus, though I kinda agree with him. If he doesn't at least try, he might not ever get the opportunity, especially if it were up to Katie.

"Babe, just let him," I try to calm her. "What's the worst that can happen? She slams the door in his face?"

"Exactly!" Gemma shouts. "And never talks to *me* again."

"Maybe she won't," Noah counters. "I just want to see her. *Please*. It's been so long," Noah pleads, and Gemma instantly melts.

"Alright, fine. But if she pushes you off the porch or slaps you, don't say I didn't warn ya."

Knowing Katie, she'll probably do one of those, but I won't deny Noah the chance to at least try.

Less than an hour later, I'm turning into Katie's driveway, then park. "Well, this is it."

Noah crouches down and looks out the front window. "This is where she lives?"

"It needs a little TLC." I chuckle. "She's planning to fix it up."

"She hasn't moved in yet, but she comes here every evening and weekend to work on it."

Noah inhales a sharp breath. "Okay, wish me luck. Here goes nothin'." He pulls the door handle, then steps out.

"You gotta give him credit," Belinda says. "He wants to mend their relationship."

"It's gonna take a lot more than just showing up ten years later with an apology," Gemma mutters.

We watch intently as he climbs the steps and nervously knocks on the cracked wood.

"Fifty bucks she slams the door in his face before he gets a word out," I say with amusement. Katie isn't gonna take his shit, and if I've learned anything about her since I've been here, she's fiercely independent and literally depends on no one.

"I'll take that bet," Jerry chimes in. "Fifty bucks she tells him off."

"Fifty bucks she slaps him," Belinda adds.

"You guys!" Gemma scolds. "Fine. Fifty bucks she lets him inside!"

We wait in anticipation until she finally opens the door.

As soon as Katie sees Noah, she immediately steps back and slams the door in his face.

"Told ya." I smirk, holding out my hand.

Noah's head drops, and I feel bad for the guy. He looks so defeated.

"Dammit, Katie," Gemma mutters. "I was hoping she'd change her mind when she actually saw him."

"She's too stubborn," I remind her. "Y'all are."

"That's true," Gemma agrees. "But still."

Noah hangs his head as he walks back and slides inside. "Yeah, she hates me."

I turn and face him. "Give her time."

He scrunches his nose. "*More* time? How much more time should I give her?"

"Give her space," Gemma clarifies as we leave. "She'll come around."

"Or here's an idea…" I arch a brow as I pull onto the street. "She needs help on the new house, and Noah just so happens to be pretty good at fixing shit."

"Katie will never hire me," he retorts.

"She works during the day. She can't say no if she doesn't know…"

"Noooo…" Gemma shakes her head. "She'll kill you for sure."

"Actually, that's not a horrible idea," Jerry blurts out.

"She might think it's romantic," Belinda adds.

"Absolutely not. She wants to do it all herself." Gemma shakes her head, crossing her arms.

"Well, if she won't give me a chance to talk, then I'll show her how sorry I am instead," Noah decides. "Start fixin' things little by little until she notices. She won't be able to slam the door when I'm already inside the house."

"This is seriously a bad idea. How are you guys agreeing with this?" Gemma glances over her shoulder, furrowing her brows.

"I've pushed her away long enough, Gem. Let me do this," Noah begs. "I have to win her friendship back."

Gemma's shoulders slump as she blows out a breath. "Alright, but on one condition…" She pauses. "She must never know I knew about this plan. Got it?"

Noah smiles victoriously. "Deal."

I can't help but grin because it's about to get *a lot* more interesting in Lawton Ridge.

AVAILABLE NOW

**Continue the Only One series with
Noah & Katie's story in *Only Us***

I had a picture perfect life. At least everyone thought I did.

But behind closed doors, my life is a mess.
My husband's far from the man I'd fallen in love with years ago.
As my rocky marriage crumbles, my best friend, Noah, stays by my side.

But then, when my husband dies, the finger is pointed at Noah.
For years, he's pushed me away, but when his life is threatened, I risk my heart to save him.

ABOUT THE AUTHOR

Brooke Cumberland and Lyra Parish are a duo of romance authors who teamed up under the *USA Today* pseudonym, Kennedy Fox. They share a love of Hallmark movies, overpriced coffee, and making TikToks. When they aren't bonding over romantic comedies, they like to brainstorm new book ideas. One day in 2016, they decided to collaborate under a pseudonym and have some fun creating new characters that'll make you blush and your heart melt. Happily ever afters guaranteed!

CONNECT WITH US

Find us on our website:
kennedyfoxbooks.com

Subscribe to our newsletter:
kennedyfoxbooks.com/newsletter

- facebook.com/kennedyfoxbooks
- twitter.com/kennedyfoxbooks
- instagram.com/kennedyfoxduo
- amazon.com/author/kennedyfoxbooks
- goodreads.com/kennedyfox
- bookbub.com/authors/kennedy-fox

BOOKS BY KENNEDY FOX

DUET SERIES (BEST READ IN ORDER)

CHECKMATE DUET SERIES

ROOMMATE DUET SERIES

LAWTON RIDGE DUET SERIES

MOCKINGBIRD DUET

INTERCONNECTED STAND-ALONES

MAKE ME SERIES

BISHOP BROTHERS SERIES

CIRCLE B RANCH SERIES

LOVE IN ISOLATION SERIES

TEXAS HEAT SERIES

ONLY ONE SERIES

Find the entire Kennedy Fox reading order at
Kennedyfoxbooks.com/reading-order

Find all of our current freebies at
Kennedyfoxbooks.com/freeromance

Printed in Great Britain
by Amazon